Pirates of Breakaway Bay

G. L. Garrett

Book Cover by Leah Palmer Preiss

Illustrations by Leah Palmer Preiss and G.L. Garrett

1st edition 2024

A very special thank-you to all those who've supported me and my passion.

As for everyone else, you're slacking ... Step up your game!

THE TARNISHED BRASS NUMBERS of the massive estate on Willowbush Court identified the address as 2-5-7-9; or was it 2-5-7-6? You see, the neglectful owner failed in his upkeep, thus allowing the last digit to dangle by a single rusty nail. Either way, it was of no consequence, because this particular home didn't need an address. For this home was the most gossiped about, highly recognizable home for hundreds of miles in any direction. You see, it wasn't the address prompting this story. It was the unusual house itself and the recluse who lived within.

The curious home was a spectacle of whimsy, to say the least. On more occasions than one cares to admit, it was described as an odd house at the end of a not-so-odd street. You see, for all of its quirky features, the stately manor was built on an affluent avenue. So ritzy was the neighborhood, in fact, doctors, lawyers, and other persons of wealth and good standing eagerly sought out and occupied most of the homes here. You couldn't find a more captivating corridor filled with extravagant homes such as these. Ornate, wrought iron fences accentuated the meticulously manicured lawns. Summer swings dangled from open porches nestled within fragrant lilac bushes. All the homes in this lovely neighborhood stood out as the most elegant and most desired in this quaint town. All but for one — 2579 Willowbush Court.

Now, without the slightest doubt in my mind, I assure you if you happened upon this home, it would immediately capture your attention; much the same as if you were to stumble upon a dead fish lying amongst rows of diamond rings in a jeweler's case. Because of that, it became a place where neighbors would encourage their visiting guests to witness for themselves. This wasn't suggested in order for someone to marvel at the estate's size or elegance. There were plenty of those to go around. Don't get me wrong, with its grand facade, stained-glass windows, eight fireplaces, and multiple cherished features you'd expect to find in a home along this avenue, this whimsical estate offered great potential. But just to be more concise, 2579 Willowbush Court was the exact sort of home children steered clear of on their way home from school. Many spectacular stories were told regarding the manor and the odd man living inside. Fantastical tales of mysterious visits from mechanical beings sent even the most curious onlooker scurrying away. There were so many oddities surrounding the home, anytime a local resident would try to explain it to someone unfamiliar, they would always get the same quizzical stare, with the following statement: "You're exaggerating!"

But they never were. In the original plans, drawn by a well-known architect, the home was designed to be an elegant Victorian residence. But as soon as the drawings left his hands, everything went catawampus. Little did he know the person who contracted this impressive home was, well, eccentric. But more precisely, the word "eccentric" was used when one was trying to be polite. In reality, it was suggested the owner needed to be fitted with a straitjacket. He was a peculiar middle-aged man named Crispus Rupina, and he had commissioned the home to be built toward the end of the Industrial Revolution. Being a rather lanky fellow with curious features, he was accustomed to unsolicited attention. With a narrow, sloped forehead and high cheekbones which protruded so far out, he was often said to resemble an inverted triangle. Muddling these features were thick, unruly mutton chop sideburns that cascaded down his cheeks and stopped just before his chin. Now, it wasn't as though the man was "unsightly." People did not turn away from him in disgust as though he was some sort of mangled creature roaming the forest; he was just "curious." Take, for instance, his long, pointed nose. Not designed as a proper resting spot for his thick glasses, he spent a fair amount of time pushing his spectacles up the bridge with his long, narrow index finger.

But for as much interest as Rupina and his estate garnered, nobody really knew much about him. It had long been suspected he made his fortune by inventing stainless steel. But I suspect Harry Brearley would strongly object to this assumption. So, when it came down to it, nobody truly knew where Rupina's money came from. Nonetheless, it really didn't matter, because he had it. A lot of it! And being wealthy certainly had its perks. As such, his fortune offered Rupina the freedom to explore an assortment of hobbies. In particular, he had a penchant for tinkering with mechanical objects. From sunrise to sunset, he would examine them and take them apart, only to put them back together. But more often than not, he would use the scattered pieces to create something different from what he started with. A toaster with a pocket watch timer to give his bread the perfect crispness was his latest brainchild. Because of his creations, Rupina's backyard was littered with the skeletal remains of steam engines, typewriters, motorbikes, and clocks. Lots and lots of clocks. Even the man himself served as a reflection of his hobby. His attire was full of frippery, accented with cogs, gears, and springs attached to his tweed vest as though they were medals he was awarded during some foreign war. However, the most ostentatious item in his wardrobe was a pressed felt top hat fitted with goggles made of brass and copper. Styled after the ones aviators wore, people surmised these protected his eyes from sparks as he worked on his "secret experiments." But what purpose did the other items affixed to his treasured chapeau serve? These included a pocket watch embedded in the center, which was surrounded by copper tubes, springs, wires, and three exposed gears which were interlocked and actually spun within the brown felt. Perhaps the gears worked the aforementioned watch, which never showed the correct time, regardless. And if that weren't enough to make you stare, wedged under this extraordinary hat, struggling to escape, was his long, pointed salt and pepper hair. So thick and unruly, it shot out both sides of his head, thus resembling the spread wings of an albatross. But for all his achievements, his hat is what he would be remembered for, aside from his house, of course. Alas, I've become distracted. Let's circle back to the house.

As I stated, his residence was a classic Victorian home. For those of you not familiar, they are quite large and astonishingly beautiful. Known for their steep, gabled roofs, decorative woodwork, and stained-glass windows, they stand tall and proud in their respective neighborhoods. Ah, and towers; let's not forget those. Most Victorian homes have at least one tower attached to the front. Large, prominent structures which stand out amongst the rest. But if these features aren't enough to make this style home pleasing to the eyes, they are more often than not painted with bright colors, sometimes several. All of which are blended alongside each other to create a whimsical, but refined, look. All but for one —

Rupina's home. He had neither the time, nor the interest in wasting his efforts decorating his home like some "child's coloring book," as he put it.

"Battleship gray!" were his exact instructions to the painters, but even this wasn't the odd part. If you'll recall, Rupina had a passion for tinkering. One so great, in fact, it couldn't be confined to his workshop, or the ramshackle shed hidden amongst the overgrown bushes taking over his backyard. Not even his home was spared.

Ah, we have now arrived at the oddity which brought Rupina the unwanted attention he struggled to escape.

As soon as the last nail was struck, and the carpenters packed up their tools, Rupina gutted the finished tower in front of his home. Within the tower, he built himself an enormous clock. That itself is not all that strange; many people have clocks, and towers are notorious for housing them. However, the bizarre feature of this massive clock was the fact he built it INSIDE OUT.

Now comes the part where you say, "You're exaggerating." No. No, I am not, so allow me to explain.

For reasons unknown, Rupina was always on a schedule and became quite unsettled if he didn't know the exact time. This seemed strange, because for as far as people could tell, he never traveled anywhere, and he certainly had no job. The man barely stepped foot outdoors, but whenever he did, he found himself obligated to talk to the nosy bystanders purposely passing his front stoop. This was something he anguished over, and it made him quite uncomfortable. Thus, after a brief conversation, he would shift and gyrate like a small child in need of a restroom. Just as the nuisance was about to ask if he was alright, Rupina's cheeks would swell up with air like a balloon about to burst before the question, "Do you have the time?" exploded from his mouth.

Startled, this left the poor soul standing there in disbelief as they glanced up from Rupina's eyes to his hat, which clearly had a functioning watch embedded right into it.

Is he not aware? they would ponder.

But it didn't seem as though he was, for what followed was an awkward silence along with not-so-subtle nods directed to the aforementioned watch fitted into his hat. But those signals never worked, for shortly after, Rupina would abruptly excuse himself with no further explanation.

Nonetheless, this burdensome prattle he endured every time he stepped foot outdoors irritated Rupina so much so, he built a clock face, roughly twelve feet in diameter, INSIDE the tower. Truly it was so, because you could actually catch a glimpse of it through a small window on the side of the structure as you walked past. There it was, a gigantic, white porcelain clock face, with black, cast-iron hands and numbers. But what fascinated most of the horologists ... (sorry, these are people who repair clocks for those of you not familiar with the term). Anyway, the horologists were aghast when they witnessed the monstrous metal gears for this impressive clock were affixed to the outside of the home. The oversized, weighted wheels with impressively large teeth were interlocked and stacked upon each other as they spun and ticked away for all to see. Even the winding mechanism, an obscenely large key, had been fitted to the back of the house and jutted out past the garden wall, giving the home the appearance of being a windup toy. As cumbersome as it was, this setup allowed Rupina to wind his masterpiece without constant interruptions from "chatty" neighbors. On the first day of every month, you would hear a door slam and some exasperated grunts as Rupina struggled to wind his clock. A short time later, the door would slam again, and you wouldn't see or hear from the odd fellow for another month, except for the days of his semiannual greasing, for as awkward as this sounds.

Again, some context needs to be placed here.

You see, all clocks need to be oiled and greased; at least the older ones, and especially the ones built with their movements outdoors, which cannot be many. Even though the large, peaked roof of the tower overhung the massive gears, they were still exposed to the elements and susceptible to rust. And Rupina's was no exception. So, twice a year, without fail, he would step out in the early morning hours wearing his nightshirt, tweed vest, and top hat before threading a thick rope through a series of large wooden pulleys. Once he secured his rope, he would toss the line over the roof and fit a wide board onto it to serve as his seat. After squeezing his way through the aforementioned tiny tower window, he would sit upon the board and pulley himself up and down the immense structure. From side to side, he'd scale the clock, squirting oil and slathering grease on the plethora of gears using his comically frayed paint brush. It turned into an all-day affair, to be certain. From sunup to sundown, the townspeople would stare at this odd man wearing an unusual hat as he scaled his tower and lubricated his clock. But this brought a question to mind; at least for me, but I'm certain there are others.

"Why didn't this unfortunate man just wear a watch?"

There were plenty of them to go around, of all shapes and sizes. Ones for the wrist, others for the pocket, they were plentiful. Rupina himself used them in some of his creations, so obviously he knew of their existence. So, why go through all the trouble of building this quizzical monstrosity? That is the mystery now, isn't it?

Now, as I was when I first heard the tale of Rupina's tower, most people became curious as to how he was able to tell the time from inside his home. The massive clock face took up most of the structure itself, and there were no bells or chimes to announce the hour; at least none anyone heard or even wrote about. For the longest time, nobody knew for certain how all of this worked, since very few visitors ever stepped foot inside. But as fortune would have it, one day Rupina received a package much too large to just leave on the front porch. A deliveryman had to help him move the massive wooden crate into the house, which proved to be quite the struggle for even though there were two husky men to assist with this task, Rupina insisted on only one entering his abode. As soon as the delivery was complete, the man was promptly ushered out of the house, and the Model T delivery sedan sputtered away. But before it got too far, a crowd of curious onlookers swarmed the truck. After which, they snatched the confused driver out of his vehicle and inundated him with a litany of questions.

"What did you see?"
"Are there any prisoners in there?"
"Does he have a robot butler?"
"Does he sleep in a coffin?"
"What's with the gigantic clock?"

According to this startled man, he saw little as he was quickly rushed out of the house. But even in the short time he was in there, he noticed dozens of mirrors oddly situated throughout the home. No matter where he looked, he could see what time it was by the reflection of the monstrous clock face. Apparently, Rupina had arranged the plethora of mirrors just for this purpose!

Unfortunately, the deliveryman's story did nothing to quell the interest in Rupina's home, and the speculation grew. But as the years passed, this recluse's curiosity faded and became tedious, so most of the townspeople just forgot about him. It wasn't until several years after his last sighting before people noticed the clock had stopped, precisely at 11:59. Whether it was a.m. or p.m., nobody knew for certain. Nor could they remember the last time the clock had been wound, let alone oiled. After a fair amount of time had passed with no further sightings, the authorities went to his home, knocking and hollering until their knuckles were raw. However, Rupina never appeared. To be certain, the town council requested the local police department break into the home and conduct a search. On one warm summer's afternoon, the constable and his team jimmied the lock to the door, and once inside, fanned out, but there was no sign of Rupina. However, his legendary top hat was prominently displayed on a stand next to the fireplace in the grand hall. Before leaving, they searched every inch of space in the massive estate, or so they thought ...

Years later, streaks of reddish-orange rust ran down from the clock gears, staining the dull gray paint on Crispus Rupina's enormous tower. Whatever grass remained had turned brown and the sparse shrubs which peppered the landscape either died or had become more unruly than before. Yet, there was still no word from the legendary man. After several public meetings regarding tearing down his "unsightly home," along with a somewhat contentious court hearing, the determination was made to issue a death certificate for "Crispus Egnatious Rupina." Now, mind you, the man's body was never discovered. However, this crucial fact did nothing more than add an air of mystery to these unfortunate circumstances. Even odder was the reclusive Rupina filed a Last Will and

Testament with the town court several weeks prior to his last known sighting! But this was not the only thing out of the ordinary for a man with a penchant to do things outside the ordinary. In the uncommonly short legal document, there was just one line which read:

"In the event of my final sighting upon this particular world, I bequeath all of my fineries to my nephew."

"He had a family?" was the common response to the news.

The aforementioned nephew was just as shocked when he was told.

"I had an uncle?"

You see, in every family, there's always that one person for whom relatives are forbidden to speak of, and in all the Rupina households throughout the world, Crispus was that person. Therefore, when the telegram of his disappearance arrived, his mere existence came as a complete shock to his nephew. Regardless, Charles B. Cornsuckle, the aforementioned nephew, inherited the infamous Clock Tower House. Not long after, Charles moved into the estate with his lovely new bride, Anastasia. Up until now, Cornsuckle never truly "found his calling" as they say and spent most of his years searching for it by taking different classes as he bounced from one university to the next. His father, a prominent doctor, and his mother, a renowned socialite and philanthropist, constantly pushed for Charles to make something of himself and not "sully" the family's good name. They grew weary of his travels and urged him to choose one location where he could accept a position with a steady income. After much struggle, he gave in and settled on becoming a history professor, but he was never truly satisfied. He taught his lessons, speaking of many wonderful places, but begrudgingly found himself stuck in a dusty classroom, being crushed under the weight of his own undeclared ambitions. However, as good fortune shined down on him, it was at the university where he met his dear Anastasia.

Anastasia was a slender woman who could bend steel. She had a soft beauty, with delicate porcelain skin and thick, wavy straw-colored hair, which struggled to free itself from the tight bun she spun on the back of her head. Even though she had grown up on a farm full of military men, she maintained a refined, dainty look, expected of ladies during the time. But after losing her father, and two of her five brothers who fought in "The Great War," it was she and her mother who took over the duties of the farm: fixing the equipment, bringing in the crops, tending to the animals, and keeping the house together. At night, Anastasia received great joy reading her brother's letters from the front lines. The words captured her attention and clung to her imagination as they spun fantastic tales of adventure. All the while, she was back home, stuck on the farm.

When the war ended, her remaining brothers returned home. They took over the duties of the farm and forced Anastasia off to college. It was of their opinion, as well as their mother's, that Anastasia had paid her dues, and it was time for her to venture out and experience life. Reluctant to leave at first, she finally accepted an invitation to study at a nearby university, choosing archaeology as her major. While attending Cornsuckle's history class, Anastasia became enamored with Charles' ability to travel the world through his imaginative tales, and the two fell in love. They shared their dreams of trekking through the jungles of South America, digging in the sands of Giza, and sailing the seas around the Cape of Good Hope. It wasn't long before Charles asked for Anastasia's hand in marriage, and as soon as he did, they made a promise to each other that once wed, they would begin their adventures. At least, such was the plan until the arrival of their lovely baby boy — Preston.

Although it was a fortuitous opportunity for Charles to inherit his uncle's home, the estate was nowhere near the university. Even before Rupina's Will was read, Anastasia and Charles had discussed him leaving behind his career as a professor and finding something which would truly make him happy. So, when this opportunity arose, they decided to move there with young Preston, and fix up the old place. Afterward, they would use the money to hire a governess to bring with them as they began their long-awaited journeys. But once they saw the estate, they questioned their plans.

"It's such a beautiful home, Charles. I'm afraid after we fix it up, I'll never want to leave."

"Nor I, dear. But just think, with the proceeds from the sale, we can begin our travels, just as we've always talked about."

This was certainly true. The sale of such a magnificent home would provide them with the resources needed to travel, but truth be told, Cornsuckle proved to be a perfect fit for the not-so-perfect home. Whether or not he would admit it, Charles turned out to be just as quirky as his dear Uncle Rupina. Even so, he was far more outgoing than his uncle. Charles and Anastasia hosted weekly dinner parties to the joy of the townspeople, because everyone, and I mean everyone, was curious about the odd house.

"What a lovely home," their guests would say just before casting a sideways glance at their partners while covering their mouths. It wasn't a subtle affront; most people thought they were too refined or important to be seen with such people in such a home. But curiosity erases many barriers — at least for a short while. And the home didn't disappoint. As soon as you entered the grand foyer, a pair of taxidermy rhinoceroses wearing suits of tarnished armor stood sentry to the rest of the home. Their undersized helmets rested askew on top of their heads. Instead of holding swords, they held umbrellas. Between them was a beautiful, mahogany staircase with white marble steps which led to the upper levels, as one would expect a staircase to do. But as with other parts of the home, this staircase was just as peculiar. Every other marble step was missing, but the plush, carpet stair runner lay stiff and intact, as if to form a step of its own, floating above the missing marble stair. Young Preston would often use this feature as a hiding spot during bath time. Tucked away beneath the stair runner, he was easily overlooked until his muffled giggles revealed his location. However, this was not the only issue, as the oddities continued, for it was the most unwelcoming of staircases. Not only did you have to navigate the seemingly missing steps, but once you got to the top, there was no landing. The stairs simply came to a dead-end in front of a bare wall.

"Seems like a lot of effort for an utterly useless staircase," Charles lamented.

But not to be disappointed, the bizarreness of the home continued. Hung from the erratic papered walls throughout the home were oil paintings of other artists, painting oil paintings of all things. And since I mentioned the wallpaper, you would be remiss not to take notice it was peculiar in its own right. Whoever hung it did so with such haphazard disregard, they rolled the sheets sideways, upside down, and overlapping other rolls, as if a toddler were given free rein of paper and paste. Some rolls of intersecting stripes were set next to mismatched colors of polka dots and geometric patterns. To continue, the furniture seemed normal enough; at least until you sat upon it. For reasons unknown, the fluffy batting had been replaced with compacted sand. The result was a cushion as hard as stone, making it torturous to sit upon for any length of time, thus ensuring guests weren't long to stay, which could have been by design. And of course, there were the clocks. Lots and lots of clocks. The shelves, cabinets, and floor were covered with them, which made little sense considering the twelve-foot clock face reflected through every square inch of this home. But perhaps this monstrosity was built out of necessity because none of these superfluous clocks seemed to keep the proper time, while some missed the required parts to do just that. What I mean is some of them only had one hand attached to the face, and most others were without gears, making them nothing more than ornate paperweights. At one point of the renovation, Charles opened the back of a grandfather clock and found a stash of glass jars filled with jellybeans had replaced its workings.

Once the novelty of the home wore off, most of the "proper" people who visited the home and attended the parties had no further use of the Cornsuckles, so they became an oddity unto themselves. As such, they soon found themselves without friends and often avoided during their evening strolls.

With their newfound free time, Charles and Anastasia returned to fixing up the old place. Even Preston chipped in, becoming enamored with repairing broken fixtures. Aside from the mechanical repairs to the home, they replaced the conglomeration of wallpaper with bright paint colors, while on the outside, they hauled away the scattered remains of machines littering the yard. The gardens received a long overdue makeover as the plethora of wilting shrubs, if you could still call the spindly, brown stalks "shrubs," were yanked out and replaced with aromatic, blossoming lilac bushes. Overgrown grass, which once gave the home an unsettling, abandoned feel, was neatly trimmed, and the walkway swept. They repainted the dank gray exterior siding with a welcoming, soft yellow tone, like you would see when you purchase expensive butter. To accentuate the intricate gingerbread porch trim, the Cornsuckles painted it with several shades of lavender, white, and pink, which complimented the home and showcased the elaborate woodwork. But when it came to the one eyesore they couldn't paint away, they relented, thus leaving the gigantic clock and all its gears untouched. Unfortunately, Charles didn't have the tinkering expertise which his departed great-uncle possessed.

With the ghastly exterior now revitalized, Charles and Anastasia slowly became "tolerable," and were more often than not met with smiles and nods as they strolled down the boulevard. Even Charles himself received a makeover. In an attempt to further distance himself from the stigma of his uncle, Charles trimmed his brilliant red facial hair, replacing his own mutton chops sideburns for a thick, bushy mustache that was well combed, and extended out beyond his lips, highlighted by tiny upward curls at the tips. Now that the façade was more in line with the other homes along the avenue, the young couple turned their attention to tidying up the inside. Perhaps it was not only to increase the value of the home, but to also make the Cornsuckles more accepted. Either way, nobody knows for certain, but what was initially an arduous task of going through Rupina's extensive collection of ... "stuff" became an adventure all its own. That's because during their dusting, scouring, and purging of old items, they discovered hidden passages secreted throughout the estate. Each of these mysterious doors and panels had elaborate mechanical workings, which was a testament to Rupina's skill, and captured the interest of Preston. Even the dead-end staircase proved to be a functional one, but only after you twisted the fourth newel post while standing on the third step. This maneuver would release a latch, which would cause the wall at the top of the landing to spring open. Charles was quite proud of himself for figuring that one out. Even though the hidden door was a mechanical marvel, it was the first thing Anastasia wanted replaced because, "you simply cannot sell a home with a staircase that leads nowhere." But that was not the end of the secretive doors.

"You really need to do something about this floor, dear."

Charles walked into the study. "What's wrong with the floor?"

Anastasia nodded to a giddy Preston, who immediately jumped up and down on the polished floorboards, causing the room to fill with an obnoxious sound so loud it could most certainly raise the dead.

SQUEAK – SQUEAK – SQUEAK

After the third squeak, a thunderous snap sounded, followed by an explosion of dust, causing the trio to jump back. Across the chamber, a large wooden panel shifted to the side. Preston immediately darted for the opening until Anastasia's motherly instinct took over.

"Dear, stop!" she called out to Preston, who skid to a halt.

Charles came up behind her. "What is it?"

Anastasia popped her head into the opening. "You won't believe this."

Upon further inspection, they discovered this elaborate entry only served to hide a secret bathroom. There was nothing grand about the space. It was your typical bathroom with a white porcelain sink, a toilet bowl resting below a high-water tank attached to the wall, and a brass clawfoot soaking tub.

"What a peculiar way to access the loo," Charles exclaimed as he inspected the room. "Let me see if the plumbing still works."

With that, he twisted the porcelain handle on the sink and, as expected, water gushed out of the spigot. Charles used this opportunity to wash the dust from his hands.

"Well, the sink works," he told Anastasia.

"Wonderful. I will check the toilet."

She tugged the pull chain attached to the high tank toilet. Instead of the expected flushing noise, the mechanical sound of gears turning filled the room as the tub slid to the side and revealed a hidden staircase.

"Hello! What is this?" Charles exclaimed as he got down on all fours and examined the opening. "It appears as though the tub is attached to the wall here, and the feet just barely hover above the floor. Fascinating!"

"Is there anything behind the wall?"

"A dark staircase. Very dark, indeed."

Anastasia walked through the threshold next to Charles and set her foot on the first brick step, reluctant to go further. "Well, this is unexpected," she said, leaning forward and searching through squinted eyes. "A hidden room inside a hidden room? There must be something truly important down there for your uncle to go through all this trouble, but I fear it's too dark to see how far down this goes."

"I'll go!" Preston said, racing for the opening until his father grabbed him by the scruff of his shirt.

"Hold on there, champ. One cannot be too careful."

Preston rolled his eyes as Charles held a lit match between his fingers. Before it burned down too far, he blew out the flame, reached into the dark, and pushed up on a wooden handled, two-armed electrical knife switch he'd found attached to the brick wall. As soon as the metal contacts touched, a pop of sparks erupted, and a string of lightbulbs illuminated the stairway.

"Well done," Anastasia said, continuing down the passageway.

"I'm right behind you, dear."

Preston, in the meantime, wedged his way past the two and took the lead.

A pungent, musty odor filled the entry as they twisted down the staircase, entering a small chamber carved into the bedrock. On the far side of the room was a thick, metal door, which resembled one you would find guarding a bank vault, complete with a six spoked handle, and combination locks. Yes, "locks," plural. You see, most vaults and safes have a single combination lock on them. However, this one had seventeen! Each one randomly positioned on the massive door.

"How in the world does one figure this out?" Charles asked as he pulled on the spoked handle while Preston took great joy in spinning the numerous combination locks.

"Well, how do you propose we open this beast of a door?" Anastasia asked, standing in awe with her hands on her hips.

Charles backed up and mirrored her stance. They both inspected the metal barrier, flanked on either side by thick granite walls.

"Perhaps a stick of dynamite?"

Anastasia chuckled. "Certainly. If your plan is to entomb us down here."

Around the door was a steel frame, etched with random numbers. Preston stood, chin in hand, staring at the numbers.

"What is the mystery behind these?" Charles asked, running his hand over the metal.

Every inch of space on the frame was covered with numbers, from 0 to 99.

"Well, maybe there's a pattern which reveals the combinations," Preston suggested.

The trio stepped back and stared at the door in its entirety. It was a menacing door, to say the least.

"Even if the numbers do reveal a combination, I'm not certain that would help," Charles concluded. "Which dial would need to be turned first, second, and so on?" He glanced up the stairs. "We have yet to find any sort of code book containing the instructions. Perhaps this is like everything else in the house and there is a trick to it. Let's scout around for some type of trigger or latch."

"I do love a puzzle," Anastasia said, wiggling her fingers together excitedly before dragging her hands across the stone walls, searching for a hidden switch.

The three sleuths scoured the space, which was no larger than the bathroom they just descended from. After failing to locate the release mechanism, Charles used his handkerchief to twist each heated lightbulb leading into the chamber, hoping one would unlock the formidable door. Alas, the opening remained sealed.

"I must admit defeat, dear. This has me stymied," he declared, replacing his handkerchief and rubbing his hand along the metal door as he spun the locks once again.

"It's getting late. Why don't we retire for dinner and come back tomorrow? Maybe getting a good night's sleep will give us a fresh perspective in the morning."

The morning sun beamed in through the windows, filling the home with warmth before slowly dissipating into a star-filled night, as did dozens of other days following their discovery. Unable to breach the imposing entry, the Cornsuckles became enthusiastically sidetracked with other parts of the house and forgot about the door altogether. Since the house was all but complete, at least to where they were no longer shunned by most of their neighbors, they began their journey as what one might call "a normal family." They had their afternoon outings in the park, their evening strolls, and attended Sunday church services. Not much had changed during their hiatus. Each time they cleaned, they made a new discovery, and their discoveries often revealed a hidden room. The latest one was found by Anastasia after she pulled out a kitchen drawer while the back door was inadvertently swung open by young Preston. This combination of moves caused several stacked plates to rattle and tumble as a cupboard in the butler's pantry slid to the side, exposing Crispus Rupina's private office.

"Dear, come have a look at this!"

Charles came in off the porch with Preston following close behind.

"Well, what have we here?" Charles asked, using his hand to sweep away a spread of webbing.

Beyond the entry was a room lined with tall bookshelves. Situated in the center was a grand table stacked with books and papers, which were blanketed in a thick layer of dust. Charles was reminded of a library when he saw it; an abandoned, unkempt library, but a library nonetheless. Aged, leather-bound books were not the only things filling the shelves, for there were rolled up scrolls and maps tucked away in every available nook and cranny. Where there was wall space, celestial maps and charts hung down. However, none of these objects held the Cornsuckle's interest. Nor did the telescopes or creepy taxidermy animals scattered throughout the space, for across the room stood some peculiar globes; seven in total. Well, let's correct this. There was one "familiar" globe — Earth, to be exact. The other six outlandish spheres were aligned as though they all shared the same galaxy. I say "outlandish" for aside from being round, they were unlike any other the Cornsuckles had ever seen. Some globes were speckled with vibrant colors while others were covered in unusual topography, such as purple plains, golden lakes, and bright red mountains. The oddest globe in the collection looked as though someone experienced a fit of rage and punched the planet, thus forming a massive crater as their fist pushed the land downward toward the core of the sphere. As if this was not enough to pique one's curiosity, there was a corner hutch which displayed a series of glass jars filled with nothing more than dirt. Shoved in between these jars were a multitude of notebooks and journals.

There was so much to see, the intrepid trio strolled through the space as though they were in a museum and had been given free rein to explore the artifacts as they wished. And why wouldn't they? Within these walls could be answers to so many questions. However, looking around, it would more likely make them wonder what sort of eccentric mind would assemble such bizarre creations. This was evident as Charles picked up a strange-looking box.

"Well, now I know what all the parts of those clocks were used for," Charles declared, holding the metal container which resembled a jack-in-the-box. Attached to the bottom was the grip of a tennis racquet. No head or strings, mind you ... just the grip. Attached to the outside of the peculiar box were dozens of clock gears. Charles turned a small metal crank, which caused the gears to rotate. The lid of the box flipped open and a mechanical scissor arm holding a comb extended out from inside the container. Each turn of the crank caused the comb to make several sweeping motions. Charles brought his head closer until the teeth of the comb wriggled their way into his thick hair.

"Fascinating!" he exclaimed as the comb dragged its way through. After several passes, he pulled the box away.

"Well?"

Anastasia giggled and Preston burst out laughing as they stared at the peak of hair, which stood straight and tall on top of Charles' head.

"What? Does this not make me even more dapper?"

"Oh, quite," Anastasia said, walking up to him and kissing his cheek.

"What an elaborate invention just to comb one's hair," he said, setting it down and flattening his disheveled hair.

"And there are even more of these strange boxes," Anastasia said as she inspected another, which was almost twice as large as a shoebox.

This metallic box also had the same type of gears attached to the exterior, but in addition, there were coils of wire and four copper tubes pointing upward like tiny cannons. Each tube had a unique label: Barium, Strontium, Copper, and Sodium. Anastasia turned the handle, causing little puffs of cotton to launch out from each tube.

"How cute, but why?" she asked, continuing to turn the handle.

Inside the box, there was a resounding click. Each cotton ball being expelled from the tubes now did so with a muted "shoomp" noise and were engulfed by different colored flames: green, red, blue, and yellow. Just before the small balls hit the floor, they crackled as little pops of sparks encircled the projectiles. Preston tossed aside the journal he was reading and rushed over to his mother.

"We have our very own miniature fireworks show!" he exclaimed with a broad smile across his face.

"How on earth?" Charles asked, opening the lid of the container.

Inside, there were small trays of tiny cotton balls covered in a grayish-white powder. Four miniature bellows puffed out tiny blasts of air, which pushed the balls through a flame and into the tubes, launching them into the air.

"Uncle Rupina must have coated the cotton with bismuth trioxide to make them sparkle and pop," Charles said as he examined the coarse powder.

"May I see it?" Preston asked. After Anastasia handed it to him, Preston began to disassemble the device.

As though he were a child in a toy store, Charles made his way through the room, examining everything he touched until he settled on a stack of tattered documents on Rupina's desk. The thick sheets of tea colored parchment were crinkled with age.

"Interesting," he said as he examined the pages, one after the other.

"What are they?" Anastasia asked.

"They are detailed sketches of the globes." Charles shuffled through the sheets. "Each one is identified here as a 'Realm,' and they are numbered from one to seven." His eyes jumped across the sheets. "Since Earth is clearly marked on this page, I can only assume the others are named as well. Do any of these sound familiar to you? Kringson, Corsite Storvot, Simenea, Vosture, or Kersippea?"

"Not at all," Anastasia admitted, coming up to Charles and looking through the sheets.

Preston glanced up from the journal he was now reading. "This is interesting," he said, flipping through the pages. "It seems Great-Uncle Rupina fancied himself a poet. However, I cannot understand his prose."

"Pardon?" Charles said, with his nose still pressed against the papers he held.

"Well, take this one, for instance."

The cat with brown whiskers continued to purr,
its checkered scarf used to capture fish, like a lure.

If it were not for the thick ice spread on the lake,
I fear the key would be forever consumed by the snake.

The unusual lyric caused Charles to lift his head while Anastasia squinched her forehead.

"I mean, what sort of poetry is that?" she asked.

"Did you mention a cat with brown whiskers?" Charles asked.

"Yes, I did. Why do you ask?"

Charles hurried out of the room, followed by Preston and Anastasia.

Now, before we go on any further, I feel it necessary to remind you of a few details. As you can clearly see, Rupina's home was filled with oddities, and these included numerous works of art. Well, I believe the term "art" would depend on one's perspective and I shan't say anything further on the subject. Anyway, oil paintings of all sizes hung throughout the hallways. Works, which I believe any admirer or critic would describe as the oddest sort, in that each piece portrayed an artist. This, albeit, was not unusual. However, each artist in these paintings were painting portraits or landscapes as well. One might ponder as to why one just didn't paint the portrait or landscape on its own? Nonetheless, I digress and now the Cornsuckles were focused on one piece in particular.

"I've always been fascinated as to why this artist would paint a cat with brown whiskers wearing a checkered scarf. Look."

Anastasia inspected the composition. There was indeed a cat with brown whiskers, wearing a mustard yellow and black checkered scarf. Next to the cat was an elderly man standing in front of an easel. Upon the easel was a canvas, which the elderly man was painting upon.

"Perhaps Crispus enjoyed writing poems about the paintings," she said.

"But why?" Upon further deduction, Charles stroked his chin as he paced. "Preston, what were the other lines of the poem?"

Preston read the poem once more, causing Charles to lean in close to the painting.

The elderly man was painting a fisherman adrift in a small boat on a lake. After several moments, Charles tapped his finger toward the image before leaning back and placing his chin in his hand.

"My word, this is unusual."

"What is?" Anastasia asked.

"Well," he said, pointing his finger to the image, "the artist in the portrait is holding 13 paint brushes. And his boat has the number 63 painted on the side with a cross beneath. I'm intrigued ... Would you grab the bible for me, dear? Historically, numbers have always held great meaning and concealed many secrets."

Anastasia and Preston hurried into the living room and retrieved the bible. After returning with the book, Preston read psalm 63 several times.

"I cannot see how this connects?"

"Perhaps the next verse," Charles said, pacing as he repeated the poem. "If it were not for the thick ice spread on the lake, I fear the key would be forever consumed by the snake."

They both stood, staring at the painting as Preston ran down the hall. "I've got it!"

"Got what?"

Preston, being keenly observant, recalled a painting hanging in a dark corner of a small sitting room. Charles and Anastasia caught up to him as he moved a potted Dragon Tree away from the print. On the canvas were several men harvesting ice from a frozen lake.

Charles beamed when he saw the portrait. "Well done, Preston!" He leaned into the painting and counted with his index finger. "There are 27 blocks of ice stacked. Let's keep that in mind." Upon further examination, Charles focused on the artist depicted in the image. Bundled up in a heavy jacket, the woman stood along the water's edge, a fair distance from the men who were gathering the large blocks of ice. On her easel, she was painting a pyramid in the middle of a desert. "Has anyone seen a magnifying glass about?"

"I have!"

Preston returned with the glass, handing it to Charles, who used it to examine the pyramid. "There is a snake in the image. Its head is pointing to the number '10' painted on one stone, and there is a cross underneath. Could you read verse ten of that psalm?"

Anastasia searched the verse. "They shall fall by the sword: they shall be a portion for foxes."

As they dissected the words, Anastasia beamed with excitement.

"Wasn't there a stuffed fox in your uncle's office?"

There was in fact. And not only was there a fox prominently displayed, but in its paw was a letter opener. Unusual, but significant as well, for the fox was pointing the letter opener outward as though it were leading a charge. Not quite a sword I agree, but then again, we're discussing a fox, and for it to be grasping a weapon of war of any sort was just absurd. Nonetheless, Charles pulled the abundance of cobwebs away from the critter and examined the aforementioned paw grasping the letter opener.

"Perhaps the tip is pointing to something across the room," Charles said, staring toward the far wall.

"I don't think so," Preston said. "If you'll notice, the pattern of fur on the body and arm do not match."

He pressed on the fox's paw, which lowered with a distinct clank. A familiar series of clicks sounded from inside the fox before its mouth sprung open, exposing a tarnished brass key. Preston reached inside and grabbed the key, which had a black tassel and a small porcelain tag attached.

"Is there anything on the tag?"

"Just the number 7."

"The mystery continues," Charles said, peeking into the fox's mouth to make certain nothing was missed. Aside from the key, it was empty. He grabbed a piece of paper and pencil from the desk. "So, we have a bible script, and two paintings. The most prominent characteristics of the paintings, aside from what we found, are the first had 13 brushes; the second had 27 ice blocks. There was nothing further involving a set of numbers." He scribbled these numbers on the paper. "Now, we also have psalm 63, and the number 10, which of course brought us to our friend the fox. What could it all mean, and how precisely does this key play into it all?"

Charles walked around the room, staring at the numbers and tapping the pencil against his lip. "13, 27, and 63 ..."

He kept repeating the numbers until he glanced up and noticed the jars of dirt had labels on them, and each had a unique set of numbers scribbled on it. After scanning each of them, he realized the numbers did not have any order to them. Perplexed, he continued his review until a stray jar caught his attention. It sat away from the rest, isolated on a small captain's desk in the corner. Charles picked up the jar, revealing the label, which was marked "1327-63," and beneath it was a gold coin.

"I believe I've struck gold!" he called out.

"Dear, you've found treasure?"

"Where?" Preston asked, sidestepping a desk and rushing over.

"Sort of, but that's not all," he said, handing Anastasia the jar as Preston snatched the coin.

She wiped her hand across the dusty label. "1327-63? Do you think it's connected?"

"I'm not certain, but it seems to be an odd coincidence."

"What of the treasure?" Preston asked, examining the coin. "Are there any more coins?"

Charles rummaged through the loose papers, drawers, and even under the desk, but there were none. "I'm afraid not."

Anastasia arched her brows. "Is there anything of significance about the coin?"

Bolted into a nearby table was an obscenely large magnifying glass attached to an expandable scissor arm. Preston pulled the glass close and examined the coin. "Well, there's a strange sort of image stamped into it."

"Something strange, you say. Well, that stands to reason." Anastasia said as she spun in a circle with her arms extended. "I'd expect nothing less."

This brought a chuckle from the trio.

On the golden coin was a raised image of a sailing vessel. The profile was small, but it appeared the ship had large gears attached to the side. Much like the ones attached to Rupina's clock tower.

Anastasia walked over and looked. "Where did you say you found this?"

"Just beneath this jar filled with what appears to be sand. But why sand? What is the significance?"

"And why did he number all these jars?" she asked. "What do these numbers mean?"

There was nothing on the shelves displaying the curious jars, which would indicate what they might be or what their intended use was for. Most of the jars were filled to the top, but several were only half full. However, this particular jar was the only one out of place. And why was it used to conceal the gold coin?

"Let's see," Charles said, examining the label. "Hmm, '1327-63.' What sort of category markings are these?"

Anastasia walked over to one of the towering shelves containing numerous volumes of books.

"Here is a newer publication which identifies objects with something called 'Atomic Numbers.' Perhaps this will give us a clue." She flipped through the book and stopped on one page, running her finger down the text. "Well, it states here the atomic number 63 is for a substance known as 'Europium.'"

Charles removed an encyclopedia from another shelf. "Europium is a lanthanide, which is a rare-earth element," he read. "This is clearly sand, so I do not believe they are connected."

Anastasia spread a map across the table. "Well, perhaps map coordinates. Your uncle certainly fixated on those. Let's see, latitude 13 and longitude 27 puts us in Umm Kaddadah, in the Sudan."

"That would explain the sand. But what of the number 63?"

"I'm not sure. But everything else appears to fit."

A twinkle appeared in Charles' eyes. "What do you think, dear? Shall we travel to the Sudan? Preston? Are you ready to take an adventure?"

"On a treasure hunt? You bet!"

When one hears of a "treasure hunt," the image presented in their heads is one involving tropical beaches; at least this is what is conjured in my whimsical imagination. This journey, however, was not so glamorous. It involved a month-long voyage across the choppy Atlantic followed by a balmy train ride through Morocco, Algeria, and Libya. Even the most adventurous traveler would second guess their life choices after a trip like this. Add to that a rambunctious child bent on discovering riches and, well, you see where this is going. That being said, the trio persevered, venturing through the mosquito infested jungles and sweltering deserts before reaching Umm Kaddadah. Unfortunately, after nearly a year of exploration, archaeological excavations, and street markets, their trip seemed to be an utter waste of time. They came up as empty as the deserts they wandered.

To add to their misfortune, the dispirited travelers now found themselves stuck in a train station in Casablanca on their return trip. Unbeknownst to them, they had arrived during the rainy season and with no doors, nor glass on the windows, water cascaded into the station, pooling onto the rustic, terracotta tiled floor. Hundreds of stranded passengers sought refuge within these walls as they waited for the mud to be cleared from the tracks. Huddled together to avoid the puddles covering the floor, their only relief from the overwhelming humidity came from the underpowered ceiling fans above their heads. Each squeak of the spinning blades pushed a breath of air, that albeit small, was a welcomed relief. Anastasia secured one of the few, highly sought after benches, which provided the only sanctuary for families looking to get off their feet.

"Well, this trip was a bust," Charles said, his elbows resting on his knees as he sat, staring at the floor.

Preston was sound asleep, leaning up against Anastasia. As she removed his shoes, so much sand emptied onto the floor it created a small pile.

"I think we brought half the desert back with us."

Charles looked at her and smiled. "Cleary, it wasn't latitude and longitude. I should've known the jar of sand and coin weren't clues. What sort of ship would be found in the middle of a desert, anyway?"

"At least Preston seemed to have enjoyed himself."

"Of course he did. It was a gigantic sandbox. What kid wouldn't love that adventure?"

"So, where do we go from here?" she asked.

"We really have nothing more to go on. Perhaps we should return home and dissect Uncle Rupina's journal even further."

While the couple commiserated, a short, stocky man wearing a white suit and bright red fez paced in front of them, glancing at the couple out of the corner of his eye. The black, stringy tassel on top of his hat captured Anastasia's attention. Her eyes grew wide as she jammed her hand into her bag and pulled out the brass key.

"Charles," she said, holding the key up and nodding toward the man.

Charles slowly raised his head, and as soon as he saw the man's hat, he looked at the key in Anastasia's hand. A broad smile swept across his face as he snatched the key and leapt from his seat.

"Over here!" he said, sprinting to a section of parcel lockers. In several of the locks were matching tassels with porcelain tags attached.

Anastasia grabbed their luggage cart, laying Preston across the bags before catching up to Charles, who was standing under an ornate, metal sign, which read "Section 63" in scripted numerals. A short distance away from the sign was locker number 7. She looked into his eyes and grabbed the key before inserting it into the lock.

"It fits!"

After taking a deep breath, she turned the key. The glorious click of a lock releasing made them burst with excitement. Perhaps this hellish journey wasn't a waste after all. Charles yanked the door open and retrieved a black canvas pouch from within.

"Would you like to do the honors, dear?"

Anastasia's eyes twinkled as she dropped to the floor and untied the bag. After peeking inside, her eyebrows shot up as she stared inside.

"Well, what is it?"

She looked up at Charles and pulled out a triangular, tarnished brass scope. "It's a sextant," she said, fiddling with the many lenses and dials.

"A sextant? I was half-expecting a bag of coins, or a treasure map."

Anastasia turned the bag inside out as Charles swept his hand into the locker.

"No, nothing more," he said, turning his attention to the sextant. "That's odd ..."

"What is?"

He flipped through several shades while looking through the scope. "Where there is normally a horizon mirror, there isn't."

Anastasia laughed, shaking her head. "We couldn't even find a working one? It had to be broken?"

"No, I don't believe it's broken. You see here? There should be a mirror. Instead, there are extra shades." He looked closer. "Each is marked with what appears to be a series of moon sizes. Plus, there is a dial here with settings for seven 'Realms.'"

"The globes!" Preston muttered, coming out of his slumber.

The three of them stared at one another. This was far too coincidental. Even after all the odd things the Cornsuckles had found, this was the one thing making their spines tingle.

"I've never used a sextant before. Is having no horizon mirror uncommon?"

"I'm no expert. I have only read about them. And none of the ones I've studied mention any of these other features. But I am certain I can find someone who knows more about this back home."

They returned to their bench, only to find the man in the white suit had shuffled his extended family onto it. Exhausted, he sat with his head back, fanning himself with his fez. The dark bags under his eyes gave cause to the blank stare he shared with the frazzled woman sitting next to him. As the despondent couple sat silent, unmoving, eight children of all different ages clambered over them. Some shouted at one another, while others wailed incessantly. Charles and Anastasia turned to Preston, shook their heads, and returned to their spot on the floor by the lockers.

As soon as they arrived home, Charles contacted a colleague of his who was an astrophysicist and professor of astronomy at Charles' former university. Along with the letter, he sent a sketch of the unique sextant. Several months passed before he received a reply, which he held in his hand as he walked into the living room.

"Anastasia, darling. Trevor returned my letter," he said, ripping the envelope open. His eyes danced across the page as he skimmed through the letter, but then his shoulders dropped.

"What's wrong?"

"Hmm? Oh, nothing. He said he has never seen such a piece before. So we are back to square one, I'm afraid."

"Oh, that is a shame."

"However, Trevor is very interested in the device. Oh, wonderful! He said he would research it and share it with his colleagues to see if they could determine if such an instrument exists. Ah, he is attending a symposium later this year, which isn't far from here. He's hoping to stop by and examine the sextant more closely."

"Wonderful! Perhaps one of his associates will recognize it."

"I hope so. I will write back to him and invite him to stay with us while he's in town. It would be grand to see him again."

While the Cornsuckles awaited Trevor's arrival, they returned to their efforts in decoding Rupina's book of poems. After cracking the first code, the rest were somewhat less challenging, and the prize awaiting them at the end of the mystery was often not as exciting as an antique sextant. In fact, their latest scavenger hunt took them throughout the house, the dense woods out back, and up to the large fountain in the center of the town park only to discover a jar of raspberry preserves.

"I fear my great-uncle was odder than we first thought," Charles said, standing with his pants rolled up, knee-deep in the fountain water, tasting the aged spread with his finger. "Mmm, not bad."

As you can see, Charles was showing himself to be just as peculiar as his dear uncle. This, however, did not deter them from their quest for answers, but as they would soon find out, their next mystery may in well be their last.

IT HAD BEEN NEARLY a year to the day since Trevor's letter made its way to Charles, and now, here was their esteemed guest, arriving late in the evening. The sputtering taxi could be heard in the parlor, signaling an excited Charles to peek out the window.

"Wonderful! Trevor has arrived, dear!" he announced, scrambling to the door and opening it just as Trevor reached up for the brass knocker. If you were passing by, you might mistake him for a well-dressed child, for Trevor was a shorter man. Much, much shorter than all his colleagues. But his intellect stood tall over all others. Ranked at the top of every class he attended, he was a highly sought after scholar when he took a position in the same university as Charles. Within two years, he was tenured, and had published over a dozen papers on the cosmos.

"Trevor, my dear friend!" Charles said, holding the door wide and helping Trevor with his luggage. Once inside, they dropped the bags and conducted a traditional greeting they had learned while working together at the university. With a bent knee, the two men bowed to one another, followed with a tip of their imaginary hats before locking arms and dancing in a circle. The ritual ended with a salute and grabbing the other's forearm for a shake, which prompted a burst of laughter from the two friends.

"You look amazing! Haven't changed one bit."

Trevor was always meticulous in his appearance, and even after his long journey, his pinstripe suit was as smooth as if it had just been pressed. Even the red pocketed handkerchief was crisp and folded neatly. His thick, dark hair was combed straight back; not one follicle dared to be out of place.

"You are too kind," Trevor said, patting his head, making certain his hair remained flat. "I was so delighted to hear from you!" Trevor sat down and removed the handkerchief from his breast pocket. After polishing the tips of his shoes, he looked up at Charles. "But when I saw the sketch of your sextant, I knew I had to come see you as soon as possible!"

"Well, here it is," Anastasia announced, entering the room as she held the sextant with both arms outstretched as though she were presenting a large roasted turkey for Thanksgiving.

"Anastasia, my dear! You are just as captivating as I remember," Trevor said as he stood and walked over to her. She leaned down as Trevor kissed her on both cheeks. "Why, it is even more brilliant than I imagined," he declared, reaching up and taking the piece from her. He adjusted his round glasses and carefully examined the sextant.

"We're you able to discover anything more about its existence?" Charles asked.

Trevor smiled, unable to take his eyes off of it. "It is unlike anything I've ever seen," he muttered. "Uhm, no, sorry, Charles. Nothing like this exists, as far as I could find. Nor has anyone at the university ever seen such a device."

"Can you navigate the oceans with it?"

"I wouldn't know how," he said, chuckling and spinning the device. "You see, the horizon mirror is not here, as you pointed out in your letter. There would be no fixed point to help you pinpoint the stars for navigation. This particular piece seems to work in reverse."

"In reverse?"

"Yes. It appears these shades are used to align the sextant with a particular moon or planet. This would serve as your starting point; your 'horizon', you might say. Once you established the horizon as it were, you would set the azimuth to a point to sail to from there."

"Am I hearing you correctly? Are you saying this would be used to sail to a particular location from SPACE?"

Trevor looked up as though the answer was written across the ceiling. "Why, I guess I am. Unless you're starting from a planet with several visible moons or planets orbiting it, for as odd as this sounds. The place, not the moons," he said as he rethought his theory.

Charles' jaw dropped, and he stared at his friend. "That's mad!"

Trevor considered this for a moment and nodded. "Indeed, it is. But aren't preposterous theories the very thing which drives science?" he said with a hearty chuckle. "Nonetheless, I believe someone was just tinkering with a real sextant and created the one you have here as a piece of art, or an oddity to create conversation, as it has done."

"Well, my great-uncle did fancy himself to be a tinkerer. This home is loaded with all sorts of objects of his creation."

Trevor smiled. "Ahh! Well, there you go. Of course, it would stand to reason after seeing the whimsical clockworks affixed to the outside of your home."

All three shared a laugh.

"Still, I would like to know more. On the off chance this was created by design, it would be wise to learn for what purpose. Do you have any other information on it, whatsoever?"

"I'm afraid not. As I explained in my letter, we were on an exploration in the Sudan and came across this piece at a train station in Morocco."

"Was someone selling it?"

Charles and Anastasia glanced at one another. "No. Actually, we found a key, here, in Great-Uncle Rupina's study. This key opened a parcel locker in the train station. The sextant was there, inside a canvas bag of all things."

"Curious," he said. "A canvas bag, you say?"

"Yes. Would you like to see it?"

"Please."

Charles retrieved the bag and handed it to Trevor. "Just as I suspected."

"What is?"

"These white streaks on the canvas. Were they present when you recovered the bag?"

"Uhm, yes, I believe so. Why?"

"Well, I would expect they are made from salt spray, similar to samples which would be created from the ocean," he said, scratching at the marks and rubbing his fingers together. "One would assume this sextant was on a ship at some point." Trevor held the bag up to the lamp. "This bag may have been made from an old sail."

Charles looked puzzled. "I've never known a sailing vessel to have black sails."

"They were rare, but they existed. Interestingly enough, the only ones I've ever read about were ones found on pirate ships."

"A pirate ship!"

They all turned and saw Preston, who had come bounding into the room.

"Well, now I suppose this must be the boy genius Charles has told me so much about."

Charles laughed and beamed with pride as Preston stood before Trevor and shook his hand. Charles never missed the opportunity to brag about his dear Preston.

"Do you really think this was from a pirate ship?" Preston asked, rubbing the coarse material between his fingers.

"It wouldn't surprise me. Each ship sailed within a particular location, and each of these waters have their own unique salt and mineral signatures. That being said, with your permission, I would like to take this canvas bag back with me. There's a brilliant professor, Noreen, who is a dear friend of mine. She came to work shortly after you left. As part of a research project, she is experimenting with a process to determine the location of an object taken from an ocean by the salt signature associated with it."

"Can she do that?"

"Well, she is in the infancy of her research, but she is trying. Her latest experiment is on a piece of wood from an old shipwreck to determine where it originated from. So far, the results have been inconclusive. However, with luck, she will be able to tell us from which ocean this canvas sailed. The downside is she is still gathering saltwater samples from around the world. Although the answer could potentially be a few years away, perhaps this would give us another piece of the puzzle."

Without hesitation, Charles and Anastasia turned to each other and nodded. "Well, by all means, give her the pouch. Anything that would enlighten us is more than welcome."

"Brilliant. Now, it's been a long journey, and I'm famished," Trevor said, patting his stomach.

"Of course! Where are my manners? My dear Anastasia and I have been quite creative in the kitchen today. Please, let's all eat."

Trevor and Charles spent the week together before Trevor returned to the university.

"If you ever get bored, we would love to have you back at work."

"Many thanks, my friend. But as you can see, there is so much going on, my mind is quite occupied."

"Well, I must admit, you've never looked happier."

Outside, the "ahooga" from a car horn sounded.

"I believe my cab has arrived," Trevor said, adjusting his coat. "Charles, my friend, you certainly have a lovely family and a fascinating home. I hope everything works out for you."

"And you as well. Promise to stay in touch!"

"I most certainly will."

Charles helped Trevor bring his bags to the cab. After the car was out of sight, Charles turned and stared at the tower clock. "You're my next project," he said with his hands on his hips before returning inside.

"Dear! Trevor has left."

Anastasia walked into the parlor, carrying a thick book.

"What have you there?"

"It's a book on sailing ships I found in uncle's office. Trevor's mention of pirate ships had me intrigued!"

She sat down on the sofa with Charles taking a seat next to her.

"When he spoke of black sails and pirate ships, I recalled a reference in the text. A ghost ship had been spotted in Georgia, just off the coast of Savannah. This ship was said to have black sails and always appeared to be on fire, as if it sailed out from the gates of hell."

"On fire?"

"Yes. From accounts of sailors who witnessed the ship, they said it brought raging clouds filled with lightning, and rain of fire fell from the sky. Some even said the storms dwarfed any hurricane they had ever experienced."

"May I?" Charles asked.

"Of course."

Charles looked at the cover. "*Fantastic Fables of the Seven Seas*? Interesting, but this appears to be nothing more than a children's book meant to create intrigue and scare the young ones."

"On the surface, yes. But then why would your recluse uncle have it among his collection of science journals and texts? Perhaps there is something to this ... this ghost ship. It's the only one mentioned to have black sails, and if you read further, there are several other references to the same ship being spotted all around the world."

Charles thumbed through the index of the book. "Well, this certainly proves one thing. Sailors are a superstitious lot!" He laughed. "I mean, look at these stories: sea monsters, mermaids, ghost ships. It's somewhat comical, actually."

Now, Charles was a brilliant man — most of the time. This, however, was not one of those times. His dismissive response caused the room to fall silent, and he swore the air had turned icy cold. As he reluctantly looked over to Anastasia, he was met with a glare so intense, a lump rose from his chest and became lodged in his throat.

"It was just a thought," she snarled through gritted teeth before snatching the book away from him and storming off to the study.

Charles dropped his head and stood. "Dear, I'm sorry," he said, following her. "You're right. You'd think I'd learn to approach things with a more open mind. Especially after all our discoveries here."

She set the book down as Charles kissed her on the forehead.

"I guess I still have some professor left rattling around inside me. Proof and facts after all, right? How shortsighted can I be?"

Anastasia pursed her lips. "Well, truth be told, if you had tried to explain I'd be living in a mechanical house with an absurd clock face staring at me every morning, I would have thought you were mad as well."

Charles smiled. "We should vow to keep an open mind in all matters and not be swayed or tainted by our own beliefs without knowing all the details."

"Agreed," Anastasia said, extending her hand as they shook.

Now, most parents will lament how quickly time passes when you have a child, and the Cornsuckles were no different. Within the proverbial blink of an eye, their rambunctious son was in high school. These passing years made it easy to forget the sextant, and most other things, until one morning during breakfast, Anastasia walked out of Rupina's private office holding a metal tube.

"Look what I've come across."

"What is it, dear?"

"I believe it is a cylinder cipher."

"A cylinder cypher? I've only studied these. May I see it?"

The foot long aged-copper tube was dull compared to the six polished brass rings, which encircled the casing and rotated around the center. Each ring had twelve symbols engraved into them. Both endcaps appeared to be oil-rubbed bronze, and each end had three tiny gears affixed to them, their teeth interlocked with one another.

Anastasia handed it to him. "What do you know of them?"

"They're fascinating, and quite difficult to open unless you solve its secret code," Charles said, twisting the endcap; but it didn't budge. "It's deceivingly light, but I don't recognize this metal."

He walked into his uncle's office and grabbed a magnet from the drawer. After placing it against the cipher, the magnet fell to the floor. Charles shrugged his shoulders and, in a flash, smashed the puzzle box against a solid marble tabletop. The force of the strike caused the marble to break apart and Anastasia to jump at the noise; the shattered pieces of table scattered across the floor.

"Charles!"

"What happened?" Preston asked, dashing into the room.

"Your father is being incorrigible."

"Fascinating!" Charles said, unfazed by the trauma he just created.

Anastasia shook her head in disbelief. "Have you gone mad?"

"No, look. Not a scratch or dent on it. This metal is unlike anything I've ever seen. Perhaps this relic is not as old as we thought. This could be some sort of new alloy."

Anastasia crept up to Charles, shaking her head. "You really must control your outbursts." She stuck her neck out and looked at the strange cylinder.

"Well, I can assure you it is not new. At least according to the writings." She took the cipher and walked into the parlor. "These symbols are ancient text. That much, I am certain of."

"How can you be so sure?" Charles asked.

"I've seen this language before. It's Sinhala." She stepped over to her roll-top desk and retrieved a stack of letters before sitting down on the sofa and shuffling through the papers. Once she found the one she was looking for, she unfolded it and pulled out a newspaper clipping. "My brothers spent time on a small island at the southern tip of India during the war. They said the people wrote the most beautiful language they had ever seen. Have a look."

Charles took the newspaper from her and examined the headline.

යුද්ධය නිසා අපේ පෞරාණීක ඉඩම් විනාශ වෙනවා

The script was indeed stunning. The letters flowed smoothly and looked more like a work of art than a newspaper. "What was the name of the island?"

"Ceylon."

Charles compared the clipping to the cipher. "But it seems this news article has the same script as the cipher. How can you tell it is older than the date on this paper?"

"Through my studies. You see this symbol here? The one that appears to be an inverted heart with a loop?" she said, pointing to the tiny mark. "This is 'ka' and was only used during the 12th century."

"Fascinating!"

"Can I try?" Preston asked.

"Of course."

Preston took the cipher and immediately began twisting the rings as he grabbed his mother's letter and walked out of the room.

"He is definitely your son, dear," Charles said. "Always seeking a challenge."

"Should we help him?"

"Do you suppose he would let us?"

Anastasia laughed. "No, you're right."

"Where did you find it?"

"I was in your uncle's office, cleaning the fireplace, when I noticed a loose brick in the back of the hearth."

"Was there anything more?"

"No. I removed the brick and found it rather empty aside from this. I was hoping for something to indicate where to find the combination."

"My understanding is they are a nightmare to solve."

"Got it," Preston said, walking back into the room.

"Got what, dear?"

"The cipher, of course."

Anastasia turned to Charles and then back to Preston. "How did you solve it so quickly?"

"It ended up being rather easy." He spun the rings as fast as he could while speaking.

"Preston! Did you just lock it again?"

"What?" Preston looked down at the cylinder. "Oh, no. I just enjoy the clicking noise. Actually, these rings have nothing to do with the locking mechanism itself. I believe they are just used to distract the person trying to crack the code. In actuality, the key to opening this is at either end of the cylinder. You see these gears? They are the actual puzzle that needs to be solved."

"And you solved it?"

"Yes. As I stated, the rings in their entirety have no connection to the lock. However, they do provide us with the combination. These symbols here," he said, pointing to the ones his mother described as 'ka,' "direct you to which gear to turn. You see, there are six of these symbols, and that is the same number as the sprockets on the endcaps, three on either side, so I focused on those."

Charles and Anastasia looked at each other. They weren't certain whether to be proud or scared of their young boy's brilliance.

"Now," Preston continued, "aside from the ancient symbol mother pointed out, this symbol here, the one I believe resembles an apple, is the only other one that appears on all six rings; I concluded this to be the starting point. From there, you focus on mother's symbols, and where they are in relation to this apple looking one."

Anastasia looked at the symbol Preston described as an apple. "That's 'cha,' dear."

"Oh, very well, but the name doesn't really matter for this purpose. Now, on the first ring, the ancient symbol is the third letter after the apple. Therefore, you go to the right side of the cipher and spin the first gear three times."

Preston spun the gear. Each rotation had a resounding 'click' to it.

"How do you know to go to the right side?"

"Oh, right. Well, the stem of the apple — sorry, mother, the 'cha,' points to the left or right side."

Anastasia bent down and looked. "My word. You are correct. Well, what did you find inside?"

"I wanted to finish the puzzle with you both."

"Well, let's see what we have," Charles said.

Preston continued the puzzle until he counted the last symbol.

"Five," he said before turning the final sprocket on the left side of the cipher five times.

As soon as he counted the final "tick" of the rotating gear, a series of clicks sounded as the cylinder vibrated. The endcap sprung open and Preston handed it to his mother.

"It was your discovery, mother. Would you like to do the honors?"

She smiled, arching her brow as she took the cipher from him. After peeking inside, she slid several fingers in and retrieved a purple silk pouch. With a nod of her head, she untied the gold chord from the pouch and reached her hand inside.

"It's a gear, and a gold coin; like the one we found in uncle's study."

Preston took the gear and examined it while Charles looked at the silk bag and turned it inside out. "No, nothing else."

Anastasia stared inside the tube and pulled out a slip of paper.

"What does it say?"

"I'm not exactly certain. On top is a red triangle with the number 7 written inside it. The only other entries are what appear to be coordinates. The paper has dozens of them: 32.0781° Norte, 81.0841° Oeste; 35.1361° Norte, 119.6756° Oeste; 19.4721° Norte, 155.5922° Oeste, it goes on and on."

Charles took the slip of paper and headed into the study, where he spun the globe.

"The first numbers appear to bring you to Savannah, Georgia." He swept his finger across the globe and located the next two coordinates. "The others are in California and Hawaii! What importance do these places hold?"

"What if we isolate each location? Perhaps it will show us something they all have in common," Preston suggested.

"What an excellent idea. I think I have a book in the library that can help us."

Charles headed to the library, but stopped when the front doorbell rang. "Are you expecting anyone, dear?"

"No."

He went to the foyer while Anastasia continued to review the paper, only to return carrying a small box wrapped in brown paper.

"We've received a parcel," he said. "My, word. It's from Trevor! He also sent a letter with it in the post."

Once he removed the paper and opened the box, Charles pulled out the black canvas bag Trevor had taken with him.

"I had completely forgotten about this!" he said. After setting the bag on the table, he unfolded the letter.

"Trevor apologizes for the delay and said the best Noreen could tell, the bag contains remnants of salt and minerals consistent with the waters of the Laccadive Sea, off the coast of India."

Charles looked up from the letter and raised an eyebrow to Anastasia, who was beaming with excitement.

"So many adventures in one day!" she said.

They both glanced at each other with an expression only too familiar to Preston.

"Here we go again," he muttered, shaking his head as he took the cipher into the study.

"Do you think we should?" Anastasia asked Charles.

"Travel to India? I think we must, especially after finding the cipher with writings seemingly from that area."

"But what of Preston?" she whispered.

"He can come with us."

"No, dear. School resumes next week. He's missed far too much as it is."

"So, how exactly should we proceed?"

After much discussion, Anastasia called Preston into the room.

"Preston, please, sit."

Anastasia poured some tea and handed Preston a cup, but he waved her away.

"Preston, your mother and I have to travel to India; Ceylon in particular."

"Have to? Like as if it's a matter of life and death? You can't be serious."

Preston had a point, and his rebuttal caused his father to purse his lips. After all, what response could he provide other than, "Fair enough," which in fact he did. But as I pointed out some time ago, long before Preston was born, Charles and Anastasia made a pledge to fulfill their dream of travel and adventure. Would one trip such as this truly hurt? Preston was of the age where he could manage on his own. So, Charles sat Preston down to explain.

"After much discussion, we concluded it would not be fair for us to take you out of school once again. We would choose to hold off until your next break, but we feel this is too pressing to wait, so we believe it would be best to leave you behind and take this journey."

"How long?"

"How long for what, dear?"

"How long will you be gone?"

"Just for a short while."

"A short while is a few hours, days even. You're talking about months," Preston said, rolling his eyes as his father stared at him. "That being clarified, I don't know what you want me to say. Every other time

I asked for us to stay home, you decided we were to leave, anyway. It's no wonder I don't have any friends. I've never been around long enough to get any."

"Son, we would love nothing more than for you to come with us, but your education is far too important. It's not like when you were younger, and we could all just go off on some wild adventure."

"I never wanted to go on those either. But if I wanted to be with my parents, I didn't have much of a choice, did I?"

Charles held Preston's shoulders and frowned. "Son, your mother and I discussed this at great length. We will take this final trip and return within two months ... three, tops. Afterwards, we stay together, and if such an occasion arises where this is not possible, then we postpone our trip until you are off to college."

"You're going to do what you want regardless of what I have to say, so enjoy your trip."

Anastasia stood and reached out to him, but Preston stormed off, pushing past her, leaving his parents staring at each other.

Outside, the crickets were chirping as Preston's parents sat on the back porch, listening to the sounds of the night. Preston crept down the stairs and headed into the kitchen, stopping short of the back door.

"Perhaps we should postpone the trip," Anastasia said. "Ceylon will still be there in another year. Once summer comes, we can head off with Preston."

"I suppose it would be for the best."

Preston smiled as he turned quietly and disappeared into his room.

As the morning sun beamed through the window, warming Preston's face, he woke up to a reflection of a large clock staring at him from the corner mirror. He smiled as he leapt from bed and came bounding down the stairs, eager to make up with his parents for his crass comments the night before.

"Good morning mother, father," he said as he turned the corner into the kitchen.

But nobody was there. "Hello?"

With an empty feeling in his chest, he turned toward the door, where tacked upon it was an envelope.

"They didn't ..."

It was the same sort of envelope he'd been greeted with several times in the past; pink with his name scrolled across it and a large red heart drawn in the upper corner. He let out a deep sigh as he yanked the letter off the door and dropped to his chair.

Preston, my sweet. Your father and I have left for India. This trip could provide so many answers for us, we feel we cannot postpone it. We wanted to talk to you about this directly, but we did not wish to wake you. No matter what you think, we do love you with all our hearts. All the cabinets are full of food and necessary items to make you comfortable until our return. There is also money in the safe should need arise. You are our most precious gift, dear Preston, and we are anxiously awaiting the day we can continue our explorations with you by our side.

With our hearts full of love,

Mother and Father

Preston closed his eyes and shook his head. Taking a deep breath, he crumpled the note and threw it to the floor.

"I should've known."

Preston heaved out a sigh. He was conflicted as to what angered him most; being left behind or having to start school once again. After buttering his morning toast, he squeezed the juice out of several oranges and scrambled two eggs. Once he cooked breakfast, he sat at the kitchen table and stared out into the conservatory. At times like this, his only connection to his family was his great-uncle's odd hat. He walked into the study and removed it from the mantle. Now, the reason I mention this is you must understand and accept that there are many outlets where one might go to seek comfort; some being odder than others! For instance, I once knew a woman who would dip her fingers into her fishbowl to pet her goldfish while singing Broadway musicals ... However, now that I come to think of it, the fish was stuffed, and it wasn't a fish after all; it was a teddy bear. Although she had a wonderful singing voice. I do remember this, but I digress. In moments such as this, Rupina's hat resting on Preston's head proved to be an indispensable distraction for the poor boy. However, it wasn't just the hat. It was a combination of things which brought him solace: the warmth of the felt upon his head, the gentle clicking of the tiny key he wound to turn the gears, and the subtle ticking of the mechanism embedded in the hat itself. The moment he set it upon his head, he closed his eyes and a sense of calm washed over him. He felt whole once again.

Ahh, the first day of school had begun, and excitement permeated through households everywhere — only from the parent's point of view, of course, for the students were miserable to say the least. Now, as mentioned and affirmed by Preston himself, he had become a sort of recluse. A situation he certainly didn't cherish or seek out. Since most of his adolescent years were spent abroad while his parents fulfilled their desire to travel, Preston missed out on years of birthday parties, ice cream socials, sports, and a litany of other activities one experiences during their childhood. While others his age went fishing, rode their bikes, or played baseball, Preston's youth was spent trudging through jungles and rainforests. That being said, as soon as Preston walked through the front entry to his school, he lowered the brim of his uncle's hat to shield his eyes from the overzealous, snarky classmates. The halls became a sounding chamber as some of the more abusive students spewed muffled insults. Most of the berating revolved around one thing.

"Get a load of the magician. Maybe you can amaze us by pulling some popularity out of your hat?"

"Here's a riddle. What's weirder, the hat or the kid?"

Not the wittiest of insults, I agree, but then again there are those who need to be the social representatives for what not to do and who not to become in every school, and Preston was greeted by them on most days. But there were those who liked the hat and were curious about it, as well as Preston, the "world traveler" as he was known. Unfortunately, their voices remained silent, hoping not to get caught up in the ridicule. This left Rupina's hat as his only source of strength to help him carry on throughout the day. By focusing on the gentle ticking of the gears, he could drown out the crass remarks and snide comments.

But even the strongest seawall can only repel the constant onslaught of waves for so long before cracking. This, unfortunately, was one of those days. As he often did during particularly trying moments, Preston sought refuge within the solitude of Anderson Hall. Most students steered clear of this section of school because it housed the administrative offices as well as the teacher's lounge. As he leaned against the wall to wind his hat, Preston overheard a conversation he would later wish he hadn't.

"This shall not do," a woman exclaimed.

The door to the lounge was open, so Preston crept closer. Through the opening, he saw the principal talking to one of her teachers as they sipped their tea.

"The poor boy seems to have become more reclusive than last year. He has no friends I am aware of. I've sent several letters detailing my concerns to his parents, but so far, they have fallen on deaf ears. I fear something may have happened to them. As such, I've alerted the authorities."

Letters? I never sorted through the mail! he thought, cursing himself for overlooking this detail.

"But he is such a nice boy. If in fact this is true, won't they put him in Iron Hills? I've heard many dreadful stories about what takes place there. Rumors, I can only hope. But either way, that's a place I wouldn't wish upon my worst enemy!"

The principal lowered her cup. "Oh, dear. I hadn't thought about that. I must call the constable immediately!"

PRESTON LEANED AGAINST THE wall with Rupina's hat dangling from his fingertips. Even the mere mention of Iron Hills sent shivers through every child in town. It was an odious name used quite often as a threat by frustrated parents to alter unruly behavior or by schoolteachers to restore order in a disrupted classroom.

You see, Iron Hills was an orphanage at the edge of town, but that's not how it started. Built almost one-hundred years ago during the industrial revolution, it began its life as a steelworks plant. It had its heyday during the war, producing materials needed for ships and tanks. After the war, the owner felt the cost to run the plant outweighed the profitable return, and the plant fell into disrepair. Perched on top of the highest hilltop in the county, Iron Hills stood tall as it overlooked a dead river. It was the sort of place which, even in daylight, gave a foreboding appearance. But at night, it made a graveyard look like a park to gather for picnics. With spindly limbs stretching out from the dead oak trees lining the drive to the bleak, gothic building worthy of any haunted mansion, it was one of the creepiest, most decrepit places you could ever imagine. If this weren't enough to make one turn away, the fog hovering over the ground gave the twin smokestacks a resemblance to pale, demonic arms, which seemingly appeared to be reaching up from the grave.

By rights, the place should have been condemned and torn down years earlier, but an overzealous investor took interest, and now, an extraordinary number of orphans are housed in this wretched place, making one wonder where exactly all these children had come from since the town wasn't terribly large. And where they were housed was just as concerning. Unbeknownst to most, the creosote-soaked towers were converted to ramshackle dorm rooms for the multitude of "unwanted children." But it was these same children who provided an opportunity for the owner to squeeze money from the state. Besides being an orphanage, the owner converted the gothic office building into a school, putting herself in charge. And I would challenge you to find a more disagreeable, acrimonious headmistress.

If you'll indulge my loathing for a moment, I feel it necessary for you to understand this ill-tempered headmistress, for it is her vile behavior which will later change someone's life in the most profound way. Now, as it has been throughout history, evil goes by many names, but in this case, it was called Matilda Crownickers. Crownickers was a dandelion in a field of roses; willing to overtake and suffocate the beauty around her for her own benefit. Nonetheless, she was a brilliant woman with a stout build and crooked nose. When she first opened the orphanage, some called her a pioneer with a strong heart and a passion to help those in need. These people should be institutionalized. Granted, she was passionate — about money. Because of that, she was more than delighted to welcome new members to her "family," but it wasn't because she enjoyed children — far from it. She found them repulsive. But as I said, she did enjoy money, and she received a handsome sum every month from the state for each child she housed, and even more money for educating them! Plus, as a well-planned benefit, the children under her care provided an ample supply of free labor. In-between classes, Crownickers would send out her army of ragamuffins to scavenge for any scraps of iron ore, coke, or limestone left behind by the previous owner. People assumed this was done because she was under-funded and forced to sell the raw materials to provide the children with a better life. Again, these people were wrong and should consider leaving their bubbles to take a realistic look at the world around them. Concealed to all but Crownickers and her "family," the goods she gathered were used in a new style of smelting plant nobody knew about. The gases created were far less than before, and because of this, most were expelled deep into the river by blowers in underground vents. As far as outsiders were concerned, the toxic plant had been shut down and was being put to good use. In reality, it was more active than ever. And this is the catalyst which led to the orphans being sheltered in her toxic chimneys.

"What callous sort would do such a thing?" you may be asking, which is a significant question indeed. You see, it happened one gloomy day while Crownickers stood in front of her grand window, wiggling her crooked toes and staring at the towers as she tried to figure out a way to save money.

"That's it!" she beamed. Her black heart raced as her mind bristled with activity. "This is my most brilliant idea yet!" She yanked open her desk drawer and retrieved a pad and pencil. "I can use the towers for dorms!" After scribbling a few notes, she poured herself a celebratory glass of scotch and threw her head back as she gulped down the swill.

But as soon as the golden liquid passed her lips, her eyes grew wide as she spit it out and grabbed her jaw.

"Wretched tooth," she howled, wincing in pain. "Those miserable children will be the end of me."

She rifled through a nearby cabinet until she found a bottle of aspirin and a straw to slurp her scotch through, avoiding her teeth altogether. After gobbling down a fistful of pills, she kicked her chair aside and paced.

"But how do I make this happen on the cheap?"

She struggled with several ideas, one of which involved stacking dozens of bunk beds on top of each other. Rising high within the towers, the children would be forced to climb endless ladders to their assigned bed. But in her miserable head, an imaginative scene unfolded as she pictured several small children climbing a mountain, bundled up in heavy parkas as the wind and snow whipped around them. Each of the climbers yanked down their thick wool caps over their ears, wiping the ice and snow off their encrusted goggles. With every reach, they threw hooks and ropes up into jagged rocks, climbing to the summit of a snow-capped mountain. As one reached down for the hand of a struggling orphan, their gloved fingertips touched just as the child's rope broke, sending her plummeting down through the thick clouds and disappearing with nothing left but a fading scream. As Crownickers blinked and came back to reality, she shuddered.

"Hmm. There is a chance the little scamps can fall to their death. That would cost me laborers." She kept thinking, staring up at the ceiling. "In order to fit more of them, what if I were to have them sleep standing up, secured to the walls in sleeping bags every night?"

This idea transformed her imagination into an ancient tomb built with stacked limestone blocks. Torches along the walls flickered with light as a young child, wearing an explorer's pith helmet, inched her way across the sand floor. After waving away the sticky spiderwebs filling the corridor, she entered a sarcophagus filled room, discovering dozens of upright mummies strapped to the walls. With torch in hand, the intrepid explorer crept up to one. Its eyes were closed, and their hands bound tight across their chest. Drawing closer, the adventurer smiled wide at her discovery until a growing wet stain spread across the mummy's nether region, causing the child to step back with a scrunched-up face.

"Eww!"

Crownickers blinked her eyes and shook her head quickly. "Well, that won't work. If they can't free themselves to go out to the bathrooms, it will cost a fortune to constantly be cleaning those sleeping bags. Plus, I will have to hire someone just to release them every morning."

But Crownickers wasn't about to give up. Even with the new factory design, some residual gases still needed to be exhausted from the stacks. However, those amounts were small, therefore the massive towers no longer needed to be as wide as they were. This left an abundance of unused space to house all these "urchins." But as you could see, Crownickers did not relish spending money. She plopped down with a clenched fist and bashed it against the desk. As she reached for her drink, she noticed the straw in her glass, and a wicked smile grew across her face. "Oh, Matilda my dear, you are a genius!"

After several months of construction, a thin sleeve of brick and mortar was built into the middle of one tower to serve as the new exhaust stack. This "masonry straw" started at the bottom and rose all the way to the top. What was left was a gap between the inner and outer walls of the smelting tower. Floors of decking were built within this cramped space, thus allowing thirty students to be housed on each level. After an exhaustive day, the children would access the dorms by climbing rickety wooden ladders through small hatches built into the floors, and even though each section was barely wider than a closet, Crownickers felt it provided enough room for her minions to sleep. Plus, in the winter, the exhaust from the blast furnaces would heat the space, thus offsetting her costs!

Now, the townspeople were not completely oblivious to Crownickers' scams. But don't for a minute think her the fool. I assure you, she was one of the most cunning and manipulative people ever to exist. If too many questions started to be raised about the wretchedness the children suffered, an elaborate ruse was already in place to throw off the meddlesome do-gooders. In order to further her "enterprise," she would run her errands while parading the children through town. Preston recalled seeing their dismal faces several times before as Crownickers marched them in and out of stores for supplies. As she exited the shops, you would often see her eating an ice cream cone while one child held a black lace umbrella over her head. Perhaps this was for health reasons you might suggest. No, not at all. This exhibit of elitism was to ensure her favorite treat didn't melt. Behind her, marching in an orderly line, were a dozen other orphans who served as pack mules, carrying armfuls of packages larger than they were. As for the ice cream, she was not foolish by any means. Each week, she would reward the top three children who collected the most scrap metal with an ice cream cone; single scoop, mind you. This kept them motivated to work, and she could always tell curious onlookers the other children did not want any. None of the slighted children dared to contradict her for fear they would lose their meal privileges once they returned. And if that weren't sinister enough, these poor orphans were forced to wear the most atrocious uniforms; gray bib overall shorts which were loose and frumpy, almost resembling burlap sacks. Underneath these were black shirts and matching black socks that rested well below the knees. Her frugalness even spared worn-out uniforms from the incinerator. For those whose shoes had fallen apart, Crownickers tied the remnants of old uniforms to their feet with string. Most of the younger children had ratty shoes with splits in the leather, but the older kids, the ones who could potentially cause problems for her, would receive the newer shoes and clothes, albeit the same ashen ones as the rest of the lot. She took advantage of her dismal parade to make certain the squalor of her students was on full display. The last thing politicians want is for their constituents to think of them as uncaring or inhumane. This fear and her elaborate facade gave Crownickers leverage when she renewed her contract with the state, arguing she needed more money for the proper feeding and clothing of the children. And on the off chance she were to be confronted in the street as to the condition of the children's attire, she would have several boxes staged with new shoes and outfits, however, these were never handed out and were only used as props should the need arise. In sharp contrast, Crownickers wore a black hoop skirt made from the finest silk, with a crisp white blouse and ruffled collar. The wide skirt made her appear plumper than she actually was. On top of her head was a large, veiled hat with colorful plumes extending out from it in every direction. Buried within the fluffy feathers was a stuffed speckled bird peeking through. While she kept herself pristine, aside from the excessive amount of red rouge on her face, most of the children's faces were covered in soot, however, the dark uniforms helped to hide their true disheveled appearance. But even though this seemed like a scam to the wiser, no one dared question her methods — in the open, at least. Behind closed doors, it was a different story. Even though a fair amount of people were indignant at the site of the ghastly children and the seediness associated with Crownickers, the sanctimonious gaggle were willing to turn a blind eye.

"Out of sight, out of mind," was their approach.

For after all their chest thumping and patting themselves on the back, they were no better than Crownickers herself. One foolish politician made the mistake of suggesting Iron Hills be closed and the children placed within the community to attend the local schools. He was run out of town before the ink on the bill was even dry because when it came down to it, nobody wanted the impoverished next to them, driving down the market value of their homes. So, the facade of compassion continued among the smug do-gooders, as long as Crownickers kept the "miscreants" away from them.

Now that you've digested all this information regarding the infamous Matilda Crownickers, you can understand why Preston stood silent, his back pressed against the wall, hoping what he was hearing from his principal wasn't true.

"Perhaps this, this place is not the best," he heard her say, "But would it not be for the better of the child? You've seen that dreaded house he lives in and listened to the whispers of the strange things taking place behind those walls. I even heard a rumor this Rupina character conducted ghastly experiments on stray dogs, turning them into some sort of bloodthirsty hounds he would send out at night to gather up orphans."

"I can't let them send me to Iron Hills," Preston whispered as he crept away.

Back home, Preston flung the back door open and grabbed the box of mail, dumping it onto the kitchen floor. As he sorted through the pile, he found several envelopes from the school, all of them marked "URGENT!" He fell back into his chair, crushing the envelopes in his fist. So many thoughts filled his head. They were relentless, and as soon as a new thought popped in, another one crammed in as well. It got to the point where he was certain his head would burst like a dam. He needed to focus! He needed a plan. As he yanked Rupina's hat down onto his head, hoping the steady ticking would calm his nerves, another letter caught his attention.

"What's this?"

The envelope had a red, white, and blue border and was marked "VIA AIRMAIL."

"It's from them!" The postmark showed it had been sent five weeks ago. "Maybe they're on their way!" he said, ripping open the envelope and reading the letter.

Preston, my darling. We are leaving next week to return home. Your father and I have missed you so much and cannot wait to be with you again. I know it was difficult for us to be away for so long, but wait until you see what we've found! See you soon!

After doing a quick calculation in his head, Preston realized his parents could return within the week.

“I just need to hold out until then!” he said, smiling as he settled into the chair.

As though he were given a new lease on life, Preston turned his attention to his homework. No need to miss an assignment and draw even more unwanted attention to himself. As he thumbed through an atlas, he stumbled upon the slip of paper from inside the cipher.

"All these numbers. Uncle Rupina must have written them down for a reason, but why?"

Coordinates in hand, he cross-referenced them on a map. Most of the locations were centered along fault lines, but then he checked the last marking: 32.0781° Norte, and 81.0841° Oeste.

"It can't be!"

Preston leapt from his chair, for not only was this tiny speck of land tied to a fault line as were the others, but it was also associated with a place known as ...

"The Pirates House!" he shouted as he ran over to a shelf where there was a collection of history books. Several of the texts referenced Savannah, Georgia. It's in one of these books he discovered the site was known as “The Trustees Garden," which was developed as a residential section of Savannah during the 1700s. More importantly was that the inn located there was frequented by pirates.

As he read the passage, he now knew there was a connection to the black pouch containing the sextant. And even more curious was an early photo of the inn, where, looking closer, Preston noticed a triangle with the number “7” carved into the door frame. This symbol kept showing up, and it reminded Preston of the first place he saw it; in his uncle’s book of poems.

Is there something I’m missing? he wondered as he went to grab the book. But as he snatched it off the shelf and flipped through the pages, he found nothing but poorly written poems. However, there was one faint scribbling which he couldn't quite make out. In a search for better lighting, he took the book over to a nearby lamp and removed the shade, holding the paper next to the bare bulb. As he did, letters began to form and spread across the page between the lines of poems. The heat from the bulb revealed words — invisible ink!

More so than all the secret doors, passages, and scavenger hunts combined, this was the most exciting thing he found in Rupina's whimsical house. He cast aside everything else and meticulously went through the journal, scorching each hidden letter written within, and what he discovered was astonishing! Detailed descriptions of technology unheard of, unthinkable in fact, were scribed within these pages. Technology where one could make "jumps" between galaxies! Preston scoured each word, each sentence. According to the writings, there were seven realms in all; each one sharing similarities with one another: the same sort of atmosphere, similar rotations around their particular sun, common calendars and time. But what of the fault lines under the coordinates he discovered. How did all this tie together? After several hours, Preston discovered something he wished he hadn't. But it couldn't be true! His uncle must be mad, delusional, or maybe just a writer of science fiction, for the information he discovered spoke of a plot so devious, it would bring about mass destruction throughout the world. But just as he snickered dismissively, he saw it! The moment the hot bulb turned the ink brown, his heart stuck in his throat. Where there was once a blank page before him transformed into a sketch of fault lines spanning the earth, and above it the words, "Celestial Domination/Realm 7 - Elimination of 93% population". If this were indeed true, if what he saw had been based on scientific evidence, there were three fault lines encircling the earth, and they were all connected. What was worse is the largest one on the map ran directly beneath Iron Hills!

"What was Uncle Rupina planning?"

Preston's imagination took hold as his head filled with strange and ominous thoughts. Sure, they joked about Rupina's peculiarity, but this was far beyond an old man's quirkiness or eccentricity — this was mad scientist worthy. The only thing missing was the evil lair on an isolated, volcanic island. *Perhaps that's what happened to him!* This insanity continued on into the early morning hours. Preston couldn't bring himself to think of anything else, but the hour was late, and he wasn't thinking clearly. All of this had to be nothing but mere fiction; a fantastical tale of nonsensical ramblings. But why hide it with invisible ink? Before Preston knew it, his head was flat against the table, drool puddling next to him as the sun beamed through the windows. Before he even had a chance to open his eyes, there was a loud knock on the door.

His head shot up off the table as he listened intently.

"Preston Cornsuckle! This is Constable McGreary — open the door! We have something to discuss!"

"Oh, no! No — no — no!" A wave of nausea spread through Preston as he leapt from his chair and grabbed his top hat.

Creeping across the room, he dropped to the floor as another knock echoed through the foyer. Frozen, he listened intently — for what, he wasn't certain, but when nothing happened, he belly-crawled to the back staircase which led up to his parent's room. Now, unlike the other stairs, these had an excessive creakiness to them, and now was not the time to alert anyone that the house was indeed occupied. As such, Preston gingerly placed his foot upon the first stair, then the next, cringing each time the wood moaned. When he finally made it to the top, he tiptoed across the floor and peered out through the curtains, but the wide porch roof blocked his view. Perhaps, by some misguided wisdom, he felt if he remained perfectly still, they would go away.

"PRESTON CORNSUCKLE! I DEMAND YOU OPEN THIS DOOR!"

They didn't ...

Preston dove under the bed, knocking his uncle's top hat off his head. His fingers spider-crawled out, grabbing the chapeau and yanking it behind the dust ruffle and onto his head.

"Preston, this is Principal Thatcher. Please open the door."

But the constable was having none of this. "Step aside, ma'am!"

The chilling squeak of the front doorknob turning caused Preston's heart to stop.

"Hello? Is anyone home?" the constable called out as the door creaked open and the dull thud of footsteps clomped through the entry.

Preston crawled out from under the bed and scurried over to the landing, hiding behind a large fern. As one might do on an African safari, Preston peered out from between the leaves and eyed the intruders, hoping to stay undetected.

"Does the headmistress know we are coming?"

Principal Thatcher nodded. "She does. I'm still not sure how I feel about this."

"You contacted us, madame, and the law is the law. The boy's parents haven't been seen in months and have failed to return your correspondence. Worse yet, Mister Crispus Rupina disappeared from this residence as well. Perhaps it is far too dangerous for a child to be left alone here," he said, using his police baton to prod the inside of a closet. "I do believe this is in the boy's best interest. If and when his parents return, they can file a petition with the courts to have him returned."

"How long does that take?"

"It's up to the presiding judge. However, since his parents have to prove they are responsible pillars of the community, I would think no longer than ten to twelve months, tops."

Ten to twelve months? Preston couldn't allow himself to be taken! His eyes darted about as he tried to come up with a plan. All he had to do was stay hidden until his parents returned, then they could figure it out. They're the ones who got him into this mess in the first place.

"I think we should search the upstairs chambers," Constable McGreary suggested.

"Is that allowed?"

"Madame, this is a welfare check. Please, do not tell me how to conduct my business!"

Principal Thatcher nodded, skulking behind the constable as they climbed the stairs. Before they made it to the landing, Preston had already crawled into the cramped dumbwaiter and began lowering himself down to the kitchen. Just beyond the wall, he listened to the intruder's muted voices as they urged him to show himself.

The moment he reached the bottom, he scooted out of the box and snuck over to the back door, but just before he stepped out, he paused. Was this the best plan? There could be others waiting outside, ready to snatch him up. Plus, why leave? This house was loaded with a litany of hidden rooms. And who knew them better? But which room had been the most difficult for him and his family to discover? Then it dawned on him — the hidden bathroom! Even if they revealed the opening, there was no way they would find the staircase concealed within.

While the constable and his principal clunked along the upper floors, Preston dashed through the foyer and down the hall next to the living room. Skidding to a stop, he stood over the floorboard he needed to press three times to release the latch. Unfortunately, this would not be some small, mousy squeak. This was sure to be loud! Certainly loud enough to alert those two meddlers! But if he was going to get out of this, he had to do it.

"Okay, here we go," he said, inhaling deeply. He got set in a runner's position and then stomped on the board.

SQUEAK–SQUEAK–SQUEAK

Everything upstairs went silent as the hidden door across the room slid open.

"Quickly, madame! He's downstairs!"

Preston hadn't realized the policeman was already standing at the top of the stairs.

"Dang it!"

Preston dashed across the room and toward the open panel. Mistakenly turning to see how close they were, Preston failed to avoid an end table, which he promptly smashed into, causing him to tumble. *Why does everyone fall when they're trying to escape?* he thought, rubbing his now-bruised elbow, but there was no time for such needless questions. After throwing the table into the hall, Preston leapt to his feet.

"Preston Cornsuckle, you stand still this instant!" the constable ordered. After reaching the first floor, McGreary grasped the newel post for balance as he launched himself around the staircase, sliding across the marble tile. Before regaining his footing, he collided with the same wretched table as Preston, knocking the policeman to the ground as his legs became entangled. "You'll pay for that, boy!" he cursed, grabbing his shin and wincing in pain as he scrambled to his feet.

This gave Preston just enough time to scamper into the bathroom and slide the weighted panel shut behind him. His heart raced as he pressed his ear against the wall.

"I saw him run in this direction!" the infuriated constable announced.

Their footsteps stopped short of where Preston stood, but it was close enough to cause Preston to back away. The wall was thick, but he couldn't risk making any noise.

"I'm certain he ran in here, and there's only one way in or out!"

Principal Thatcher stuck her head out into the empty corridor, but then remembered something.

"You know, a friend of mine attended a dinner party here and said this place was full of trap doors and hidden rooms!"

"Is that so?" The constable removed his police baton and, with a sinister grin, crept along the walls, rapping on several sections of paneling. "Hmm, interesting."

"What is?"

"Well, that section of wall sounds much different from this one here. Have a listen."

Principal Thatcher approached the wall and leaned in as the constable tapped it with his baton. There was a discernible, empty thud.

"It certainly does," she said, placing her hand on the wall. "Preston?"

They listened intently, but there was nothing but silence.

"Please come out, dear. We are just trying to look out for you. You must trust us. As an educator, I know what is in your best interest."

What unprecedented arrogance one must have to consider themselves to be the voice of others. Preston rolled his eyes at this. "Typical," he muttered as he turned, struggling to remember the secret to unlocking the hidden staircase. Once his eye caught the pull chain dangling from the high tank toilet, it reminded him how to access the hidden cellar. He walked over and pulled on the chain, which created a cacophony of rattling pipes and rushing water.

"No, no, no!" Preston said in an excited whisper, waving his hands in a feeble attempt to fan away the commotion. But once everything settled, the entry to the stairs remained sealed. Preston hurried over to the wall and pressed his ear against the panel. Fortunately, the trespassers seemed far too distracted to have noticed the ruckus.

"Perhaps it is a book on a shelf," Principal Thatcher said. "I've read several mysteries where pulling back on one releases a hidden door."

The dull thud of books dropping to the floor gave Preston some relief.

"Wait one moment," the constable said, standing in a pile of discarded books. "I distinctly recall hearing the sound of a squeaking floor just before the boy disappeared."

He figured it out! Preston stepped back, beads of sweat gathering on his forehead. The room was large, but it wouldn't take long to find the right floorboard. Overwhelmed with stress, Preston sat on the edge of the tub. "I need some water," he said, reaching forward and gripping the smooth porcelain sink. Cold, refreshing water flowed from the spigot, splashing into the bowl. He took off his hat and grabbed a nearby towel, wetting it before dabbing his forehead.

That's it! With the water flowing, he ran over to the pull chain once again and gave it a tug. There was no flushing noise this time. It was replaced by the sound of the tub sliding to the side.

"Thank you!"

He turned off the faucet, causing the tub to slide over to its original spot, but before it completely closed, Preston dashed into the stairwell, disappearing into the darkness just as the entrance sealed itself. He fumbled around until his hand found the light switch, which he yanked up. In a pop of sparks, the long line of lightbulbs burst with life, leading Preston down the stairs.

"My hat!" he said, tapping his head, only then remembering he had taken it off to dab his brow.

"If they see it, they'll know I was in there and they'll keep searching the room. They're bound to unlock the door and find me down here."

He couldn't risk it, so he shot back up the stairs and jerked the metal release for the tub. It took all his strength to push the heavy tub aside, and just as he reached his hat — SQUEAK, SQUEAK, SQUEAK — The noise echoed in his head as everything seemed to move in slow motion. The moment the metallic click of the latch released the door, Preston's feet had barely cleared the opening, and the tub settled with a resounding thud, covering his escape. Once the last sliver of light from the bathroom fleeted behind the closed panel, he turned out the lights on the stairwell and waited silently, frozen, his heart about to explode out of his chest.

"A bathroom?" The voices were muted, but he could still make out the words.

"Well, there is no place to hide in here," Principal Thatcher said, feeling slight relief at not finding him.

"Ahh, or is that what he wants us to believe? What if there is yet another hidden entry?"

He listened as the two invaders walked across the tile floor, tapping on the walls and stomping their feet. One of them even wriggled the tub, but fortunately it didn't budge. However, they persisted, checking every inch of the room.

In the midst of darkness, nary a sound being heard, one's imagination begins to deceive them. And in Preston's case, he kept feeling an imaginary hand grabbing his shoulder — caught! As he shook away the phantom feeling, he decided to not sit idly by to be captured. After all, he was never one to give in and accept defeat. Then again, maybe he was. He'd certainly find out on this day. Regardless, he turned the lights back on and stared down the stairs. The only chance he had was at the bottom; in a dank room full of emptiness, completely void of anything other than air ... damp, stale air. If surrender could be bottled as a fragrance, this is what it would smell like. Even so, he stared at the only other way out. At least the only other POSSIBLE way out, and it stood tall before him — the massive vault door.

In an act of desperation, Preston grasped the handle and turned, but as expected, it didn't budge. He spun several combination locks before stepping back. If this house had taught him anything, it was things are not always as they seem. There was always some sort of gimmick or trick. He deduced since there was clearly no pattern for these locks, perhaps this was by design, only to serve as a distraction from prying eyes attempting entry. And why wouldn't they be? The same construct was something he encountered with the cylinder cipher. It was at this moment of insight when his eye captured a minuscule detail, so small it was easily overlooked. Deep within the recess of the spoked handle was a depression in the shape of a sprocket.

"Could it be?"

Preston removed his hat and examined the three attached gears. Each was a different size, and one of them appeared to match the recess in the door handle. After plucking the gear off the hat, he pressed it into the handle — it fit! The gears were not only gears after all — they were keys!

Grabbing the spoke of the wheel, he took a deep breath, and turned the handle, which clicked as it spun freely. His heart raced with renewed hope. Perhaps the space was filled with canned goods or preserves — a safe room of sorts. He just needed to hide out for a few days. Just until his parents returned. Once he heard a resounding metallic clank, he pulled the door open wide. The musty stench of a damp basement washed over him as he peeked inside the darkened chamber. After retrieving the gear, he replaced it on his hat and ran his hand along the wall, where his fingers bumped a wooden handle. He threw the switch up, illuminating the space. But there was nothing ... Well, that's not entirely true. What I meant was there was no food or provisions of any sort to be found, and there certainly were no riches one would expect to be locked behind such an impressive door. But what was there was a solitary steamer trunk; one which had been oddly modified. The trunk sat in the center of the room on the cold stone floor.

"All of this for a piece of luggage?"

He crouched down and examined the dome lidded trunk. This long sought after discovery gave him a momentary distraction from the search taking place just above his head.

But as I said, the trunk had been tinkered with. Why? The reason was not certain. However, fitted to the outside of the chest were an array of polished brass gears and sprockets. Groups of them interlocked with each other on different portions of the trunk. Affixed to both sides were copper pipes that twisted and turned along the wooden slats before disappearing into the chest itself, and arranged evenly on the lid were several gauges displaying: Pressure, Temperature, and Velocity. Above those stood a brass steam whistle, much like the type you would see on a locomotive. Just below the latch was a clock — a pocket watch, to be precise. It was the exact size and style as the one on Preston's hat. He continued his examination until some hushed voices and rumblings coming from the top of the stairs distracted him. He feared the intruders were getting closer to discovering the secret basement.

Regardless of what happened, he absolutely needed to see what was inside. This door had been a mystery for so long, and now to see what was behind the elusive opening couldn't be left unchecked. As he hurriedly tried to open the steamer trunk, he found the lid to be locked as well.

However, it had the same type of spoked recess in the latch. He removed the gear from his hat and tried to press it into the latch, but it was too large. He plucked out a smaller gear and slid it into place. Even though it snapped into the recess, the latch remained locked.

"This doesn't make sense. It should've worked!" He stared at the trunk. "Why would a lock not unlock if the key fits?" Certainly, a riddle to ponder, and as he did so, the sound of the ticking clock in his hat captured his attention. Could it be? He removed the hat, placing it next to the trunk. The other clock wasn't keeping time.

With his index finger, Preston spun the minute hand on the trunk's clock until the two timepieces were synched, and just as soon as they were, the latch sprung open! Immediately, several interlocking gears on the outside of the steamer trunk came to life, and the lid raised.

Preston stretched his neck, eager to get a peek inside the elusive chest as the top lifted. However, instead of finding gold or jewels like one would expect, Preston was astonished to see the trunk was some type of machine, or vehicle of sorts. Inside was a wooden control panel fitted with glass vacuum tubes, metal coiled wires, and an absurd number of toggle switches and gauges. There was also a tufted, red velvet seat secured to the bottom of the trunk, with a tall brass pull handle next to it. But before he could figure it out, he heard the latch on the tub release.

"They got through!"

He grabbed the sprocket from the trunk's latch, shut the vault door, and scrambled around the room.

"There has to be another exit," he said as he twisted the lightbulbs and stomped on the floor. But there was no hidden switch.

His only option was to hide in this odd trunk. It was such an obvious spot, but what else could he do? As soon as he stepped inside and scrunched down onto the seat, a series of lights on the panel flashed and the gauges came alive as their tiny arrows fluttered. Worried the flashing lights would give him away, Preston slapped his hand against the panel, accidentally pushing several buttons. Within seconds, the lid slowly dropped.

"Wait, no!" he yelled as the closing lid forced him to hunch over, knocking the hat off his head.

With a loud click, the trunk sealed itself, and the latch locked. Now, I don't know about you, but being trapped in a tiny box such as this would certainly cause an explosion of panic to spread through me! Preston was no different. He grunted and called out for help as he pushed his hands against the top, but it didn't budge. Once he realized his efforts were futile, he paused. The silence surrounding him was deafening, his only comfort being the lights, which continued to blink yellow - blue - green; yellow - blue - green. With each flash of light, shadows danced inside the trunk. The only thought in his head at the moment was giving himself up, for no matter how bad he believed Iron Hills to be, he was certain he wouldn't run out of air there!

Preston dropped his head against the panel. "This is ridiculous," he said, searching for a lever to release the lid. The only one which looked as though it was some sort of release mechanism was the one next to the plush seat. He squeezed the handle and clicked it back until it came to an abrupt stop. This turned out to be a major mistake, for as soon as the lever came to rest, an alarm bell rang out from inside the trunk, causing a startled Preston to smash his head against the lid.

"What the —" he started to ask, rubbing his head, until the bell stopped and was replaced by the clanking of metal gears. There was a slight shudder when the gears stopped and, shortly after, the steam whistle above him shrieked out an ear-piecing howl. Preston covered his ears, groaning in pain before a burst of intense white light filled the compartment. Blinded by the flash, Preston huddled in the trunk, concealing his head with his arms as he sat silent and unmoving. The trunk rumbled and shook violently for a moment, and then all fell silent. As he uncovered his head, he heard the latch release just before the lid lifted.

PRESTON DARED NOT RAISE his head, fearing he'd be snatched up by the constable as soon as he popped out. But something odd piqued his curiosity; the trunk was rocking. Not a rough, jerky jostling, like being shaken by the shoulders; this was a relaxing, steady motion, like softly rocking a baby to sleep. Actually, it felt as though he was — floating in water!

A million thoughts raced through Preston's head as he remained hunched over. Nobody was there to yank him up by the scruff of his neck — they would've done so already. Scrunched over, he remained silent, listening to the steady creaking of wood. With no lights to show him his surroundings, he waited a short while longer before deciding it best to figure out what was happening. Unfortunately, his brain couldn't convince his body to move. After much internal struggle, Preston mustered up the courage to raise his throbbing head and peek out from the trunk.

This is useless. I can't see a thing!

Darker than before, Preston couldn't even see beyond the tip of his nose. He blindly reached his hand out and felt around. The ground was solid, so some good news there. But as he dragged his fingertips across the rough surface, they dipped in and out of jagged channels. Wood, it definitely felt like rough wood. Perhaps a wood floor? This didn't quite make sense. He was positive the trunk was on a stone floor, unless, with all the jostling, the trunk shifted and ended up on a section of wooden floor he hadn't noticed. Nonetheless, now that he was confident he wouldn't be stepping into a flooded basement, he took hold of the armrests and stood, retrieving his hat in the process. But his newfound confidence didn't take into account the rocking, and as one foot settled on the floor, a sudden pitch tossed him to the side. In a flurry of losing his balance and tumbling out of the chest, his hand slapped against the control panel, pressing a switch which triggered the lid to close.

After hitting the ground, Preston momentarily stood steady before another pitch launched him backwards, slamming into what could have been a barrel. As he tumbled, so did the barrel, which rolled away and smashed into something else buried within the shadows. What was once a quiet chamber was now filled with sounds of chaos and carnage. Preston was aghast at everything happening, but any concerns he had quickly vanished as a sliver of light filtered into the space.

Maybe there was another secret door!

In a way, he was correct — a secret door of sorts was opened. You see, these trunks, or at least the technology built into them, were developed in a distant realm by a populous much more advanced than Earth or any of the other realms. Unbeknownst to Preston, or a whole many more, I would presume, this technology allowed travelers to cross galaxies and land within one of seven realms. Each planet bearing a startling similarity to one another. Now, this is a whole lot to take in, and our story is far from over. That being said, my rambling on about this subject at this particular point doesn't address the issue at hand, which is Preston's issue at the moment, to be certain. So, on we go, for now.

Now, with some much-needed light, Preston wriggled himself free and crept toward the glow, feeling his way with his outstretched hands. But before he made it across the space, his foot became entangled in a loose coil of rope, causing him to trip and crash into what felt like a small table. Something he was quite familiar with. As he and the table smashed against the floor, the sound of shattering glass filled the air. Careful not to get cut, Preston reached down and untangled the thick rope from around his foot.

"What is —"

"Eh, who's down there?" a voice from the top of the stairs called out. Next came the sound of shuffling feet scrambling down some creaky steps.

The constable!

Preston searched for a place to hide, but it was still too dark to see clearly, and until a few minutes ago, he was positive the room was empty. But there was no time for him to ponder this, for whatever door he thought had been opened flew open even wider and slammed against the wall with a crashing thud. More light washed into the room, allowing Preston to take notice of a stack of crates behind him. His immediate concern was not what these were or where they came from; he could sort that out later. Bound together with netting, Preston used the roping to climb over the top of the crates, diving behind the mound and blending into the darkness. Afraid to move, he peeked out and watched as two shadowed figures entered the space. They were being led by a soft light flickering from a lantern one of them held.

"Seems we have a stowaway," a terse female announced, sweeping the light around her feet as she inspected the clutter.

"Eh, what's this?" asked a man with a gruff voice, which sounded like he swallowed a mouthful of sand.

Through the shadows, Preston watched as they approached his trunk with their swords drawn. Yes, actual swords!

"Why, it's nothing but a trunk," the repugnant pirate said, kicking it with his foot. "Odd, we didn't bring one of these with us."

"See what's inside," the tall woman said.

"It's closed."

"Well, open it!"

The man jiggled the latch.

"I can't. It's locked."

"Hmm ... You better go get the Captain. I'll keep looking around."

The man sprinted up the stairs as the woman skulked her way around numerous stacks of crates, barrels and — a cannon? Of course, after seeing everything in Rupina's home, a cannon would be one of the least odd things Preston had run across. As she approached through the shadows, it was obvious this woman wasn't Principal Thatcher.

"Come on out, you little rodent. I won't hurt you."

As she circled a large box, she leapt forward and slashed her sword.

"Blast it," she cursed before continuing her search.

What happened to not hurting me?

Preston watched as she inched closer to his hiding spot. Unable to rely on the darkness to keep him hidden any longer, he reached down and grasped the closest thing to use as a weapon. It felt heavy and had a solid handle, like a hammer, so he gripped it tight in his hand. As soon as she got within inches of his spot, Preston launched himself at her, but was immediately snatched by his shirt in mid-air.

"Argh, and what do we have here?" a deep, rancorous voice asked. If Preston were to survive all of this somehow, he felt certain he'd hear this cold, angry voice in his nightmares. For now, he would have to come to terms with this terrifying situation, which at the moment had him dangling with his arms and legs flailing about.

"Ey, Chuggs! If ye find the stowaway, the Captain wants 'em on deck," the man called down from the top of the stairs while the woman walked up to the pirate bobbing Preston up and down as though he were a puppet.

"Not to worry. It looks as though the search is over," she sneered.

Chuggs grunted as he yanked the hammer out of Preston's hand. If you took a hundred Prestons, and stuffed them into an oversized man suit, this brute would still tower over him. He had to be the largest person Preston had ever seen. The hulk of a man raised the hammer, ready to bring it down on Preston's head.

"Don't even think about it, Chuggs," the woman ordered. "Take this urchin topside. The Captain will deal with him."

As if someone snatched a toy away from a child, Chuggs frowned with a timid groan as he dropped the hammer and carried Preston like he was nothing more than a sack of rubbish. The enormous man stooped low to avoid hitting his head on the beamed ceiling. His hand alone was as large as Preston's head and held the boy with a viselike grip. As soon as they climbed the stairs, the sound of seagulls squawking and waves crashing filled Preston's ears, but the intense light temporarily blinded him.

How did I get on a boat?

As his eyes adjusted to the sun, he saw three towering masts, each fitted with sails billowing high above — black sails!

This is the ship!

Fastened to the deck were three bulky copper tanks, which had a thick pipe running through them and the masts as well. High above, steam lazily drifted upwards from the top of the towering masts. All around him, men and women dressed as pirates scurried about. Still suspended in the air, he turned his head and now clearly saw the owner of the meaty mitt holding him prisoner. The man was bald; his skin as dark as the eyepatch he wore. He released his grip on Preston, who crumpled to the ground. Preston pushed himself up by his elbows as he stared up at him. The imposing beast of a man wore nothing other than cream-colored khakis, which were tattered below the knees. The leather strap tied around his bulging bicep strained to stay knotted. There was a sword tucked into his wide leather belt, but against this behemoth, the blade seemed nothing more than a tiny dagger. With an aloof approach, Chuggs reached down and lifted Preston to his feet. Now, it wasn't the ease of him lifting Preston which made the boy cower; it was, in fact, the arm to which he used. You see, where there should have been flesh, there was metal.

A mechanical arm? Preston was dumbfounded! He stared at the exoskeleton of the man's limb, which was crafted from hammered copper sheets, molded to the same proportions as his other arm. Along the prosthetic were openings in the forearm and elbow. Each movement by Chuggs caused separate gears to spin and pistons to extend. Below the covering were silver rods, which served as bones and supported the copper plating. The prosthetic continued up to his shoulder, where it became attached to the man by a series of rivets. The burnished metal had a soft, green patina around the fasteners. Preston scooted away until his back hit a wall. He had seen plenty of mechanical workings in the gadgets his great-uncle designed. However, this was beyond anything he could've imagined.

"What ... what are you?"

"We should be asking the same question of ye," a gruff voice announced. "Or more precisely, WHO are ye, if we are not trying to be rude." A stout man in a buccaneer coat and a tricorn hat hobbled up to Preston. "In a civil world, it is customary to introduce oneself. I, for example, am Captain Barnabus Hornswaggle, otherwise known as 'Redbeard!'"

Preston was absolutely certain that as soon as Redbeard announced himself, even the waves of the ocean paused to listen. With his face shadowed, Redbeard approached, his presence exuding a confidence Preston had never experienced. The man presented a subtle refinement to a seemingly malicious being, as if one encountered a shark wearing a tuxedo. But as soon as the man's hat blocked the sun, his bushy, red beard captured Preston's attention. Attached to his twisted strands of beard, dangling like Christmas ornaments from some spots and embedded deep within others, were loose gears; much like the ones on Preston's steamer trunk, and similar to the ones affixed to Rupina's hat.

My hat! Preston had all but forgotten his treasured chapeau. He reached up and tapped his head. *Did I have it on when they found me, or is it still in the trunk?*

At the sight of this, Redbeard quirked an eyebrow, the wrinkles on his forehead growing as deep as the ocean itself.

"Are ye missing something, boy?"

A lot! My sanity, for starters. "No, I was just noticing your hat appeared crooked, so I was worried the wind might blow it off or something."

"Hmm," Redbeard grunted as he shifted his worn, black tricorn hat. Much like Preston's hat, Redbeard's had three interlocking gears on the side, but his did not spin.

"Well, ain't that gentlemanly of ye? Now, hows about we get back to the point at hand? I believe ye were about to tell me yer name."

"Uhm, yes, right, sorry. It's, it's, Preston. My name is Preston," he said, covering his mouth as he let out a muted burp.

Redbeard smiled as Preston succumbed to seasickness. "What be the problem, Squire Preston? Yer looking a bit green around the gills." The crew let out a roar of laughter as Redbeard reached into one of the wide cuffs on his heavy, blue wool coat and pulled out a red silk handkerchief, handing it to Preston. "Ere ye go."

"Thank you," Preston said as he covered his mouth. To take his mind off the swaying ocean, he fixated on the large, shiny brass buttons on Redbeard's coat. "Sorry, I've never been on a boat before."

"Nor have ye still since this be a ship."

Again, the pirates burst out laughing. If you want to feel unsettled, and a bit worrisome, find yourself stuck in the center of a gaggle of sword-wielding pirates.

Preston went to stand, but paused when he noticed Redbeard's pants. But it wasn't the pants themselves. His focus was on the cream-colored material that disappeared into his black leather boot. Boot, as in singular, for he only had one. Where the other boot should be had been replaced by a large wooden peg leg. From the tall tales of scavengers of the sea, it was the sort of prosthetic you'd expect to see on a salty dog like Redbeard. However, similar to Chuggs' arm, the leg had several compartments carved into it. One of the copper plated covers was open, and inside were several gears and switches. But one might question what a leg like this controlled? It's not as if tendons and ligaments were being manipulated by the spinning gears. Granted, I'm not an expert in the subject, however, it is my understanding a device, such as this, was something created more for balance than mechanical, or so it should've been.

"So, young Preston, what might I ask brings ye here aboard my ship?"

"I'm sorry. I'm not exactly sure where 'here' is."

"Well, 'here' at the moment is aboard the Dragon's Curse; and 'here,' in the not-too-distant future, is being ashore in the jewel of the sea, Breakaway Bay."

"Breakaway Bay?"

"Aye! Am I to believe this name is unfamiliar to ye? Tis the location of my fortress, and the port of call for The Steampunk Pirates."

Steampunk Pirates? "No, I'm sorry, but I've never heard —"

"Captain! This is the trunk to which I spoke."

Redbeard turned, and his eyes grew wide.

"It can't be!"

Preston spun around to look. The tall woman he encountered earlier emerged from the doorway, followed close behind by two other pirates who were carrying Preston's trunk.

The beaming sun highlighted the woman's exotic features. Through her shoulder length wavy black hair, she leered at Preston. Her appearance was a contradiction to the senses. She wore white pants, which clung to her long legs, but were partially covered with a long black trench coat. But those mesmerized by her beauty might miss the dagger hidden in her black boots, or the pistol tucked away in her lace corset. She exuded fear and respect from her shipmates as her boots clunked across the soaked wooden deck planks, but as she passed, some drew a scowl.

"And what do we have here?" Redbeard asked as he hobbled over to the trunk. For a dour brute such as Redbeard, a smile of any sort seemed as out of place as a fish riding a bike. Yet, here it was. An unsettling smile crept across his normally stolid face as he bent down and ran his hands along the smooth wooden slats of the steamer trunk. "Beautiful," he said, spinning the gears and fiddling with the gauges. Leaning in close, he took a deep breath, inhaling the oak scent of the wood as he rubbed the leather strapping. “Ahh yes,” he said, looking to the side. “At long last.”

“What is she, Cap’n?”

“She be a steamer trunk. The last of her kind, if I’m inclined to believe the scuttlebutt.”

“Last of ‘er kind?” one pirate chuckled. “Me mother’s got three of ‘em in ‘er attic!”

The other pirates burst out laughing until Redbeard cast an icy stare. “Not like this one, ye fool! Much like the Dragon’s Curse, this one can make the jump from one realm to another.”

There was a gasp amongst the crew.

“Realm jump?” Preston whispered, reminding him of his uncle Rupina’s writings.

“Aye, this beauty was built decades ago in the 7th realm, in a city called Savannah.”

“Savannah?” the woman squeaked.

Redbeard glanced at her over his shoulder. “Aye. The city for which ye were named after, my dear. I spent a fair amount of time at a fine tavern called the Pirate's House back in my youth. It was during my sea captain’s training,” he said, looking up and smiling. “I’d recognize the work on this trunk anywhere.” He continued to stare at it before turning to Preston. “Hmm,” he said, jiggling the trunk’s latch and stroking his beard. “Where is the key, boy?”

“Key?” Preston coughed.

Redbeard’s face turned as red as the handkerchief. “Ye best belay that yarn, boy! Ye didn’t just get spit out of the sea only to land on my ship, flopping around like some scared tuna. This trunk brought ye here, and for that ye needed a key,” he snarled, his words skipping across his tongue. “Now, where is it?”

"I'm sorry, but I just found this trunk, and when I got inside, the lid closed. The next thing I know, I ended up here. I don't know anything about a key, or what this thing even is."

Redbeard scowled at Preston. "Show our uninvited guest to his accommodations!" he roared, thrusting his finger at Preston.

Savannah and another pirate grabbed Preston by his arms and dragged him off.

"Ye'll tell the truth, boy. This, I promise!"

What have I gotten myself into? Just those six words was all it took to fill Preston with dread and sorrow. How many times are these words uttered every day? Some situations prompt a more dire use of the phrase, and this was as dire as one would expect. Preston's heels bounced down the stairs and as he glanced around, the once brilliant sunlight had been replaced by a smattering of lantern light deep within the ship. Along with everything else he had suffered, now he would be imprisoned in some shadowed corridor.

Savannah stopped in front of a thick door and grabbed the rusted bars covering the window, pulling it open. The wood moaned against the corroded hinges as she shoved Preston inside. He slid across the straw covered floor. The dank room only had one tiny window, which allowed a scant amount of outside light into the space. With no cover, the sea spray misted into the chamber, coating the timbers with a gritty white layer of salt. As the door slammed shut and locked, Preston walked up to the window. It would be a tight squeeze to be certain, but he was confident he'd be able to scrunch himself enough to wriggle his way through. But then what? After all, there was nothing but a vast ocean as far as the eye could see. Even the strongest swimmer wouldn't attempt such a foolish quest. He dropped to the floor and stared up at the ceiling, turning away from the swaying oil lantern. He had just gotten over feeling nauseous, and sitting in a puddle of his own vomit wouldn't enhance his current situation. What was he to do at this point? Redbeard wanted something he didn't have. And even if he had the key, that is, his uncle's hat, how could he just hand over something apparently so valuable to these "Steampunk Pirates?" What if the hat turns out to be his only way home? What would he do then? He dropped his head into his hands as the salty spray misted over him.

Two identical twin pirates, with faces as narrow as a broom handle, carried Preston's trunk into Redbeard's quarters and heaved it up onto the dining table. Redbeard didn't bother to look up as he shuffled through some papers at his desk. As they turned to leave, one twin reached for the door, but was thrown back against the wall as Savannah barged in, pushing her way past the befuddled man, who was now lying on the floor searching for his misplaced hat. His brother rushed over and helped the lanky man to his feet, grabbing his matching stocking cap and replacing it on the poor man's head. Both twins looked at each other, shrugged their shoulders, and shuffled out of the room.

"Why do you not speak more of my birthplace?" Savannah asked.

"And why would I do that?" Redbeard muttered, obviously bothered by the incessant interruptions.

"Oh, I don't know ... so I would learn something about myself. Perhaps I could understand your desire to abandon me there."

"Abandoned?" he scoffed, giving her a quizzical stare. "Yer one for theatrics, aren't ye?" The cantankerous pirate grunted and shook his head. "What possible difference could this information make in yer life?"

"I could have learned more of my mother. Perhaps had a sense of normalcy to my childhood!"

Redbeard dropped his head. "Ye know enough about her. She was a serving wench and nothing more. I told ye this. Anything beyond would be a distraction to our mission, and I cannot, nor will I allow that!" he said, slamming his hands onto the desk as he launched out of his chair and pointed to the door. "Now forget this nonsense and return to yer duties."

Savannah's jaw dropped as she glared at him. "Aye, sir," she said through gritted teeth before stomping out of his quarters.

The moment the door closed, Redbeard opened his desk drawer and removed a small, red velvet sack. He jiggled the pouch in his hand as he carried it over to the trunk.

"Aye, ye are a beauty," he said as he ran his hand over the latch, and then emptied the contents of the bag onto the table. Dozens of brass gears of all sizes spilled out across the wooden surface. Like a jeweler examining diamonds, Redbeard picked through each sprocket, scrutinizing them before choosing one and placing it into the recess on the latch. The first gear fit snug, but nothing happened. The trunk remained locked. He removed the gear and replaced it with another — still, nothing. He searched the remaining gears, trying one after another. None of them released the stubborn latch!

"Argh!" He yanked out a dagger from the red sash around his waist and held it high.

"Ye can't be doin' that, Cap'n."

Redbeard scowled at the short, stocky man who entered, uninvited.

"What do ye want, Quinton?" he asked, stabbing the dagger into the table.

"I want to make sure ye don't get angry and destroy this one like the last."

Redbeard swung around and yanked the blade from the wood, pressing the sharp tip against Quinton's throat. Unimpressed, Quinton raised his hands.

"Easy, Cap'n. Ye know I meant no disrespect."

"Then ye best knot yer tongue!" he said, withdrawing his knife and sliding it back into its scabbard.

Quinton dropped his arms. This had become an all-too-familiar routine for the two men.

"I just want to make certain I help ye in any way I can," Quinton said, bowing. "The job of the quartermaster is to protect the captain, and I feel it was I who failed ye last time."

"The last one was cheaply built," Redbeard grumbled as he picked through the sprockets. "But this one ... this is different. I recognize the craftsmanship. This is the one!"

"The one?" Quinton asked as he swept the dangling tassel of the red-striped stocking cap away from his eyes to get a better look.

"Aye! Inside this trunk is a hidden compartment only known to me! And protected inside this compartment are many secrets, more valuable than all the gold in all the realms. One of which will give us the means to set any jump points we choose."

"Any jump points? I thought we had but a handful in each realm?"

Redbeard chuckled. "Aye! Ye speak the truth! But the founders of our technology used many more. When I found their bones, I found a design to build a portable beacon; one which would guide our ships to a point of our choosing! So precious was this design, I hid it in this here trunk. For many years, this trunk was secreted in a safe place until some wretch stole her from me. And now I'm closer to getting back those designs and the answer to who stole this beauty from me."

"How can ye be so certain this is the one, Cap'n?"

"I have my ways of knowing."

Quinton bent down and adjusted his glasses as he examined the latch. "Why don't none of the gears work? I mean, they fit and all."

"That's the brilliance of this design. Each trunk has two unique gears cast at the time of construction." He held one gear in his hand as he examined it in the light. "Each imperfection of the metal, the calculated weight of the sprocket, all play a role in releasing a particular lock."

"Seems like a nasty bit of nonsense for one to be makin' it so difficult."

Redbeard squeezed his eyes shut while letting out an exasperated gasp. "Bollocks! Then why have a lock at all? Ye know nothing of these trunks, so I wouldn't expect ye to appreciate the design. Is there some work ye can be doin'?"

"Aye, Captain. We're approaching Breakaway Bay. I'm preparing the Dragon's Curse for our arrival."

"Then get on with it! I'll be topside shortly."

After Quinton left, Redbeard glared at the trunk. "Soon, I won't have to rely on that wretched woman any more. Iron hills, indeed."

Savannah threw open the door to the crew's quarters and collapsed into her hammock. With one leg extending out, she swung back and forth, staring at the ceiling while several pirates sat around a barrel, using its lid to play cards on. Most normally ignored her outburst, but one of the older pirates shook his head and scoffed at her.

"And what's yer problem this time, princess?" he asked, not bothering to look up from his cards.

"And to what concern is it of yours?"

He slapped the cards down and stood. "It is of concern because every time ye have an issue with someone or something, ye start tearing OUR things apart and throwing OUR stuff around! I want to make sure none of my trinkets are ruined by another one of yer childish tantrums!"

Savannah leapt out of her hammock and lunged at the man, ripping his shirt open before pressing a dagger against the pirate's chest. But where there should have been skin, there was an open box of exposed gears. The tip of her blade embedded into one of the rotating gears, causing the tiny brass wheel to stop turning. She cocked her head to one side and glared at the man from the corner of her eye as he gasped for air.

"Your tongue is sharper than your blade, Slits! Wouldn't it be a shame to share your slumber with the crabs just because your mouth outran your brain?"

The pirate scowled as he grabbed her hand and pushed it away. Now free, the gear turned once again, allowing him to draw in a deep breath. After tying his shirt closed, he sneered and clenched his fists tight, but he knew better than to raise a hand to Redbeard's daughter. There was only one allowed to scold her, and it certainly wasn't him.

"All I'm saying is we all have to share this space," he muttered through gritted teeth. "And when ye go around and destroy everything we 'ave, it doesn't help matters."

Savannah kicked over the soiled ditty bag next to his bunk and scoffed at him. "You think those scraps you keep are worth anything? If you don't like your accommodations, then you can go sleep in the crow's nest. Now stop your bellyaching so I can get some shuteye."

Savannah returned to her bunk, dropping into it so hard, the ropes whined as they stretched. With her feet crossed, she covered her eyes with her hat while several pirates threw icy glances at each other. A few of them even stood, gripping their daggers tight in their hands. It hadn't been the first time they considered slitting her throat and tossing her over the side of the ship, but as they pondered their next move, Savannah casually pulled her pistol, laying it across her chest.

"If any of you dogs get some wild idea, it'll be your last."

"Get yer worthless selves above deck!" Quinton yelled, kicking the door open and staring at the pirates lallygagging in their quarters. "Breakaway Bay is just over the horizon!"

Savannah didn't budge as the rest of the crew leapt out of their hammocks and scrambled past Quinton. Once the room cleared, the frustrated pirate glared at Savannah. Regardless, she made no effort to move or entertain his demands. With not even a whisper, or exasperated breath, he turned to leave.

"Hey!"

Quinton stopped in the doorway as Savannah removed her hat and sat up.

"Make sure you get these old codgers upgraded. Slits still wears an open chest box. Won't do much good to have a pump in him if he gets shot in the box and his gears fail."

"Are ye one to be given me orders now?" Quinton asked before heading up to the deck.

"Obviously somebody has to," she said, placing the hat back over her eyes.

Savannah drifted in and out of sleep as she reflected on her youth.

I never had a chance.

It wasn't as though Savannah resented her life; she loathed it. But what of it? The iceberg may dislike the cold, but it is the cold that allows it to exist; and Redbeard was the bitterest cold she'd ever known.

At a time when Savannah saw her friends being sent off to school, she was loaded onto a ship, exiled to a distant realm, training to become someone she had never wanted to be. Because of Redbeard's ... well ... "ambitious nature," let's call it, he didn't want to be constantly burdened with a headstrong, petulant child. Of course, he had only himself to blame. With Crownickers as her mother, and Redbeard for a father, she'd never actually had the opportunity to live what one might call a "normal" life. And yes, Crownickers and Redbeard had been wed at one time, although I'm not certain this is still the case. Nonetheless, can you imagine those two insufferable narcissists immortalized in effigy on top of a wedding cake? But getting back to Savannah, whatever the intent for her banishment, she was boarded at a place nicknamed the "Pirate's House." A little on the nose if you ask me. However, pirates weren't the most creative lot, so the name should come as no surprise. Plus, if I'm being forthcoming, they were technically correct; it was a house, of sorts, and it was always full of pirates. That much is certain. While in port, raucous gaggles of marauders ate at the infamous establishment, slept in its beds, and — well, we will just say they entertained themselves there as well.

By any standards, civilized people would attest the Pirate's House was no place for a child — and most adults would surely agree if I am to be perfectly honest. But it was the ideal place to send someone if they were destined to be an up-and-coming leader in the pirate world. The intention was for the young girl to rotate among ships, allowing her to experience different leadership styles, but the crew aboard these vessels followed the old ways and never wanted her around. There was a long-standing notion that having a female aboard a ship was bad luck, and pirates were a superstitious bunch, to be clear. Worse yet, some believed she was placed there in order to spy on them for Redbeard. But when it came down to it, none of this mattered, because they were too afraid of Redbeard to send her back, so she remained isolated.

Even before Savannah's exile, her relationship with her father was that of fire and ice. Of course, her relationship with Crownickers wasn't any better. You see, Crownickers had her own plans of conquest, and having a young daughter clinging to her side would interfere with her desire to court a wealthy suitor. After her husbands (yes, plural) mysteriously died, she inherited their fortunes. To Crownickers, marriage was nothing more than a money-making scheme.

Before you ask, I assure you Redbeard knew of Crownickers' ... well, outside interests, we'll call them. You'd think he'd care, be outraged, but he didn't and wasn't. His only interest in the woman was Iron Hills. A place Crownickers purchased from her illicit inheritances. Iron Hills was one of but a handful of jump points in the Seventh Realm, what we'd call Earth, and Redbeard would endure whatever he needed to in order to secure this location. Plus, Crownickers produced and supplied him with stainless steel. Something he needed to strengthen his fleet if the vessels were to survive jumping between realms.

With regard to her daughter, Crownickers' relationship with Savannah is one of convenience — or at least it used to be. At one point, Savannah actually thought her mother loved her, and Crownickers played the mother angle perfectly, making Savannah believe they were growing close. But she later found out Crownickers was just using her. You see, Crownickers needed workers for her new smelting plant, and since Savannah had been isolated, she was desperate for companionship. This forced the young girl to seek out friends among the local street children who hung around the Pirate's House, scrounging for scraps of food. But as soon as she became close with anyone, they would mysteriously disappear. Come to find out, Crownickers kidnapped them and forced them to work in her smelting plant. Word spread among the orphans about Crownickers, and they accused Savannah of collaborating with her. Even though she had nothing to do with it, none of the children trusted her any longer. Because of this, she was shunned even further. Not only forsaken by the children around her, but also her parents, her solitude went on for years. Even Crownickers stopped visiting since her daughter's so-called "usefulness" ended.

While all this was taking place, the pirate's reign of influence was coming to an end (at least within this realm). When the governor of Georgia learned about the Pirate's House and its clientele, soldiers were sent to the city to round up whatever pirates they could find. But they were a cunning lot. For such an emergency, they had dug a tunnel which ran from the tavern to the river. When the soldiers arrived, the whole lot of pirates escaped through the tunnel, leaving Savannah behind. You see, this provided the perfect opportunity to be rid of her, while also saving face with Redbeard. But since she was still too young to venture out on her own, she was forced to take a job as a serving wench in order to survive. It was during this time when she met a particular soldier who frequented the establishment. Immediately, he was enamored with the bright, strong-willed girl with mysterious eyes. It wasn't long before he began courting her and soon thereafter, they fell in love. Their love was a tale made for the ages; one which only became stronger after they had a child of their own.

When word of this got back to Redbeard, he sailed back to take Savannah home because he would not let his legacy die because of a summer's romance. But as soon as he learned the child's father was a soldier rounding up pirates, Redbeard wanted nothing to do with the young girl whose blood was that of an enemy. Upon his arrival, he and Savannah's betrothed faced each other in battle. This encounter would change her life forever.

Savannah often dreamt of her lover. It was these precious moments which reminded her of happiness. In her dream, she reached for the chiseled face of her soulmate just as a flash of light and a thunderous boom caused the man to grimace in pain before his face dissipated into nothingness.

Preston was awakened by the same distant explosion rattling the ship. He leapt to his feet and scrambled over to the window. In the distance were two towering rock formations jutting out of the water. Their peaks curved toward each other like two outstretched arms looking to hold hands. A puff of white smoke drifted up from the stone bluffs before another boom from the second cliff echoed across the water. "They're shooting at us!" he yelled, ducking below the window. He didn't know what to do; he'd never experienced anything like this! Not wanting to die, he crawled over to the corner, grabbing a nearby bucket, and slipping it over his head. Huddled against the wall, he was somewhat relieved to hear the crew cheering. "Wait, what? It must just be a signal."

Preston cautiously stood, glancing out the window once again. As they drew closer to the twin peaks, he noticed the pair of massive cannons perched high above. Both pointed out to sea and were mounted on round metal pedestals attached to large gears which were built into the side of the cliffs. Another set of gears closer to the water clanked loudly as they lowered a steel net protecting the entry to the bay.

The ship heaved and a splash of seawater sprayed across Preston's face. The cold, salty mist brought the surrealism of the situation into reality. For a short while, Preston fought to convince himself all of this was a bad dream, but he couldn't fool himself any longer. The burst of cannon fire had destroyed his hope and replaced it with an unsettling tightness exploding in his chest. He crumpled onto the hard floor and buried his face in his hands.

"I have to find my hat before they do. It's my only way out, but how?"

Perhaps it was his imagination, or was it just kismet taunting him, for each time the ship rolled, the hefty deck timbers squeaked three times, reminding him of that stupid floor back home. "Three squeaks and I can remain hidden." He snickered at the imbecility of it all. "Why didn't I just come out when they called for me?"

The door swung open and smashed into the wall. Preston looked over and saw Chuggs filling the opening; seemingly more so than the door did.

"The Cap'n wants ya up on deck, runt."

They say words cannot hurt, but these did! Each syllable felt like a bullet ripping into Preston's chest, tearing apart his soul. Throughout his body, his nerves erupted as he reluctantly stood, wondering if this was the beginning of Redbeard's promise to extract the truth from him. A truth he wasn't sure he even knew, or believed for that matter. Nonetheless, images of sadistic punishment flashed before his eyes. Medieval torture devices of spikes, racks, whips, and rat infested dungeons were all he could imagine. His mind became a pervasive playground of fear, turning against him as he climbed those steps. Since they were approaching land, Preston considered jumping over the side of the ship until the thought of razor-sharp shark's teeth popped into his head, forcing him to quickly dismiss this idea. On the main deck, Redbeard stood tall at the ship's wheel while Savannah was by his side, staring through a monocular. It's an unsettling feeling of loneliness to be filled with so much angst and anxiety, only to look upon someone who has none. The mind struggles to overcome emotions of jealousy, rage, and guilt, wanting so badly to be the person who is free from concern. While the mind clashes with its thoughts, the body is left to wait, anxious to learn how it should react. For the moment, Preston was finding it hard to breathe.

I don't see a table to strap me to. Are they going to whip me? Preston thought, looking over at the towering mast of the ship. *There's nobody standing there with that cat-o'-nine-tails thing.*

"Ye hungry, boy?" Redbeard asked, not bothering to look at him.

This man didn't seem the type to care much for Preston's well-being, but Preston nodded, nonetheless. "Yes, sir."

The brutish pirate snorted as he pushed past and grabbed the spyglass from Savannah. "Well, as soon as I get the key, ye'll get some grub."

As odd as it sounds, even more so to Preston, he breathed out a sigh of relief hearing this. Granted, starving to death wasn't his idea of a pleasant death, but at least he wasn't going to suffer any pain — for the moment. Too exhausted to even hold his head up, Preston's shoulders slumped down as his head purged all his previous thoughts. For the last several hours, he had endured an emotional upheaval, more so than he had ever experienced in his life. And, unfortunately, this unheralded adventure of his had just begun. He glanced around, trying to see if he recognized any landmarks identifying where he was. Always on the alert, Redbeard took notice and creaked out a smile at this futile effort.

"It might fancy ye to know we're headed into Breakaway Bay," Redbeard said, adjusting the lens on the scope. "The jagged rocks ahead of us surround the island. There is only one way in or out, and nothing but open ocean for as far as the eye can see." Preston had no reason to doubt this. His eyes saw it just as Redbeard described.

As they sailed between the towering granite arches, the clifftop cannons spun as the massive guns rotated and tracked the ship. Redbeard slid his peg leg into a fitted recess built into the deck, which had a brass plate next to it labeled "Gateway." Once his leg clicked into the opening, he reached down and spun a small wheel attached to his prosthetic. With each turn of the wheel, the gears on the cliffs turned in unison, causing the net protecting the bay to raise from the water and secure the opening once again. Preston noticed several other holes in the deck where Redbeard could fit his leg into. Each one had its own label: Guns — Sails — Navigation. His leg served as a control panel of sorts.

"Put the young squire in chains before we make landfall."

Quinton and Chuggs attached thick iron shackles onto Preston's ankles and locked them in place. The iron rings weighed heavy and dug into his skin. But why the chains? Where was he to go? Unless, of course, it was a tactic to cause fear and angst, to which he already had plenty of both.

Within the harbor just ahead, long piers jutted out like massive fingers looking to snatch the approaching ship. To either side of the seaport, the white sand beaches spread wide, while just beyond was a quaint coastal town. So pristine was the scene with its swaying palm trees, one might expect to see this picturesque panorama on a postcard. The town was peppered with a melange of stone and wood timbered buildings, where just beyond, hills ebb and flowed across the countryside.

Close enough to make out faces, Preston was surprised how refined the townspeople were. After all, up to this point, his only introduction to the inhabitants of this world had been the unkempt, ruffians currently surrounding him. Away from the ship, however, the men were well-groomed and cordial as they strolled along the cobblestoned avenues in suits or pressed linens, tipping their hats to one another. The women were just as refined, wearing billowing bonnets of feathers and lace.

As the ship nestled up against the deep-water dock, the massive sails of the Dragon's Curse wound themselves around the boom like some monstrous window shade being drawn. There was a mechanical hum of engines as water churned from the side of the ship, pushing it against its mooring. As soon as it was snug, the crew tossed thick ropes to awaiting dockworkers who secured the ship to hefty bollards made from old cannons. By the way people reacted to Redbeard entering the harbor, it was clear he was in charge. Every dock worker stopped what they were doing to tend to the Dragon's Curse. Townspeople glanced over upon their arrival but continued on with their daily activities. It in no way appeared to be an oppressive society. There were no others being dragged around with their feet chained. Resentment swept over Preston as he watched everyone else meandering about, carefree. They all seemed happy and yet he was imprisoned because — actually, he wasn't sure he even committed a crime. Why was he in chains?

"Ahh, it pleases these tired eyes to see the bay," Redbeard told Savannah, staring across the water. However, once the ship moored, his smile wavered, and Redbeard looked down at Preston as though he was a stray dog begging for food. "Make sure this wretched boy stays warm!"

Savannah nodded and grabbed Preston by his collar, but he wasn't too worried. After all, he wasn't going to get tortured, and he was going to be kept warm. How bad could it be? After the gangplank was laid into place, Savannah led him off the ship and past a crowd of gawking children. He felt like one of Crownickers' orphans, on display for all to pity as he was paraded through town. Preston took a moment to glance back at the Dragon's Curse, hoping to catch a glimpse of his trunk. Patches of metal sheets riveted along the battered, wooden hull made him wonder if they were covering damage caused by battles or storms. In different circumstances, he'd love to study the ship some more. Toward the bow and stern were hefty metal gears, interlocked with one another, much like the ones on his uncle's clock tower. Preston had tinkered enough with his uncle's steam engines and gadgets to see the ship was not only sailed by the wind but also with steam. Besides the gears positioned on the hull, a series of them were affixed to the masts as well. The ones near the stern were linked to iron bars welded to the massive rudder. Mechanical ships were nothing new to Preston, after all, back home, this was the norm. However, the Dragon's Curse was a concoction of technology, intermingled and pieced together to form a primitive version of a modern warship.

But getting back to the town itself; aside from his current situation, this was the sort of place Preston believed anyone would enjoy living in. There were no beggars scavenging for food, no squalor, it all seemed pristine and well maintained. The flower boxes in the windows burst with colorful bouquets, and white picket fences surrounded the homes. Horses trotted past, pulling wagons loaded with crates and barrels. In sharp contrast to this nostalgic ambience were modern trolleys, which clanked past Preston. They resembled train cabooses and were carrying villagers who sat comfortably upon cushioned benches. Underneath, the trolleys were propelled by a steam-driven hook which ran along a channel in the road.

If one dared venture to the edge of town, they would find themselves standing before a towering cliff of black and gray stone — basalt to be exact. The mound grew straight and tall; so tall in fact, it blocked out the sun, causing the air to grow cold. It was a stone Preston recognized from the books in his uncle's study. But wait, basalt meant volcano ... Surely, they weren't planning on dropping him into a volcano! This seemed a ridiculous notion. If this were to be Redbeard's intent, why go through all this trouble? Then again, he was told he would be warm! The earlier fears of torture he happily dismissed had returned. Perhaps his concern was warranted after all!

As this thought festered inside Preston's brain, Savannah continued leading him along the winding path. But with rows of planters full of cascading greenery and fragrant flowers, this didn't seem as imposing as he first thought. Maybe he was overthinking this. For a brief moment, he felt relieved. But this feeling of euphoria was short-lived for as he raised his chin, several levels of cannons jutting out from openings in the cliffside painted a different story of what awaited him.

A high-pitched squeak permeated the air as a box made of metal mesh rattled down the side of the rugged stone.

"Is that an elevator?" Preston asked, staring at the rattletrap creeping along. But Savannah continued ignoring him. The last thing she wanted to be doing was entertaining an impudent boy's annoying barrage of questions, all the while losing ground to her father's lapdog back at the ship. Certainly, at this very moment, that insidious cutthroat Quinton was cozying up next to Redbeard, filling his head with tales of treason and betrayal while she was forced to babysit this miscreant.

With wheels attached to the back of the elevator, it more resembled a rickety automobile dangling over the side of a cliff with nothing but a frayed rope to keep it in tow, the likes of which Preston wouldn't trust to hold back a dog, yet alone a weighted elevator. Savannah slid the scissor door open as Preston stared in disbelief. Certainly, she didn't expect him to get inside this thing — she did. Not with a warm invitation to step inside, more of a not so elegant shove. Once inside, she slammed the gate shut, reached down, and yanked back on a rusty metal lever built into the floor. The lift made a horrific whine as it shuddered and clanked its way up the steep cliffside. Its wheels bounced along the stone as they ascended, causing ungodly creaks and squeals from the metal coffin surrounding him. The higher they climbed, the more the elevator swayed in the wind, causing Preston's knees to buckle as he gripped the steel mesh tightly.

Perhaps it wouldn't be the worst thing to tell them of my uncle's hat. As soon as he was about to speak, the entire harbor came into view and that's when Preston saw several pirates unloading a steamer trunk; his steamer trunk, which they packed onto a nearby wagon.

It's still shut, he thought. *Where are they bringing it?*

He scanned the town for a warehouse, or ... well he wasn't exactly certain where one might store a trunk such as this. Nonetheless, he had to keep track of it in case he was given the opportunity to get inside it once again and escape all this madness. But in reality, none of this mattered at the moment for he was a prisoner — shackled, hungry, and possibly facing horrific miseries. More now than ever, he needed a friend, and his only course of action was continuing with a barrage of questions, hoping one of them broke this woman's hardened exterior.

"Uhm, is this your home?" he asked, somewhat apprehensive.

Savannah gave him a dull stare before looking back out at the sea.

Well, she's not going to be it.

The rest of the ride felt awkward. Almost the same feeling as though he had asked a girl to a school dance and got laughed at — well, almost as awkward. But THAT only happened one time, and he didn't want to talk about it! Anyway, once the elevator jerked to a stop, Savannah opened the rear gate and shoved Preston out. Lined along either side of the cliff were dozens of cast iron cauldrons.

"What are those for?"

Savannah flashed a crooked smile. Finally, he caught her attention!

"It's so we can pour boiling oil on anyone foolish enough to try to escape and climb down the side," she said with a sinister chuckle. "Nothing quite like blistering skin and torturous screams to brighten one's day!"

Preston's breath stuck in his throat. Maybe not speaking was the way to go.

They passed through a solid metal gate, intimidating enough on its own, but this one was also flanked on either side by towering stone walls. Nearly twenty feet tall, they were topped with cannons and an army of pirates screaming obscenities at one another.

"These gates are impossible to escape from, so don't get any ideas," Savannah warned.

What? Preston raised an eyebrow. "If it's impossible, then why all the cauldrons of oil?"

Savannah skid to a halt, swinging around with her fists clenched she grabbed hold of Preston's shirt, twisting it as she glared at him, her nose a hair's width away from his. "Look, you scurvy little dog, you give me any sass whatsoever and I'll crush your barnacles! Savvy?"

Preston quickly nodded, his tousled hair flying everywhere. He didn't know exactly what she meant by "crushed barnacles," but it didn't sound pleasant. With a deep grunt, she released him and continued on with Preston reluctantly in tow. Just ahead of them stood a grand building constructed from white brick and dark glass, which rose from the plateau.

The entire keep was an odd setting where old met new; a place where antiquated oil lanterns lit the way to steam powered elevators. But this was nothing compared to the guarded building ahead. At first glance, the structure resembled more of a factory than a fortress. In a flurry of activity, its exterior elements of gears and mechanics were churning along the facade as though it was some sort of child's wind-up toy. A scene which reminded Preston of his home, and its much-maligned clock tower. But this ... this was so much grander! You couldn't help but wonder what fantastic creations were being assembled inside. Over the entryway were two colossal, black metal gears interlocked with a rotor drive, all of which were swirling and spinning. A pair of identical black smokestacks, trimmed with shining copper, sprung out from the top of the building and belched out clouds of steam. Opposing wings with smoked glass windows were set off from this grandiose entrance. At the end of one wing were three riveted copper tanks, which stood half as tall as the building itself. Each was fitted with its own pressure gauge. So large were these gauges, you'd think they were Rupina's clock faces. At the end of the other wing was a black cast iron tank which was big enough to be a building of its own. On top of this container was a black iron chimney which resembled the stack from a steam locomotive. Not to be outshined by the other wing, this tank had a massive copper pipe running out of it, which disappeared into the building as well.

On either side of the entry stood two grungy guards, each of them fashioned with a small cannon prosthetic attached to their arms. Preston wanted so badly to ask how they lit the fuse, but that thought quickly left his head when one turned and glared at him.

"Whaddya lookin' at, runt?" he asked, prompting Preston to forego his question as he cowered behind Savannah.

The inside of the keep was just as industrialized as the outside. Certainly not what you would expect in a pirate's fortress. Polished white tile covered the floor of the foyer, reflecting the array of copper pipes which weaved their way along the ceiling. Shiny brass gears, twice as large as Preston, spun on several sections of the walls. Aside from this, the space was empty apart from the smattering of shelves, which displayed an assortment of gadgets and gizmos. Some contraptions were eerily similar to the ones in his uncle's office, which piqued Preston's curiosity.

Centered in the back of the entrance was an iron spiral staircase, which twisted its way down further than Preston could see. As they descended the stairs, the chain attached to his legs clanked along each metal step, echoing a high-pitched "ting" deep into the bowels of the building. Farther and farther, they descended, passing dozens of hallways, each branching off from the stairs and all leading in different directions. Some of these exits had massive doors at the end of the walkway, while others just disappeared into darkened corridors. But none were any Preston cared to travel into. By the time they reached the bottom, Preston's mouth had become bone dry. For as far below ground as he assumed they were, he'd hoped it to be damp and cold. But instead, it felt as though he had climbed down into a raging furnace.

"It sure is hot down here," he said, sweat dripping from his forehead. Savannah let out a soft chuckle, which caused Preston to clench up. *Why was that funny?*

There was no need to throw a switch or light a torch, for where she led him, a soft, red glow filled the chamber and guided them down a narrow corridor dug into the rock surrounding them. Just beyond the confines of this hallway was an ominous cavern. A chamber even hotter than where they just emerged; something Preston thought impossible until this moment. Shadows from the pulsing red glow flickered along the walls, causing jagged shadows to stab outward from every crevice. With a scene as eerie as this, Preston was almost certain he was standing before the gates of hell.

Once they traveled deeper into the cavity, he noticed the light filling the space was created by a river of lava flowing through a channel, deep below the chamber. Staged ahead of Preston, suspended from the ceiling, were a dozen massive, round copper boilers, interconnected to each other with pipes, which made the arrangement look like a giant string of pearls. With a series of pulleys, the boilers could be raised or lowered as needed.

"What are those for?"

"Never you mind."

They walked to the edge of the lava flow, where Savannah pulled on a lever embedded into the hard ground. As soon as she did, a set of gears clicked beneath a metal bridge, which extended itself over the river of molten rock. While the walkway clanked its way across, Preston stared down at the red river, watching it slowly creeping its way through the deep channel. Its casual movement likened to toothpaste being squeezed out of a tube. He was mesmerized by the molten liquid as it glided along, flames shooting up from the thick red magma, which would crust over with a hard, black shell before bursting open and being swallowed up by more red liquid.

"Move it," she barked, snapping Preston out of his trance.

She led him across the bridge and up to a thick wooden door. After removing a key, she pushed Preston into the cell before slamming it shut.

"If I were you, I'd tell the Captain everything he wants to know," she said, twisting the key in the lock. "Enjoy your stay," she snickered as she crossed the flow and retracted the bridge.

Preston turned and surveyed his accommodations as the sweat continued to drip from every pore in his body. It was a tiny cell. Not even large enough for him to lie flat on the floor without cricking his neck. Made from nothing more than a dugout recess in the bedrock, there were no windows other than the one on the door. And that was barely large enough for Preston to fit his head through. Being right next to the deep recesses of flowing lava made the heat in the cell unbearable. The air was so thick, so heavy, it was a labored effort just to draw in a breath. Desperate for relief, he stuck his face into the opening, trying to suck in whatever air he could, but it was just as stagnant, and he struggled to breathe. His eyes tingled and his vision narrowed as he became lightheaded, his knees wobbling. Unfortunately, there was no place to sit, other than a dingy, rusted bucket. More than likely, this was done in an attempt to maximize the discomfort thrust upon Redbeard's "guests." No doubt, on more than one occasion, it helped to speed up one's confessions, but even this wasn't enough to break Preston's stubbornness. Although he came close when he relented and picked up the bucket, cringing as he looked inside.

"Don't tell me this is my toilet."

Suppressing a gag, he flipped the bucket over and used it as a stool, rubbing his hands on his pants in case there was any "residual" excrement.

"Maybe I should just tell them where the hat is," he said with his head between his knees. "Or at least where I think it is."

Preston thought of the hot summer days back home. A place now at risk of fading away into a distant memory. How long would it take for him to forget all he knew as he suffered his imprisonment? His future full of uncertainties as he withered away in this tomb he found himself in. Quite a difference from his swanky home where he had enjoyed breakfast hardly a day ago. One day ago! How could so much bad happen in so little time?

Drenched in sweat, Preston's shirt clung to his skin. Seeking even the tiniest relief, he dragged his tongue across his dry, cracked lips, which gave him the most unwelcome sensation as though he just licked sandpaper.

"Maybe it'll be cooler if I lie on the floor," he mumbled as he kicked the bucket away and slid down the wall, contorting himself along the floor. Just as he had hoped, it was cooler. However, his comfort quickly faded. Whatever relief he momentarily enjoyed had vanished and his eyes weighed heavy.

"I'm not going to make it," he muttered before everything went dark.

PRESTON AWOKE TO A sharp pain in his ribs. Through heavy eyes, he saw the cause of his discomfort — Savannah was kicking him.

"On your feet, wretch."

Preston shook his head and shakily rose. With his eyes half-shut, he staggered out the door. Each step he took caused an excruciating drumbeat to echo in his head. He'd give anything for some water right now — well, almost anything.

Stupid hat.

He smacked his lips together, cringing at the roughness.

"Where are we going?"

But there was no response. Then again, there could have been, but in his condition he couldn't be certain. Either way, he wasn't sure he really cared. Right now, every bit of focus he could muster was keeping him upright. Nonetheless, the irritating sound from the clanking of shackles only exasperated the pain of the iron digging into his raw skin.

They trudged up each step, winding along the spiral staircase, haphazardly retracing their route. Preston stumbled several times, but once outside, the cool ocean breeze gave him a renewed vigor. By the time the so-called elevator reached the bottom, Preston's head started to clear; at least enough to question whether his time in the cell was less torturous than the ride in this infernal contraption. However, those thoughts quickly jumped out of his head as several explosions shook the ground.

"What was that?" Turning his head, he saw smoke rising from the top of the cliff. When Savannah continued on, unfazed, he assumed they had just been testing the cannons. He deliriously chuckled at this since his feet felt as heavy as cannonballs. They shuffled down the avenues until he felt he couldn't go any further.

"Are we almost there?" he mumbled.

"Keep moving!"

Fortunately, they stopped in front of a stone building with bright red shutters and window boxes full of fragrant flowers. The sign hanging from an iron bar above the door read, *The Rusty Bucket. Food and Spirits.*

"Rusty bucket ... How fitting," Preston mumbled, thinking back to the disgusting bucket he was forced to sit upon. For good measure, he rubbed his hands along his pant legs, hoping they were clean, but refusing to look. Before he was done, Savannah pushed him into the tavern, where Redbeard sat at the largest table, ripping apart a roasted chicken with his bare hands. Of course, all Preston fixated on was the moist meat dangling from the pirate's mouth. This could have easily been another form of torture, being forced to stand there and watch as Redbeard's lips and fingers glistened with the juices.

"Keep him here!" Savannah ordered the two guards standing at the door. She walked over to Redbeard and sat on the bench next to him. "You sure we should be doing this?"

Redbeard scowled at her. "He's as prickly as a sea urchin, just like ye! Plus, what are ye squawking about? It isn't like we're torturing the boy."

"You can just make another key!"

"We've covered this," he groused, throwing the chicken onto the plate. "Ye know that's not possible. It has to be the exact size and weight to be the true key. Each tool mark has to be identical — precise," he said, squeezing his thumb and forefinger together.

Now, it isn't as though Savannah was skittish when it came to mind games, or torture, for that matter. But this was a child after all, albeit an excessively annoying one. Apprehensive, she shook her head and turned toward the door. "Can't we just break it open, set a new lock, and patch it up?"

Redbeard closed his eyes. "So, I guess what we have here is an expert on these particular steamer trunks, eh? Have ye not considered me wise enough to entertain these thoughts? Let me assure ye, I have — thousands of times!" he said through gritted teeth. "Once the trunk is tampered with, a failsafe engages, and the trunk sends itself to a predetermined location. We risk the chance it to be never found again!"

"I apologize, Cap'n. Of course you know more about these matters than I."

He settled back and leered at her as he wiped his hands on a towel and drew in a deep breath.

"It'll be fine. Ye were younger than him when ye had yer first swallow of ale."

"Yeah, and look how well I turned out," she said, kicking the bench away as she stormed over to Preston and yanked him by his shirt.

"Well, look who we have here," Redbeard said, swallowing a mouthful of ale so sloppily it dribbled down his beard.

Savannah pushed Preston down by his shoulders onto the bench. He couldn't stop staring at the ale, its white, fluffy foam floating over the rim of the mug, cascading down the side, leaving a trail of tiny, wet bubbles. Still lightheaded, he said nothing as he sat, his head wobbling. Redbeard smiled and slid a fresh tankard over to him.

"Ye seem to be suffering from the thirst. Why don't ye have a sip?"

It was one of the most beautiful sights Preston had ever seen, reminding him of a root beer float. Even though he had never tasted ale before, seawater was preferable to this crippling thirst he suffered. Without a second thought, Preston grabbed the mug with both hands and slurped down the entire pint. Before he could set the empty mug back onto the table, the room started to spin, causing him to grip the wooden bench with both hands, hoping not to fall off.

"Did ye enjoy yer drink?" Redbeard's voice sounded hollow and echoed as though it was coming from inside a tunnel.

Preston's head popped up, and he became unsettlingly aware of his eyelids as he blinked slowly, struggling to force them wide.

"Very wonderful and refreshing," he said, slurring his words. "Sir!"

Redbeard burst out laughing, watching as Preston's eyes drooped.

"Would ye like some chicken, boy?"

"You know something? I would love some," he said, using his hands to hold his head up as he eagerly nodded, swaying in his seat.

Redbeard motioned to a man wearing a white apron who brought a pewter tray with a full roasted chicken over to Preston. Even before the server set the platter down, Preston was leaning in, his mouth salivating at the sight of the golden, crispy skin. The smell was intoxicating, but as he reached for it, Redbeard slid the plate away from him. *What just happened?*

"What say we have a parley first?"

"A what?"

"How did ye get aboard my ship?"

Preston presented a crooked smile and raised his finger to his lips. Or at least he tried to, missing his mouth several times before finally succeeding.

"Shh, it's a secret."

This prompted another burst of laughter from the pirate. Savannah stood next to Preston, unamused, with her arms crossed.

Redbeard, however, leaned in close and scanned the room. "What if I promise not to tell yer secret?" he whispered.

Preston squinted at the man and gave him half a smile as he poked his finger at him. "Okay," he said. "You seem very trustworthy." He whipped his head around and jumped at the sight of Savannah. With quivering eyes, he tried to glare at her, but the effects of the alcohol had taken over and his stare became nothing more than a fluttering wink. "She's scary," he said, turning back to Redbeard and pointing his thumb at her. He then placed his hand to the side of his mouth and leaned in. "It was in — it was in a magic box."

Redbeard nodded and stared at him with a broad smile.

"A box you say?"

"I know, right?" Preston said, pushing himself back and throwing his arms out to the side as he himself broke into laughter. "Who would've thought?" he asked, slapping the table so hard it rattled the dishes. "Ow!" he squeaked in pain as he brought his hand back and tried to shake the pain away. "Anyway, all I was trying to do was get away from my teacher and BAM! Here I am!"

"Well, my young lad, ye tell quite a tale!" Redbeard said, sitting back in his chair and nodding as he stroked his beard, looking up at the ceiling. "Quite the tale indeed!"

Preston closed his eyes, smiled, and nodded quickly, which brought Redbeard in closer once again. The pirate raised his finger and tapped the air as he rubbed his beard with his other hand.

"But, I'm confused," he said. "How did ye get this magic box of yers to work?"

Preston stared at the hat on Redbeard's head, in particular, the three gears on the side. With a crooked frown, he drew in close. "Looks just like those! Can you believe it?"

Redbeard removed his hat and examined the gears before raising an eye to Preston. "Ye like hats, do ye?"

"Love 'em! Got a pretty special one myself ... Kind of."

"Really? Ye don't say. I bet ye have it all fixed up nice. I'd fancy a look." Redbeard smiled at Preston with his yellow teeth showing wide.

Preston's eyes raised up. "Me too!" But before he could say anything further, his shoulders slumped down and his lip quivered.

"Tsk-tsk," Redbeard mouthed, extending his lower lip as he raised his eyebrows high. "Oh, dear boy, are ye saying it's lost?" He stared at Preston with sorrowful eyes. "Please, tell me yer not without yer wonderful hat?"

Preston struggled to hold back his tears. With a deep sniff, he nodded. "My poor hat. It never did anything wrong. It must be so lonely."

"What an awful thing to happen to a gallant lad such as yerself. I cannot stand for this!" he bellowed, dropping his fist onto the table, which caused the empty mugs to topple. "I'll tell ye what," he said, placing his heavy hand on Preston's shoulder, "perhaps me and my crew can help ye get yer fancy hat back. What say, ye?"

Preston shot up, but lost his balance and fell flat across the table. His arms spread wide, pretending to fly as he looked up with a big smile. "That'd be amazing! You'd really do that?"

"Ye bet I would," Redbeard said, leaning across the table and raising Preston up, steadying him by the back of his shirt. "Where do ye remember seeing it last?"

Preston thought back, rubbing his chin with his hand. "On your boat! What a pretty boat. You're so lucky. I want a boat." But then Preston closed his eyes and his head sunk into his shoulders until a plate breaking in the kitchen woke him. Without hesitation, he picked up the conversation. "I had a hat, did you know? But I think it fell into the box." Preston's eyes filled with tears. "Wait! It could be in the dark, scary room!" His head dropped once again. "My poor little hat. It's probably scared in the dark, all alone."

"Ah, don't ye fret about it, lad," Redbeard assured him, patting him on the shoulder. "We'll find yer hat. Ye think you can describe it for me? Just so my crew knows exactly what to look for."

Preston rubbed the tears from his eyes and pointed at Redbeard's hat. "It's tall, and brown, and soft, and fantastic! You know what? The gears on it even turn!" he said, his face twisting with sadness before he began blubbering.

Redbeard's eyes lit up. He grabbed Quinton by the collar and pulled him down. "Get those two idiots to search the hold again!"

Without another word, Redbeard stood and darted out of the tavern. Preston dozed off but snored himself awake. When he raised his head, he saw Savannah sitting across from him, which caused him to jump back and look around. "Have you — have you been there this whole time?"

Savannah rolled her eyes and pushed the platter of chicken over to him. "Shut up and eat your food."

Preston smiled as he tore into his meal. The waiter brought over another pint of ale and set it on the table. As Preston reached for it, Savannah slapped the tankard to the ground, the refreshing brown liquid spilling across the floor.

"Why?" he whispered.

"Water!" Savannah growled. "Bring it to him and don't ever let me catch you giving him anything else!"

"Yes, ma'am," the waiter said, bowing his head and rushing over to retrieve a fresh cup.

Savannah scowled as she stared at the door.

In Redbeard's cabin, all was deathly quiet. That is, if you were to ignore the sound of chattering teeth coming from the two pirates huddled together — twins, to be exact. They shook uncontrollably, staring at the floor as another pirate stood sentry. An intimidating man, to say the least, as half his skull was made from riveted copper plating and exposed gears, while a red-lensed monocle, which had replaced one of his eyes, glowed bright. Just as the twins' nerves settled, Redbeard stormed into the room and sneered at the duo.

"Grimms and Gramms!" he growled as he slammed the door, his voice filled with distaste at the names. "How many times have we found ourselves here?"

Like scared puppies cowering in a corner, the twins raised their heads and nervously looked at him with sorrowful eyes. It was Redbeard who had taken in the two young orphans so many years ago after he found them huddled under a wooden crate on the streets. Now grown, they were tall and skinny, hunched over with extremely poor posture. Their clothes were raggedy and dangled off their bony bodies. In order to tell them apart, Redbeard ordered them to wear different colored shirts. Grimm wore a red and white striped shirt, while Gramm wore a bright blue and white striped shirt. Gears embedded within their chests spun wildly as their stocking caps absorbed the sweat beading down their foreheads. Redbeard grunted as he circled them.

"It ain't our fault, Cap'n," they both said in unison. "We wasn't told where we was to find it," Gramms explained.

"Are ye telling me neither of ye two idiots thought to search the hold? The same place to which the chest AND the boy were found?"

"We did, Cap'n," they said, looking at each other and nodding furiously. "But it's dark down there," Grimms said, bringing his hands to his quivering lips.

"And cobwebby," Gramms reminded Grimms as they turned to each other and nodded in unison.

Redbeard dropped his head before slamming his fists on a nearby table, which collapsed in pieces.

"Get out! And get yer worthless, scrawny selves down there and find me that hat or I'll use yer skins to make another!"

Grimms and Gramms spun around on their heels like they were performing some sort of drunken pirouette. Once they regained their balance, they turned, crashing into each other as they whipped the door open and scurried out of the room. Redbeard let out an exasperated sigh, dropping down into his chair and burying his face in his hands.

The guard watched in amazement as the two men bounced off the walls and up to the deck. He pushed the broken table aside and walked up next to Redbeard. After taking a deep breath, he bent down to speak.

"If I may say, Cap'n, and mind ye, I only want to help ease yer troubles. I know yer their ward, but why do ye keep those two scallawags around?

Beg yer pardon, sir, and maybe it ain't me place to say, but it could make ye appear weak to the crew."

Redbeard raised his head, his eyes straining to quell his growing anger. As he turned his head, the veins in his temple throbbed while his face burned with rage.

"Weak to the crew," he repeated through gritted teeth, nodding his head as his fury boiled over.

He shot up out of his chair and, with a deep grunt, thrust his hand forward with such force, his fingers dented the metal portion of the man's skull as his fingers dug deep into the spinning gears. Redbeard yanked his hand back, causing the sprockets to explode off the pirate's head and scatter across the floor. The man's shocked face froze in place as he crumpled to the ground, leaving Redbeard panting as he tried to quell his fury — it didn't work. After flipping over his desk, he picked up the guard by the scruff of his neck and dragged the limp body up the stairs. The crew on deck were joking and laughing as they lay about, but sprung to attention when they saw what was taking place. As Redbeard pushed through the crowd, he picked up the lifeless body and threw the man over the side of the ship. Everybody stood perfectly still until Redbeard turned toward them and sneered.

"Any of ye lot be thinking me weak?"

Nobody said a word as they all scattered, scrubbing the deck and rigging the lines. Redbeard snorted and returned to his cabin, slamming the door so hard the drooping sails fluttered.

The twins came stumbling into Redbeard's quarters, tripping over each other as they ran up to his desk, hooting and hollering.

"I found it!"

"Did not, I did!"

"What are ye talkin' about? Ye weren't even near it —"

The arguing went on as they tussled, trying to pull the hat free from the other.

"Enough!" Redbeard yelled, causing the twins to drop Preston's hat to the floor. "The two of ye put that on my desk and get out of my sight before I run ye through with a lancer and feed ye to the sharks like some moronic shish kebab!"

The brothers picked up the hat and set it on the desk before sprinting out of the room. With a deep breath, Redbeard picked up the hat and smiled.

"Ah, ere we go!"

After examining the three gears, he plucked the one which was the same size as the recess in the latch of Preston's trunk. He pressed it into the lock and stepped back with a giddy smirk on his face, like a child waiting for a present. After a few moments, when nothing happened, his face dropped, and his mood soured. He removed the gear and placed another one in it, but it was too small to set correctly and kept falling out. The last gear he tried wouldn't even fit into the recess. By this point, sweat was dripping from his forehead as he jammed the first gear back in and yanked on the latch, but it didn't budge.

"Ye temperamental bottom dwelling lump of sea slime!" he snarled as he hoisted the chest over his head and heaved it across the room. The weighted trunk smashed against a large oil painting and bounced off the wall before knocking over a water pitcher and basin. Shards of ceramic scattered across the floor. All the commotion brought Quinton running into the room, but when he saw what was taking place, he retreated. Unlike the last poor soul, Quinton knew enough not to interrupt Redbeard's fit of rage.

Not yet finished, Redbeard reached down and hoisted the displaced painting above his head, only to slam it down against the back of a chair. In a frenzied rampage, he continued to smash the frame until it fractured and broke apart into a dozen pieces. Kicking his way through the debris, he grabbed a chair and hurled it through the grand windows on the back of the ship.

All fell silent as Redbeard took a moment to catch his breath. Quinton took this opportunity to step in, clearing his throat, which caused Redbeard to swing around, glaring at the foolish man.

"Get this blasted trunk out of 'ere and make sure I never stumble upon it again!"

Without another word being spoken, Quinton grabbed the handle of the chest and dragged it out of the room, quickly shutting the door behind him.

By the time Quinton made it back to Redbeard's quarters, several glassmakers were already replacing the windows on the back of the ship. He entered the room and stood quietly as Redbeard covered his eyes with one hand, while using his other to massage his temple.

"Perhaps that wretched boy was telling the truth," he muttered. "None of those gears in his blasted hat worked."

"Should I send him to Iron Hills?"

Redbeard looked up, his forehead still red from rage. He stood and walked over to Quinton.

"Nah. We'll keep him around for now." Redbeard picked up a large jug from a nearby table. After pulling out the cork, he exhaled a deep, calming breath and lay the jug across his bent elbow. After taking a swig, he nodded to Quinton and slid his sleeve across his wet lips. "Where's he at now?"

"Savannah went to fetch him."

Redbeard settled into a chair and stared blankly into the air.

"By the way, Cap'n, the port side ratline netting needs replacing before our next voyage."

"Well, get on with it then."

"Aye, Cap'n. Uhm, Browners was out of 'em, so we'll have to get a new one elsewhere."

Redbeard lowered the jug from his lips. "Shackles' place?"

"Aye."

The name alone caused Redbeard to close his eyes and shake his head. "This day gets worse and worse," he mumbled. "Fine! Have her send the boy. Alone! Let's see how much the old man tells him."

Compassion is a fickle beast, for it can build a person up yet destroy them all the same. I'm not suggesting one should not be benevolent, but they should tread lightly when striving to be. However, this warning will fall upon deaf ears to those who are true to its calling. They would never change their humanity, even if they knew the eventual repercussions of their actions. This was the fate, the downfall as it were, of one Captain James Dorian. But this was the name as he was known in the long-ago past, well before Preston was birthed. For it was Captain Dorian who would inadvertently ignite Redbeard's lust for conquest and his desire to rule the seven realms. A once brilliant sea captain, Dorian would live out the remainder of his days cast aside in a shanty, bearing the moniker "Shackles." Now, after all he endured, would he change his actions if given the opportunity? Would he pass by the remote island which brought him to where he is today? Had he seen what would become of his precious ship, what direction in life his cabin boy would take, would that be enough to snuff out the compassion burning bright within his soul? Perhaps not, but what of his son who would later die at the hands of Redbeard? Stuck down by his former crewmate, a cabin boy no less. What then? Alas, we will never know, for you can jump realms, but none of them open a doorway to the past.

Of course, this brings us to today where Shackles remains an irritating barnacle on the side of Redbeard's ship. Metaphorically speaking, I assure you. The man is very much human, and very much alive, although a former sort of his previous self to be certain, something which Preston was soon to discover.

On the other side of the island, the cool morning air blew over Preston, stirring him out of his alcohol induced slumber. What followed came an incessant itching; one so utterly irritating, he kicked his way out from beneath his covers, hoping to rid himself of this antagonizing sensation. But the itching would be the least of his discomfort on this day. After squinting through the blurriness of the early sun's gaze, he sat up, only to grimace in an explosion of excruciating pain. His head felt as if it were being cracked in half and pried apart, followed by shards of gravel being dragged across his brain. A most unwelcome, regrettable sensation that even to this day, people find themselves willingly encountering after a night of excessive consumption.

"Ohh ..." he moaned, pressing his hands against his ears, hoping to keep his delicate skull intact. As he regained focus, he glanced around the room. To his surprise, he found himself on a straw bed with a ratty wool blanket covering him. "How did I get here?"

Multiple stacks of small barrels marked "Gunpowder" lined the walls, filling the room with the pungent smell of exploded fireworks. So strong was the smell, in fact, Preston could taste the grittiness in the back of his throat. Pyramids of cannon balls were neatly arranged next to a massive cannon, which pointed out the embrasure in the thick wall. Preston tried to stand, failing as he stumbled, forgetting about the chains entangled around his feet.

"Not a great way to start a day," he mumbled, wobbling as he stood.

Still unsteady, he shuffled over to the opening and hung his head out for some fresh air. Through his strained stare, he gazed out past the cannon toward the harbor. You couldn't see the ocean from his window at home, but you could smell the lilac bushes and dogwood trees along the avenues. All of that now replaced with swaying palm trees and a subtle tropical wind, which reminded him how far away from home he was. The door slammed open, causing him to grab hold of his head once again. Turning around, he saw a young girl had walked into the room. She was about his age, and her golden bangs spilled out from under her blue headscarf, falling flat against her forehead. For as stunning as she was, it was her bright blue eyes, which captivated him the most. They were as brilliant as the clear morning sky and glistened while her long eyelashes swept out and curled up. In her arms she carried a pile of clean clothes, which she set on the bed. She herself wore a ratty peasant dress with a white apron tied to it, which made Preston think she was trapped, much like he was. Beneath the patches of soot covering her face was the smoothest porcelain skin Preston had ever seen.

"Good ... good morning," he managed to say, stumbling over his words.

His efforts were met with a dull expression just before the girl walked out of the room.

"Okay, then," Preston said, rolling his eyes. But she returned a short time later, carrying a bucket of water. In her other hand was a pair of new boots with a thick sea sponge tucked into one of them. She set everything down next to him and turned to leave.

"Who are you?" he asked.

"I'm not supposed to talk to you," she said, avoiding eye contact as she hurried out of the room and shut the door.

Preston stared at the door momentarily before walking over to the bed. He picked up the garments and shook them out. They were clothes similar to the ones the crew wore aboard the ship; his sullied school attire had now been replaced with a cream Bastian shirt, complemented by a black leather sash to tie around his waist, and black canvas trousers, which Preston was certain were made from cast away old sails.

"What are these loops on the belt?" he asked, examining the leather strap. "Is this where they put their swords?"

Before he could figure it out, Savannah came into the room and unlocked the shackles from around his legs, tossing the chains into the corner. The metal clanking noise caused Preston to cover his ears and squint.

Too loud, he thought, still suffering from the effects of the ale.

"Get dressed," she said, walking toward the door. "The captain wants to see you in his cabin."

Preston scoffed. "Why, so he can get me drunk again?"

His insolent remark stopped her dead in her tracks. She spun around and grabbed Preston by the neck. "The CAPTAIN wants to see you, so the reason doesn't matter," she sneered. "I'm personally hoping he wants to go fishing and is in need of some large bait." She cocked her head, looking Preston up and down. "Hmm. Maybe your new name will be 'Fishbait'."

Her grip remained like a vise around his throat, allowing little air to enter until she gave it one last squeeze before releasing him.

"I suggest dispensing with your brazen comments and make haste! The captain is not as forgiving as I!"

Preston collapsed onto the bed, relieved he could breathe once again. After Savannah stormed out of the room, snickering, Preston sat up, gasping for a moment as a wave of nausea spread through him. Whether it was from the effects of alcohol, or unmitigated fear, the reason mattered not. What did matter was him making it through this day — and the ones to follow, which he hoped were many. As he rubbed his throat, he felt the filth along his skin. Eager to get clean, and clearly in a rush, he dunked the sponge into the bucket, filling it with cool water. Even this felt amazing; but the relief washing over him when he squeezed the water over his throbbing head was glorious. That is until the water trickled down to his chafed skin, where his joy was replaced by a searing pain. Even so, after his somewhat unpleasant bath, it was a welcomed relief not to stink like a can full of week-old rubbish. When he heard Savannah give an exasperated sigh from outside his door, he hurried to finish.

After sliding on the boots, he walked over to the door and turned the thick iron ring. Outside, Savannah was standing in the hallway with her foot propped up against the stone wall.

"Well, it's about time! Let's go."

What was this day to bring? Preston couldn't be certain, however, he remained somewhat confident he'd be safe. After all, why present him with a new wardrobe only to ruin it with soot, sweat and — blood? He shuddered at the thought, quickly pushing it out of his head as he followed Savannah down the hall, running his hand along the smooth stone walls. They passed a half dozen rooms similar to his, which lined the outer side of the corridor. Preston peeked in each one as they passed. Every one of them was a staging area for cannons.

Just ahead they entered a carved-out stairway where lanterns set in chiseled out niches throughout the passage provided a scant amount of light. The staircase itself was built wide enough for two people to fit, but only if they were standing shoulder to shoulder. This was clearly by design to protect the gun embattlements above from an inside attack. For additional security, every few floors had an iron gate blocking their way. Each time, Savannah would stop to unlock the gate and make sure it was secured before they continued.

Maybe it is impossible to escape.

Once they reached the bottom, two guards pushed open a thick metal door, which led them out behind the keep. A small path brought them to the edge of town, and unlike his last stroll, this time he was free of the leg irons clanking away. To the townspeople, he was just another kid, and they barely gave him notice. Even in his current situation, he was starting to feel like a normal person. But this feeling wouldn't last.

Before they reached the ship. Quinton walked up to Savannah and whispered in her ear, which made Preston nervous. She scowled and turned to Preston.

"Change of plans."

"What? Where are we going now?"

"There's an old codger who lives in a shed at the end of the beach. You need to go there and pick up some netting for the Dragon. The fool has already been paid, so don't let him give you any back talk. Remind him what happened the last time he tried to short the Captain."

"What happened?" Preston asked.

"Never you mind that! Now get going."

"What's his name?"

Savannah stopped and rolled her eyes.

"What do you need it for?" she asked with an exasperated huff. "He's the only old man living in the only ramshackle shed out there!"

"Okay, sorry."

"If it's so important to you, you can call him Shackles."

Shackles? Well, that gives me an idea of what happened to the poor guy.

"I'll be returning to the Dragon. Once you get the net, meet me there."

Preston nodded as she walked away, but he stood steady. *Is she really going to leave me alone?*

Grasping his intention, she glanced over her shoulder. "It's an island. There's nowhere for you to go."

Unfortunately, she was correct. All Preston could do was let out a deep sigh as he trudged through the ankle-deep sand. Just ahead, he spotted what he assumed was Shackles' shed. Built at the water's edge, what this man called his home was nothing more than a one room building, pieced together with discarded wooden planks for walls, and some rusted sheets of tin for the roof. Dozens of fishing nets were strung from nearby trees, drooping down like deflated balloons. As Preston stared at the display, a raspy voice from inside the shed caused him to jump.

"Ooh are yeh?"

"My, my name is Preston. I'm, I came for a net? Savannah sent me."

"Is she here?" asked the old man, peeking out the door with wide eyes. The breeze tousled his unkempt, bleached hair, which exploded from the sides of his balding head. His beard was just as wild and sparse, making him look like he slapped his face down into a tray of sticky cotton candy. One of his eyes fixated on Preston, while the other darted around.

"Uhm, no, she just sent me." *Does anyone like her around here?*

The old man stroked his beard, causing scraps of food and dust to sift through his fingers. Once he was certain Preston was alone, he hobbled out of the shed, grabbing a driftwood staff which was leaning against the wall. By the looks of him, you'd think he'd been shipwrecked on this tiny stretch of beach all his life. The only clothing covering his tanned skin was a ratty loincloth, which was tied tight around his waist and resembled a large diaper. Hunched over, the man drew close. Preston prepared for an affront to his nostrils, but much to his surprise, the man smelled tropical, like coconuts.

"Pretty young to be sailing with that lot, ain't ye?"

Preston tried to answer, but couldn't stop staring at the man's teeth. Every other one was missing, giving the resemblance of a picket fence.

"Uhm, I wouldn't know, sir."

The old man circled Preston, digging the tip of his staff into the sand with each stride. He was rickety as he moved, but even though the skin dangled from his bones, he had an underlying, subtle strength to his build. But what gave pause were all the deep scars along the man's back, which made Preston wonder how much he had endured in his life.

"Hmm," the old man muttered as he headed toward a stack of folded nets, directing Preston to follow him with his bony index finger.

"Are you Shackles?"

This caused the man to stop abruptly, cringing at the name. He spun around and gritted his remaining teeth.

"For all intents and purposes, aye."

As he closed his mouth, one tooth remained out in front of his pursed lips, seemingly rebelling against the imprisonment of being shut away with the others. Once again, he motioned for Preston to follow him. As he did so, Preston noticed the old man only had three fingers on his left hand.

"So ye want to be a bold, swashbuckling pirate, ey?"

"Pardon?"

"What's a young scamp like ye doin' joining Redbeard's brood?"

Preston looked confused. "I wasn't given much choice."

Again, the man stopped in his tracks and glanced back over his shoulder.

"Interesting," he said, his voice elevated. "So, what's yer story?"

"My story?"

"Ye got barnacles in yer ears? Yer story, yer tale, how did ye get tied to that riffraff?"

"Oh, I was, well, I was captured when they shot up my boat."

"Boat, ye say? So, yer a sailor, are ye?"

"Sort of."

Shackles raised an eyebrow. "Uh-huh. Well, this is yers just ahead."

They passed the pile of nets and headed into a small patch of tall palm trees with ropes intertwined between them. Hanging from these lines were several nets, spread wide and dangling down like some monstrous spiderweb. Shackles reached up with his cane and unhooked one net. The massive gathering of intertwined rope collapsed and bunched up on the ground. Preston stared at the impressive pile.

"Well, don't just wiggle yer toes in the sand! Give me a hand! Grab the far end and bring it to the middle."

While Shackles stretched out and held the opposite end of the lengthy net, Preston walked his forward. They did this several more times until they stacked the net into a neat square, which grew as tall as Preston, leaving him standing there, staring at the heavy bundle. This prompted a not-so-subtle grunt from Shackles.

"Ye got a cart?"

Where would I have put a cart? "Uhm, no."

"Mule?"

Preston shook his head.

"Someone comin' to give ye a hand?"

Is he serious? "I, I don't think so."

Shackles ran his hand over his forehead and gave an exasperated gasp. "Well, c'mon with ye," he said, weaving his fingers into the pile of netting.

Preston followed his lead and wriggled his fingers into the net. With a mighty heave, both of them plowed a trail through the deep sand as they dragged the weighted lump of netting over to the water. Once there, they pulled it up onto the dock and hauled it over to one of the several moored longboats. While Shackles prepared the boat, Preston took a much-needed break, massaging his aching legs while he examined Shackles' fleet. It was a hodgepodge of wrecks and — well, more wrecks. A few of the boats appeared to be somewhat seaworthy, I guess ... I mean they were still above water, and somewhat dry. Several others were barely afloat. Although, if it weren't for the ropes tying them to the docks, this may not be the case, since water easily flowed in and out of the holes rotted into the hulls. Much to Preston's delight, Shackles was fiddling with one which seemed sturdy enough to stay above water. It was roughly twelve feet long, with a single mast in the center. In the back of the boat was a smokestack, half the height of the mast. Barely breaking a sweat, the old man shoved the bunched-up netting down onto the bottom boards. The weight of it caused the tiny boat to bounce up and down in the water.

"Well, hop in."

Preston stepped down into the boat as Shackles untied the line and jumped in after him.

"Do you need any help?" Preston asked, staring at the small mast in the center of the boat.

"Can you sheet in the jib?"

Preston turned as white as the sail he was grasping, causing the man to cock his head.

"And ye say Redbeard found ye on a ship?"

Preston didn't know what to say.

"Interesting," Shackles said, reaching over to the dock and grabbing a toppled stool. "We'll just putter over." He sat down next to a small console and flicked several switches and levers before leaning back; whistling as though he had not a care in the world. As the boat hummed and whirred, Shackles reached into a cabinet where he retrieved a long-stemmed clay pipe.

"Where do ye hail from, kid?" Shackles asked while he lit the pipe and took a few puffs.

"Me? Oh, it's a place far away. You've probably never heard the name before."

Shackles nodded and lifted a metal hatch in the bottom boards where he tossed the lit match into. Almost instantly, smoke rose from the stack and the boat rumbled as a whirring noise grew louder. With a steady hum, water gurgled from underneath.

"Hold on," Shackles said as he pulled a lever, causing the boat to motor away from the dock.

After sliding his staff into a coupling attached to the boat's rudder, he used it to steer while his other hand fiddled with the switches. As they picked up speed, Shackles guided the boat toward the Dragon's Curse. Preston sat back and watched Shackles as he motored along, the salty mist spraying against the old man's smiling face. He wasn't sure if he had ever seen anyone so happy before. But once they were able to see Redbeard's crew scampering about the deck of the ship, Shackles' smile disappeared and he steered the boat ashore, gunning the motor to punch the bow into the sand.

"This is as far as I go," he said as he stepped onto the beach.

Wait, what? Preston begrudgingly jumped over the side and helped him pull the netting from the boat. They dragged it on to the beach before Shackles got back into the boat.

"Yer gonna have to figure it out from here," he said, staring at Preston. "Oh, and watch yer back." With that, he yanked on a lever and spun a dial, which got the water churning a great deal more as the boat dragged itself off the sand. Without so much as a wave, Shackles motored away and became a small dot on the water's surface.

"Okay, then," Preston said as he turned toward the ship. *What did he mean by watch my back?* With a deep grunt, he grabbed the net and pulled, but it barely budged. He went around to the back of the lump of rope and gave it a shove, but all this did was topple a bunch of netting over the side of the mass.

"Now what?" he said, scratching his head. Befuddled, Preston stood there with his hands on his hips. "How do I get this all the way over there?"

Circling the net, he came up with an idea. If he unfolded all of it, the weight would be dispersed across the sand, so that should make it easier to drag. Just as he started to stretch out the net, Savannah walked up, followed by two pirates from the crew.

"Forget about that. We need to go."

"Okay."

The pirates easily lifted the net and walked off with it as Savannah and Preston headed toward the ship.

"Did he give you any trouble?" she asked.

"Who, Shackles? No, not at all."

"Did he have anything to say to you?"

"Like what?"

Savannah stared at him. "Never mind. We're late."

When they reached the ship, they climbed the gangplank and found the crew frantically hammering oakum into the gaps to seal the deck, while others coiled rope, polished the copper tanks, or just stayed out of Redbeard's sight. Savannah had seen this many times before — someone got on her father's bad side. Curious as to who it was, she peered over the side of the ship, looking for the one who caused this activity (secretly hoping it was Quinton). After not finding anyone treading water, she led Preston down the hallway and knocked on Redbeard's door.

"What?"

"I've got the boy."

"Well, get in here with it."

It? Preston thought.

Savannah twisted the thick iron handle and pushed Preston into the room. They found Redbeard scribbling on a piece of paper. He looked up and stared at the boy, who stood silent, fumbling with his fingers as he glanced at the broken table.

"Aye. This is more befitting for a cabin boy," Redbeard told him.

"Cabin boy?" Preston muttered.

"What say ye?" Redbeard asked.

"Nothing."

The back of Savannah's hand collided with Preston's cheek. "You either address the Captain as Cap'n or sir. And none of your back talk!"

Preston cringed from the blow and rubbed his cheek, which had turned cherry red. "I'm sorry. I'm just not sure what a cabin boy is ... sir."

Savannah chimed in. "You will serve the Captain his meals, clean his room, polish his boot, and anything else he demands of you."

Redbeard stood and walked toward Preston.

"Ye see, my last cabin boy and I had a bit of a misunderstanding, ye might say," Redbeard said, tossing some loose gears onto the table. "Take this one into town and pay a visit to the sutlers. Yer gonna need help gathering the provisions we need. We sail at dawn."

"Aye, Cap'n."

As they left the ship and entered town, Preston reflected on his decision to hide in that, to use his words, "stupid trunk." He'd nearly been roasted, suffered through a hangover, and just now got smacked in the face. Who starts their day like this?

It was just before lunch when they headed to the sutlers, whoever they were. With families passing him all around town, Preston wondered what he'd be doing back home right now. He certainly wouldn't be working as a cabin boy. However, he felt relieved. This new job of his seemed much, much more preferable than being trapped in a cage next to a sweltering furnace. But the reality of it all was this place wasn't his. He wasn't even sure what this place was. There were so many questions popping into his head, he felt as though he was going to burst if he didn't get them out. As he'd experienced, though, it was in his best interest to keep his mouth shut; Savannah clearly wasn't a conversationalist. But as you might expect, given his inclination to find answers, his silence didn't last long. Before they even made it past the waterfront, he couldn't hold back any longer, feeling as though he was going to hyperventilate from the anxiety filling his chest.

"Excuse me, Miss ..."

"Savannah."

"Miss Savannah."

"Just, Savannah. None of that 'Miss' nonsense."

"Sorry, it's just that I don't know anything about ships, or sailing, for that matter. The closest I've been to water was filling my tub."

"You'll learn. And heed my advice, you better be quick about it. Our captain has a low tolerance for lallygagging."

Preston gulped.

"Miss Savannah, can we stop and get something to eat?"

Savannah rolled her eyes, reached over to a nearby street cart, and haphazardly grabbed a loaf of bread from the display, causing several others to fall to the ground. "There! Enjoy your meal," she said, tossing the bread to him.

Preston looked back at the exasperated vendor who was scrambling to pick up the fallen loaves. The poor man wanted more so than anything to scream out at Savannah, demanding payment for the bedraggled bread — he didn't. Only a fool would cast that stone, and it would certainly not end well.

"What are we shopping for?"

"When I have it and give it to you, then you'll know."

This is going to be horrible. Preston's shoulders slumped as he bit into the loaf. There was a subtle crunch to the flakey crust, followed by his mouth filling with the soft, warm dough inside. As he bit into another piece of the delicious, buttery loaf, his eyes rolled back as his head filled with thoughts of home. He missed his morning routine, making toast and enjoying his breakfast on the back porch

I should've just gone to Iron Hills. At least then I would have had a chance at getting back home.

His heart stuck in his throat as the fear of never returning home or seeing his parents washed over him, but he couldn't think of such things. It's much easier to give in to a challenge, and Preston would never allow himself to do that.

Savannah stopped in at least a dozen stores and tradesman's shops. A ship and its crew needed a plethora of supplies when beginning a journey because if you ran out of food in the middle of the ocean, there were no stores with which to shop. But let's say you are able to reel in some fish — problem solved, right? No. With no drinking water, you'd need to rely on the rain to save you, for drinking ocean water would dehydrate you quicker as the body struggled to remove the salt. Perhaps now you can see why Savannah ordered everything from sails to gunpowder, yards of silk, salted pork in hefty barrels, needles, thread, and countless other items, including some Preston didn't recognize. Each time she paid, she pulled out a crimson velvet pouch and retrieved a gold coin. Glancing over during one of their stops, Preston saw something on the coin he thought he recognized, but he couldn't get close enough to make out the image. While at the next shop, he snuck up behind Savannah as she paid. Hearing him breathing right next to her caused her to cringe.

"Get away from me," she said, kicking him away as though he was nothing more than a street rat.

The clerk took the money and went around to the back of his shop, reappearing with a two-wheeled wooden cart. However, this one came without a horse.

"Let's go."

"Where to? There can't be too many stores left in this town."

"My orders should be ready. Now, we'll double back to the shops and load the cart," she told Preston. He piled all their wares he had been carrying onto the cart as Savannah walked away. After a few steps, she turned and threw her arms up. "Well?"

Preston had to look twice at her, cocking his head before his eyes grew wide. *Is she serious?* "You want me to pull this thing? It weighs a ton!"

Savannah raised her eyebrows and nodded. "Fair enough, Fishbait. Why don't I set off and find someone else more willing to help me? We'll just bring you back to your cage in the keep. The lava is flowing heavy today, so it should be nice and toasty for you. Would that be preferable?"

Preston shuddered at the thought. "No," he muttered, begrudgingly picking up the yolk of the cart. *What happened to me being a cabin boy?*

Granted, the weighted cart was quite difficult to pull, and it became a much larger task than Preston anticipated. Even on a smooth surface, the thick wooden wheels wouldn't be very forgiving. Here, along this cobbled avenue, it was a thousand times worse since each stone created a tiny hill for Preston to climb. One rock would be bad enough; here he had hundreds, and each bump rattled his bones. Add to this the additional weight of provisions, and you'll understand why it took all his weight and straining his leg muscles just to get the cart moving. The worst of it was that as soon as he got a steady roll, Savannah would stop to get more goods and the process would start all over again. This assault upon his muscles continued throughout the day. By late-afternoon, his shoulders ached from the constant strain and jostling, and his palms were rubbed raw from the wooden yoke. He had never worked this hard in his life. The smart thing would've been to keep his mouth shut and continue on — he didn't.

"This is ridiculous! Do we have much further to go?"

Savannah paused and raised her eyebrows. "You know what? We do now." She turned away from the road leading them down to the docks and headed back up the hill.

"Are you kidding me?" Preston yelled, throwing down the yoke. But as soon as he said this, he wished the words he uttered would magically vanish in midair before reaching Savannah's ears — they didn't.

Before he could pick up the yoke and apologize, Savannah had her dagger pressed against his throat.

"Hmm," she said, leaning in close and staring Preston in the eye as a tiny trickle of blood dripped down his neck. "I think this would hurt much more than your legs or hands do now. Perhaps we finish when I say we finish and you say nothing more for the rest of the day. Savvy?"

Preston's heart raced as he took short, rapid breaths, trying not to push the blade further into his skin. *What happened to my life? Is this what I'm going to deal with every day?*

Upon seeing this, the townspeople turned away, pretending he didn't even exist.

"Now, how about we make a few more stops, then we'll see if you're ready to return to the ship? What do you say?"

"Okay," Preston whispered.

Savannah removed the knife away from his neck and slid it back into its sheath. She shook her head, snorting as she walked away. "Lazy! That's the youth of today!"

With his blistered hands, Preston wiped the blood from his neck. Before he lost sight of her, he lifted the heavy yoke and strained to follow, bounding his way along the cobbled path.

At the top of the hill, Savannah turned down a narrow street and under a brick archway. The road opened to a long-forgotten square surrounded by dilapidated buildings. Anyone happening upon this location of town would think it abandoned. Most of the windows on the decrepit buildings had been shuttered, while the others were filled with broken panes of glass. It was an eerie place to find oneself in; devoid of any sunlight, the air was heavy and dank. This place was so seedy, only the outcasts with nothing left to fear traveled this far. Neglected by all, this little corner of Breakaway Bay was a far cry from the bustling village they had just walked through. There were no people present, not even a stray dog dared to venture alone here. Even the rats knew better than to come out of hiding. The crash of broken glass from one of the darkened alleys caused Preston to clench up.

"Where — uhm, where are we?" he asked, getting close to Savannah as he glanced around.

"Wait here."

She walked toward a passageway and was immediately swallowed up by the shadows, leaving Preston alone. Now, in case you've never experienced it, once you're truly alone, every sound becomes magnified. Not long after she disappeared, Preston heard another glass bottle break, followed by some muttering in the darkness of the alley closest to him. Melded into the shadows, three scraggly men emerged and stepped out into the dim light. They seemed surprised, never seeing a child left alone in this part of town. Dressed in tattered clothes, their eyes never left the visibly shaken boy as they sauntered up to him. None of these vagrants wore shoes, leaving the soles of their feet as black as coal. The rags they covered themselves with were so soiled, the fabric had stiffened with years of caked on dirt and sweat. Preston tensed up as they drew closer, their dull expressions driven by their gaping mouths as they grunted words to each other. Beneath the rugged scruff on their faces, they sneered at him with vengeful scowls.

"An what do we 'ave 'ere?" the tall, skinny man asked, his breath reeking of cheap wine.

Preston couldn't take his eyes off this man. His teeth resembled baked beans, and over one eye, he wore a patch, which partially covered a pronounced scar, carved long ago, deep into his face. The glaring wound split his sullied skin from above the covered eye, down to his chin. Preston turned as the man's cohorts approached from different sides.

"It looks as though yer cart is too heavy for a scallawag such as yerself. Per'aps we can help lighten yer load?"

Preston said nothing, standing his ground in front of the cart.

"Keep an eye on this one, Bitters," the tall man said to the shortest of the bunch. "If there ain't much 'ere, I'm sure we can get some hefty coin fer this l'il stray."

The thieves laughed as they rifled through the contents of the cart, opening packages and shaking boxes until Preston threw the yoke down.

"Get away from here!" he yelled as loud as he could, pushing the small, stout man away. "This isn't yours!"

After scowling at each other, the three men burst out laughing. One of the ruffians, a sloth of a man with sleepy eyes, pulled out a rusted sword and swung at Preston. The blade sliced through the sleeve of Preston's shirt and across his skin. Preston fell backward and grabbed his stinging arm as the man approached him.

"This'll teach ya some manners, ya lousy street urchin."

As he raised his sword high, the sound of shattering glass exploded from behind the man, showering Preston with tiny shards. The man's eyes rolled back into his head as he collapsed, his face smashing against the cobbled stones half-buried in the road. Savannah stood behind him with the handle of a serving pitcher, which was the only part still left intact after she pummeled the stranger. Bitters, a person who thrived on self-preservation, scrambled to his feet and ran off into the darkness, not wanting any part of what was about to take place. Savannah spun around and pulled her cutlass as she approached the tall stranger, who yanked the tattered felt hat off his head and fumbled it between his fingers.

Even in pain, Preston couldn't help but to stifle a laugh as the man's yellow hair, now free from its restraint, exploded at the top of his head. With his lanky build, tattered green clothes, and a head full of puffy yellow hair, the hooligan resembled a dandelion.

"Eh there, Savannah," the man said, his brow now dripping with sweat. "We did'n know this was yer booty or we would've never —"

"Skinny Pete! I should've guessed. It seems as though you've grown accustomed to wearing an eyepatch. Are you now wanting another one?"

"What?" he asked as his hand shot up and covered his good eye. "No, not at all. We was just —"

Savannah stared down at Preston. A small stream of blood soaked into his shirt. "Why is he still on the ground?" she asked, replacing her sword into its scabbard.

"Sorry, miss," the man said as he darted over to Preston, grabbing his good arm and helping him to his feet. "That weren't me," he said, backing up and shakily pointing to Preston's bleeding arm.

Savannah sauntered up to Skinny Pete and leered into his good eye. She reached up and grabbed the straggly hairs on his chin, jerking his head to the side as she examined his face.

"I always thought you would make a somewhat competent member of our crew. With a few modifications, of course."

The man's eye grew wide as he stared straight, not daring to whisper a word.

"Perhaps I should deliver you to the transition center?"

There were few things in Breakaway Bay which instilled as much crippling fear in somebody as did the transition center. It was the most heinous of places, known by all. A place where a person was transformed into a sort of machine. Someone designed to be helpful to the great pirate king — and expendable!

I'll die before I go there! This is what Skinny Pete wanted to say. I assure you, he didn't. As for Savannah, she took great joy in seeing a man suffer at her hand, but the hour was drawing late, and she had much to do.

"I'll tell you what. You can use your extra energy to drag my cart down to the Dragon. And you best be quick about it!"

"Yes, ma'am. Of course," he said as he sprinted over to the wagon and lifted the yoke before bounding down the street toward the docks.

Preston straightened himself up, wincing as he squeezed his arm. "Sorry, I thought I could scare them away."

Savannah burst out laughing. "You? You couldn't scare the flea off a dog. Let's go."

Now, you'd think by the way Preston hobbled along, he'd been run through by a pike, and blood was spewing from every pore in his tender, broken body. I assure you, this wasn't the case. People had suffered worse cuts from shaving, and his dawdling, followed by subtle moans, were annoying an already aggravated Savannah. The anger percolating in her came to a full-blown boil, causing her to come to an abrupt stop. With an exasperated grunt, she spun around and stormed up to him.

"Let's see it then!"

Preston grimaced as he raised his arm, still grasping it tight, hoping to stop the flow of blood, which quite frankly, barely trickled. Savannah pulled his hand away, and in one quick motion, ripped his tattered sleeve away from the shirt. The sudden movement made him want to scream out in pain, but he bit his lower lip and held it in. Once she took hold of his bare arm, she raised her eyebrows and shook her head.

"Hmm. I'm not gonna lie. It's not good."

Preston's mouth dropped.

"Whaddya mean?" he asked, trying to pull his arm away so he could see, but Savannah held firm.

"Look, I'm gonna be straight with you. It might have to come off."

"What? My arm? No, that can't be! I can move it," he said, struggling to release Savannah's grasp on him.

"Easy now, you're making it worse. There are tendons dangling from the flesh, and I can see bone."

The mere mention of tendons and bones turned Preston as white as snow.

"Am I going to die? Will they put a fake arm on me like Chuggs?"

Savannah burst out laughing. "No, you milksop! That butter knife of a sword he swung barely broke the skin. You're not even going to need stitches."

She walked over to a bench under a window and picked up a jug, pulling the cork out with her teeth.

"Wait, what is —" Preston started to say before Savannah poured the rum onto the wound.

Now, if you've ever experienced alcohol being poured over an open wound, or a scratch in this instance, you'll certainly be able to relate to the feeling Preston was now suffering.

"OW!" He bellowed, feeling as though she just shoved his arm into a raging fire. "Are you kidding me?"

He squeezed his eyes shut while Savannah took the scrap of sleeve she had ripped off and tied it over the wound. As she pulled the fabric taut, Preston's body stiffened from the stinging.

"My lord, Fishbait. I've seen people lose limbs and not put up this much of a fuss." She knotted the makeshift bandage and dropped his arm. "There, now let's go! I've got things to do."

He nodded to her as he inspected the bandage. No blood was seeping through, and the pain had dulled.

Now Savannah wasn't totally void of feelings. After all, she was a nurturing mother — well, let's drop the nurturing part. At least she was a mother. Actually, disregard what I just said. She found all of this amusing. Seeing the young lad grimacing in pain, she stifled a snort as she turned, shaking her head.

"You know what? After all you've been through, Fishbait, I think I can help you feel better."

"How's that?" Preston asked, happy to get some relief.

"Well, there's a lovely place for a spot of tea up ahead. Why don't I drop you off so you and the other ladies can compare bonnets and catch up on your knitting? Tomorrow, before we sail, I'll come by and fetch you," she said, bursting out laughing.

Well, let's just hope for the best in a person and say the nurturing side of Savannah was still asleep and had not yet greeted the day. Nonetheless, by the time they reached the ship, Skinny Pete had already unloaded the cart and stacked the supplies next to the gangplank.

"All set and square for ye, Miss Savannah," he said, twisting his hat in his hands.

Savannah scowled as she inventoried the items before turning to the quivering mess of a man. "Make sure this cart gets back to Browners, savvy?"

"Yeah, yes, of course. Anything to help," he sputtered before picking up the yoke and pulling it away.

"Hold on there."

Skinny Pete flinched as Savannah strolled up to him. "You got any gold on you?"

"Gold?"

She leered at the man. "Your mates ruined a perfectly good shirt and damaged my help," she said, pointing to Preston. She then sniffed the air. "Plus, causing me to stand so near to you makes me want to take several baths to get your stink off me. I think a few coins might help me forget about the troubles you caused me."

"Right, yes, of course. That's only fair," he said, nodding his head as he dropped the yoke.

Pirates, in case you are unfamiliar, are quite the selfish bunch who would sooner give up an appendage rather than their "loot," which was like family to them. But this tight-fisted attitude carried over to thieves as well. As was the case with Skinny Pete. However, in this unsettling situation, the alternative would be quite unpleasant as Savannah would kill him and take his gold, anyway. This for certain is something Skinny Pete was quite aware. So, with some trepidation, he pushed his hand into his tattered trousers and retrieved a small pouch. His hands quivered as he tried to untie the leather cord, but he was shaking so much, the pouch slipped from his hand. As he bent down to pick it up, the sharp, polished tip of Savannah's sword pierced the coin purse, forcing Skinny Pete to yank his hand back.

"This should cover it," she said, causing the disheartened man's shoulders to slump. As he slowly rose, his face fell, and he became sullen.

"Yes, ma'am," he muttered, picking up the yoke and slowly wheeling the cart away.

Savannah lifted her sword and retrieved the pouch from the tip. She dumped the coins into her palm, six of them, and picked one out, flipping it to Preston.

"Make sure all this gets loaded onto the Dragon before dark," she said as she replaced her sword and walked up the gangplank onto the ship.

Preston glanced down at the golden coin, his stare growing intense. But not from Savannah's unexpected grand gesture; this befuddlement grew from the image on the coin itself.

"Wait, what? That's the one!"

COINS, BACK IN THE day and perhaps in some instances today as well, were often made by leaders who had a penchant for subtle, or perhaps not-so-subtle reminders of who held power. Take, for instance, Julius Caesar, whose face was prominently displayed on Roman coins, making certain his subjects had no doubt as to who the absolute ruler was. Centuries later, Redbeard boasted the same tactics. His coins were minted to remind the realms of the power he held. So, it was no surprise that the coin in Preston's palm was embossed with an image of the Dragon's Curse. Arguably the most powerful ship to sail the seven realms. But this mere coin beckoned a litany of questions. The foremost being, how did Uncle Rupina get one of these?

While loading the provisions onto the ship, Preston's head was scrambled, buzzing with questions. Had his uncle been a pirate? Did he pillage side by side as one of Redbeard's notorious crew? Had he ever killed anyone? Was this how he financed his eccentricities? Then a worrisome question arose, for perhaps this was the reason for his great-uncle's disappearance! Was Rupina the victim of Redbeard's rage? Was he in hiding? Or worse ...

Although he had never met the man, everything seemed to be intertwined: the coin, the mechanical limbs of the crew, the technology of the town. Perhaps his uncle's tinkering led him to help Redbeard create these — humanoids? After all, the workings inside their prosthetics were eerily similar to the creations scattered throughout Rupina's home. And what of the many whispers of mechanical beings roaming the halls of Willowbush Court? At one time, not so long ago, Preston could dismiss these as fantastical tales. But those moments were gone.

Lost in his thoughts, macaws and parrots weaved in and out of the palm trees as they made their way back to their nests for the night. The evening sky was cast into a purplish, orange haze. However, his moment of tranquility was short-lived.

"Captain says you need to take a slumber in the box!"

Preston jumped at Chugg's voice. There was no way he could go through that again! Should he run? What could he have done wrong? His heart raced until he saw Chuggs wasn't talking to him; he was dragging a befuddled woman down the gangplank.

"I did'n do nuthin'! Check me pockets! I got nuthin' on me."

Preston fell back, quivering as he watched the two disappear into the night. He hadn't been here long, but of all the people he wouldn't argue with, Chuggs came in a close second behind Redbeard. As expected, Chuggs wasn't swayed by the woman's pleas. Since the giant seemed more mechanical than human, Preston wondered if his heart had been replaced by a machine as well.

Regardless, the spectacle he'd just witnessed only served as a dark reminder of his own predicament — trapped, a prisoner of sorts. But even that was confusing. As another parrot disappeared into the evening sky, it seemed to be an appropriate depiction of his situation. He was nothing more than a bird with clipped wings. Free to venture out but unable to fly away. This was his new reality. Worse of all, if he didn't prove his worth, he was certain to be right next to that wretched woman; locked away in the bowels of a bubbling volcano, suffering what he was certain would be the least torturous punishment he'd endure.

By the time the last barrel was stored, the Dragon had grown quiet. Since there was to be an early morning departure, most of the crew had long since settled in for the night. Shadows danced across the deck from the flickering golden flames of lanterns staged along the rails. With the waves splashing against the hull and the subtle creaking of the rolling ship, Preston's eyes grew heavy. It had been an agonizingly long day, to say the least. Curious as to whether he was finished for the evening, Preston sought out Savannah, assuming she was below deck with the rest of the crew. As he approached the forecastle, he paused, and rightfully so. Nobody ever explained his station among the others. Was he allowed to roam free on the ship, eat with the crew, or share their quarters? He had no desire to do the last, since what waited below was a gaggle of bloodthirsty cutthroats who would likely invent torturous games for their amusement at Preston's expense. However, he hadn't had anything to eat besides a meager loaf of bread, so onward he went toward the front of the ship.

"Bow is the front, stern is the back," he whispered. "This is the fore-room, fore-door? I'm never going to get this right."

He opened the door leading into the forecastle where the sound of laughing and mugs clinking filled the hallway. Still uneasy, Preston paused, but only for a moment because the smell of roasted chicken filling his nostrils overpowered his rational thinking. Overcome with pangs of hunger, he crept along the narrow hallway until a door creaked open, sending a burst of light into the corridor along with the sonorous tone of accordion music. Preston quickly ducked behind a barrel as a shadowed figure pushed a food trolley into the hall before returning to the festivities. After several moments, Preston crept up to the cart where amongst the piles of empty plates were portions of chicken, fish, small chunks of bread, cheese, and empty casks of ale. Forming a pouch with his shirt, Preston piled in as much food as he could before retreating up the stairs. As he tiptoed across the deck, he nearly tripped over a drunken pirate, flat-faced and doing his best to mumble out a sea shanty. Oblivious to the world around him, he didn't even take notice when Preston snatched the mug of ale from his hand. Unfortunately, a waft of the vulgar drink reached Preston's nose, causing him to gag. Refusing to ever allow that vile liquid past his lips again, Preston dumped the ale into the bay and took the empty mug over to a rain barrel, scooping it full of water. Now he could comfortably search for a quiet, out of the way place to settle in and enjoy his meal. But where? Ahh, but why not under the lifeboat? It seemed to be the perfect place to ensure some much-needed solitude. However, stealth and exhaustion aren't agreeable companions. Add to that his raging hunger and Preston may not have been as careful as he strived to be, for as he slinked his way across the deck, he tripped over the anchor chain and dropped the mug. The clanking of chain and mug created more than enough noise to alert the unseen sentry.

"Eh, ooh goes there?"

Preston froze when he spotted the guard leaning against the ship's wheel. Not wanting to get caught with his pilfered chicken, Preston stood silent, stiffening his body and sucking in his stomach as though it would help him blend in amongst the sparse shadows. Fortunately for him, it was late, and the apathetic sentry half-heartedly stretched his neck as he looked out over the ship before settling back into his spot and drifting off to sleep once again. Within a few breaths, the man was snoring, thus giving Preston the courage to retrieve his mug and dash over to the overturned lifeboat. At first, Preston thought to only use this as a discreet spot to enjoy his meal and rest his eyes, but the mere definition of the craft sent a whisper of excitement coursing through his body — Lifeboat!

This was exactly what he needed to escape; to reclaim his life! Against the rail was a wooden bucket, which Preston dumped his food into before leaning over and searching out into the bay. Unfortunately, without a moon, it was too dark to see, leaving him with nothing to do but stare out into the night, cradling a bucket of food.

Where would I even go?

Sure, he knew he was on some sort of volcanic island, surrounded by miles of ocean, but what ocean? Plus, he wasn't sure what direction would take him to the nearest continent. He glanced out at the small boats tied to the docks. Just as he inventoried whatever sailing knowledge he had in his head, he became distracted by squeaking coming from the dimly lit pier. Through the shadows, he spotted the girl from earlier, all alone, pushing a cart full of dirty linens away from the ship. As he watched her, Preston shook his head.

"Not yet. I need to be smart about this."

A breath of cool wind swept across the deck, causing his arm to prickle with goosebumps. Returning to his shelter, Preston grabbed a nearby lantern and crawled under the lifeboat. It wasn't much, but it was warm and dry. As he swallowed his last morsel of dinner, he dragged over a small sack of cornmeal and settled his head down onto it. Within moments of wrapping himself in a loose piece of canvas sail, his eyes grew heavy. A faint shuffling caused him to stir, but Preston was far too tired to scrutinize the noise. Had he, he may have learned Savannah had kept sight on him the entire time. Once she was certain he had drifted off to sleep, she replaced her pistol into her corset and headed down to the crew's chambers.

The barking of orders invaded Preston's slumbering solace until the commotion grew too loud to ignore.

"Make sure ye batten down the hatches before we set sail!"

Heavy thuds of boots across the deck and the squeak of rope being slid through pulleys surrounded Preston as he untucked himself from his cocoon. Every muscle in his body bristled with pain as he struggled to emerge from beneath the lifeboat. The sun was just peeking over the horizon, awakening the shadows of the crew climbing the tall riggings as the sails were hoisted. Thick iron bars were slid into brackets, securing the numerous windows and hatches throughout the ship. Below deck, bags bursting with coal were tossed from one person to the next as they were stacked in the ship's storeroom. Next to them, a dozen prisoners shoveled heaps of coal into the blazing furnaces, fueling the fires that caused steam to steadily drift out from the masts. After checking his bandage, Preston found Savannah standing at the bow of the ship, staring through a telescope. He stood next to her, dodging her long hair as the wind swept through it.

"Sorry, I must've been exhausted. I didn't hear anything this morning."

Savannah turned to him with a raised eyebrow. "I'm not sure why you're standing there pushing down wood," she said, returning to the monocular. "The Captain's fierce appetite is only second to his ferocious temper when he is left waiting for his breakfast."

Preston's heart jumped. "What? I didn't — where do I get that?"

Savannah dropped her hand, scowling at Preston before nodding toward a nearby staircase leading below. Never have you seen anyone move as fast as Preston who sprinted across the deck, weaving his way in and out of the busy crew. As he dodged a cannon, he spun around before suffering the misfortune of bouncing off Chuggs, who was carrying a thick anchor chain over his shoulder.

"Get off me, ya barnacle!" the enormous pirate bellowed, shoving Preston against the ship's mast.

"Sorry!"

Preston scrambled to his feet and leapt down the stairs as he chased the smell of bacon and eggs cooking in the galley. He threw himself through the door and stood in the entry, panting. The cook, a grisly old curmudgeon to say the least, spun around and waved his steel cleaver at the intruder.

"Ooh, are ye?"

"I'm, I'm Preston. I'm supposed to get the Captain's breakfast."

"Well, be quick about it! It's been sitting 'ere for an hour now."

"An hour?"

He slid the covered tray over to Preston, who grabbed it before turning back to the cook. "Excuse me, but where would I find the Captain?"

"Argh! As if I don't 'ave enuff to do round 'ere! Up the first set of stairs last door at the end of the hall."

"Thank you!" he yelled, running out of the room. As he came to Redbeard's quarters, he slid to a stop before crashing into the closed door. The tray wobbled as he tried to balance it with his free hand. Once he did, he shakily reached forward and knocked.

"What?" Redbeard yelled.

Preston jumped back, almost dropping the tray. "I have your food, sir."

"About time! Get in 'ere!"

He hurriedly brought the food inside, setting it on the table where Redbeard was sitting, waiting with fork in hand. The pirate stroked his beard before reaching over and lifting the cover. Unfortunately for Preston, this wasn't the type of breakfast a pirate king expected to be served, for on a beautifully prepared bed of lettuce was a rat — a dead one at that. Jammed into its mouth was a tiny tomato. Redbeard was incensed, turning purple with rage as Preston stood frozen, his eyes fixated on the deceased rodent. Before Preston could blink, Redbeard launched himself off the chair and flipped the table over, sending everything on it into the air, including the rat. Preston's apology came quick, but not quick enough, for Redbeard had already grabbed him by the neck and lifted him off the ground.

"What sort of nonsense is this, boy? Ye think yerself to be funny?"

Preston's feet were kicking wildly. He couldn't speak with Redbeard crushing his throat.

"Talk quick, gutter-rat!" he said as he removed a pistol, cocked it, and pressed it against Preston's temple.

"I, I, didn't do —" Preston sputtered.

Redbeard bit his lip, then burst out laughing as he dropped a befuddled Preston. Savannah and the cook charged into the room beside themselves with laughter.

"Get up, boy," Redbeard said, grabbing Preston by the shirt and lifting him to his feet. "Savannah told me how ye stood up to those scallawags yesterday."

Preston rubbed his throat. *This was all a joke? What is wrong with these people?*

"Go get yerself some breakfast and a fresh shirt, then make sure ye clean up this mess," Redbeard told him. He walked out of his cabin, still laughing with Savannah and the cook sharing in the amusement.

"It wasn't that funny," Preston grumbled, staring at the dead rat.

Now, it had been quite some time since Preston had an actual meal, so he wasn't about to let one throat crushing encounter spoil his feast. However, his escape to normalcy was short-lived. After breakfast, he reluctantly returned to the scene of the unfortunate rat's wake. While stepping over the carnage, Preston realized this was the first time he had been in Redbeard's cabin alone. An opportunity which could shed some light on his situation, and perhaps help him escape the madness. Inside, the captain's cabin was certainly spacious. However, he had never been on a ship before, so he had nothing to compare it to. Nonetheless, it was certainly much larger than his room in the keep, if you could call it such, and this room was filled with an array of interesting items. The grandest of which was a massive shark's jaw, or so it appeared. It was so colossal, this beast could've swallowed Preston whole. Inside its gaping mouth, Preston measured one of its many razor-sharp teeth.

"They're as big as my hand!"

As he stared at the teeth, he shuddered to think what would have happened this morning if it hadn't been a prank. If he'd actually ignited a rage in the callous captain so fierce, he would've tossed Preston overboard, potentially causing a face-to-face encounter with a beast such as this. His young life becoming nothing more than a grotesque spectacle of his demise for these hooligans to enjoy before their voyage. He'd never pondered thoughts such as these before. Why would he? What sort of person is forced to live a life fearing absurd scenarios as the ones bouncing around in his head?

Hoping to escape these thoughts, he stepped away, focusing on his cleaning. On the other side of the room was the dead rodent, staring blankly at him.

"Don't blame me. I didn't think it was funny either."

Once he swept away the shattered glass, he bribed an older pirate with a pilfered plate of mutton to pick up the rat and throw it overboard. However, this mere exchange caused an epiphany. Was this just the beginning for him? Would this be his first step to becoming a Steampunk Pirate? It was only a scrap of meat after all, but he took great pride in his efforts to swipe it from the kitchen. An act which would normally be unthinkable to him and create an abundance of angst had become a challenge to overcome; and for this, he had concerns. Nonetheless, there was no time for such distractions, so he moved to the back of the cabin where, up several steps, was Redbeard's personal workspace. The captain's ornate desk took up most of the space, where just behind was a massive picture window, offering a sweeping view of the bay. Plants hung down from the ceiling, soaking in the sun beaming through the glass, as did an orange tree in the corner. On the wall, hung like a tapestry, was a map the size of a bedsheet. Breakaway Bay lay in the center, surrounded by seven planets, each labeled and marked with a list of coordinates. But what made Preston shudder was the one planet labeled "Earth."

"This can't be right," he said, backing away until he brushed against a stack of papers at the edge of the desk, knocking them to the floor.

"No, no, no!" He dropped to his knees, frantically gathering up the sheets. "Were these in some kind of order?"

As he scooped up several stray sheets of paper, his attention was diverted at the sight of an intricate carving on the side of Redbeard's desk. The scene was of two ships battling, but one of them was above the other, dropping from the sky as if it was — flying?

"Can this be?" Preston pondered the implication of the scene, rubbing his fingers across the nooks and crannies of the carving. But then he looked back at the tapestry and noticed a drawing of the Dragon's Curse crossing the celestial plane. While fixated on this, the ship pitched and a squeak from an odd-looking display of planets next to the desk caught his attention. *An orrery!*

But this orrery was like no other. Instead of planets rotating around the sun, as it is in our universe, this model's planets orbited around a model of the Dragon's Curse. It was as though this narcissist Redbeard fancied himself to be the center of the universe. But what universe exactly? The planets depicted in this model were unrecognizable for anyone with even the slightest degree of astronomical reference. Albeit there was one which was easy to spot — Earth, obviously. As for the others, well, there were six additional with a spot for another, but that one seemed to have long since been removed. The oddest sphere in this array had a cone shaped recess bored into the center, as if a tremendous tornado drilled itself into the planet. The cone covered almost a quarter of the sphere, and inside were several tiny moons, which appeared to be spiraling into the funnel, destined to be swallowed by the planet forever.

"Wait a minute," he said, reaching for the globe. "This is exactly like the one in —"

But a soft knocked startled him.

The papers!

Before the door opened, he scrambled over to the stack and patted the jumbled papers together into a slightly less disheveled pile. The hinges squeaked as someone stepped into the room. Pretending not to notice, Preston peeked out of the corner of his eye and saw a tall man enter the room. He was wearing ankle chains, similar to the ones Preston was imprisoned with when he first arrived. The stranger shuffled into the room; his strides restricted by the length of the weighted chain. He was a lanky man with scraggly hair as white as snow. It burst from his head like white rays of sunlight. His clothes were tattered, his bare feet blistered and bedraggled. The man held an unrolled scroll in his hands.

"Oh, pardon me," he said, reeling back, surprised when he spotted Preston bent over, sweeping the floor. "Is uhm, is Captain Redbeard here?"

Preston stood and shook his head.

"Right, of course," the man said, looking around. "Would you happen to know where I might find him?"

Again, Preston shook his head, doing his best to conceal the disarrayed stack of papers.

"Oh, very well," the man said, glancing at the globe Preston stood next to. "Well, have a pleasant day."

The man turned and clanked away.

"Wait!"

Startled by Preston's outburst, the man hunched over as though he had just been struck upon the head.

"Could you tell me where I am?" Preston whispered.

The befuddled man looked around and clanked over to the map, shakily pointing to one planet — and it wasn't earth.

"You need to jump through the stars to get here," the man said with an eager whisper.

"Wait, what?"

Preston wondered if this had been a huge mistake. With his wild hair and ridiculous answer, the man must've been deranged. Preston closed his eyes and shook his head, refusing to believe what he had just been told. However, the man was much smarter than Preston realized. Sensing the boy's apprehension to this revelation, the man nodded to a stack of papers. Before he could utter a sound, a sudden creak caused him to wince. "I cannot tell you anything further," he said, shaking his head furiously as he scurried out of the room, lamenting on what he had just done. "You cannot trust anyone. When will you learn?" he muttered, chastising himself as he disappeared down the hallway.

Even before the man was out of sight, Preston was flipping through the papers until — Iron Hills?

Below the heading was a list of names. First initials only, followed by a surname and nothing more. Of all places to be named, why Iron Hills? Maybe there was something else in the stack. He shuffled through the pages: Schedule for Tides, Inventory List, Provisions, Repairs ... nothing gave him a clue as to why that wretched place would be catalogued here. He kept skimming through the documents until he stopped on one, which had a sketch of a steamer trunk, similar to the one he arrived in.

"There are others?"

Each part on the diagram was labeled as to what its function was:

- Venting

- Pressure Feed

- Thermostatic Delineator

- Gamma Density

- Granular Residuum Tray - Fill prior to beginning Realm Jump

"Realm jumps? Then it's true? That's why Redbeard is so eager to get the key!"

"What are you doing?"

Preston jumped, once again causing the stack of papers to launch from his fingers and scatter across the floor. As he spun around, paper continued to rain down upon him, one sheet fluttering down upon his head. It was quite a sight to behold, amusing in any other situation, however, not this particular one. In front of him stood the girl from earlier, presenting the most unpleasant scowl she could muster.

"Nothing! I was cleaning up. Just like the Captain told me to do."

She set down the pile of folded bedsheets she was carrying and glanced down at the papers, and then at Preston. Without a word, she picked up the sketches from the floor. After examining them, she organized the stack and set it on Redbeard's desk.

"I would strongly advise you do what you're told and don't stray from that."

"Right, of course."

She rolled her eyes and headed to the door.

"Wait!"

The girl stopped and turned, giving him a look of ... well, actually she almost seemed to be looking right through him. A mixture of annoyance and disdain is the best way I could explain it. For as awkward as Preston was normally, it took on a whole new meaning now as he stumbled over his words.

"You — you're not going to say anything about this, are you?"

The girl frowned, shook her head, and left the room.

"How can I be so stupid? Pay attention or you're gonna get killed," Preston said, smacking the side of his head with his hand.

"You need to clean that wound," she said, enjoying the spectacle of his self-deprecation.

Startled, Preston looked down at his arm. Before he could stitch together an intelligible response, she had left, only to return with a crisp, clean shirt.

"I'm Amelia," she said, before disappearing once again.

"Are you sailing with us?" he yelled out.

"No."

He stood there for a minute, mesmerized. After ripping a strip of material off the old shirt, he tied it over the wound and put on the clean shirt.

"Amelia," he said with a smile.

By the time he made it up on deck, the Dragon's Curse was well underway, escorted by two smaller ships on either side. Dozens of fishing boats, laden with the morning's catch, were making their way back into Breakaway Bay, cheering on the Dragon as they passed. Even in the early afternoon sky, several planets were visible high above the billowing black sails. Preston fixated on the largest one. From this distance, it could have been any other planet; even one within his own solar system. Unable to fathom the possibilities of space travel and what he now needed to do to return home, Preston stood frozen until the cool, salty mist splashed his face.

Shaking his head, he found himself questioning his surroundings. The water was wet, the air was cold, but was anything actually what it appeared to be? Perhaps this was an elaborate dream filled with unimaginable detail. He pondered the possibility of this until he caught sight of Savannah on the quarterdeck, where she and Redbeard stood at the ship's wheel, directing Quinton, who sneered at Preston as he passed him on the stairs.

At the helm, Redbeard stood next to the binnacle of the ship, but this one was unlike any other compass Preston had seen. As with most others, the compass was set atop a tall wooden stand, but this one had heavy gears interlocked along the side of the base. Constellation maps were painted on the two spheres flanking the compass. Each sphere had its own set of golden numbers, with one side representing latitude, and the other, longitude. While both spheres rotated independently of each other, they worked in conjunction to operate the ship. Positioned above the binnacle was a crescent moon, made of brass, which swiveled around the compass.

"If yer ready, Cap'n," Quinton said, returning to the deck carrying a wooden box.

In the box was a sextant, just like Preston's parents had found. If nothing else, its mystery would soon be revealed. Once thought to be broken, in this world it worked as intended. Raising the sextant to his eye, Redbeard peered through the lens, pointing it at two of the smaller planets. Satisfied with his alignment, he flipped through several lenses until he found one to use as his fixed point. Once he found it, Redbeard adjusted the crescent moon on the binnacle. When he swiveled the moon, the gears on the base turned, as did the ship's massive wooden wheel. As soon as the ship corrected itself, Redbeard faced the bow and adjusted the sextant, finding another point. He spun the sphere on the port side of the binnacle, causing the foremast to move. He then faced the stern and did the same thing. Once he completed his calculations, he rotated the starboard sphere. This movement turned more gears on the binnacle, which adjusted the mizzenmast.

"Have the nonessentials been transferred to the other ships?"

"Aye, Captain."

"Then prepare for departure!" he yelled out to the crew. "I'll be in my cabin setting the jump. And make sure there's not too much pressure in the tanks!" he said, watching the steam blasting out of the vents. "If they blow and we get scuttled, it'll be all yer heads!"

He handed the sextant back to Quinton and disappeared to his cabin.

"What was the Captain doing?" Preston asked Savannah, who was staring through a monocle.

"He's plotting the ship's course within the other realm. Now I suggest you get below deck before you're washed overboard and end up in deep space."

"Then it's true," Preston muttered, the fear in him swelling to the point he became lightheaded. "Uhm, what did the captain mean by nonessentials?"

"Those are the people he doesn't want to risk getting killed during our mission."

"Wait, what?" Preston yelled just before a horn blasted out an ear-piercing scream. With his hands pressed tight against his ears, he yelled out to Savannah. "How do I get to be a nonessential?"

As the horn blared a second time, the two escort ships fell back and turned toward Breakaway Bay. The crackling sound of grinding gears filled the air as the Dragon's Curse creaked and rumbled. The crew did not seem bothered by this. But as the wooden planks along the deck flexed and heaved, Preston gave serious consideration to jumping over the side, sharks or no sharks. Regardless, as he tried to move, he couldn't. It may have been the ship vibrating the blood out of his legs, or the paralyzing fear coursing through him, but either way, he wasn't moving. However, everything else around him was a flurry of activity. High above, the gears on the masts spun, causing the main sails to raise and pivot, becoming giant umbrellas above the towering stacks. The steam spewing out of the masts filled these sails with hot air, swelling the canvas like some sort of rectangular balloon. Moments later, the ship pitched and lifted from the sea. Given that this could be his last chance to remove himself from this insanity, Preston sprinted over to the rail and threw one leg over the side — it was too late. Far below, a thick cloud of steam now surrounded the hull.

Several additional blasts from a horn echoed through the afternoon air as jets of steam continued to blast out from under the ship. By now, the thick steam clouds had dissipated enough to where Preston could see water pouring down from the side of the ship, splashing into the sea far below as the Dragon's Curse continued to climb.

The ship groaned from the strain as the fierce dragon figurehead spit out a breath of steam from its gaping mouth. Along with its glowing red crystal eyes, Preston was overwhelmed with a sense of foreboding as he stepped back across the deck. Ahead in the distance, storm clouds billowed and swept the sky, encircling the ship. Cracks formed within the black clouds as a brilliant red light beamed through from just beyond. They continued to stretch even further, curving upward and filling the horizon until they gathered together. As soon as the massive clouds met, thunder erupted as lightning crackled within the opening. Ever so slowly, the mass began to swirl, picking up speed until it appeared as though the ship was sailing directly into the mouth of a tornado.

"I don't feel so good," Preston said as he hunched over and held his stomach.

Covering his mouth with his hand, he ran to the side of the ship as the wind howled. Wisps of steam continued to shoot out below them, and even though they were no longer in the water, the ship thrashed about as though it were stuck in the middle of a hurricane, fighting against the raging seas. The sails ballooned, straining the towering masts, which bent and creaked from the force of the storm. The violent, erratic swaying tossed Preston across the deck, causing him to crash into a wall. He went to scream, but there wasn't enough air for him to draw into his lungs. Still nauseous, he crawled over to the door where Savannah stood waiting, shaking her head.

"I warned you!"

After throwing himself inside, a crew member, wearing what appeared to be a diving suit, slammed the door closed and spun a large wheel, which sealed the opening. As one would expect, Preston became too curious for his own good, leading him to peer through the porthole.

"What's happening? Why are they dressed like that? Is this a hurricane?"

The face of another pirate flashed into the window, causing Preston to retreat. After gathering his senses, he approached the glass and watched. Made of copper, the pirate's helmet was fitted with small round windows, making the crew member look like a giant, metallic spider. Two coiled hoses came off either side of the face mask and connected to a pair of copper tanks attached to the back of a thick canvas suit. Each joint on the crew member's body was covered with layers of black, riveted metal, fitted to protect the elbows and knees, yet allowing ease of movement. Preston watched as other similarly dressed pirates fought through the wind and positioned themselves on deck. Meanwhile, two other pirates struggled to climb the ratlines. After reaching the top of the mainmast, they hooked themselves to the crow's nest. The rest of the crew grabbed thick chains anchored to the deck and secured them to the belts around their waists. Two hulking pirates stood strong, clinging to the ship's wheel while the remaining crew did their best to control the sails, trying to keep them from shredding apart by the force of the wind. The storm grew worse as chunks of hail the size of baseballs pelted the Dragon, while streaks of brilliant blue lightning exploded all around them. Long, thin arrows of white light streamed past, slowly at first, but then picking up speed. The beams shot past the ship faster and faster until they became lost within clouds of purple smoke, which poured onto the deck like waves on the ocean. The ship steered into a swirling vortex of flashing lights. Even from inside the cabin, Preston could hear the seams of the sails stretching as they strained to stay together. Unable to withstand the relentless pummeling, several sails shredded apart, the torn pieces being sucked up into the whirlwind encircling the ship. After another sail was ripped free, one deckhand became entangled in the twisting lines and was dragged across the ship, disappearing over the side. The masts bowed so much from the intense storm, Preston expected them to snap apart like twigs. Panes of glass cracked as the wide deck boards creaked, heaved and settled, some of them flexing so hard, they fractured, sending splinters of wood shooting through the air like tiny daggers. Just when it appeared the ship was about to split in half, everything froze, and a booming echo filled Preston's ears before swallowing all other sounds. Unable to blink, Preston watched as the world around him moved in slow motion. The flickering flame from a nearby oil lamp stood motionless, as though the torch itself was painted within the glass. It only took the blink of an eye before things snapped back to normal and the ship crashed into the sea, sending towering waves of water over the crew.

Preston slowly stood, overcome by the throbbing in his head. He bent over, pressing his hands against his skull, hoping to ease the pain. A pain far worse than the day Redbeard filled him with ale.

"What was that?" he muttered.

"We've completed our jump. Don't worry, you'll get used to it," Savannah said as she brushed past him and spun the wheel on the door, releasing the seal. After yanking the hatchway open, water washed into the room as she headed out onto the slippery deck with her pistol in hand.

Overcome by the effects of the jump, the deck mates who had withstood the storm collapsed to the ground. Pirates who had remained below deck for the journey scrambled out from every opening, yelling as they manned the cannons and carried out new sails. Several of them stopped to help their fallen shipmates to their feet before taking them below deck.

Preston stepped out into the now clear blue sky. The sails shifted down to their original position and were once again filling with wind. Seeing the crew lying about writhing in pain, Preston ran over to help.

"Are they alright?"

"They will be." Savannah lowered her scope and turned to Quinton. "She's just over the horizon! Let the Captain know we've arrived." She turned to the crew. "Prepare for battle!"

IT IS SAID SEVERAL Greek gods were born of the earth; if that is to be believed, then Redbeard was born of the sea. It had long been fabled that the pirate's left hand beckoned the wind while his right tamed the waves. So frightful was the man, even Poseidon sought out his approval. That is, if you are to believe in such fantasy. Nonetheless, no matter what one chooses to believe, it was certain Redbeard's presence instilled fear and respect, and as he stood firm in front of the ship's wheel, the crew scattered in a frenzy of activity, fearful of the repercussions for not hastening their duties. By the time he took the helm, the carpenters had already replaced the broken planks from the deck while the riggers removed tattered sails and hoisted new ones in their place.

"Huzzah!" the crew called out in a collective grunt, alerting Redbeard the deck guns stood ready.

Prepared for battle, Redbeard pushed Preston aside and inserted his peg leg into a hole in the deck. Next to it was a brass placard marked

"Cannons." Once his leg connected with a click, he twisted it, causing the small guns on the bow and stern of the ship to rotate. Before Preston could ask what was happening, explosions of cannon fire shook the Dragon's deck. The blasts were so strong, Preston lost his footing and fell against the ship's wheel. Redbeard lifted him off the ground and threw him aside.

"Mind yer ways, boy! We're in the midst of battle!"

From across the waves, a muted sound, similar to banging drums, echoed through the air as the other ship returned fire. A barrage of red hot leaded balls screamed toward the Dragon's Curse. Preston fell flat as the thick wooden walls of Redbeard's ship splintered from the assault. Newly replaced sails were shredded from the broadside, leaving them limp and dangling from high above as Redbeard spun the ship's wheel.

"Well, what are ye waiting for ya scurvy dogs?" he yelled down to the crew. "Fire!"

Two decks below them, the ship rumbled once again as the Dragon's heavy cannons returned fire. The deck filled with clouds of smoke, the air thick with the smell of sulfur. Preston looked toward the other ship with its massive white sails. As soon as he spotted the galleon, it was struck with the weighted lead balls, which continued to scream across the water and blast into their target, punching holes into the side of the massive ship as they exploded. Sailors yelped as they were propelled through the air and came crashing down into the sea.

"The Captain always likes to greet new friends with his own blend of exploding rounds and chain shot!" Savannah screamed over the booming of the guns.

"Chain shot? What is that?" Preston yelled, covering his ears.

"Watch!"

Another burst sent cannonballs attached to one another with a thick iron chain twisting through the air. They wrapped around the galleon's masts, slicing through them like a hot knife through butter. Two of the towering masts collapsed on the sailors below as the ship was set ablaze, fire bursting out from several holes in the hull's side. But Redbeard wasn't done. Before the other crew had time to recover, Redbeard yanked on a lever jutting out from the deck next to the wheel. Steam exploded from the top of the Dragon's masts before a whistle screamed and gears along the hull spun, releasing the hefty anchor which plunged down into the dark water. The crew grabbed hold of whatever was near them before the ship came to a crashing halt as though they ran aground. Redbeard spun the massive wheel and the large vessel whipped around, confusing the sails, which collapsed and fluttered. The starboard side of the Dragon's Curse now faced the burning ship.

"Fire, ya dogs!" he screamed out.

Another bellowing rumble of cannons exploded below Preston, shaking the ship violently. As with the last volley, more gaping holes were punched into the galleon's hull. Most of the crew from across the way were forced to jump into the ocean as they tried to escape the raging fires. A loud crack echoed across the waves as the final mast of the galleon snapped in half, tossing the sails over the side where they plummeted into the deep water. The ship was floundering and taking on water as it listed to one side. Before it could sink any further, Redbeard flipped open a metal cover on the helm, revealing a dozen levers and switches. He toggled a switch, and yanked back on another metal lever, which caused more steam to billow from the stacks as two monstrous harpoons extended out of the bow. Redbeard spun the ship's wheel once again, raised the anchor, and headed directly for the crippled ship.

"Ramming speed!" he hollered, causing the crew to hoist whatever sails were left. With the canvas full of wind, the Dragon's Curse raced through the water, its fierce dragon figurehead leading the charge, steam spewing from its frightful mouth. With a jarring crash, the Dragon's Curse slammed into the side of the galleon, the twin harpoons piercing deep into the now brittle hull, impaling the ship and preventing it from sinking any further.

"Now get yer worthless selves over there and present me with my prize!" Redbeard growled. "If ya lose any of it, I'll keelhaul the lot of ya!"

The pirates scrambled to the front of the ship and tightroped across the harpoons, using them as a bridge to board the other ship. The sound of muskets firing and blades clashing filled the air, but the thick smoke obscured the battle. Several of Redbeard's pirates fell from their wounds, one of them taking a sword through the ribs. But as they lay momentarily still, the gears in their bodies churned even faster and they rose to their feet, continuing the fight while blood spilled from the wounds. Slowly, the clanking of swords and the bursts of musket fire diminished before a hearty cheer erupted. Once the winds picked up and pushed away the dense smoke, Preston saw the pirates had taken over the crippled galleon. Survivors of the crew were either bound to what remained of the splintered masts or tied together and marched across the harpoons. The rest lay on the deck, motionless. But none of this mattered to Redbeard. He was far too distracted to concern himself with this. His neck strained as he peered over the ship's wheel, looking as though he was waiting for a long-lost love to return.

"He must be trying to find Savannah," Preston said, searching as well.

Redbeard's eyes darted about until a giant smile grew across his face. Preston looked over to where Redbeard was staring, expecting to see Savannah, but instead saw two pirates carrying a pallet piled high with jagged black stones. They were followed by other pirates escorting a well-dressed woman bound in chains.

She must be the captain, Preston thought.

Soon after they boarded, Redbeard's crew laid boards across the two harpoons, creating a makeshift ramp. Once they finished, small teams carried over dozens of other pallets filled with the same jagged black stones. Speckled within these stones was a tarnished, copper-colored metal.

"What is that?" Preston asked.

Like a child on Christmas morning, Redbeard's eyes gleamed with excitement. "That is what we was searchin' for," he said, pushing past Preston. "Bring it all aboard quickly!" he yelled. "That wreck of a ship won't stay afloat much longer and if it goes down, it'll drag us into the briny deep with it."

As the precious cargo was loaded onto the Dragon's Curse, Redbeard hobbled over and grabbed a stone off one pallet. "This, lad, is Zimponium," he said, tossing it up and catching it. "It has the strength and durability of stainless steel, but this'll also stretch when it gets hot, and snap back when it cools."

"Do you chisel the metal out of the stone?"

Redbeard laughed. "That would take too long and make it tainted. It needs to be 100% pure, and the only way to ensure the quality is to melt it out of its shell with enormous amounts of heat." He tossed the stone to Preston. It was about the size of a lemon, but lighter than a snowball.

"Cap'n! There are chests of gold!" one pirate yelled, running up to Redbeard and holding out two fists of coins.

"Forget yer pilfering ways!" he said, slapping the gold from the man's hands. He grabbed him by the scruff of his shirt. "Make sure ye get every last bit of Zimponium or ye'll be tonight's dinner for the kraken!"

"Aye, Captain," the pirate said before sprinting back across the harpoons.

Redbeard shook his head and took Preston by the arm. "Get over there and make sure those idiots recover all the Zimponium! She's about to be swallowed up by the dark waters!"

Preston looked at the ship engulfed in flames, and then at Redbeard.

"Well, what are ye waiting for? Ye have yer orders!" he said, shoving the boy away from him.

Preston stumbled over his feet before running to the bow, where he stared out at the stricken vessel. What was he supposed to do with these "orders"? The mere fact someone hadn't thrown him overboard by this point was nothing short of a miracle. Now, Redbeard expected him to confront a bunch of cutthroat pirates and somehow sway them to throw down their prized gold to collect a bunch of rocks?

The closer he got, the more intense the heat became. Like ants, Redbeard's crew scampered back and forth with loads of Zimponium, pushing past Preston who stood unmoving, his toe pressed firm on the makeshift bridge. Just beneath his feet, the sea raged, sending pangs of fear shooting through his body. But if he didn't cross, he was certain to suffer Redbeard's wrath. This realization forced him to gather whatever courage he could muster and tiptoe his way over. By the time he was halfway across, an enormous wave crested so violently, part of the crippled ship's hull gave way and broke apart. One harpoon piercing the galleon shifted, flexing the walkway, causing Preston to stumble. He crumpled and rolled as another wave washed over the bridge. Frantic, he blindly grabbed the air, taking hold of a stray rope dangling from the bowsprit. As he rubbed seawater from his eyes, he held tight to the rope until he stood steady. He couldn't tell if he was shivering from the cold water, or from fear. Nonetheless, he regained his footing and made haste as he sprinted across the walkway. Once he reached the galleon, he dodged the flames and scurried down into the cargo hold. Water poured in from the multitude of holes punched into the hull. Pirates were scattered throughout, trudging through waist deep water as they scrambled to gather all the remaining Zimponium until a loud crack of timber caused everyone to stop and listen. The snapping of boards signaled their fate as the hull started splitting apart.

"She's about to go, lads! Fill yer pockets with whatever gold ye can!" Quinton yelled.

The pirates abandoned the Zimponium and started shoving fistfuls of coins into their pockets. As Quinton filled a burlap sack with treasure, he spotted Preston staring at him. Just as Preston was about to say something, Quinton growled as he sloshed his way up to him. With a firm grip on his dagger, he grabbed Preston by his shirt and pressed the tip of the blade into Preston's chest.

"Ye say anythin' to the Cap'n about this and I'll gut ye like a fish! Savvy?"

Preston quickly nodded as Quinton pushed him away and returned to collecting his loot. With water continuing to fill the chamber, Preston ran up the stairs to what was left of the deck. As he choked his way through the thick smoke, he came across a dozen prisoners tied around a split mast.

"Get back to the Dragon!" Savannah yelled to Preston over the sound of the roaring fire and snapping wood.

"What about them?" he asked, coughing the smoke from his lungs.

Savannah looked at the bound men, screaming for their lives.

"They refused to fight for Redbeard, so they sealed their fate! Now, go!"

Preston ran past them over to the harpoons.

"Lad! Please help us! I beg of ye! I have a young daughter!" one prisoner called out.

Preston skid to a stop and looked at the defeated crew, then at Savannah, who was preoccupied hustling the remaining pirates along the walkway. As the deck flexed, even Preston could see this heap was about to sink into the sea. He picked up a discarded cutlass and ran over to the prisoners. With a broad swipe of his blade, he sliced through the thick rope. As the crew freed themselves, Preston tucked the sword into his belt loop and ran back across the walkway. Just as he reached the other side, the massive harpoons broke loose from the splitting hull of the mangled ship. The remaining wood holding the galleon together fractured as the ship, now free from its restraint, rolled to its side. Desperate, pirates swung across from ropes in a last-ditch effort to escape the raging sea swallowing the galleon.

"Where is she?" Preston asked, searching the deck for Savannah before spotting her, trapped on the floundering ship. As she tried to grab a rope to swing over, the hull of the stricken ship rolled further, causing her to lose her footing, and she was cast into the turbulent waters. Submerged for several moments, she resurfaced and swam over to a line dangling down from the Dragon's Curse. Meanwhile, Redbeard was busy directing the crew to secure the Zimponium below deck as the helmsman tried to pull the ship away.

"Cut the remaining lines before she drags us down as well!"

Several pirates with axes and hatchets chopped away whatever lines were connected to the galleon. Now unburdened, the taut ropes snapped back at them like cracking whips.

"Be quick about it!" Redbeard hollered until Savannah's pleas for help caught his attention. He looked over the side of the Dragon and grabbed a coil of rope. Just before tossing it down to her, one pallet broke apart, sending Zimponium rolling across the slick deck. Ignoring Savannah, Redbeard threw the rope down and yelled to the crew.

"Grab my spoils before it's swallowed up by the sea!"

Under Redbeard's watchful eye, the pirates rushed over to make sure they gathered all the loose stones. Preston watched Savannah dip below the waves as she struggled to swim away from the capsized ship. With the galleon's hull slipping below the surface, Savannah was being sucked down in its wake.

"Hold on!" Preston yelled as he rushed over and picked up Redbeard's rope, tossing one end down to Savannah. Once it hit the water, he heard her heave as she struggled to swim over. With a desperate stretch of her arm, her head disappeared below the surface just before her hand grabbed hold of the rope. Preston sprinted over to the mainmast and tied the other end of the rope around it. Savannah coughed out water as she tried to climb against the force of crashing waves while Preston darted back and pulled on the wet rope, straining to help her up to the deck. The relentless, crushing waves kept smashing her against the hull until she lost her grip and dropped back into the water. Two pirates rushed to help Preston, but as soon as Redbeard saw this, he pulled out his pistol and fired it into the deck next to them.

"Get yer lily-livered carcasses over there and secure the Zimponium!"

The men immediately dropped the rope, which sent Savannah back into the raging water. Once the last of the stone was loaded into the hold, Redbeard nodded and the two men went back to help Preston retrieve Savannah. The three of them heaved on the lifeline and pulled her up the side of the ship. As soon as she made it back on deck, she collapsed, coughing out a lungful of water. She gasped in some much-needed air before rolling to her side and crawling up on all fours. As she tried to stand, she fell back to the ground, grabbing her ribs and panting until she finally caught her breath. Preston bent down to help her up, but she pushed him away and threw the rope to the side, glaring up at the quarterdeck where Redbeard stood, unfazed. He scoffed as he returned to his cabin just as the galleon's wooden figurehead disappeared below the surface.

"Stop your sulking and get us home!" he yelled to her before slamming his door shut.

After everything she'd endured, Savannah wasn't going to let this pass. With a hearty growl, she bolted up the stairs and into his cabin, leaving Preston to stand there, his mouth agape, as he watched debris from the sinking ship float to the surface.

"What just happened?" he asked, dropping to his knees, his eyes wide.

Savannah reached Redbeard's cabin and kicked the door open, barging into the room while seawater steadily dripped from her. Outside, the crew prepared the Dragon's Curse for the jump back to Breakaway Bay.

"You left me to die!"

"Stop yer bellyachin'! This shouldn't surprise you. These loads are more important than any of ye, and nothin' will get in the way of me fulfilling my destiny!" he said, his face red with anger. "And if any of ye scallawags have a problem with that, ye can take a walk on the plank and find yer own way home, if ye think ye can make it!"

It took everything she had in her to keep from screaming out. Clenching her fists, she leered at Redbeard, her face twisted with rage.

"Aye, CAPTAIN!" she blurted out, turning and stomping away. But before leaving his cabin, she stopped in front of Preston's top hat, which Redbeard had on display. With a bold sneer, she snatched it off the stand before storming out of the room, leaving the ornery pirate shaking his head and smirking.

"Here!" she said, shoving the hat into Preston's chest.

"My hat!" he said, beaming as he placed it on his head and followed Savannah onto the deck.

Before he caught up to her, six pirates came out of the hold dressed in the same apparatus as when they departed Breakaway Bay, but this time, each of them carried an enormous wooden harpoon with a razor sharp serrated metal tip at the end.

"What are those for?"

"To make sure we get back home."

Each guard positioned themselves along the sides of the Dragon's Curse; two at the bow, two at midship, and two at the stern. Other members of the crew ran up to them and attached a pair of thick chains from the deck to a belt around their suits. After securing one guard to the deck, the crew member removed her helmet and stared at the other. She gave her a nervous smile before hugging the woman and placing the helmet back on her head. Just before they began the jump back, each defender squatted low into a battle-ready stance, their heads on a swivel as they looked out nervously.

"Get below, Fishbait! And stay away from the doors and windows!" This time, Preston didn't hesitate.

Savannah gave a thumbs-up signal to the pirate manning the ship's wheel. After taking a deep breath, the helmswoman secured her helmet, then pulled back on a long lever. Almost immediately, steam poured from the mouth of the Dragon's figurehead as the ship prepared to jump realms. As she turned, Savannah saw Preston with his head out the door.

"I told you to get below! Now, stay back!" she said, pushing him back and sealing the hatch.

"We have serious damage to the deck beam!" someone called out from the bottom of the stairs.

"Argh! I'll be back," she said, running down to the hold as the violent rumblings began.

Curious, Preston crept up to the window, unable to see through the pale mist covering the deck. The swirling vortex of clouds surrounded the ship and before he knew it, everything had shifted into slow motion. But just as quickly as it began, it ended as the Dragon's Curse came to a bone crushing halt. Whatever caused the ship to stop did it with such force, Preston was thrown across the room, crashing into the far wall, and knocking him unconscious.

"Are you alright, dear?"

That voice.

"Why don't you get up? It's almost time for lunch."

Preston opened his eyes and saw his mother standing before him. His father was behind her, setting up a picnic in the town park next to the fountain. The fragrant smell of lilacs filled the air as a gentle breeze swept over the bushes.

"You must have fallen asleep."

Preston smiled as he looked around. *It was all a dream!* The town had never looked so beautiful. The sky was bright blue, and multitudes of flowers burst with color. From a deep haze, he heard his mother calling to him again.

"Hey! Wake up!"

But as his vision cleared, he came face-to-face with Savannah.

"Snap out of it, Fishbait!"

The sound of shattering glass caused Preston to jump.

"Feeder, port side!" someone yelled as a long slimy tentacle slithered into the space and grabbed one of the crew.

Preston struggled to his feet as the purplish-gray snakelike arm coiled around the man. As he watched, frozen in fear, Preston saw the suction cups of the tentacle pulling back to reveal circular rows of sharp teeth which pierced the pirate's flesh. The poor soul screamed out in agony as the tentacle pulled him back through the window, the remaining shards of glass shredding the man's skin. Preston scooted back against the wall as Savannah withdrew her sword and pulled a nearby copper tank off its hook. She turned and threw it to Preston.

"Tie this to your face! It'll help you breathe!"

He quickly tied the cup around his face and strapped the tank to his back as he started breathing again. Savannah wasted no time with hers as she readied herself for battle. What sounded like a tremendous explosion shook the room as another tentacle crashed its way through the thick wooden door and slithered its way around, searching for another victim. Before Preston knew it, the snakelike arm had grabbed hold of his boot and dragged him across the floor. Unaware of what was taking place behind her, Savannah swung her blade, fighting off another arm slinking its way through the window. As Preston slid along, he pulled the sword from his sash and sliced into the creature's scaly skin. The tentacle stiffened as orange puss oozed from the wound. It released Preston and pulled back as Savannah sliced into another arm. Preston threw his back against the far wall, barely able to catch his breath. Just outside through the thick haze, he caught a glimpse of the two terrifying creatures attacking the Dragon's Curse. Part of the beasts were wrapped around the hull, squeezing the thick planks of wood, while their other tentacles grabbed whatever they could as they strained to pull the ship apart. With a horrific howl, the larger creature ripped several boards from the hull.

"This can't be real!" Preston said, staring at the horrific monsters.

Over thirty feet long, it was as if several sea creatures morphed into one deadly beast. The creature's body resembled a shark, but with protruding wings on its back, like a stingray. Six squid-like tentacles, twice the length of their bodies, extended out from their chests. As if choreographed, each creature had four of their arms grasping and pulling on different parts of the ship, while the remaining arms searched for food. Dozens of the crew scurried up onto the deck, climbing the ratlines into the crow's nest to assist other pirates swinging swords at the monsters, who were now tearing the ballooned sails apart.

"Keep those devilish beasts away from the sails, lest we plummet and perish!" Redbeard yelled at the top of his lungs.

On deck, cannons and lifeboats flew through the air as the voracious beasts latched onto anything they could grab hold of. One creature devoured a crew member as the other wrapped its tentacle around the torso of a guard who was frantically stabbing at the beast with their harpoon. Wounded from the assault, the creature coiled its arm, tightening the grip it held until the defender's bones cracked and they slumped over. The monster then yanked the limp torso up off the deck, effortlessly snapping the chains as though they were nothing more than a piece of thread. The beast lifted the body up to its shark-like head and opened its gaping mouth, flashing several rows of serrated teeth. Just before it tore into its victim, another guard plunged their harpoon deep into its side. With an ear shattering scream, the beast's tentacles shot out straight as orange aqueous goo spewed from the puncture and across the deck. The wounded beast released the dead crew member, who disappeared into a wave of purple smoke alongside the ship. Writhing in pain, the creature uncoiled itself from the Dragon's Curse and dropped off the side, vanishing into the swirling storm. The sudden release from the weighted beast caused the ship to lurch, dropping everyone to the deck. The remaining creature released the mainmast and followed close behind its mate, both disappearing into the purple, smoke filled sky. Blue lightning flashed and howling winds strained the sails as Savannah leapt out over the smashed door onto the deck. Through the whipping wind, she waved a red flag as she ripped her mask off.

"Get us out of here, quick!" she screamed over the labored moans of the mangled ship.

About to be swept away in the storm, she replaced her mask and dashed back inside, pushing Preston through the carnage and down the stairs. Once they were below deck, she sealed the second hatch as the ship rumbled and returned to making its jump. Before he even had time to process what had just happened, the Dragon's Curse crashed down into the water off the coast of Breakaway Bay with a jarring thud. Snaps of fractured wooden planks throughout the hull popped like fireworks as the ship settled, leaving the crew to scramble about as they fought to keep the ship intact.

"What, what just happened?" Preston asked, ripping his mask off as his eyes darted about. A broken sword lay next to him, covered in orange slime. "What were those things?"

Savannah collapsed onto the floor with her head resting against the wall and her eyes closed. Blood trickled down her right temple as she tried to catch her breath.

"When you make a jump, the rippling effect of a ship this large splitting the space between realms awakens the Gorknots, or as the crew calls them, Feeders. Our initial jump is sudden, catching those devil-beasts off guard. The transfer out is too fast for them to catch us. But now, they've adapted. They know where to wait for us upon our return. This is when we're at our most vulnerable. What makes it worse is after a battle, when the Dragon's Curse is at its weakest. We move slower through the jump. This is why we were easy prey for them to catch. They just plucked us out of our jump like a cat snatching a wounded mouse."

"Savannah! There's a breach in the hull!"

"What's next!" she screamed as she jumped up and ran out with Preston following her.

Passing through the debris of the demolished cabin they once stood in was surreal, especially to Preston, who now longed for the days where his worst fear was being tormented at school. Only one portion of wall remained, while the rest of the room was a cacophony of splintered boards, broken glass, and blood, both red and orange. As Preston crossed the deck, the damage was just as severe. One mast was split in half, with the upper portion missing completely; presumably floating somewhere out in space, or wherever they just were. Several railings were either missing or struggling to stay attached to the deck. Loose cannons rumbled back and forth as the ship pitched. Snapped free from their restraints, their wheels rolled through pools of blood, leaving trails of red throughout the ship. With all the damage sustained, the Dragon's Curse was listing to the right. Preston looked over the side and noticed a gaping hole in the hull, broken planks of wood drifting away from the ship.

"No!" a woman screamed, causing Preston to turn. On her knees, the woman Preston saw earlier held the broken chains where her partner once stood.

As the Dragon's Curse limped into Breakaway Bay, it barely made it into port without sinking. By the time they reached the moorings, the waterline was just below the main deck. Once they secured the mangled ship to the dock with extra rope, the crew marched the prisoners up to Redbeard's fortress. Behind them, guarded by at least twenty heavily armed pirates, were dozens of wooden crates piled high with Zimponium.

"Make certain the doctor puts this booty to good use," Redbeard told Quinton, pointing to the long line of treasure.

"Are ye sure he'll stay focused once he hears of all the new prisoners?"

Redbeard smirked. "Ye send Chuggs over to help him stay focused. He can tinker with his new playthings once my fleet is assembled."

"Aye, Cap'n."

"Hold on."

"Yes, sir."

"Before she goes runnin' off, tell Savannah to get herself cleaned up, then to come see me in my keep. When yer done with all that, get a damage report and meet me back there. We need to make sure the Dragon is prepped and ready for another run."

"Aye!"

Quinton left Redbeard standing tall at the rail, watching with pride as the line of pirates made their way through town. The townspeople cheered, clearing a path for the procession as though the Zimponium was a queen making her way through her kingdom. As his eyes followed, Redbeard spotted Preston sitting on a crate alongside the Dragon's Curse. Hunched over, he held his head with one hand, while his treasured top hat dangled from the other. No amount of soothing gears ticking above his head could help him settle after what he witnessed this day. Nonetheless, Redbeard smirked as he made his way back to his cabin. He remembered his first battle as though it were yesterday. The young lad did well. Amelia, however, was not so easily impressed. Even though she was too young to remember, she still knew of her father's death, and was disgusted at the sight she now witnessed. She stood over

Preston, leering at him with her arms crossed and a broad scowl across her face — her standard greeting for the boy as of late. Had it been anyone else, she may have pushed them into the bay and been done with it.

"So, how many people did you kill?"

Unaware she was even there, Preston jumped, nearly dropping his hat into the water as he turned to her.

"What are you talking about?" he asked, cocking his head at her. "I didn't kill anyone."

She raised her eyebrows and nodded her head to the cutlass still tucked into his sash.

Preston stood, pulling out the blade and gladly handing it to her. "Here, take it! And if you must know, I used it to cut some rope to —" But he stopped. He didn't know who to trust. What if it got back to Redbeard he had freed some prisoners as an act of compassion? But wait, did Redbeard even know what the word compassion meant? And if he tried to explain what it meant, would he be insinuating Redbeard was too illiterate to understand his actions? His eyes crossed as his head filled with questions. *I'm getting off track.* "Savannah needed help. She fell into the water, so I had to cut some rope and help her get onto the ship."

Amelia huffed at him. "You must feel like a big man," she said as she walked away, throwing the sword into the bay.

"Hey, you don't even know the half of it!" he yelled after her. "What I've been through! The things I've just seen!"

"Whatever," she called out, leaving Preston standing there, dumbfounded.

"Do you even know what's out there?" he screamed. "Because I don't!"

Now, I dare say, throughout history, there may have been a smattering of pirate leaders more sadistic and repulsive than Redbeard. Perhaps some existed who even made him look like a sheep among lions. However, this realm had never known any other. And as Savannah entered the keep and stood outside his door, it took everything in her to suppress the rage boiling within her soul. After all, it was in her best interest to keep her mouth shut. But this was not how she was built, and something deep inside kept gnawing at her, refusing to allow her to move on from being abandoned. And for what? A pile of rocks, of all things. She raised her fist and pounded on the door as if it were his big, disgusting face.

"Get in here!"

Not much on manners that one, but she was used to it. Even so, all she could do at this point was to throw her head back and bite her tongue before turning the handle and entering his lair, still wearing the wet clothes from earlier as though they were the uniform of the scorned.

"You called for me — SIR?" she asked with a contentious snarl; drawing out the words as though she were spewing hate from her lips.

Seeing this affront to her father, Quinton handed Redbeard a report of the ship's damage before he used this opportunity to leave. As soon as the door closed, Redbeard scowled as he looked Savannah up and down.

"Yer gettin' me floor wet," he grumbled, walking over to a massive framed map hanging on the wall. Attached to hinges, Redbeard swung the map to the side, revealing a hidden safe. Inside was a thick, brown leather text, which he threw onto the table. The aged leather cover was scuffed and discolored.

What does he present me with now? Another paltry treasure deemed more worthy than I?

"Ye feel yerself slighted, cast aside, I presume."

There was so much Savannah wanted to say, but as she witnessed many times before, disobedience meant being cast into the briny deep; sometimes alive, more often than not — well, you can guess.

"My feelings matter not, Captain. Whatever is for the good of the cause. We serve at your pleasure," she said with a subtle bow.

Redbeard snorted and nodded, turning to the book.

"Let me ask ye something. What be our greatest ally?"

Savannah paused. "I don't know what you —"

"What is the one thing we can rely on above all else?"

She thought for a moment. "I don't really know. If I had to guess —"

"History!" he said, cutting her off. "History is our greatest ally! Take this book, for instance. Of course, yer aware there are seven realms. Perhaps yer too young to remember, but there used to be eight," he said, waving his finger in the air.

"Each realm is in their own stage of technological advances." Redbeard walked over and swung the hinged map closed, concealing the safe once again. "We, here on Kringson, are toward the bottom of that list," he said, pointing to the realm on the map. "We've accepted and played our role as bottom-feeders for centuries now. I may be many things, but I am not, nor will I ever be, a bottom-feeder! Fortunately, fate shined down on us, and we captured advanced technology decades ago from the eighth realm, just as it was swallowed up by a black hole. Before Kinarly was destroyed, its cowardly leaders abandoned their people and fled in a small vessel. As good fortune would have it, this ship of theirs was struck by debris from the planet as it broke apart, just as they were beginning their jump. They were still able to launch, but enough damage was done to knock it off its course and this rabble of recreants crashed onto our world. The elders found themselves stranded on a remote island with no way off. Unfamiliar with this world, they weren't prepared for what awaited them, and soon perished."

Redbeard walked over to the desk and flipped the book open, thumbing through the water stained pages.

"Tis this book they left behind which has guided us to where we are today. It tells their story, their history as it were. Within this book is the key to my destiny. I dare say the most valuable key known to all for it unlocks a treasure trove full of information. And information is power!"

Redbeard smiled and nodded as he closed the book and paced.

"Ye see, I was a young lad serving on a ship when we found those refugees; or what was left of them. Since I was with the initial landing party on the island, we was the first to make this discovery. Their remains were nothing like we had ever seen before. The flesh had been picked away by the crabs and what not; their bones pale from the sun, but they was the prettiest bones one did ever see," he said, smiling and shaking his head.

"Even as they stood toe-to-toe with the grim reaper, these fools made certain they exposed their true selves; flaunting their fineries, their flowing silk robes, all the trinkets used to stroke their egos in life. Even til their last putrid gasp of breath, they wore their jewel encrusted hats. It was wealth beyond anything I could've ever dreamed about. But even all their riches couldn't buy their salvation when death came calling. We knew the rare jewels and metals they covered themselves in would make all of us rich ten times over."

Savannah's hair dripped onto the table. Redbeard walked up to it and dragged his fingers through the puddle, rubbing them together as he glared at her, which prompted her to step back.

"I was young, stubborn, rebelling against authority, just like yer doing now. But what I lacked in discipline, I made up for in perception. Unlike some —" he said, glaring at her, "I was smart. I didn't let my emotions cloud my visions. While those cutthroats were busy fighting each other over these mere trinkets, I knew there was much more to this discovery. Therefore, I stepped away as they divvied up the loot; leaving to search the island, away from all the baubles and gimcracks that captivated the attention of weak men. And my efforts paid off because I found this artifact before the others," he said, tapping the cover of the text. "Having a sense of its value, I hid it deep within a cave on the island, vowing to return later to see what fortunes of my own I could find. When my mateys finished stripping the dead of their wares, they tossed me a token to help them load all their treasure onto the ship." Redbeard twisted a thick gold ring on his finger. Embedded in the center was a massive emerald. "We returned to the ship, and I immediately charted the island to make certain I was able to find it once again. Years passed, and I continued working on the ship until I could purchase a small vessel of my own. Aye, it weren't pretty, but it was solid. I sailed her back to the island and found the book I had buried, and within this book was a map, which led me to their hidden vessel. The damage weakened it during the jump, and by the time I found it, it was nothing more than some scraps of metal barely holding itself together. It took some doing, but I removed the operating console and returned with it to my ship."

He paused and raised his eyebrows as he focused on the ceiling. Almost as though he was peering through some distant portal, watching his past unfold before him.

"It was a sight to behold," he said, beaming at Savannah. "But for as quick as I retrieved it, word had spread throughout the realm about the riches we had found. An oath of silence is a strong one, but a belly full of rum often gets a tongue to dance. Once word got out, many began searching for the treasure — this book, and the secrets behind the realm jumps. The powers to be, the 'Kings of Kings,' as they called themselves, also learned of this mysterious technology and from whence it came. They became obsessed, determined to capture it for themselves. Many suffered because of their resolve. Their ruthlessness knew no limits. Torture, razing of villages, murder, their fury spread throughout the realm as they searched, desperate to find it before the others. My plan was to escape with this console until I could understand it, but since there were blockades throughout, I had to find a way to smuggle it out of the capital. So, I devised a plan to do that; hiding it in something that would be overlooked in case we were stopped — a steamer trunk! Those self-professed brilliant men had grown accustomed to things of magnificence. Because of this, the buffoons searched for a ship worthy of the cosmos. Something capable of carrying kings like themselves. They didn't concern themselves with a pauper's steamer trunk."

He laughed and shook his head.

"Fools! Later, once I learned the secrets within this book, I gathered some brilliant minds to help me replicate their technology. To keep our secrets our own, I directed my people to build my fleet of steamer trunks out of Zimponium. They were things of beauty, that is certain!" he beamed. "Over the years, the steamer trunks have served us well. Not only for their effectiveness in hiding our treasured technology, but they also proved to be of solid construction for the jumps, and to this day, this captured technology still powers our fleet."

"Fleet? I thought we only had but a handful of vessels?"

Redbeard paused, then smiled. "My spies informed me a large vein of Zimponium had been mined on Corsite, but the precious stones were already being moved to an extraction plant. In order to intercept it, we had to make our recent voyage there."

"How did we learn of this ... this rock?" Savannah asked, sneering at the power this stone held over her father.

"Long ago, we brought it aboard before we scuttled a ship carrying it in their cargo hold. At first, we believed it to be copper, thought we'd make a tiny profit. But when we found this not to be true, we interrogated one of the captured crew. They confessed to us the true power of the stone, and it proved to work better than expected in building the framework for vessels to make the jumps. Over the years, we used some of it to shore up the Dragon's Curse. But as you saw from our last hunt, the poor gal cannot handle many more of these excursions without a further, more extensive retrofit."

"Is the haul from Corsite enough?"

"It's never enough!" Redbeard said, slapping his hand against the desk. "But we make do." He smiled and walked back over to the map. "We've acquired all we can from Corsite. This shipment was the last, I'm afraid. It will only be enough to rebuild the framework for the Dragon's Curse, or assemble our new fleet of steamer trunks, but that is all. I've made the decision to go ahead and complete the trunks. Once the fleet is finished, we can move forward with my plan to conquer the other realms."

"But how can we do that? You said so yourself. Our technology is outmatched in some realms."

"Aye, it is true. Aside from a few stray provinces still fighting us, we have Kringson secured. Corsite can be taken," he said, pointing his dagger at the map, "but without implementing my plan, it will be some time before we overcome their defenses. Storvot and Simenea are in their infancy in development. They are ripe for the taking. But Vosture, Kersippea, and Earth are far ahead of us in military strength and arms technology. However, there is one force that makes them shudder to their core."

"What force is that?"

Redbeard smiled. "Nature."

Savannah stared for a moment. "I don't understand."

Redbeard nodded. "Yer young, naïve; ignorant to the history of things."

He saw the fire in her eyes burn from the perceived slight, which caused him to chuckle.

"Lower yer sails! Ignorance is not something one should be offended by. It should drive a person to learn more. And here we are, learning, every day. Ye see, throughout history, countless numbers of armies have been lost because of nature." Redbeard's face lit up as he explained. "The destruction of the Spanish Armada in 1588, Kersipeas's Legions of Death wiped out in 1673, Vosture's loss of its Zeppelin fleet in 1902, the list goes on. Ice, lightning, wind, rain, volcanoes, avalanches, tornadoes — the power of nature is endless and cannot be contained once it is unleashed. All these elements have played a role in massive destruction. Lives lost, kingdoms destroyed, all in one swipe. Even the largest ships, or the thickest walls, cannot withstand the power behind a tsunami! If ye can control nature, then ye can control the realms; and that's where our fleet of steamer trunks comes in."

Redbeard walked over to a shelf and retrieved a long wooden tube. He twisted the cap off and pulled out a thick scroll wrapped tight. Within this roll were six more, just like it.

"Fortunately, we are the only ones who can make jumps. But given time, we risk the other realms stumbling upon our trunks secreted throughout the seven, and our advantage will be lost. We've seen it already with the Preston boy. His arrival is why we need to act and act quickly! Those three powerful realms I spoke of will consume the lion's share of our efforts in order to bring them in line. The others should be relatively easy pickings."

"How do you plan on getting this done? We don't have the ships, or the armies."

Redbeard unrolled the lengthy scrolls across the table. Savannah watched as the paper trailed over the edge like a waterfall.

"Charts?"

Redbeard smirked as he swept his hand across the parchment and smoothed it out. "This, my dear, is so much more. What we have here is my destiny!"

Savannah looked over the top parchment, which was labeled "Kersippea."

"Kersippea? I've never been."

"Beautiful realm. Rich in resources beyond yer imagination," he told her.

Below the name was a sketch of the planet, split in half, showing both hemispheres. Within the drawing, red circles highlighted different regions. Each circle had a line drawn to a corresponding box, and within each box were enlarged topographical drawings of that particular section. Scattered across these regions were red dots. Savannah flipped through the maps, and as Redbeard said, Vosture, Kersippea, and Earth each had more red dots on the paper than all the other realms combined.

"Ye can see the seven realms as they appear in the cosmos. Within each realm are the dots which show the locations of their armies and navies."

Savannah looked over his shoulder, being careful not to drip on the paper.

"Captain, Kersippea alone has so many points on the map. Then you come to Vosture and Earth. How can we overcome those numbers?"

Redbeard nodded. "Very good point. However, between wars and disease, these realms have been weakened, still unable to fully recover. Kersippea, for instance, has struggled with insurmountable droughts, causing their food supplies to dwindle. Widespread starvation has swept over the realm and diminished their numbers. Vosture has suffered a pandemic which has wiped out a third of their population. And Earth has just finished a great war, which has depleted all of their militaries!" he said, slamming his hand on the table, causing Savannah to jump. "Our time has come, my dear," he said, smiling wide. "None of these realms have the resources, or the desire to endure any further hardships."

"I've heard tales of Earth's military might. Our fleet will be decimated. How is it we will have enough power to overtake them all?"

Redbeard scoffed. "None of these realms are united. They pick each other apart every chance they get."

He stepped over to a shelf and grabbed several books, which he threw down in front of Savannah.

"These texts are full of tales of wars these groups have waged upon another. Without thought, this takes place in every realm time and time again. They've wasted their resources, their populations bickering against one another with their petty squabbles. Even if those buffoons could set their differences aside and come together to confront my forces, it would be too late."

Savannah squinted her eye. "The battles will rage for generations. Eventually, they will unite against us."

Redbeard laughed and then stared at her, arching his eyebrows. "Nature."

She said nothing.

"Even before ye were born, I've been preparing for this moment. Ye speak of generations, but yet ye fail to see what I've seen. What I've sacrificed to get us here."

In one quick motion, his arm swept across the table, causing Savannah to step back as books, lamps, and mugs scattered across the floor. The only thing left on the table were the charts, which Redbeard slapped his hand against. With his other hand, he flipped through the sheets and pressed his index finger against several spots: "Gernsun, Croscko, New York, California, Brentose, the list goes on. These fools stage their militaries in cities along their coasts as if they are building walls to protect the inner sanctums of their so-called nations! Yet, deep below their fortresses, under the boots of their armies are sleeping volcanoes, fault-lines in the very bedrock they build their empires upon. Within each circle ye see is the location of our targets; places we'll need to detonate our bombs. They remain hidden from our enemies; buried deep in the mouths of the volcanoes, wedged into the cracks of their fault-lines. They scatter about, unaware their demise is upon them. And once all our bombs are in place, we'll dispatch our fleet to trigger these explosions! What follows will be cataclysmic destruction as lava flows burn through their cities! Billowing clouds of volcanic ash will choke out their suns; monstrous tsunamis with their crushing towers of water will wash the scourge from their lands — MY lands. All these mighty militaries ye speak of will be annihilated by the ensuing destruction. After our initial attack, we will wait for the waters to recede, for the skies to clear, then all of the realms will be up for grabs. That's when I come in, sit upon my throne, and proclaim myself to be Commandant of the Seven Realms!"

He walked over and set his hand on Savannah's shoulder. "And yer gonna be a part of it, my dear," he said, speaking softly before rage filled his eyes. "But only if ye can learn to keep yerself together!"

Savannah's head shot up at this news. "You want me to be a leader?"

Redbeard relaxed his tone and smiled. "Of course, I do. What do ye think I've been doin' all these years? It's not because I didn' want ye around. I have been preppin' ye to take over one day. Yer going to be the future of this great civilization we build together. But I will not extend my hand to some petulant child who prattles on about things for which she does not understand! Savvy?"

Savannah nodded, erasing the slight from earlier. This was so unexpected. Her father had never given her any leadership role until now. She stood tall and looked him in the eyes.

With a broad smile, Redbeard nodded and walked over to his desk, where he removed a box made from polished wood, accented with shiny brass hinges and handles. As if it were a small puppy, he delicately set it down before her.

"What's this?"

Redbeard opened the box. Purple velvet lined the inside, cushioning a silver pin in the shape of a Kraken, which he removed. Savannah's eyes grew wide.

"I am promoting ye, my dear." He lifted the lapel of her coat and set the pin into the fabric. "Yer now one of my most trusted advisors. The relationship with the Steampunk Pirates and the Kraken are one and the same. All the creature's tentacles work together and exist to serve the body. I see my crew as being those tentacles. Because of this relationship, the Kraken and the Steampunk Pirates are a stronger, more formidable force feared by all."

Savannah's eyes widened. "I, I don't know what to say, Ca — Captain. This is such an honor," she said, staring down at the pin.

"It's been a long time coming, my dear."

"What would you have me do, sir?" she asked before bending over to review the plan with Redbeard.

He rolled up the papers and stuck them back in the tube.

"All in good time, my dear."

FROM A DISCARDED, RUSTY sheet of tin roof Shackles had given him and a spare length of rope from the ship, Preston fashioned himself a sled to help pull the Dragon's repaired nets across the sand. Without it, the trips had proven to be burdensome to say the least, but nonetheless, he looked forward to them for being away from the Dragon meant less chance of upsetting Redbeard. In his short time in captivity, he had seen far too many instances of Redbeard's explosive temper. Mangled crew members, bursts of furniture-smashing rage, and the horrific, torturous screams periodically waking him throughout the night back at the keep. But his new sled wasn't going to help him today. This trip involved picking up a new boarding net because the last one was shredded in the battle at Corsite. Since this net was much larger and heavier than his normal load, it would be too cumbersome for the sled. Therefore, knowing he'd be relying on Shackles to help him out, he hit the stores on the ship before departing, because Shackles' help came with a price. In most cases, this price was bota bags full of rum, and this trip would certainly cost him at least three of the leather pouches. Fortunately, the ship's hold had barrels upon barrels of the sweet spirit since the crew consumed it like water. As long as Preston swiped a little at a time, nobody seemed to notice. In exchange for the rum, Shackles helped him load the larger nets into his boats, and ferried them back to the Dragon's Curse. Well, perhaps I should clarify this. He would drop Preston and the nets NEAR the Dragon's Curse. For no matter how much rum he was offered, Shackles still refused to get close to the ship, leaving Preston to wonder what horrors had caused this man so much angst.

Now, even though Shackles exuded an appearance which would repel even the most welcoming of persons, Preston soon found him to be quite an interesting fellow. Once you scratched through the rough surface of his painfully limited personality, he was actually personable. Preston and Shackles even reached the point in their "relationship" to where the old man was teaching him to sail.

"When did you meet, Redbeard?" Preston asked, adjusting the boom in the boat.

Shackles didn't respond. Instead, he retrieved his clay pipe, lit it, and took a few puffs. But his silence didn't bother Preston. Being a man of few words, he had learned this was Shackles' way of expressing his displeasure in certain questions. Since this wasn't going anywhere, Preston changed the topic.

"What type of ship is this, anyway?"

Pulling the pipe out of his mouth, he looked up at the sail. "She be a boat. A jolly, to be more precise."

"A jolly?"

"Aye. Some might call it a dinghy, but I've made some of me own modifications to make it so much more."

"Like the motor?"

Shackles nodded. "Aye! For when the winds aren't too keen on helping me along."

"Have you ever sailed something as large as the Dragon's Curse?"

Shackles returned to smoking his pipe, blowing out tiny rings that faded into the wind. *How was this a bad question?* But Preston soon understood why...

"She used to be me own, but that was a lifetime ago."

Preston's eyes grew wide.

"You? You were the captain of the Dragon's Curse?"

Shackles pulled his pipe out of his mouth, tapping it on the side of the boat to empty the tobacco. "Aye. She's a thing of beauty, ain't she?"

"I didn't know you were a pirate."

"I wasn't one of them!" Shackles yelled, leaping up and kicking his stool across the boat. "Never have been, never would be!"

"Sorry, I didn't mean to suggest —"

"She was stolen from me!" he said, stabbing his pipe toward the ship. "That lumbering, red-haired cask of sea sludge was part of my crew."

"What?" Preston gasped, releasing the rope, which caused the sail to become loose and flutter in the wind like a flag. "Redbeard was part of your crew?"

"Now look what ye gone and done!" Shackles said, reaching up and grabbing the quivering sail.

"Right, sorry." Preston snatched the line and threaded it through the wooden pulley. After readjusting the sail, it filled with wind.

"What happened? How was he on your crew?"

Shackles scowled as he inspected the sail. "He was on my crew because he was a good sailor. For all his faults, he was showing himself to be a fierce leader; he could motivate the crew when needed. But he was young, and overly ambitious. Thought he knew better than the rest of us. On one voyage, I sent him ashore on a small island we happened upon. I made it a habit to check every island we came across. Ye never know if anyone be shipwrecked. I'd want someone to do the same for me, so I tried to set my karma right. Anyway, he and some others searched the island. When they rowed back, I knew they'd found something. No castaways, but something they weren't speaking of. I figured they'd found some treasure and were keepin' it for themselves. I never really cared about that sort of thing. We was making good coin being merchant marines and all. Plus, a few trinkets here and there kept the crew in line. Nonetheless, Redbeard had changed when he returned that day. He became more distant, always questioning my actions."

"So what happened?"

Shackles stared at Preston, then at the sail. "Ye be needin' to adjust the leech line."

Preston pulled the rope taut, which straightened the sail. It was obvious Shackles was done talking about the past. But Preston had something on his mind, and as the Dragon's masts were coming within sight, he thought it was best to ask before they got too close.

"Captain, I was wondering if you would sell me one of your boats."

"Captain? What sort of nonsense are ye spitting?"

"Well, you were a captain, weren't you? Plus, 'Shackles' doesn't seem to be a name you deserve."

The old man frowned and shook his head. "Shackles is just fine. And it's not up to ye to tell me what should bother me and what shouldn't. That's just as demeaning as any name being thrown my way."

Preston sat back and looked away. "Sorry."

"Ye put too much thought into a label, son. It's a weak one who calls others names to make themselves powerful; but it's an even weaker person to be held down by these words."

Shackles picked up the sleeve of rum Preston brought him and took a big swig.

"Ye can call this drink bilge, bile, or whatever other name ye want to give it, but the taste will stay just as sweet!" he said as he burst out laughing.

Preston smiled and nodded before looking off into the bay. Shackles pursed his lips, sealed the sleeve of rum, and set it down before taking a deep breath.

"What for?"

"Excuse me?"

"What exactly are ye bein' in need of a boat for?"

"Uhm, well, I'm hoping to become better at sailing. It's kind of fun, so I thought I would continue to practice on my own."

Shackles stared at him out of the corner of his eye. "Can't imagine Redbeard wanting one of his scallawags to have a boat of their own. Especially since the Dragon's Curse has a few of its own."

Preston went to speak, but the words weren't willing to leave his mouth. His fumbling jaw and unsteady hands caused Shackles to nod his head.

"How ye plannin' on payin' for this boat?"

Preston's face lit up, and he thrust his hand into his pocket, pulling out the coin Savannah had given him.

Shackles laughed at the sight. "That'll barely buy ye a sail. And the one ye get will be full of holes."

“Oh,” Preston said as his shoulders dropped and he returned the coin to his pocket.

It stayed quiet as they bounced along the waves.

“So, ye think ye can sail away from here?”

Preston froze. “No, sir, I was just —”

“Where ye think ye can go? How far ye think ye can get in one of these?”

Preston sighed and turned away. “I, I have to at least try.”

Shackles thought for a moment as Preston stared out into the bay. “Well, let’s hear this plan of yers then.”

The murkiness of the water was only made creepier by the starless sky. But if one expected to have a successful escape, one couldn’t just simply venture out in broad daylight now, could they? So, as unpleasant as this evening was, it was the exact type of setting Preston needed. And just across the vast emptiness of the bay, the roaring fires on top of the twin peaks formed a golden halo over the cliffs. They would be the only light guiding him away from Redbeard’s grasp. Once he reached the sandy shore, Preston spotted a burlap tarp, which he pulled back, revealing the longboat Shackles let him “borrow” for the cost of a gold coin. On the bench, he found a lantern along with a metal box full of matches. Next to this was a crate filled with fruits and vegetables, a fishing pole, and a jug, which he hoped contained water and not rum. Then again, Shackles would never give up his rum freely.

Aside from the waves gently rolling ashore, all remained quiet. There was nothing more to do, and Preston was at a turning point. So, with a heavy breath, he leaned against the bow and dug his feet into the sand before giving the heavy boat a hard shove. The wooden keel slowly slid through the deep sand. As he glanced toward the docks, lantern lights flickered along the rails of the Dragon's Curse, which gave him pause.

"This is crazy," he whispered. "I can't do this. What if I get caught? Redbeard will send me to be converted, or worse."

One look is all it took for him to stop pushing and slide down into the sand. Staring up at the sky, he reflected on his time back home. Had he known what awaited him, he would've insisted on going along with his parents to India. If he had done so, he would've never become trapped in this horrible place. But his desire to return couldn't compete with his will to live. After all, was it really all that bad here — at least for now? Besides, he knew at least one steamer trunk was hidden here — his steamer trunk. There was a good chance others may be scattered about the island as well. So, what was the harm in staying? He could keep looking for the trunk, and as long as he kept out of trouble, nobody would hurt him. This seemed a much better plan than trying to navigate the open sea in a boat pieced together by a man whose sanity Preston often questioned. Comforted by his decision, Preston stood and covered the boat, but a dull thud made him drop down into the sand.

Shackles gave me up!

The thud happened again. Preston lay silent with his face pressed into the sand. He was panting so hard, the sand blew away from his gaping mouth. Even though he had changed his mind, what was Redbeard to think if he were to find Preston next to a boat full of supplies? Preston needed to remain hidden, but when nothing happened, he lifted his head, his face covered with sand creating a gritty beard. After wiping his cheeks, he checked the area.

Nobody's here, he thought. However, the thuds continued. *It sounds like something bumping the boat from the water.*

Slowly, Preston raised his head over the bow. He peeked out but couldn't see anything other than empty water. Fumbling his hand into the boat, he grabbed the lantern and matches. To stay out of sight, he crouched low to the ground and lit the wick, being careful not to raise the flame too high. With the lantern extended out in front of him, he crept his way around the boat. Every little sound caused his heart to skip. By the time he reached the water, he had to pause for a moment to steady his nerves.

"You can do this," he whispered before closing his eyes and counting his breaths, which helped keep his imagination in check. Careful not to make too much noise, he popped out from behind the rudder and breathed a sigh of relief. There was nobody there.

"I'm just hearing things," he said, glancing around.

But another dull thud made him jump. Waving the lantern in front of him, he noticed the waves pushing a dark lump against the hull. Preston tiptoed forward and as soon as his feet touched the surf, he turned up the beam of light. Below him was a pile of seaweed. The wet, gooey lump was covered with crabs crawling in and out of the leafy pile. Relieved to discover this blob was the thing making all the noise, he grabbed an oar from inside the boat, using it to knock the crabs away. As he dragged the clump to the side, a bloodshot eye stared at him from inside a partially eaten skull.

"Ahh!" Preston's screams filled the air as he fell backwards and kicked his heels into the sand to get away.

Great! There was no way to conceal himself after that. Fixated on the decomposing head, he saw part of the skull still had flesh attached to it, while the other side was metallic — Redbeard's cabin boy! That was enough for him! He jumped up and sprinted to the front of the heavy boat. There was no way he was going to risk letting this happen to him. So, with all his strength, he kicked his feet through the sand as he pushed the boat so hard, he bulldozed over the corpse, never stopping until he was waist deep in the bay. In one hastened move, he launched himself into the boat and used the only oar he had left to paddle through the shallow water. The waves were unrelenting as they slapped up against the hull, pushing the boat sideways as Preston stared at the body, which, now, unencumbered, washed up onto shore. The crabs returned to continue their feast, causing a queasy feeling to wash over Preston. Some muffled voices in the distance caught his attention. He'd expected nothing else for as loud as he screamed at the sight. However, there was no time for self-loathing. He scrambled over to the control panel, but with everything happening, his thoughts escaped him, and he forgot how to operate this thing.

Think, think! But it would be easier to focus if these ridiculous waves weren't spinning him around like some amusement park ride! Panic swept over him as he gripped the panel and stared at the switches. "Got it!"

He pulled out a match, lit it, and threw it into the hatch, just as Shackles had done. Back at the panel, he ran his hands across the switches.

"It's gotta be this one," he said as he flicked the center switch, which caused the boat to moan and slowly spin in a circle.

No, no, no! Too loud! His hand shot over to the switch, and he cut the engine. *Use the sail, you idiot!* A yank of the lever caused the canvas to raise and fill with wind, but he was headed back to shore. This wasn't going well and now several lanterns were visible on the Dragon's deck.

"Dang it!"

Preston spun the wheel, correcting the boat, which was now headed toward the twin peaks. After making a few adjustments, the gentle breeze filled the sail, causing the boat to slice through the water faster and faster. As you'd expect, he was relieved to be away from the corpse, and breathed easier as the wind whipped through his hair. For all his worry, there didn't seem to be too much activity along the docks, and there were no longer any lantern lights on the Dragon. Perhaps his encounter with the aforementioned cabin boy didn't garner the attention he feared. And now, as he quickly approached the twin cliffs, his attention shifted to the cannons perched high above. Before he began this "excursion" of his, Shackles had assured him the cannons couldn't track a small boat, and as he passed undetected, he was relieved the words held true.

Almost there!

Not sure how much time he had to get past the outposts without the night watch spotting him, he trimmed the sails, hoping to get more speed out of the little boat. Just as he was about to pass in between the cliffs, something obvious and horrifying popped into his head.

"The net!"

But before these words had time to pass his lips, the bow of the boat slammed into the metal mesh protecting the entrance to the bay. He hit it with such force, he was nearly thrown into the water. Brass warning bells tied to the netting rang out from the jostling. Even before he could raise himself up off the deck, a flurry of activity broke through the silent night as Redbeard's guards came pouring out of their cliffside embattlements. Thinking there was a breech from the ocean side, they grabbed torches, using them to light the oil lamps affixed to giant round mirrors. Bursts of light shot out from the spotlights and the bright beams were focused on the water directly outside the net. Preston heard the gears from the cannons spin as the pirates pointed them outward, screaming orders to each other.

"Sound the signal! Alert the Dragon!"

After the call to arms, a thundering boom from a cannon echoed across the sky.

For all his efforts, it was over. He was certain to be placed in chains once again, and there was no way to salvage Shackles' boat, which was now entangled in the netting. Preston had two choices: stay in the boat and come up with some excuse as to why he was out there, or swim for it. The choice was obvious and right after the splash of a tiny barrel came the splash of Preston hitting the water. You shouldn't be surprised. I mean, who in their right mind would try to spin a tale such as this to a person such as Redbeard? Once his head broke the surface, he spotted the barrel and swam toward it. Preston hated cold water, and this was even colder than cold. So cold, in fact, his muscles immediately stiffened, making each stroke torturous. Relief swept over him as he reached the barrel and held tight, using it to stay afloat.

"Over 'ere!"

Preston spun his head around and saw the guards had spotted his boat.

My hat! He patted his head, realizing his uncle's hat must've been knocked off during the crash. *If they find it, they'll know it was me!*

With every ounce of energy left in him, he swam back to the boat. Between his heart thundering and his lungs aching from the strenuous swim, Preston's chest felt as though it would explode. After dipping below the waves several times, a burst of nervous energy gave him a much-needed boost.

Please don't let me drown, he plead as he reached the boat. Wasting no time, Preston threw his hand into the boat and grabbed his hat. Clenching it between his teeth, he kicked away until he was out of sight from the night's watch. Before he got too far, he heard grappling hooks splashing into the bay as they tried to snag the entangled boat.

"It's over 'ere ye miscreants! Shine those blasted lights this way!"

A second round from the cliff top cannons echoed across the bay. Soon after, the Dragon's Curse came alive. Deck guns were loaded and longboats from the ship were dropped into the water, immediately making their way toward Preston. He kicked his feet as fast as he could, scrambling to get away before he was spotted. Exhausted, he spotted his barrel bobbing in the waves. He grabbed hold and swam away from the Dragon's longboats. This was the longest night of his life!

By the time he reached shore, the beach was speckled with lantern lights as Redbeard's crew scoured the area. After crawling out of the surf, Preston scrambled over to a patch of scrub trees, taking cover within the blanket of leaves. Once he gathered enough courage, he peeked out toward the water. Smaller ships sailed through the bay, shining searchlights into the water. Bonfires burned along the roads leading into town as sentries checked everybody passing. Far ahead, Redbeard's keep glowed brightly. Everyone would be out looking for Preston tonight, and he had no idea what to do or where to go. Cold and scared, he tried to come up with a plan until a growling voice broke through the night air.

"Get in 'ere!"

"Shackles!"

Preston dropped to his stomach and crawled into Shackles' hut. With all the lights turned out, he could barely see the old man's silhouette as Shackles stared out a crack in the wall. Light flashed through the spilt boards of his walls as Redbeard's crew made their way through the property. Everywhere you looked, lanterns swung wildly as the pirates weaved in and out of the trees, searching for whoever piloted the boat. As the specks of light disappeared, Shackles lit his own inside the shed.

"Thank you!" Preston said as he looked around, noticing a captain's uniform adorned with silver medals and gold epaulettes on the sleeves prominently displayed in the corner.

"Yer gettin' me floor dirty."

Preston realized he was covered in white sand. *I look like a sugar cookie!*

"Sorry," he said, spinning in a circle, trying to see where he could brush himself off.

"Never mind that now." Shackles peeked out again. "Well, ye poked the pufferfish this time, did'n ye? How far did ye get?"

"The entrance at the cliffs. I didn't realize they always keep the net up."

"Wouldn't do much good if it weren't up and protectin' the openin' to the bay, now would it?" Shackles carried the lantern to the back of the shed. "This way."

"Where are we going? The guards are gone. Shouldn't we just lie low?"

"Aye, they be gone for now, but it won't take them long to realize that's one of my boats. They'll be back soon. That I promise ye."

Shackles turned out the light. Along the back wall, he grabbed a wooden plank and slid it to the side. After peeking his head out to make certain it was clear, he made his way into the night with Preston following close behind. Before they got too far, Shackles picked up a palm frond lying nearby.

"Keep going that way and step into the water."

"Into the water? Why?"

"Ye know, for someone in as much trouble as ye are, ye sure ask a lot of questions."

"Sorry."

"Now get movin' before I change me mind about helpin' ye."

Preston had just started to dry off, and here he was once again, back in the bay. While he kept watch, Shackles used the palm frond to sweep away their footprints pressed into the sand. Ingenious really. Now, with their path concealed, Shackles stepped into the water and guided Preston toward a small mound at the end of the beach. With the search parties at the other end of the beach, Shackles led Preston up the mound.

"Help me with these," Shackles whispered as he kneeled next to several boulders.

Preston grabbed hold of the heavy stones as they moved them aside, uncovering a small opening barely wide enough for either of them to squeeze into.

"Ye need to go through here. Someone will meet ye on the other side."

Preston peeked into the opening, which was even darker than the night sky.

"I can't see a thing."

"Well, I ain't gonna shine a light in there for ye and have everyone come this way. Stick yer squabbly arm in there and grab the ladder."

Preston reached in and felt the rung of a wooden ladder. He looked at Shackles before removing his hat and stepping into the hole.

"Hold this, please," he said, handing Shackles the hat.

"What? Just get rid of this thing!"

Preston's head shot up. "No! It's my only connection I have to home."

Shackles rolled his eyes and took the hat. Once Preston wriggled his way into the opening, Shackles handed him the hat and lantern.

"Take this."

After adjusting his hat, he grabbed the light and shoved his hand into his pocket, retrieving a match. Before he could light it, Shackles slapped it out of his hand.

"Not yet, ye fool!"

"Okay, sorry!"

"After ye help me plug this hole, climb down to the bottom, walk for about ten minutes, THEN light the dang blasted thing!"

Preston hung the light on the side rail of the ladder before reaching up to help Shackles replace the stones. When the last one was slid into place, he climbed down.

"Thanks, Captain."

Shackles stayed silent.

Descending through the abyss was unsettling, and the air wreaked of dead fish. Kind of made sense, considering where he'd found himself. Nonetheless, it seemed to take forever to reach the bottom, but all at once, Preston stepped into knee deep water — more water, of course. Consumed by total darkness, Preston stuck his hands out, trying to feel for this elusive passageway. His hands rubbed along the cold, wet stone until he found the entry.

"It's so creepy down here," he whispered, hoping his voice gave him comfort, and possibly even some courage in this most unsettling of situations. But he heeded Shackles' warning to not light the lantern right away. "I can't even see what's in front of me. How long before I smack into something?"

On alert, his senses heightened, Preston tried to force his ears open wider as though it would help him pick up on the slightest noise. A splash in the distance made him jump. He strained his eyes, hoping to gather some glimmer of light to help him see.

"That's useless!" he said. As his voice echoed down the corridor, something dawned on him. *Stop talking! You're only making it easier for someone to find you and cut you to bits.*

The only sounds filling the unsettling silence were his heartbeat pounding in his ears, and the sloshing of water. Ten minutes was beginning to feel like ten hours. *How long does it take to freeze to death?* But even though the air was chilly, Preston was relieved to feel the water level had dropped below his knees and his boots would help keep his feet dry.

Between the brisk air, and his damp clothes, Preston's teeth chattered continuously, sounding like a pair of castanets clicking throughout the hollow. Eager to light the lantern, if for nothing else a bit of warmth, he fought the urge and held off, still fearing someone or something would spot him.

Certain enough time had passed, he traipsed his way through the corridor a little further, just as a precaution. By now, the water had receded, and he was walking on sandy ground. He pulled out a match from the sealed metal tube and lit it. The bursting flame's warmth felt wonderful against his icy fingers. Honestly, his hands were so numb at this point he could've grabbed the flame and not even noticed. After shakily lighting the wick, a welcomed soft glow chased away the shadows around Preston, but returned when he grasped the glass. For the moment, he didn't care about the dark returning. He was just hoping to warm his hands.

"Ouch! What was that?" has asked swatting at his stinging leg. With a quick jerk, he swung the lantern low to the ground. Gathered around his feet was an army of crabs scavenging the surface. One had scurried up his boot and was furiously pinching his leg.

"Get off me!" he yelled, knocking it away.

After setting the lantern on the ground, he kicked at the pesky crustaceans, causing them to scatter. "What else is down here, waiting for me?" he asked, retrieving the lantern and shining the light ahead of him.

Shackles crouched under the cover of some scrub brush as he searched the area around his cabin. All was silent, and there was no movement, so he crept his way across the sand and opened the door, skulking his way into the shed. After lighting a lantern hanging by the door, he set it on the table.

"Where ye been, Cap'n?"

Shackles jumped, seeing an unwelcome face silhouetted by the shadows — Redbeard. So brazen was he, sitting in Shackles' favorite easy chair! Chuggs stood to the captain's left with a female guard opposite him. The gruff woman wore two leather whips, one on each side of her belt. She gave the old man an ominous glare; one familiar to Shackles, often appearing in the deep recesses of his nightmares, causing him to wake up screaming, drenched in sweat. With an uneasy scowl, Shackles shook his head and threw a burlap sack onto the table.

"Crabbin'. Ye hungry? I did'n catch enough for everyone."

Chuggs walked over and dumped the sack out. Several crabs scurried off the table and, as soon as they hit the floor, they shuffled out the door.

"Well, I guess I'll be hungry now too."

Redbeard didn't seem amused.

"Why was one of yer boats tangled up in our net?"

"One of my boats?" Shackles asked, walking over to the door and sticking his head out. "Did ye bother to bring it back?"

Chuggs grabbed him by the back of his neck and threw him down in front of Redbeard as the other guard removed her whip and snapped it between her hands.

"Now, now, Chuggs ..." Redbeard said, rising and helping Shackles to his feet. "Ye need to take it easy. We're guests in this man's home, such as it is. Now, what say ye, Captain?" Redbeard asked as he walked over and rubbed the sleeve of Shackles' old uniform between his fingers. He spotted Shackles staring at the red-haired woman. "Where are my manners? I'm certain ye remember, Aralia. Or as ye might remember her from yer last time together, 'Shredder'."

Shackles grabbed his lower back as he straightened. Aralia was coiling her whip, replacing it on her belt as she smirked at the old man before tipping her hat. He just leered at her and grunted.

"Ye know darn well that drunken lot of yers is always over here getting into mischief and taking my boats out to go fishin' or just having a jolly good time. Did ye bother askin' them?"

Redbeard smirked and walked over to the door. With a muted scowl, he turned to Shackles. "If ye think our last meeting was bad, let me find out yer spinning yarn."

As Chuggs walked past the old man, he looked down at him and gave a deep snort. Aralia brazenly shoved the burlap sack into Shackles' chest as she followed. "Yer gonna need more crabs," she said with a villainous chuckle, sending chills through the old man's body.

Once they were out of sight, Shackles slammed the door and threw the bag into the corner. He hobbled over to the chair, dropping down into it as he winced in pain.

Free from the restraints of sloshing through knee-deep water, Preston moved quicker down the lengthy tunnel. However, even with the lantern's wick at its highest point, Preston could only see several feet ahead of him. Beyond the reach of his outstretched arm was darkness and uncertainty.

"Who is this person I'm supposed to meet?" he wondered as he crept along.

Every sudden noise caused him to pause. This place seemed like the perfect breeding ground for a variety of things — none of which he cared to encounter, especially rats. But realistically, rats were the least of his worries. Rats wouldn't give him up. Nor did they swing swords or shoot guns! But for the moment, his main issue was he still couldn't see what was ahead, and relied on running his hand along the rough, stone wall just to stay on course.

I better not fall into a pit. What would I do if — ugh, what was that? Slime! Of course, the walls were covered in slime — at least he hoped it was slime. It felt wet and gelatinous, like the entrails of a snail. Maybe the walls were covered with thousands of snails! As disgusting as this new image was inside his head, he couldn't risk removing his hand and missing a turn or dropping into some cavernous death trap.

Shackles is insane! What has he gotten me into? He'll be sorry if I die down here, and he can't get his rum!

He wasn't certain if he was angry or scared at this point. As he tried to figure out exactly how he should be feeling, some sloshing ahead of him made his choice for him — fear! *What was that?* Preston didn't move, didn't breathe, he just stopped! Actually, the thinking part continued, and unfortunately for him, because all he could think about was what was waiting for him in the paralyzing dark. Desperate for company and distraction, he carried on a conversation with himself.

"I wonder if smugglers dug this out, or if it's always been here. It's probably always been here. Maybe. But why would someone create this hole down here? Exactly!" (It ended up being more of an argument with himself as opposed to a conversation.)

This continued on for some time until he heard a faint squeak in the distance; almost as if someone had opened a door.

Should I call out? he wondered, listening intently.

When he heard nothing else, he kept moving.

"Maybe I should just — WHOA!"

Preston gasped after his foot slipped. Apparently, the ground had ended, and nobody bothered to inform him of this change. He stepped back and crouched down, swinging the lantern along the edge.

"A river?" Just beyond his toe was an abrupt drop, where rippling water flowed along.

"What now?"

He turned and shined the light along the walls, spotting several torches, which he quickly lit. A golden glow swept through the space, introducing some much needed light, as well as a bit of warmth. Preston found himself on one side of an enormous cavern with towering ceilings. Down a rickety staircase, a small boat rested at the edge of the water. Instead of a sail being attached to the mast, there was a pulley with a thick rope strung through it. One end was attached to the ledge where Preston stood, while the other end disappeared into the darkness. Normally, Preston was the adventurous type, but a lot had changed, and those days were well behind him. Hoping to find another route, he retraced his steps to make certain there was no other way to go. When he found nothing but solid walls, he relented and stepped down to the water's edge. The only thing left to do was to get into the boat and pull himself across.

Worried he would be spotted, Preston snuffed out the torches by dipping them into the water before climbing into the boat. An iron hook at the bow provided a place to hang the lantern. Still apprehensive, and somewhat suspect of Shackles, Preston reluctantly grasped the rope and began pulling his way across.

"I wonder where this goes?" he asked as he looked to either side, but even with the lantern, it was still far too dark to see.

For what seemed to be an eternity, Preston pulled on the rope. Hand over hand, he kept going, listening to the incessant squeaking of the aged pulley. Water as dark as ink surrounded him.

"Who knows what's living in this moat," he said, peering into the murkiness.

The farther he went, the more concerned he became.

"I hope whoever I'm meeting doesn't leave. Hello?" he gingerly called out.

The sound of his voice reverberated off the ceiling and bounced his words all around him.

"That's so cool! HELLO?"

This time, he was much louder. As he stood there, counting how many times his words echoed off the walls, something bumped the bottom of his boat, nearly knocking him down.

"What the heck was that?" Memories of the Feeders filled his head.

His lip quivered as he peeked into the water; his thoughts filled with the terrible scene of the Feeders they encountered after the battle. Another bump jostled the boat once again, causing Preston to grab both sides to steady himself. He watched the water to one side, while on the other, something breached the surface and splashed back down.

"What the —"

Preston screamed as his eyes darted about, but there was nothing in the boat other than a set of oars to use as a weapon, so he dove forward and grabbed one paddle. Without hesitation, he sprung up, raised the paddle high above his head and slapped it against the water as hard as he could. Over and over he did this, all the while screaming at the top of his lungs.

"Die you filthy beast, die!"

Once his shoulders started burning from his overly aggressive assault, Preston threw the paddle down and snatched the rope above his head, yanking on it for dear life as he pulled his way across. His hands were moving so fast they became raw and blistered as the rope slid through his grip. Not paying attention to anything but the surrounding water, he continued across until he crashed into a stony ledge, which sent him to the deck, his knees sliding across the rough wood.

"Thank God!" he said, pushing himself up and jumping over to solid ground.

Eager to distance himself from whatever creature was hunting him, he got as far away from the water as he could, and through the gloom, a bright flame from a nearby torch chased the darkness away. Out of the shadows, a figure approached him.

"You?"

AMELIA WAS NOT ONE to hide her emotions, so there she stood, her arms crossed while tapping her fingers against her elbow. "I should've guessed it was you who stirred up this hornet's nest." She shook her head, refusing to look at Preston as she stormed over to the torch. "Way to keep quiet and not get discovered, by the way."

Preston looked around, making sure he wasn't about to be placed in leg irons, or worse.

"I don't understand."

"I'm not surprised."

"Where are we?"

By placing a metal pail over the torch, she snuffed out the flame before grabbing Preston's lantern. "Let's go," she said, disappearing down a nearby tunnel before he could react. Reluctant to follow, Preston stood silent before shaking his head and chasing after her.

"Why are you helping me?"

Amelia frowned. "Only because I was asked to. Had I known it was you, I would've reconsidered."

Preston rolled his eyes.

"So, how do you know Shackles?"

"Don't call him that."

"Uhm, okay. Well, what do you call him?"

She stopped and turned. "Gramps."

"Wait, what? He's your grandfather?"

"You catch on quick," she said, scouring the darkness ahead of her.

The tunnel continued on, twisting and turning, which gave Preston time to process the last several hours.

"I assumed Savannah was Redbeard's daughter."

Amelia let out an exasperated huff. "Look, everyone is out there trying to figure out what happened, so we don't have time for a history lesson. He's my father's father. Now let's go."

Is everyone related to each other on this rock?

"Why were you screaming so loud back there?"

"Uhm, some monstrous beast was trying to have me for dinner." Preston looked back toward the river. "They didn't bring one of those Feeders back with them, did they?"

"No, of course not."

"Well, what the heck lives in that water?"

Amelia turned her head and rolled her eyes. "Turtles. A sea turtle bumped your boat."

Preston sheepishly stood there with his mouth open.

"It's a miracle you're alive," she said before stopping in front of a stone staircase. "I hear they can be vicious." Quelling a laugh, she turned to Preston. "Not a word. And try not to scream if you see a spider or something."

She extinguished the lantern and grabbed Preston's hand, which caused a jolt of nervous energy to course through him, leaving his palm sweaty. His mouth fluttered as he started to say something until Amelia cut him off.

"Don't get any ideas. I can't risk you tripping over your fat feet and giving us away."

In total darkness, they crept up the narrow stairs. Sounds of chairs sliding across a wooden floor, and muted voices grew louder the higher they climbed. Amelia suddenly stopped, almost causing Preston to slam into her. She turned and pushed him back. "Stay still," she whispered. Reaching above her head, she pushed on the ceiling just enough to cause a sliver of light to creep into the stairwell before pulling out a tiny mirror from her apron, which she slid through the opening.

With the panel open, Preston could clearly hear people talking as if they were standing next to him. Forks scraped across plates and glasses clinked against one another.

"Wait, is this the Rusty Bucket?" he asked, which caused Amelia to purse her lips and clench her jaw.

Preston had never suffered a vicious scolding such as this, all without a word being spoken. He cowered while stepping back. After finishing her search, Amelia slid the mirror back into her pocket and pushed the hatch open before climbing up into the room. Somewhat apprehensive after her glare, Preston followed while keeping some distance. Inside the space, they found themselves surrounded by crates full of fruits and vegetables. Amelia pushed the panel back over the opening, using a barrel to conceal it before stacking sacks of grain and crates of vegetables around the base to camouflage it further.

"Let's go," she said, motioning for Preston to follow her as she tiptoed across the floor and stuck her head out the door.

Busy eating their meals and drinking pints of ale, the crowd in the Rusty Bucket didn't pay any attention to the pair. With everyone distracted, Amelia grabbed Preston by the shirt and dragged him out into the dining room, making their way to the exit.

"Hey, hold on you two!" Preston and Amelia jumped at the sound of Savannah's voice. Not wanting to get dragged into this confrontation, the innkeeper skulked away and disappeared into the storage room.

"What are you two doing in here?" Savannah asked, standing next to Chuggs in the doorway.

"We were going to get something to eat," Amelia quickly said.

Savannah walked up to the pair as Chuggs stood guard.

"Were you now?" she asked, one eye squinting at Amelia. "With what?"

Amelia reached into her pocket and pulled out several coins.

Savannah frowned and turned to Preston.

"You're making the lady pay, Fishbait?"

"Uhm, no, I just —"

"He didn't know we were coming here," Amelia interrupted. "I asked him to help me earlier, so I was going to treat him to dinner ... as a thank you."

Savannah cocked her head as she leered at each of them.

"Forget that now and get back to the fortress until this mess is cleared up."

"Oh, okay, sorry. I didn't realize it was so serious."

"Hmm," was the only response Savannah offered as Amelia and Preston slid past Chuggs, who snarled at them. Following them out into the night, Savannah took notice of Preston's sand covered boots.

Amelia stayed quiet, her head on a swivel as they got into the elevator and made their way up to the keep. Down below, Preston saw dots of lantern lights bouncing along the beach as the search continued. But none of that mattered to Amelia, whose gaze remained fixed toward the portion of island where her grandfather lived. As they reached the top, she pulled the gate open, but before Preston made it out of the elevator, he was met with a stiff finger poking him in the chest.

"You better pray nothing happens to him!"

Preston stood speechless. Once he lost sight of her, he breathed in deep, trudging his way into the building and down to his bedroom. After skirting around the monstrous cannon he shared his room with, he stared out the window. There were far fewer lights on the beach now, but the Dragon's Curse was still aglow as patrol boats continued to zigzag through the harbor. As the evening waned on, even fewer lights were visible until everything dissipated into complete darkness.

Once the early morning light broke over the horizon, Preston rubbed his stinging eyes. He hadn't slept a wink.

"I hope he's okay."

Even before the street vendors had arranged their carts along the avenues, Preston made his way down to the beach, venturing close enough to see Shackles' shed without bringing too much attention to himself. Several exhausted pirates dragged their feet as they trudged through the sand, while others slept against palm trees. Redbeard was relentless, keeping the patrols out all night. He would certainly be furious that no one was found, and Preston was eager to stay away from him.

As he approached the Dragon, he glanced toward Shackles' hut but didn't see any movement. Since the deck was empty, he wondered if he should head back to make certain he was alright. But even though there was nobody around, there were still patrols out, and Amelia warned him to stay away. Right now, he was just as afraid of her as he was Redbeard. Nonetheless, not knowing was gnawing away at him. There had to be something he could do. Then, as he passed the mainmast, a mischievous smirk slid across his face. He ran down the stairs into the galley and snatched one of the chef's knives. Once he got back to the mizzenmast, he checked to make sure he was still alone before grabbing several strands of netting, which he sliced through until the sound of clunking boots walking across the gangplank grabbed his attention.

Savannah!

With the scowl on her face and the bags under her eyes, she was certain to be in a horrible mood. He quickly threw the knife into the bay and climbed up the net.

"What are you doing, Fishbait?" she groaned. "I don't have the energy for your shenanigans today."

"Uhm, no, it's not like that. I noticed this part of the net was worn, so I wanted to check the rest of it. Do you think it needs to get replaced, or fixed?"

Savannah stared blankly at him before closing her tired eyes. "Since when has this become your concern?"

Preston climbed down from the net and rubbed his hands on his pant leg. "Sorry. It's just — I was headed down to clean the Captain's quarters and noticed the rope had frayed, so I wanted to mention it."

He turned to walk away before Savannah stopped him.

"Hold on. I'll have it taken down and you can haul it over to Browners' shop."

"Browners? We're not using the Cap —"

Savannah spun around. "What did you say?"

"Uhm, just making sure we're not using Shackles anymore."

Savannah stared at Preston. "Tell you what ... I'll have the crew take care of this. The captain is still onboard, so head back to the fortress and clean his office."

Preston realized his plan to check on Shackles wasn't going to work after all.

"Right, I'll head over there now."

"Eh? Who's been in me kitchen? Where's me knife?" the cook called out from below.

Savannah shot Preston a glare as he scurried across the gangplank. As soon as he disappeared into town, she examined the worn pieces of netting.

"What are you up to, Fishbait?"

"What do I do now?" Guilt was eating away at Preston as he took the long way through the village. Not the way he would normally go, but as he did, he stumbled upon a forgotten road which ran along the beach and led up a hill. It was an older dirt road, covered in an unruly overgrowth of weeds and grass. "I need to make sure he's okay."

Preston made his way up the steady incline. Since there were two narrow channels cut into the dirt path, Preston assumed this had been a staging area for cannons, which meant they would look out into the bay, and perhaps Shackles' hut. Sure enough, when he got to the top, there were the remains of several ramparts overlooking the bay. Centered between them was a small stone shed. He crept up to the doorway and leaned in.

"Hello?"

Nothing. In fact, it didn't appear that anyone had been here in years. The only part of the door remaining were small scraps of rotted wood barely clinging to the rusted hinges. Inside were a few kegs of hardened gun powder, now repurposed as a table and chairs. Discarded notebooks were strewn across the top. Preston picked one up and looked inside. The discolored pages were filled with pencil sketches of ships in the bay, a parrot perched next to a pelican, and even a portrait of someone who looked like Shackles.

"These are amazing."

Aside from rotting timbers and crumbling walls, there wasn't much else in the small building. Outside, the vast overgrowth completely obscured the beach. To get a better view, Preston weaved his way through the bushes, tripping over something concealed under some loose brush. Moving the weeds aside, he found a lantern with shutters attached to the front of the glass lens, and a lever on the side. When Preston pushed down on the lever, the shutters opened.

"A sema —"

"What are you doing up here?"

Preston jumped up and spun around, coming face-to-face with Amelia.

"Why do you always do that to me?" he asked, grabbing his chest.

"Because you're always somewhere you're not supposed to be. What are you doing up here?"

"I wanted to see if Shack — if your grandfather is okay."

"He's fine, so back off. You're going to bring unwanted attention to him." She pushed Preston aside and covered the lamp once again. "He just wants to do his work and be left alone."

"Is that a semaphore?"

Amelia ignored him.

"Does your grandfather have one too? That's so cool," he said, reaching down for it. "Is this how you guys communicate? By flashing signals to each other?"

"Shouldn't you be back at the Dragon, below deck drinking with the boys?"

"The boys? What boys? What's your problem with me, anyway?"

"I don't have a problem with you," she grumbled.

"Really? Because every time I see you, you seem to be angry with me."

"Well, maybe you should stop doing stupid things and putting others in danger!"

"What stupid things?"

"Oh, let me see ... how about trying to use a boat to get back home for starters? A boat of all things!" she said, rolling her eyes.

Preston's mouth dropped, and his eyes grew wide. "What am I supposed to do? Stay here and accept the fact I'm stuck on this rock and hope I don't get killed?"

"Seriously? And what were you going to do then?"

"Well, it doesn't really matter now, does it?" Preston closed his eyes and shook his head. "Look, I promise I won't get your grandfather involved in anything else I do. Had I known who he was, I probably would have never asked him. But don't try to get in my way and tell me to give up. I'm going to find a way home."

Amelia arched her eyebrows and shrugged. "Okay, have at it. Best of luck to you."

As she walked away, Preston followed until she turned to him with her hand up in front of his face.

"Stop."

Preston let out an exasperated breath.

"It's best if we stay apart. Go that way," she said, pointing toward the docks. "Maybe you'll find your way off this so-called 'rock.'"

"Fine!" he said, giving her a chance to get ahead of him, but started fidgeting when he lost sight of her. "Where'd she go? Does she know a shortcut or something?"

Along the shadowed walkway of the fortress, he spotted her near the elevator. Before she could slide the gate shut, he jumped in and grabbed the lever.

"What are you doing?"

"I'm just trying to be your friend. Why do you have to make it so difficult?"

"Because I don't need friends! What I do need is to be left alone so I can finish what is required of me. Then one day, maybe I'll get to leave this 'rock' as well."

She tried to push Preston out, but he shut the gate before she could.

"Don't you think we can do that by working together?" he asked, pulling back on the lever. With a sudden jerk, they started to rise.

"I honestly don't care what you want!" But her mouth spoke words her eyes ignored. Eyes which Preston couldn't stop staring at; eyes that caused his stomach to flutter.

"Listen, I—"

He couldn't make a coherent sentence if his life depended on it. Amelia caught herself staring as well, but turned away.

"Just leave me alone," she said, her voice softening. "I stuck my neck out for you, so you at least owe me that."

Preston drew in a deep breath and stepped back. "You're right. I do owe you."

Neither spoke another word as the elevator clanked up the side of the cliff. After they reached the top, Amelia yanked the gate open and headed toward the fortress, pushing past Savannah, who didn't like what she saw.

"Why is she so upset, Fishbait?"

"I honestly don't know."

Savannah spun her head toward Amelia before turning back to Preston, giving him a suspicious glare.

"You best hope I don't find out you're scheming. Now, hurry up and get inside. You need to have the captain's office cleaned before he gets here. Be forewarned, he's in an ornery mood, and obviously, you have a knack for getting on people's nerves."

Preston drew in a deep breath as he watched Amelia walk past the gate. *Obviously.*

"Hey! You paying attention?" Savannah said, snapping her fingers in front of his face.

"Yes, yes, sorry."

"With last night's incident, there's extra security. Once you get inside, you should see Chuggs standing guard. Tell him I sent you and he'll let you into the captain's office."

Preston nodded and headed toward the fortress, leaving Savannah to stare at him. *What happened between the two of you?*

At the end of the hall, Chuggs stood guard in front of the door. Actually, you couldn't even see the door, just Chuggs, who looked as impressive and as angry as ever.

"Nobody goes in!" he growled, even before Preston made it up to him.

"Savannah told me I need to clean in there before the Captain gets off the ship," he said, presenting a broom and bucket full of water as proof. But Chuggs didn't budge. Amelia walked up carrying a bucket of her own and dragging a mop. Preston glanced over to her, then quickly looked away.

"What are you doing here?" she asked, dropping everything next to him. "Stalking me, I can only assume."

"Oh, no. Of course not. I'd hate for you to get the wrong idea and think we were friends or something."

She crossed her arms and arched her eyebrows. "Right ..."

"If you must know, I'm supposed to clean up in there, but Chuggs won't let me in."

"Chuggs, get out of the way."

Chuggs looked down at Preston and scowled before turning to Amelia, who stood silent, tapping her foot. After gritting his teeth, Chuggs let out a deep grunt and opened the door. Amelia picked up her bucket and pushed past the hulking pirate, with Preston following close behind. There was one thing for certain, if Preston were ever in a fight, he'd want Amelia by his side. She feared nothing.

Redbeard's office was certainly impressive, as one might expect it to be. Polished black marble flooring carried through from the hallway, and white brick walls framed a sweeping facade of glass, offering an incredible view of the bay. His desk was centered in front of the massive window and made from black metal with a polished stone top. Over the years, Redbeard had proven himself to be an enigma, leaving others to contemplate his true self. Was he a rough, brutish sea captain or a savvy businessman? Either way, the battle trophies scattered throughout the space certainly left the impression of what he desired his legacy to be. Redbeard's trophies were more a collection of oddities from different realms which were perched on stone pedestals, including what appeared to be a rhinoceros head with three eyes and thick skunk-like fur. Preston read the plaque attached to the pedestal.

"Battle of Triston."

On display next to the rhino was a polished silver pistol. Affixed to the barrel was a glowing blue orb, which continuously pulsated. On a card tied to the trigger was a note.

"Property of ~~Arch-Minister Grizznod~~"

Another name was written above the minister's, so the card now read, "Property of *Redbeard*."

Growing impatient, Amelia cleared her throat. "Are you almost finished with your tour?"

He wasn't ... Especially after seeing something he recognized from back home.

"A stock ticker!"

He walked up to it, but accidentally bumped the pedestal, causing the glass dome to wobble. Fortunately, he grabbed the glass and steadied it before it fell over. With a sheepish glance, he peeked over at Amelia.

"Now I know why I got sent here," she said. "You can't even handle a simple task like cleaning a room without causing trouble."

"Look, I can just leave and you can do this all by yourself," Preston said.

"You should! It would be entertaining to see what torture Redbeard cooks up for you when he finds out you didn't follow his orders."

"You wouldn't."

"Try me!"

"You're insufferable, you know that?"

"And just what is that supposed to mean?"

"Oh, right. Let me see if I can put it in a way you'll understand. Ye be like a barnacle stuck to me shoe, matey! Did I dumb it down enough for you?"

Words are sometimes spoken without a moment's thought, as was the case here. And of all the dumb things Preston had done in his life, this may have been at the top of the list, for if you could somehow humanize a volcano about to erupt, Amelia would be the perfect model. Her face twisted to the point she was almost unrecognizable. As she stood there, her brow furrowed so far, Preston couldn't see her eyes, which was probably for the best. Every muscle in her body seemed to quiver with rage. Even after everything Preston had suffered up until this moment, he'd never been more afraid. He swore he could actually see the blood boiling up into her head, filling her cheeks and turning her skin so red, he thought she would explode. Fearing what came next, he took a few steps back. Amelia's knuckles turned white as she gripped the mop handle so tight, he'd assumed she was imagining it being his throat. She opened her mouth, but then slammed it shut before throwing the mop to the floor and storming out of the room, leaving Preston standing there, speechless. As soon as his legs allowed him to move, he chased after her.

"Ey! Where are ye goin'?" Chuggs yelled out, but Preston ignored him as he caught up to Amelia.

"Wait!"

"What?" she growled through her teeth, seething as she did everything she could to avoid his stare.

Preston grabbed her arm — mistake! Before he could react, she had spun around and punched him in the chest so hard he crumpled to the floor.

"Leave ... me ... alone!"

Her words surprisingly hurt more than her fist. But Preston wouldn't relent. He knew he went too far, so he jumped up and got in front of her, albeit just out of her reach. This is when his heart melted, for in her eyes, tears collected, ready to spill out. She dropped her head and turned away from him.

"I'm not stupid!" she said, wiping her sleeve across her face; aggravated by not only his words, but her weakness from them. "Not all of us got to go to a fancy school. Most of us had to teach ourselves. It's not easy here! Especially if you're a girl."

"I'm sorry," Preston said, letting out a deep sigh. "I didn't really mean it. It's just, you're, you frustrate me so much, and it doesn't help I don't have anybody to talk to. I feel so isolated here, so alone. I'm basically a prisoner. Actually, I am a prisoner!"

Preston dropped down, throwing his back against the glass window before burying his face in his hands. "I miss my mother and father so much. Every day I live in fear, wondering if I'll ever see them again. I wake up every morning worrying if today's the day I get thrown overboard because I looked at someone wrong, or the captain's soup was too cold ..."

The silence was deafening until Preston looked up at Amelia.

"I'm scared," he whispered.

Amelia sniffled and dropped down next to him.

"I'm really sorry," he said to her. "No matter what I'm dealing with, it's no excuse to say what I did. You're not stupid. Trust me, I know how smart you are. I wish I was as smart and as strong as you."

Amelia snorted.

"I mean, my chest still hurts."

Amelia scoffed. "Strong ... You don't know anything about me."

"Because you won't let me."

She didn't respond so much in words, but when Preston went to stand, she grabbed his arm. Drawing in a deep breath, she looked at him, then away.

"I knew this boy once. He was on a ship Redbeard captured. I'm not sure what happened to the crew, but this boy was imprisoned and brought to him. He became fond of this kid and kept him on as a cabin boy — just like you. After some time, we became good friends, and then one day, he just disappeared. I asked around, but nobody said anything. I couldn't find him anywhere. Then, one day, I overheard Redbeard saying I was being too 'distracted' by him, so he sent him off to this nasty woman he knows from another realm." Amelia sighed. "I never saw him again."

"Who's this woman?"

"It doesn't matter. What does matter is it's all my fault he got sent away, and because of that, I swore I would never make friends with anyone again."

Preston nodded. "I get it. Truth be told, I'm thinking it would've been better if I had just let them send me to the orphanage. At least I know my parents could've found me once they returned."

"Well, what's done is done. Anyway, we'd better get back. Redbeard will be here soon."

Preston nodded and stood. Reaching out, he took Amelia's hand and helped her up.

The rest of the afternoon, they cleaned the office in silence, for a little while at least. After Amelia knocked into the same stock ticker as Preston, they turned to each other and burst out laughing. Chuggs wasn't the most free-spirited person and became quite annoyed with their shenanigans.

"Ain't ya two done yet? I can't stand listening to yer cackling any longer."

Both of them choked on their amusement as they tried to quell their chuckles, but as soon as they looked at each other, they exploded with laughter once again, causing Chuggs to slam the door shut.

"What's behind there?" Preston asked, pointing to the two doors at the back of the office. "Do we need to clean in there as well?"

"I'm not sure. I've never been allowed in there."

"Maybe we should look," he suggested, doing his best to restrain a mischievous smile.

"Are you kidding me? I didn't make it this far by making dumb decisions like that. Keep your head down and do your job. I told you that's how you get out of here."

"Hey, I was told I needed to clean in here, and whatever is behind those doors is part of 'in here,' so that's what I'm going to do."

Amelia looked on nervously as Preston jiggled the handles — locked. *Plus, my trunk might be in there*, he thought, examining the door and pulling on the handles once more.

"You just tried that," Amelia said. "Move!"

She pulled a leather pouch from her apron pocket and removed a small metal pick, which she inserted into the lock. With her ear pressed against the wood, she fiddled with the lock until she heard a subtle click.

"There." But as she twisted the handle, Chuggs barged into the room.

"Hey! Whaddya think yer doin'?"

Instead of answering, Amelia looked at Preston and smiled. "Run!"

They both darted past Chuggs, who took a swing at them, but missed. Once they got far enough away, Amelia bent over, laughing — but not Preston. He was as white as a sheet.

"What are we going to say when Chuggs tells Redbeard?"

"Oh, don't be ridiculous. The last thing Chuggs wants to do is tell the Captain what happened. If he did, he'd suffer Redbeard's wrath for not paying attention after letting us in. Anyway, why were you so interested in unlocking those doors? Is there something you're looking for?"

"Uhm, nothing really. Just curious."

Amelia stopped. "I thought we moved past this."

"Past what?"

"You lying to me?" she said, her face filled with scorn.

"I'm not lying to you."

"You're not fooling anyone. Especially me! I've been lied to my whole life."

"I don't know what you're talking about."

She nodded and shrugged. "Fine. Have a nice life, Fishbait."

Amelia was halfway down the hall before Preston called out. "Wait!"

She turned and glared at him. "What?"

He walked up to her and glanced about. "I'm trying to find my steamer trunk. The one that brought me here," he said in a hushed voice.

"And you couldn't tell me that?"

"What do you expect? Ever since I got here, I've been told not to trust anyone."

"Maybe you should stop listening to all those idiots on the ship and start thinking for yourself."

"You're right. But most of the time, I don't even know where I'm supposed to be or what I should be doing. If I ask anyone around me, I get set up for some sort of prank or they tell me the wrong thing to do.

It's so confusing! And I definitely don't know what happened in that battle, or whatever that shark thing was! I mean, seriously, where am I? Can you explain any of this to me?"

"I could, but I won't. It's better if you don't know."

"Wait, what? Why are you getting mad at me for keeping secrets when you're not going to tell me anything, either?"

"You don't understand. This place, my grandfather, it's just — anyway, if I were you, I would leave as soon as I could."

"That's why I wanted to open those doors in Redbeard's office. Maybe my —"

"What?" Amelia asked.

"We left the mops and buckets! Redbeard is going to take it out on me!"

Amelia and Preston ran back but stopped short when they saw the door was open. Their buckets, the mop and broom, everything was out in the hall.

"Where's Chuggs?" Preston whispered.

Amelia shrugged her shoulders and crept toward the door.

"Someone's inside," she whispered.

Preston squeezed his eyes shut, worrying they were too late. But then he heard another voice — Quinton. Amelia skirted along the wall to get closer.

"We are in need of more materials. Prepare the chest. I'll be aboard the Dragon shortly."

"Aye, Captain."

Amelia yanked Preston around the corner just before Quinton walked past.

"C'mon," she said, heading back to the door.

"She's coming again?" Savannah asked.

"No. We just need to send the chest to her," Redbeard told her.

"Even better! I have a few things to do before I head back to the ship. Summon me if you require anything further, sir."

"Let's go," Preston whispered urgently as they scrambled down the hall. "Where do we —" he began to ask, but Amelia wasn't behind him. He turned the corner and saw her running her hands along the wall. "What are you doing? We're going to get caught."

Amelia smiled and pushed in on the wall. A latch behind the panel clicked, and the wall slid open.

"In here," she said, pulling Preston by the sleeve and sealing the opening behind them just as Savannah walked by.

Inside the tiny room was a spiral staircase. It was too dark to see where it went, and before Preston had a chance to ask her, Amelia disappeared down into the abyss.

"Amelia?" he whispered, just before the room filled with light.

"Sorry. The switch is in a weird spot."

"Why is everything in the keep electric, but in town they're still using lanterns?"

"They were building extra steam generators to power the town, but they reassigned the workers for Redbeard's plan."

"What is that plan, exactly?"

"Celestial domination, for whatever that means."

Preston pondered this for a moment as they descended the stairs, but he became distracted the farther down they went.

"Where does this go?" he asked. Unlike the lower levels of carved out stone, these walls were painted brick.

"All the way outside if we want to. Come on."

"What materials was Redbeard talking about?"

"I assume it's some kind of stainless steel he's always going on about. Anyway, he gets it from your realm."

"Really? From where?"

Amelia pursed her lips and paused. "From my grandmother — Crownickers."

Preston's mouth dropped. "Are you serious? Why wouldn't you tell me?"

"I didn't want you to think ill of me or get scared away because of her. That's why I didn't say anything."

"Do you know much about her?"

"No. Savannah won't let me near her. She said she's a vile woman; worse than Redbeard."

Preston barely heard the rest of what Amelia said. His focus had shifted to an opportunity to return home. "How do they do it? Do they send the Dragon's Curse?"

"Sometimes, but he said they were sending the chest. The Dragon's Curse must be worse off than I thought."

"What kind of trunk is it?"

"I don't know," Amelia said. "A steamer trunk like any other."

"Oh ..."

"But different, sort of."

"What? How is it different?"

"Well, for one thing, it's much larger. And in order for them to load more steel into it, they attached the navigation system to the outside of the trunk."

"It could work," Preston whispered.

"What could work?"

"Uhm, well, do you think if I hide in this trunk, I can get back home?"

Amelia stopped and spun her head around. "Are you insane? Even a starving mouse wouldn't bite into that piece of cheese."

"Why not? Do they look in the trunk before they send it?"

"Those lazy bums? I doubt it. I mean, why would they? It's kept behind a locked door, which is also guarded. Nobody can get to it."

"Then it can work!"

"Be quiet," Amelia said, covering his mouth. "You need to be careful what you say, and how loud you say it. Others know of these passages." She looked down the staircase, then leaned into Preston's ear. "You may be able to. But I'm not sure where in your realm you would end up."

"Okay, but it's something. It's a chance. How does the delivery work?"

"I'm not sure of all the details. All I know is Redbeard sends the chest, and it returns full of steel. But even if you're able to get into it here, who knows what happens when it gets there? Someone must be on the other end to retrieve it so they can load the cargo. You could be found as soon as you arrive and who knows what would happen to you then? Worse, if you get caught here, you'll for sure be brought to the transition center."

Preston thought about this long and hard, as he should. After all, he knew there was at least one other trunk hidden on this island, so was it worth the risk of trying to return home this way? He could just wait it out until he found his uncle's trunk, but that day may never come.

"But this is an opportunity I may never get again. I think I have to at least try."

Amelia bit her lower lip, dropping her head. "Fine. You're insane to try, but what can I do to help?"

"Where's this trunk?"

"They keep it in a vault next to the lava flows."

"How can we get to it if it's guarded?"

"They brag all the time about how this fortress is impenetrable, so only the worst crew members get sent down there as punishment. Since they spend all day in the sweltering heat guarding a locked door hidden within a secured fortress, these guards don't really care enough to pay attention," she said, rolling her eyes. "Most of the time, they wander off to a ventilation stack where there's cool air flowing, or they go to the underground springs for a swim or get a drink. But there's no way to know for sure if or when they'll do that."

"Well, if I'm going to try this, I have to do it quick. They're probably already sending someone to get it." He grabbed Amelia by the shoulders. "I know this is a big ask, but would you take me to the vault?"

Amelia drew in a deep breath and grabbed Preston's hand. "Quickly."

They sprinted down several more levels before they came to a landing. Amelia pushed on another hidden panel, causing it to inch open, allowing a blast of hot air to fill the stairwell.

"Okay, it's clear," she said, peeking her head out.

They both stepped out into a long, narrow corridor. Sweat immediately dripped into Preston's eyes, blinding him with a stinging pain as they trudged through the stifling heat.

"It's got to be over 100 degrees down here," he said, dragging his sleeve across his forehead.

"Yeah. We're close."

For years, the Steampunk Pirates had chiseled into this stone to create their fortress. Within the massive keep were dozens of levels and hundreds of doors. This particular passageway was special in that it contained the one door which stood in the way of Preston's freedom. The lone door sat apart from all the others within a cavernous opening. Aside from the soft glow of light from the molten magma flowing deep below the chamber, it was darker than the rest of the sub-levels Preston had been in. Just as Amelia said, there was only one pirate guarding the door. The duo ducked behind several stacked barrels set off in the corner. Preston peeked out at the guard, who was slumped over on a stool. The man's bare stomach burst through his dingy shirt and spilled over onto his lap. Whether it was from sweat or just normally greasy, his long, salt and pepper hair lay flat and was tied tight to the back of his head.

"I think he's asleep — or dead."

Amelia took a quick look. "Chummers. Figures."

"Who is he? Do we need to worry?"

Amelia snorted. "No. But unfortunately, that's the room we need to get into."

Both a wooden stool, and the sloth of a man sitting upon it were propped up against the reinforced metal door. Just above the latch was a sizable padlock.

A creaking door echoed in the distance and slammed shut, which caused Chummers to stir. Amelia and Preston crouched down as the pirate jumped up, worried Redbeard had sent someone to check up on him.

"This be ridiculous," he muttered as he stretched his arms. "Steal a chicken from the galley and now I'm the one to get roasted." He tried to wipe the sweat from his brow, but his shirt was wetter than his forehead. "Argh!" He kicked the stool to the side and glanced around before stumbling down a darkened passage.

"That's the way to the springs," Amelia said. "He must be going to get a drink. Quick, let's go."

They both sprinted toward the door and jumped over the slow flowing channel of lava.

"You keep watch," Amelia said, pulling the pick from her apron. She jammed the metal tip into the keyhole and fiddled with the lock as Preston stared over her shoulder.

"What are you doing?" she asked, shoving her elbow into his stomach, pushing him away. "Make sure he doesn't come back."

"Right, sorry." Preston turned and leaned against the wall, staring down the darkened opening. Torches along the walls provided enough light for him to see if Chummers returned.

Before Preston had a chance to settle in, Amelia had picked the lock and was using her apron to remove it. She raised the latch and heaved the door open.

"Be careful. The metal's hot."

Inside the vault was a wooden steamer trunk covered with wide bands of copper-colored metal. The control panel connected to the outside was similar to the one inside Preston's trunk.

"Why copper?" he asked.

"It's not. That's the stuff you guys stole from the ship the other day — Zimponium."

"Oh!"

"Hurry up! Chummers will be back soon."

Preston lifted the lid. Even though the trunk was much larger than his, there was no seat or padding of any sort.

"This is going to be uncomfortable," he said, taking his hat off and crouching down inside. As Amelia shut the lid, Preston stopped it with his hand and stood up. "Wait!"

"What?"

"Come with me."

Amelia scrunched her face. "Why would I do that?"

Preston's shoulders slumped. "Oh, uhm, well, I thought you might ... just that ... You'll be free to draw and do all the things you want to do."

Amelia shut her eyes and shook her head. "I'm fine right where I am."

Preston didn't look at her as he nodded, which caused Amelia to frown.

"Listen, I —" Chummers singing a sea shanty echoed through the halls, cutting her off.

They tired of the rotted fish he fed to the men,
so with a flick of his wrist, the mate cut him to ten;
As the crew cheered him on, the Captain fell,
and yo ho ho, they sent him to hell ...

"He's coming back! It's now or never."

"Right." Preston sank down into the chest, stopped, and popped his head up. "I'm going to miss talking to you."

Amelia scowled as she shoved him down. "Don't be such a wench." This left Preston with a dull ache in the stomach, but before he had a chance to commiserate, Amelia pulled him up by the shirt and pressed her lips against his. Preston's eyes shot wide open and his body tingled down to his toes. "Now go!" she said, pushing him away. "He's not far." Speechless, Preston sunk down as Amelia closed the lid, but now Chummers was too close for her to leave unnoticed.

"Eh! What are ye doin'?"

Amelia froze, squeezing her eyes shut as she tried to come up with an excuse.

"I'm gettin' a drink, ya filthy barnacle," Chummers said. "Every last one of ya forgot I'm down here and left me to die."

He wasn't talking to her! Just around the corner, a pirate named Bowline had distracted Chummers, drawing him away from the vault. There was no time to think this through, so Amelia quickly ran out, shut the door, and replaced the lock before sprinting back over to the barrels.

"Stop yer griping and get the chest ready. The Cap'n wants it on deck before the sun rests."

"All right, all right. Did ye bring any rum with ya?" Chummers asked, flashing a snaggletooth smile.

"And why would I be doin' that? Did ye share yer chicken?"

Chummers' shoulders dropped.

"Exactly! Now get mov'n!"

Chummers scowled as he pulled on a rope tied around his neck. Dangling from it was a thick iron key. "An ye wonder why I did'n share my chicken," he grumbled while twisting the key in the lock. Swinging the door open, he walked over and kicked the chest. "Stupid trunk gets treated better than I do." He grabbed the handle and yanked on it, but the chest barely moved. "Why is this blasted thing so heavy?" he asked before walking around it. Bending over, he took hold of the latch.

"Eh! Hurry up! I was ordered to help ya, not to spend my day listening to ye grumble."

Chummers looked back and burst out laughing. "Ye made fun of me for snatchin' the chicken, and yet here ye are! What did ye do to get sent down 'ere with the likes of me?" he asked, letting go of the latch.

"Nobody cares about helpin' a street rat like you. The Cap'n said you'd probably screw this up, so I got stuck lookin' after ye."

"What?" Chummers yelled, gripping his cutlass before Bowline pulled out his pistol, cocking it and pointing it straight at Chummers' head.

"I could just make ye do it yerself, ye flea-ridden dog."

"Right. Well, let's be quick about it," Chummers said, taking his hand off his sword. "The air stinks down here."

They each grabbed a handle and grunted as they dragged the trunk out of the vault.

By the time they made it down to the street, Chummers dropped his end and bent over, heaving.

"That blasted thing is heavy!" he groused until he heard a bell clanging in the distance. "That's it! I'm exhausted! I've spent too much time in that inferno down there. Let's take the trolley."

As the caboose turned the corner, it stopped in front of the two pirates standing in the middle of the tracks.

"Everybody out!" Chummers yelled. "Official business!"

The passengers stared at each other until Chummers removed his sword. "I said, out! Every last one of ye!"

Even though Chummers may not have been the brightest pirate in Redbeard's crew, he knew how to motivate others — especially if they were unarmed. With that, the passengers scrambled off the trolley as Chummers and Bowline lifted the oversized trunk onto the car. When it didn't fit past the first row of benches, they yanked one out and threw it to the side. After setting the trunk in its place, Bowline took a seat on another bench as Chummers dropped onto the trunk, fanning himself with his hat as the whistle blew.

"Aye, this is much better."

They rode the car for several more stops until Bowline called out to the conductor. "Hold 'er here!"

"What are ye doin'?" Chummers asked. "We 'ave two more stops before the docks."

"We'd do better to get out here before the Cap'n sees us taking it easy."

"Ugh. I guess yer right," Chummers said. "He swore if I screwed up again, I'd be sleepin' in Satan's Cradle."

They dragged the trunk off the trolley, the bottom bouncing down the three steps to the ground. The jostling forced Preston's head to smack against the lid, giving him a massive headache. With a deep grunt, they lifted the trunk and carried it down to the ship. When they finally got it up onto the deck, they both bent over, heaving.

"What's yer problem?" Quinton asked.

"That blasted thing is heavy," Bowline said with his hands on his knees. "I didn't see ye down there helping us."

"I'm far more important to the Cap'n than ye two glorified pack mules."

Amelia made it down to the ship just before Savannah came aboard. After climbing a mooring line, Amelia ducked behind a cannon.

"I'll let the Captain know it's here," Savannah said.

As soon as Redbeard emerged from his cabin, he handed Savannah a slip of paper with the coordinates.

"Get her ready to send."

Savannah crouched down and read the paper, adjusting the dials on the console as needed before nodding to the two pirates. They reached down and grabbed the handles, both of them grunting as they lifted the trunk.

"What's wrong with ya?" Redbeard asked. "Too much rum last night?"

"No, Captain. It just feels heavier than I recall."

Redbeard cocked his head and walked over to the chest, lifting up on one handle. "Hmm," he grunted as he looked around. With one swift move, he lifted the latch and whipped open the lid.

Inside the trunk, a hunched over Preston peeked up.

"And what might we have here?" Redbeard asked, grabbing Preston by the throat and lifting him out of the trunk. "What were ye doin' in there, boy?"

Preston let out a strangled gasp as he tried to choke out an excuse.

"There you are!" Amelia called out. "That was a great spot to hide, but you're not supposed to be in there."

Redbeard dropped Preston to the deck and turned. "What sort of tomfoolery are ye speaking?"

"I'm sorry, Captain," Amelia said. "We were just playing a game. Kid's stuff is all. It was Preston's turn to hide and —"

SMACK!

The back of Redbeard's hand struck Amelia on the cheek so hard she crumpled to the ground. Refusing to show him tears, she instead shot an icy stare at her grandfather, refusing to give him any satisfaction. Meanwhile, Savannah clenched her jaw while grasping the handle of her knife as she leered at her father.

"Games! This is not time for games, girl! Now the both of ye get out of my sight and go back to work!"

Preston and Amelia ran down the gangplank and disappeared into town.

Redbeard spun around and stood face-to-face with Savannah. "Those two are yer responsibility! Ye need to get them in line, or I will!" he roared, poking his finger into Savannah's shoulder.

She gritted her teeth so hard, her jaw ached. "Aye, Captain."

He turned to walk away, but then paused and turned to Quinton. "How long was that steamer trunk on board?"

"About ten minutes, Captain."

"Hmm."

"Amelia!" Preston chased after Amelia and grabbed her by the arm, but she yanked it away and kept walking. "Look, I'm sorry. I didn't mean for you to get in trouble."

Amelia turned abruptly. Her cheek was still bright red and her eyes glistening. "I'm fine. Stop following me or things are going to get much worse," she said before storming off and melting into the crowd of people filling the avenue.

Preston stood silent, searching as a lump stuck in his throat. "I need to make this up to her." He pushed through the crowd, but she was gone. Not wanting to make Redbeard angrier than he was, Preston headed back to his office to finish cleaning. When he got to the end of the hallway, Chuggs was nowhere in sight, but the door was partially open. Inside, he heard papers being shuffled, which prompted Preston to push open the door wider and peek into the room. An older man with chains around his ankles stood next to Redbeard's desk, looking through some papers.

"What are you doing?"

The man jumped and his arms shot out; the pencil and papers he held flew out of his hands and scattered across the floor. He spun around and looked at Preston with wide eyes. It was the same old man from the ship. His hands shook as he stood there, nervously glancing around.

"Who are you?" Preston asked, noticing the man was now wearing a dingy white lab coat.

"I'm, I assist Redbeard."

"Why are you in here?"

"I was trying to ... wait a minute." He cocked his head and shuffled over to Preston, his chains clanking across the floor.

What is he doing? Preston wondered as he stiffened up and stepped back.

Oblivious to Preston's reaction, the man circled him.

"Your hat — where did you get it?" he asked, reaching out several times, slowly grabbing the air, but withdrawing his probing fingers each time as though being burned by a flame.

"It was my uncle's."

"Your uncle?"

"Well, actually, my great ... my great-uncle," he said, shying away from the odd man.

"What was this man's name?" the stranger asked, his voice breathy.

"Uhm, Crispus ... Crispus Rupina. Why?"

The man's eyes grew wide and sparkled.

"Are you ... are you Charles' son?" he asked, almost in tears. His jaw dropped. "Has it been so many years?" he turned away, raising his shaky fingers to his mouth.

Preston cocked his head. "Who are you? How do you know my father?"

The stranger abruptly turned around and walked up to Preston, who drew back even further. The man then grasped his shoulders and smiled wide. "Because I am your great-uncle! I am Crispus Rupina!"

AS YOU MIGHT IMAGINE, Preston was in shock, speechless, in fact. His jaw dropped as he stared at the man, still not believing what he'd just heard. Could it be? The long slope of the man's nose was certainly the same, and as Preston looked closer, through the stranger's wrinkled skin, he recognized the eyes of the man in the portraits hanging in his home.

"Uncle Rupina? How could you ... Everyone assumed you were dead! There was a funeral."

Rupina ignored his questions and kneeled before Preston. "I cannot believe my tired eyes. But, but how did you get here?" he asked, looking around. "Why are you here?"

"I don't exactly know."

Preston explained the story to his uncle. From how he found the vault and the steamer trunk, up to what happened when the constable came down the hidden stairs, forcing Preston to hide in the trunk. How it closed and transported him to the cargo hold where he was taken prisoner, leading up to the whirlwind of events taking place ever since. Once he finished, Rupina stood and turned away.

"It's all my fault," he said, almost weeping.

"What do you mean?"

With his eyes glistening, Rupina turned to face his nephew. "Never mind that now," he said with a wavering smile and patting Preston's shoulders. "What's important is we get you back home."

Still holding his shoulders, he stared into Preston's eyes.

"For as awful as this place has been, you've brought me great joy — and concern," he said, examining Preston. "Oh! You're not wearing shackles. Are they treating you well?"

"Uhm, I guess so. It's fine, but that doesn't matter. Now that I found you, you can help me escape all this madness. Get back home!"

"Of course!" Rupina said, shaking his head. "Where is my head? We shall leave at once! Quickly, is the trunk still in the ship's hold?" he asked, looking toward the door.

"No. They took it away," Preston said. "I assume it's hidden somewhere in this fortress. Do you know what's behind these doors?" he asked, walking up to them and pulling on the handles once again, but they were locked. "Chuggs! He must've locked them."

Rupina's shoulders slumped. "If it is indeed behind those doors, then all is lost."

"Why, what's back there?"

"Our death if we are caught going in there." Rupina chewed on his thumb while pacing the floor. "Where would they have stored our steamer trunk?"

"If we can't find that one, what about another one? They seem to use them all the time. I've seen plans for others. What if we were to grab a different one and use it to return?"

Rupina didn't bother to look at Preston as he paced. His head spinning with thoughts. "We would need the coordinates for home. It's been so very long, and my mind is not quite what it used to be. I'm not certain I can remember what they were, and if I get it wrong, we could end up in the middle of the ocean, or worse." Rupina suddenly stopped. "But there might be another way."

"What is it?"

Rupina picked up the crumpled papers from the floor, haphazardly shuffling through them until he found the one he was looking for.

"Ah, yes. Here it is," he said, unfolding the wrinkled sheet and adjusting his glasses. "Since I never thought I could get hold of my steamer trunk, I worked tirelessly on a way to recreate a design I learned about that works as a transference signal emitter and receiver. The theory for the device was based on receiving signals from items in space. Quasars in particular. Even though I replicated the mechanism, the complexities of the design necessitated the need for a new alloy — stainless steel. The chemical composition of this steel focuses the electronic signal which passes through it. Therefore, it is able to serve as a long-range beacon, thus able to draw a vessel from here, wherever here is, to there, earth, home, wherever you place the device," he said, pointing to different spots in the air as if he was trying to map out the planets. "It just so happens I completed a prototype for this design before I was captured."

"There's no beacon back home," Preston said, looking at the design.

"Ahh, but there is!"

Preston was taken aback. He struggled to remember this system his uncle was talking about.

"What did you build?" he asked as he picked up several pages his uncle dropped once again. "I never saw anything like you're describing. Was it hidden somewhere in the house?"

Rupina smiled. "Yes! And it is hidden in plain sight. It's —"

"The lot of ye aren't worth the salt in these pork barrels! If none of ye can get this done, then all of ye will slumber in Satan's Cradle!"

"It's Redbeard!" Rupina warned as he turned, dropping his sketch. "He's back, and I'm not supposed to be in here!"

PRESTON SPUN AROUND. "QUICK, I think —"

"Well, well, and what do we have here?" Redbeard asked, storming into the room with his dagger at the ready. The clunking of his peg leg against the tile reverberated through the room and shook Preston, sending a shiver up his spine.

Chuggs grabbed Rupina by the arms as Redbeard walked toward him, all the while glaring at Preston with those murderous eyes. In the meantime, Rupina's head was on a swivel as sweat dripped down his forehead. With the tip of his dagger, Redbeard sliced the buttons from Rupina's shirt, each one bouncing off the tile with a soft tick. Embedded in the old man's chest was a metal box.

Preston's mouth dropped at the sight. *They butchered him!*

With a contemptuous scowl, Redbeard tapped the cold steel blade against the gears clicking away inside Rupina's chest.

"Ye must think ye be too important for me to yank these wheels from yer chest," Redbeard said, sneering at the man.

After all his time in captivity, after all his encounters with this man, Rupina knew better than to say anything. He stood as still as a statue while Redbeard looked him up and down before grabbing Rupina's chin with his free hand. He forced his head to the side and leered at him. "Perhaps we should finish the procedure and have a go at yer skull. I'm thinking that'll speed things up and you'll finally give me what was promised."

Rupina was visibly shaking at his words. With all his focus, the old man tried to speak, choosing his words carefully to mollify Redbeard's growing rage. "I, I'm almost done, captain," he stammered, still not looking at the pirate. "We needed more Zimponium, more steel, in order to continue. It was out of my hands."

Redbeard nodded. "Hands, you say?"

In a flash, Redbeard snatched Rupina's arm and laid it across the table. He placed the blade of his knife against Rupina's wrist with just enough force to cause a thin line of blood to seep out from under the steel.

"It seems to me yer pace won't be affected by the loss of this," he said dismissively. "Unless ye think ye can work quicker with both hands."

"No, please! I'm working faster than we both expected! We're making significant progress!"

"You take me for a fool?" Redbeard growled, pressing harder on the knife.

Rupina reeled from the pain and swallowed hard. "No, of course not. Please! I'm just explaining —"

"You'll be keelhauled is what you'll be doing!" he yelled, grabbing Rupina's shirt and pushing him away. "Take this scurvy dog away!"

Chuggs dragged Rupina out of the room, the chains on his ankles sliding along the ground.

Redbeard swung around and pointed the knife at Preston. "And what of ye?" Redbeard asked, staring at Preston's hat he proudly wore. "Ye been quite busy getting yerself into mischief this day. Perhaps there's more treachery taking place than meets the eye." He twirled the dagger between his fingers as he circled Preston. "So, what shall I do with ye?"

"I'm sorry, Captain. I'm not sure what you mean. All I was doing was cleaning, like I was ordered."

"Who is the old man to ye?" Redbeard asked, pointing the blade at Preston's face.

"Him?" Preston asked with surprised eyes, pointing his thumb at Rupina. "He's nobody. He saw me cleaning and stopped in to ask if I was supposed to be in here. We just started talking is all, and then you came in."

"Is that all?" Redbeard asked, nodding his head as he continued to circle Preston. "I find it odd that with all the bags of bones skulking in and out of here, he's the only one ye strike up a conversation with. And more curious is he hails from yer own realm. Yer tellin' me all this bein' nothing more than a mere coincidence?"

"Is he? From where I'm, from?" Preston said, trying to act shocked. "Wow! We never got that far. I just saw him in chains, and I was in his spot not long ago. So I was just trying to give him advice on how to stay out of trouble, is all."

"This is advice yer offering?" Redbeard burst out laughing. "He'd be better consulting a stone on how to swim!" After wiping the blood from his blade, he slid it back into its sheath. "Fetch me some food and be quick about it, or you'll find yerself in leg irons once again."

"Right, of course, sir." Preston scrambled out of the room, squeezing his way past Quinton. Once he was gone, Quinton turned and closed the door.

"Do ye believe him, Cap'n?"

"I don't have the luxury of giving my trust to others." He leered at the door, lost in his thoughts. "Let's have those two spend some time together. I want to see what this relationship of theirs actually is."

"Do ye have something in mind, Cap'n?"

Redbeard's smile grew wide. "Ye know I do."

Quinton smiled. "Of course ye do, Cap'n. Ye always do."

Once Quinton left, Redbeard sat down at his desk when a crumpled-up piece of paper on the floor caught his eye. Reaching down, he picked it up and flattened it. His face grew red, and he smashed the table with his clenched fist.

Preston walked in carrying a tray. "Excuse me, sir. I, I have your dinner."

Redbeard shoved the paper in his pocket and gave Preston a blank stare.

"Uhm, I can finish cleaning your office, Captain," he said, setting the tray of food on the desk and grabbing the mop leaning against the wall.

"Never ye mind that now," Redbeard said, lifting the silver cover off the tray. "I have a task for ye," he told him, not making eye contact.

"Of course. How can I help you, sir?"

"I understand ye like to tinker with things, and I need someone to look in on the old man; to help him finish his work. He is lagging behind, and I have a schedule to keep. Ye think ye can do that?"

Preston struggled to contain his smile. Redbeard had just presented him with a chance to escape.

"I'll start right away, sir."

Redbeard nodded. "Well, be off with ye then."

As Preston turned and left the room, Redbeard glared at the door.

Rupina winced as he heard the chain being removed, because for the past however long, he never knew what awaited him on the other side of the door: a meal, an interrogation, a subtle reminder of Redbeard's impatience, often involving some form of physical abuse. But when he saw Preston walk in, his eyes grew wide.

"What are you doing here?" he whispered, bending low and tiptoeing over to his nephew, all the while keeping a close watch on the door. Preston coughed out a laugh at the sight, for around his uncle's head was a leather strap with an oversized magnifying lens attached to the front. As he stared at Preston, his right eye appeared to be the size of a baseball.

"Redbeard asked me to help you with your work."

"He did what now?" Rupina asked, somewhat loudly, as the guard outside the door peered in.

"I swear, it was his idea," Preston explained as his uncle returned to his work table and pretended to fumble with some gears.

"This doesn't seem right," Rupina said, whipping off the magnifying lens from around his head. "Redbeard doesn't do anything out of the kindness of his heart. He is always planning, scheming." Rupina's eyes darted about as he tried to figure out the true intention of Redbeard's act.

"He doesn't know who you are, or our relationship, does he?" he whispered.

Before Preston could respond, Rupina placed his finger against his lip. "No, that can't be correct. Then why would he put us together? There must be something else. Perhaps he is just trying to get me to finish my work quicker, or ..." His words trailed off as he turned toward Preston with a fearful look in his eyes. "You could be here to spy on me." Preston squinted at his great-uncle, trying to figure out if he was thinking clearly, while Rupina now peeked at him out of the corner of his eye. "Perhaps not, but we cannot be too careful now, can we? Then again ..."

Preston didn't know what to say. He knew his uncle had been imprisoned in this workshop for longer than Preston had been alive. Did spending all these years alone cause him to go mad?

"Why would I —"

"No, of course not. That can't be it," Rupina said, cutting him off, dismissing anything Preston had to say on the matter. "You don't seem the type. Nonetheless, perhaps we should return to our work; or my work, that is, as it will become our work in a manner of speaking. Anyway, how are you, my dear boy?" He smiled and shook Preston by the shoulders before hugging him tight.

Preston stood stiff, not knowing which direction to take the conversation. He desperately wanted to ask him about the beacon back home, but would this question lead to more suspicion? More accusations of mistrust? Even though his uncle seemed lucid once again, Preston thought best to avoid planning their escape just yet. "So, do they always lock you in here?"

Rupina looked up and then to the door. "That? Oh, no. Only when Redbeard is particularly furious with me. It normally lasts for a week or so, then I'm allowed out to gather my creative senses, as it were. It's so good to see you. You look well."

"What about you?" Preston asked, walking up to his uncle, whose shirt was still open. The stainless-steel box embedded within his chest was attached to his skin with tiny rivets. Gears arranged inside ticked and spun. "What did they do?"

Rupina was momentarily confused until he looked down. "This? Ah, this is nothing, my dear nephew," he said, tying his shirt closed. "Now, you must tell me everything while we work."

"Of course. What can I help you do?" he asked.

"Well, we are supposed to be building control panels for a fleet of steamer trunks." Lined up along a table were several assemblies, about the size of a phonograph. He slid one over and stretched out the wires. "Let me explain how the design works."

Over the next several days, Preston took apart and rebuilt each device. This helped him understand the concept and design of the panel. Unfortunately, his uncle still hadn't brought up the beacon. Preston assumed he was still suspicious of Redbeard's intentions. As he sat on a bench, locking several gears into place, Preston turned to him.

"I still cannot believe we're on a different planet; in a different galaxy!"

"It was certainly a shock to me as well," Rupina said. "How fascinating though, don't you think? I mean, what an incredible opportunity. If we weren't prisoners, of course."

"Well, hopefully we won't be prisoners for too much longer." Preston paused for a moment, wondering if he should bring up the beacon. "Who would've ever imagined there was a technology out there to make this happen? How does it all work?"

"I've learned much since I've been here, but still cannot fully explain it all. What I surmise is one can only travel between realms, and not galaxies."

"What's the difference? Aren't they the same?"

"Not quite. Realms are planets, which are similar, but exist in different galaxies. The similarities of these planets form a connection with one another; they create an unseen, celestial bridge, if you will. The seven realms all have some form of human life. Beings who breathe oxygen, drink water, grow old. Beyond those attributes, their timelines are comparable as well. Their rotations around their particular sun take place at approximately the same amount of time; they also share the same type of atmosphere, climate, and seasons."

"Impossible," Preston said, shaking his head.

"All evidence to the contrary, my dear boy. When you come to terms with what has happened, you cannot help but to admire what Redbeard has been able to accomplish."

"Do you know much about him?" Preston asked.

"Redbeard?" Rupina smirked and shrugged his shoulders. "Not sure even Savannah knows much about the man. However, over the years, I've heard bits and pieces from many sources, to which the validity of their tales has yet to be confirmed."

"How did he become a pirate?"

"He was not always one. Growing up, his father was a religious man and took him on a pilgrimage across the sea. It was on this trip where he became fascinated with sailing. All of his free time was spent watching the crew as they adjusted the billowing sails. To him, it was a carefully choreographed dance, where the wind and canvas met as one. There's definitely an art to captaining a ship," Rupina admitted. "Years later, war broke out and Redbeard was called up to the air fleet. Hand me that wrench, will you?"

Rupina took the wrench and tightened a nut onto the side of the panel. When he was done, he worked a lever back and forth, which opened a valve.

"Perfect! Anyway, his time as a spotter in a zeppelin was short-lived as the war ended. However, the young man never lost his love affair with the sea. After he returned, his father insisted he resume his lessons, but Redbeard was reluctant to give up the salty mist. Instead, he left home and took a position on a trade vessel as a cabin boy. Eventually, he worked his way up to commanding his own ship. Another war broke out, and instead of enlisting, he became a privateer and received a 'Letter of Marque' from the security council, allowing him to attack other ships. When plunder became scarce in this region, he sailed to other ones, taking on ships and gathering booty, thus creating a name and reputation for himself. During one battle, he was severely wounded and taken prisoner. In the cell next to him was a doctor, of sorts," Rupina said, rolling his eyes.

"This man, Krinsworth, fixed Redbeard up the best he could with whatever parts he found or gathered during their work on the prison ships. Once Redbeard regained his strength, he was scheduled to be hung as a pirate. Back home, the security council disavowed any knowledge or alliance with Redbeard. When Redbeard presented his 'Letter of Marque' during trial, it was found to be a fake. You see, the ambassador to the security council made certain the letters he signed appeared to be real, but were changed just enough to cast doubt into their validity. For instance, the royal seal on Redbeard's letter was slightly altered before providing it to him. His letter showed a sailing ship with one mast sailing east. The actual royal seal has a three-masted sailing ship heading west. When called into question, Redbeard was tried and convicted. On the night before he was to be hung, he escaped with Krinsworth and several underpaid guards who were promised riches beyond their wildest dreams. He hijacked a ship and made his way back to Breakaway Bay. Once he returned, he waged a private war against the council. Eventually, he swayed the other privateers to join him. It wasn't long before Redbeard won his war. The first thing he did was to have all the council members rounded up and imprisoned. They ended up being the first test subjects for Krinsworth to 'perfect' his craft."

Preston's jaw dropped. "That's barbaric!"

Rupina nodded. "That's not the worst of it."

"What do you mean?"

Rupina scowled and pointed his screwdriver at the rows of control panels. "These! These are to be the feather in his cap. That's why I've been stalling as long as I can. But I fear I cannot hold out much longer," he said, checking the bandage around his wrist. "He grows weary of my excuses and has become quite impatient. If I don't finish them soon, he'll make sure I do."

"How can he force you?"

Rupina tapped the screwdriver against the gears in his chest. "This is what he wants to do to people's heads, to control their thoughts, their actions. Krinsworth has been experimenting with a procedure to do just that. I'm not certain how far along he is, but I believe if he had been successful, I would have already been transitioned."

Preston didn't know what to say.

"Anyway, I was going to hold out until they forced my hand, in a manner of speaking," he said, smiling as he rubbed the wound on his wrist. "In the meantime, I've been trying to come up with a plan to stop all of this. But now, with you here, I fear things have changed. It may be best if we take my designs and return to our realm."

"Yes, of course! What do we need to do?"

"Hand me a sheet of stainless steel, will you?" Rupina asked, nonchalantly pointing Preston to a nearby closet.

"Uhm, sure ..." Preston brought over a sheet and set it down in front of Rupina. After making sure the guard wasn't standing by the door, he leaned into Rupina. "You know," he said, quietly, "they send a steamer trunk to a woman back home who provides them with all they need. I tried to sneak into one of them, but I ended up getting caught. A friend of mine saved me."

"Oh, back home? You —"

"Open it up!"

"It's Savannah!" Preston jumped up, hitting his knee against the table.

The door unlocked and Savannah walked into the room. "Hey, Fishbait! You've got an hour to finish up in here, then meet me at the gate. We have to go into town." She turned and sneered at Rupina. "Make this codger do some of his own work for a change," she said as she left.

"Yes, ma'am."

Once they were sure she was gone, Rupina turned to Preston.

"A woman back home, you say? Do you happen to know her name?"

"Crownickers."

Rupina dropped his wrench. "Matilda Crownickers? Figures. Although, I expected her to be dead by now."

"Wait! How do you know her?"

Rupina shook his head. "Her and I conducted business years ago."

"You worked with Crownickers?" Preston said, dropping the tray, which caused the guard to unlock the door.

"What's goin' on in 'ere?"

"Sorry, I just dropped this. I'll clean it up and be right out."

The guard grunted as he slammed the door shut.

"Well, long ago, well before you were born, Crownickers came to me, asking about producing this new steel in a smelter that wouldn't draw attention. When someone asks not to draw attention to what they are doing, that is a warning sign one should not ignore! I should have said no right then, but I was weak — succumbing to greed." He arched his eyebrows and titled his head, thinking back. "It's hard to resist a pillowcase full of gold coins ... Of course, had I known then what I do now, I would've made different decisions," he muttered. "Anyway, the gold coin you found in my study was one of those pieces."

"I can't believe you worked with that nasty woman," Preston said, collecting the tools. "Why didn't you tell me? She runs Iron Hills! The place the constable was going to send me. That's the reason I ended up here!"

"Being sent there would've been most unfortunate," Rupina said. "However, I'm not sure you fared much better here."

"How do you know all this?"

Rupina snorted. "When you spend decades imprisoned, you tend to hear things. Most of my knowledge on the matter comes from a pirate who has a penchant for rum," Rupina said, tipping his thumb into his mouth like he was taking a drink. "What's their name?"

Preston stood there, confused. "Who's name?"

"The friend who helped you after you got caught in the chest?"

"Oh, Amelia."

Rupina looked up. "The blonde-haired girl who delivers my meals?"

Preston nodded. "She didn't say much about Crownickers."

Rupina shrugged his shoulders as he continued fiddling with some gears. "I'm not surprised. Nobody trusts anyone here. It seems to be part of the pirate code. Information is sometimes treated as being more valuable than gold. But perhaps there's another reason she's not to be trusted. She's family and could be part of Redbeard's grand plan."

"You know they're family?"

"Of course. I've been here a very long time." Rupina sighed and then stared at the door. "We should leave."

"Go outside?"

"What? No! We should return to our realm ... but how? That's the question now, isn't it?"

Preston's face dropped. Perhaps it was too late; perhaps his uncle's mind was too far gone. "That sounds like a great idea," he said, forcing a smile.

"Cap'n, sir, she's coming down the hall."

Redbeard drew in a deep breath and grumbled as he dipped his fingers into his pocket and pulled out a watch. With it came a piece of paper.

"In due time," he muttered, staring at the paper before slipping it under a stack on his desk.

"You called for me, sir?"

"Aye. I want ye to see something. Something I trust only ye can help me with."

"Of course. Anything, sir."

"I've just had something returned to me which will help us prepare for our final phase."

"Final phase?" Savannah asked. "What can I do to help, sir?"

"Step this way, dear."

Redbeard walked over to a conference table, which had a large map spread across.

"We need youngins to help set the explosives within our locations in each of these realms," he said, pointing to red spots on the parchment. "For this operation, we'll be using my fleet of steamer trunks to transport our young soldiers to their targets at precisely the same time. It's imperative this attack happen all at once."

"At the same time? With so many targets, is such an ambitious assault even feasible?"

"It'll have to be."

"This kind of coordination would task even our most experienced soldiers. Why the need for youngins? They have nowhere near the training."

"Because, in order to maximize the damage, we need to get the devices deep within the bedrock. Our young scamps will need to wedge their way into the tiny crevices below the soil. Therefore, as soon as they arrive at their locations, they will squeeze themselves into these holes, attach the bombs, and detonate the devices, causing the destruction for which I've planned. The ensuing carnage will bury the realms."

Savannah's head shot up.

"But they'll be killed in the explosion! It's a suicide mission. There must be another way."

Redbeard turned away; his face twisted with anger. He squeezed his eyes shut and clenched his fists before taking a deep breath. With a broad smile, he turned back to Savannah.

"No, no, my dear." Redbeard shook his head and circled the table, resting his hand on her shoulder. "These children are our most valuable asset. They are our future, and because of this, there is nothing more important to me than their well-being. As such, we have built a failsafe into the devices. The detonations don't happen until our trusted soldiers pull the return handles. This way, they'll be far enough away when the devices explode."

Savannah closed her eyes and nodded. "Very well, sir. How long before we can place you on your rightful throne?"

"Well, it will take some time for the water to recede and the land to fully recover. Only then will we have our ships return with our armies to finish conquering the realms. This is where you come in. The fleet will be broken up into squadrons and sent to their respective locations to take control. And you will be in command of the flagship for the fleet."

Savannah's eyes grew wide. She tried to hold back her smile.

"Who are the young ones you need, sir?"

Redbeard reached into his desk and pulled out a manifest, handing it to Savannah. Among the names on the list were Preston and Amelia.

"And if any of them refuse?"

"The strong ones will recognize this great opportunity and see it for the honor it is. The unworthy ones will not be given the choice. Those who resist will pay a visit to the good doctor. He assures me this new procedure he developed will allow me to control the minds of our more obstinate soldiers. He has already tested it out on some of the crew we took captive from the galleon."

Savannah didn't like this. She knew of Amelia's stubbornness. Second only to her own.

"Uhm, this is amazing ... It's the perfect plan, Captain. I ask only if, once the mission is complete, will the transitioned ones be able to return to their natural selves?"

Redbeard sensed the concern in her voice. In a rare moment of affection, he took hold of her shoulders and stared into her eyes. "Of course. Every last one of them. Especially my dear granddaughter, if it comes to that. But I'm certain you will see to it that it doesn't."

In one of the desk drawers, Redbeard retrieved a scroll, which he unrolled. Inked out across the sheet was a newly drawn map of the "7th Realm."

"As a matter of fact, I would like Amelia to take an active role in the plan as well. Once the waters recede on Earth, this is what I'm told will remain."

Savannah reviewed the map. There were three small continents remaining, with a few islands scattered about.

"My hope would be for my dear granddaughter to serve as my ambassador from a garrison on one of these smaller islands. With yer oversight, of course."

"She would be honored, Captain. Amelia has always desired a way to become closer to her grandfather. This will thrill her!"

"Over the years, I have grown quite fond of her, and only wish to strengthen our bond," Redbeard said, raising his eyebrows and smiling.

He removed a fountain pen from his pocket and scribbled "Savannah" across the top of the page, which caused her mouth to drop.

"Now, if my plan goes accordingly, and ye follow orders and do yer part, I will bestow the title of Prime Minister on ye for this realm."

Savannah struggled to find the words. "You, you humble me with your generosity, Captain. I thought leading the fleet was a great honor, but this ... I don't know how to thank you."

"Ye thank me with yer loyalty!" Redbeard smiled and nodded. "Every detail of this plan has been meticulously thought out by me. There can be no variations!"

"Of course, sir. My top priority will be following your every lead, as it has always been."

"Well, be off with ye then, my dear. The hour grows late and there is much to be done."

"Aye, Captain." Savannah backed up, smiling. Before she left, she grabbed the manifest, accidentally knocking Rupina's slip of paper to the ground.

"What is this?" she asked, bending down to retrieve the paper.

"That's nothing, dear," Redbeard told her, snatching the paper off the floor. "Plans for a new peg leg. Ye best be off. Much to prepare!" he said, waving his finger.

"Of course," she said, turning and leaving the office.

Once she was gone, Redbeard scowled and uncovered the paper. In a folded over corner was a name.

"So, the old man has known all along."

WITHIN REDBEARD'S EYES WAS a mixture of rage and glee. For so long, he had struggled to put his plan in motion when, unbeknownst to him, the key to his success was locked in a lab within his keep.

"Boots! Get in 'ere!"

An older pirate wearing welder's goggles and an iron brace around his neck hustled into the room. "Yes, sir?" he said, adjusting his brown, felt bowler hat.

"Fetch Krinsworth. There is much we need to discuss."

"Aye, Captain!"

Boots hobbled away while Redbeard returned to examining Rupina's designs. A short while later, Krinsworth entered the room, wiping his bloody hands with a dirty cloth.

"You called for me, captain?"

"Aye. I believe I have finally found the wretch who pilfered my treasured steamer trunk. But I'm not certain the plans remain hidden within."

"That's wonderful news! How will you plan on capturing him?"

Redbeard smiled, raising his eyebrows. "No need. He's been with us for some time."

Krinsworth cocked his head. "I don't quite understand."

"What do ye make of this?" Redbeard said, sliding the paper over to Krinsworth.

The doctor looked at the sheet. "The beacon! Is this the same as the elder's design?" He flipped the sheet over. "But where are the rest of the schematics? The control panel?"

"I assume the old scudder had gathered them before he left."

"The old — you don't mean?"

"Aye," Redbeard said, raising his eyebrows.

"Should I have a go at him to get the rest?" Krinsworth asked, setting the paper down. "There are several new techniques I devised, which I am certain will work. It would be my honor."

"Now's not the time to show our hand." Redbeard stood and stroked his beard as he paced, flicking the dangling sprockets tied to it. "For the moment, I have to believe the plans have been removed, and I won't risk losing them again. The codger is impudent. He values not his life, and I cannot trust a man who does not fear death. For all I know, forcing his hand would lead him to design a beacon which would send my armies into the sea, and I'd be none the wiser until it was too late." Redbeard swung around and placed his enormous hand on Krinsworth's shoulder, making certain Krinsworth felt his might. "First, I must smoke out the rest of the rats scurrying about until I rid myself of this infestation. In the meantime, I would like ye to start working on the beacons. Follow the plan EXACTLY as it is on this paper. We'll obtain the rest when I feel we're ready."

Now, you must understand, Krinsworth was a brash sort of fellow. He walked the halls of the keep with an unchallenged air of confidence, strong in his words and in his stance. But this — this was something far beyond his area of expertise. Slice open a body, create new ways to torture a traitor, grovel if needed; these were his forte. But developing a device of this magnitude was troublesome, and beyond his skill set, to say the least. But few dared to disappoint the pirate king, and he did not relish being the first to do so. Redbeard's command left him paralyzed with concern, saying nothing on the matter. This immediately captured Redbeard's attention.

"Krinsworth!"

"Sir?"

"My plan, my destiny, is within my grasp! More so than it has ever been. Are ye certain yer up to the challenge?"

Krinsworth's eyes fixated on Redbeard's cutlass, watching intently as the man tapped his fingers on the grip. "Of course, Captain. You are well-aware of my work, and willingness to achieve your goals at any cost."

Redbeard dropped an eyebrow and nodded to the door, but when Krinsworth retrieved the elder's design off the desk, he noticed something else — a map he didn't recognize. One with Savannah's name scribed across one continent.

"May I ask about this?"

"Never mind that," Redbeard said. "Just a distraction to keep someone in line."

Krinsworth bowed and exited the room, leaving Redbeard staring at the map of the seven realms. "My destiny will not die because of one man's failure."

It was a rare moment when Amelia and Savannah sat together; let alone share a meal, as if they were an actual family. Actually, this NEVER happened. At least not since Amelia was of school age. So, as they sat across from each other in the Rusty Bucket, it was no surprise Amelia was concerned as to why this was happening.

"What would you think if I were to tell you we're leaving Breakaway Bay?"

Normally, this would mean a mission, or plunder of some sort. However, this time her words took a different tone. Something foreign to Amelia's ears.

"Really? Just the two of us?" she asked, leaning forward.

"An opportunity has presented itself. If it all works out, it will be good for both of us."

Amelia beamed at this. *We can live a normal life!* "I would love to! I'm not sure how it is to live as a normal kid, but I can't wait to find out!"

Savannah nodded her head and smiled. Amelia was taken aback by this. She could count on one finger the number of times she'd seen her mother smile.

"All my hard work is finally paying off. Your grandfather is bestowing a great honor on me — on us. This is just between you and me, but when his conquest of the 7 realms is complete, I am to be in charge of one, and the role of ambassador will be bestowed upon you!"

"An ambassador?" Amelia asked, falling back into her seat. The smile faded from her delicate face. "I'm not ... I mean, what do I know about being an ambassador?"

Savannah stared blankly at Amelia. "You will learn. Just as I have had to over these many years!"

The poor girl was speechless. What could she say? What was she to do? This was not a task she wanted to take on. Amelia didn't want any part of this world. Why couldn't her mother just accept this and let her be? She creaked out a smile as Savannah fell back into her chair. She sensed her young daughter's trepidation.

"How could you not be more excited about this? You've endured much. Much more than someone your age ever needed to, and now it's time for you to be rewarded!"

Amelia could see Savannah was disappointed. She let out a deep sigh and nodded. "You know, you're right, mother. This is an honor; a shock, really. I don't even know where to begin."

Savannah smiled. "You deserve this, Amelia. We both deserve this. And now, with your grandfather's plan almost complete, we won't have much longer to wait."

Amelia nervously smiled.

"What's wrong?"

These words sent prickles through her body. She dropped her fork and drew in a heavy breath. There was no turning back now. It wasn't in her mother's nature to dismiss something blindly. She would demand an answer if Amelia wasn't willing to give one.

"Once everything is done, once everybody gets what they want, will grandfather spare Preston and his uncle?"

Savannah cocked her head. "His uncle?"

The world froze around Amelia. *What did I just say?* Her teeth clenched as she replayed the conversation in her head, all the while trying to come up with a way to distract her mother from this unspeakable revelation. Her heart raced as she pushed back her chair and stood. "Well, he, I meant —"

"What are you saying, child?" Savannah looked at the door. "That old man is family to the boy?"

Tears formed in Amelia's eyes. She tried, but she couldn't piece the words together.

"How did you hear of this? Did Fishbait tell you?"

"No!" She couldn't deny anything at this point. Her body, her mind betrayed her, and she dropped back into her chair. "It's not like that. I accidentally heard them talking one day when I walked past the workshop."

Amelia stared at Savannah, her stomach churning. She slid her plate away as Savannah stared out a window, processing this information. Amelia rushed over to her. After dropping to her knees, she took hold of Savannah's hand.

"Please, Savannah, MOM ... please don't say anything. I beg of you."

Savannah broke her trance and stood, raising Amelia up and drawing her in close. She stroked her hair and hugged her tight. "No need to fret, my dear. It'll be our secret."

Her soft words seemed to put Amelia at ease.

"Anyway, dear, the old man is not yet finished. He has yet to complete the beacons, and I'm not sure how long this will take. Why don't you sit, and we can finish our meal?"

"Where's that daughter of mine?"

Quinton was organizing some books on Redbeard's shelf. "I believe Savannah went into town for lunch. Afterwards, she was going to take that kid with her to run some errands?"

Redbeard's face twisted. "Does she spend much time with the boy?"

Quinton stopped what he was doing and turned to Redbeard. "I don't know for certain, but lately I've only seen her with the boy or Amelia."

"What are they getting at?" Redbeard mumbled.

"Pardon, Captain?"

"It's nothing. Fetch her for me."

"Aye, Captain."

Redbeard was adjusting the gears on his peg leg when Savannah walked into his office.

"Sorry, Captain, I was taking care of —"

"It doesn't matter. I need ye to learn all ye can about Port Royal." On a nearby shelf, he grabbed an armful of books, charts, and scrolls, dropping them in front of her. She sifted through the pile.

"Why Port Royal?"

"Because it is a valuable prize, and a trusted jump point. Since ye are to be in charge of the realm, this is where I foresee the capital to be placed."

Inside, Savannah beamed. She still couldn't believe the words he spoke. "*In charge of the realm.*" Those five words sent chills through her body, relieving the burdensome weight she had placed on her heart and in her mind so many years ago. Troubled memories of her childhood faded, being replaced by thoughts of exploration, leadership, and TRUST.

"Of course. What would you have me do?"

"Whatever ye want," he said, throwing his hands in the air. "Ye'll be setting policy and running my government from there. Now, let me tell ye about Port Royal. Before the city yer named after was a pirate haven, the 3rd realm laid siege upon Port Royal and sank the city!"

"I thought it was from an earthquake?"

"Some will lead ye to believe it was an earthquake, but we know better. Because of the attack, we were forced to abandon the city for some time. Once the invaders left, the dogs guarding the 7th realm set about rounding up our people and hanging them as pirates," he said, while drawing out the word *DOGS* in red pencil. A slight affront to Savannah's illicit relationship for which he had still not forgiven her. As he glared at her from the corner of his eye, she turned away. "Eventually, we were able to return and rebuild; but we did so below the water's edge, in caverns far below, and out of sight of the others. It remains this way today. She continues to be one of our jump points. Speaking of which, I have something to show ye."

Redbeard walked to the back of his office and, after unlocking the doors, he swung them open wide. Inside were two rows of steamer trunks lining the walls as far as the eye could see.

"Your fleet! It is complete?"

"Aye, just now."

"They look perfect," Savannah said, squatting down and examining the metalwork. "What is the next step?"

"That's why yer here. I have a special task for ye."

Savannah's ears perked up. She jumped up and stood straight, her heart pounding in her chest. "At your service, Captain."

Redbeard smiled. "First, I need ye to instruct the old fool about the change in plans. Then, introduce him to these beauties and order him to complete the assemblies at once. They are to fit precisely into our new fleet. If he gives ye any lip about it, use those 'persuasive tactics' ye tend to be good at," he said with a sinister glare. "Once he's been properly motivated, I need ye to get our young pilots readied for the jump. They need to learn how to operate these trunks to deliver our payloads to their locations. Do you think you can complete this task for me?"

"Of course, sir."

"I knew ye could," he said, patting her on the shoulder. "The good doctor will explain the operating procedure for these little wonders. Prepare the youngins for their mission. Ye have three weeks!" He walked to the doors and looked over his shoulder. "Perhaps ye can bring my granddaughter in on this to help ye train them. I would like to keep this a 'family' affair."

Savannah smiled. *Finally*, she thought. "As you wish, Captain. I'll get Fishbait to help as well."

Redbeard scowled at her and cocked his head. "Am I to believe the boy shares our bloodline?"

"No, sir, it was just —"

"Did ye not hear me say, 'family affair,' or am I mistaken, and another's lips spoke those words?"

"Right, yes, of course. I apologize, sir."

Redbeard slammed the doors closed and approached Savannah.

"I've taken notice ye have become quite close with the rapscallion. And that daughter of yers seems smitten as well. Perhaps I was mistaken to place ye in charge of him," he said, turning his back to her. "Maybe this task is better served by another."

"What are you talking about? The boy means nothing to me," she said, rushing up to Redbeard's desk with her fists clenched.

"I thought I could depend on you. That I could trust yer loyalty to me, to the cause, but ye speak of bringing an outsider into our circle."

Redbeard shook his head and walked over to the window. "There's been whispers of ye spending too much time with this scamp, taking him under yer wing. How can I trust ye'll do what's required of ye when the time comes?"

"You can! What reason have I given you to think otherwise?" she asked. Years of seething rage exploded as she slammed her fists against the desk. "I've spent my life in your shadow, doing your bidding, all so you could achieve your goal. And now you cast doubt on me like a net being tossed into the sea, fishing for answers I cannot give. From where does this come? Who would allow this slander to spill from their lips? I shall take great pleasure in yanking out their mechanics for these lies!"

"Drop yer sails, daughter!" Redbeard ordered as he sat at his desk. "For this to work, we need to be on the same course, and I'm beginning to have my doubts about ye."

"If you have something to say, then go about it."

"It appears that boy has become a distraction. Yer fire no longer burns bright. Not only are ye coddling the scamp, yer protecting him."

"I would fillet him and feed his remains to the kraken before I betrayed you, or the cause!" Savannah turned and walked toward the door, but stopped. She spun around and pointed her finger at Redbeard. "You're just angered over the time the old man is taking to complete his task. This poison you're spewing comes from his betrayal, not mine!" Her face twisted with anger. "I have given my all to you, and yet I have been passed over time and time again for these dogs who aren't fit to scrape barnacles off our longboats! Yet, I've said nothing! And now, after we come to an understanding, you put my loyalty on trial!"

Redbeard leaned back in his chair. "Well, it's just I hear things. Ye forget, I know all that takes place with my crew."

"Do you now?" she asked, storming up to him, squinting her eye at the foolish man.

Redbeard's forehead crinkled as he sat up. Leaning forward, he glared at Savannah. "What are ye saying?"

"If you know so much, why would you let a cabin boy into your circle who is kin to the man building your most precious prize?"

Redbeard froze for a moment, but then leaned back in his chair once more. "Ye think I didn't know?"

Savannah shook her head and unclenched her fists. "Then why do you do it?"

"Because it's better to keep the shark in front of ye, then to have it swimming out from the shadows, ready to strike."

Savannah grunted before storming out of the office, leaving Redbeard to stare at the door for a moment. With each passing moment, his intensity swelled, his muscles straining as his face crinkled, growing redder by the moment. His knuckles turned white as he clenched his fists tight, hoping to quell the storm raging inside his soul, but to no avail. Unable to hold back any longer, he leapt up from his chair, sweeping his arm across his desk, launching piles of papers and books across the room. Struggling to contain his rage, he dropped his head and leaned over the desk, heaving until suddenly a small chuckle grew inside him, growing into a burst of laughter, leaving him shaking his head.

"So, the scamp is kin to the codger?"

CHAPTER 14

SINCE THE REPAIRS ON the Dragon's Curse were finished, Preston and his uncle headed to the docks to scour the scrapyard for any leftover materials in order to complete the fleet of steamer trunks. At least this is what the guards were led to believe. However, secretly, they were hoping to collect enough Zimponium for an additional trunk. One large enough to transport the duo back home.

Along the street of this quaint village, evenly spaced approximately 100 feet from one another, were arched bronze boxes trimmed with copper. People unfamiliar would think them to be postboxes. They certainly looked similar. Each piece stood roughly five feet in height and had a copper profile of Redbeard stamped into the metal facing the street. Etched into the back panel was an image of the Dragon's Curse. Wisps of steam slowly spilled from a black iron scupper vent on top of the box. Most of the casing was enclosed except for one side, which showcased interlocked brass gears protected by glass. Curious, Preston examined the piece.

"What are these?" he asked.

"They're transfer stations to help move the trolley through town."

"Really?"

As a trolley slowly approached, the whistle at the next stop screeched while a steady cloud of steam was exhausted from its scupper.

"For all I've learned about pirates of the past, it makes me wonder why this place is so different from anything I've read," Preston said, shaking his head.

"Redbeard is certainly unique, and one would be a fool to underestimate him. He is so much smarter than he appears, and as you stated, far more advanced than the pirates we've read about back home. Gold and jewels are not what he seeks. What concerns him is stealing as much technology as he can. Breakaway Bay is decades ahead of the other continents on this planet. And it's all because of what he has accomplished. Throughout the realms, he sends his ships to plunder whatever machines or science journals they can find. And his efforts have paid off. Granted, this island is in its infancy of development compared to, well, us, but it's moving ahead at a staggering pace. Take the Dragon's Curse, for instance. True, it still depends mostly on the wind to move it along. But he's been able to incorporate steam technology to motor along when necessary."

The Dragon's Curse was up ahead. Rupina stopped Preston and pointed out some features.

"You see the scupper vents just above the waterline along the hull? The ones that look like tubas? Those shoot out massive amounts of steam that help propel the ship forward or backward as needed. But I'm not sure why there are so many. I've never been able to go below the first two decks to see how they work."

"It's because they help the ship become airborne."

Rupina froze. "What?"

"It's true. I was aboard when it did. At first, I couldn't see the tubes since there was a thick cloud of steam beneath us. When we got high enough, I saw the ocean below the keel."

"How far did you get?"

"Another realm, from what I was told."

Rupina was lost in his thoughts. "How fascinating! For a ship so much larger than a steamer trunk to not only fly, but to jump realms. It staggers the imagination."

His eyes darted back and forth as he calculated the possibility of this in his head.

"This fellow he works with, Krinsworth, he must have been able to help him with the design. That's the reason he keeps him close," Rupina said, tapping his forehead.

He pulled a scrap of paper and pencil out of his pocket before sketching the Dragon. It wasn't long before he piqued the interest of some of the crew who came to the rail.

"Oy! What are ye doin' down there?"

Rupina put away his paper and waved. This failed to appease the pirate, who seemed excessively annoyed. But yet it wasn't enough of an annoyance for him to do anything more than throw some dirty looks at them.

"Be on with ye!"

"Let's keep moving," Preston said, nodding and holding his hand up. They continued past the ship and headed to the supply depot.

"Fascinating!" Rupina said. "Imagine the possibilities if we were allowed access to those mechanisms. The creations we could design together." Rupina kept glancing back at the ship.

Long before Preston came to the island, Redbeard had big plans for Rupina, and if things had gone as planned, Rupina would have held the same position as Krinsworth. However, once Rupina saw how Redbeard treated those around him, he thought it best not to align himself with the brute, or his gaggle of Steampunk Pirates. A smart decision to be certain, however, his timing was less than ideal. One might have waited until they were off the island and away from the realm before they made their concerns known. Especially since his concerns were ones critical of Redbeard's leadership. As you can imagine, this infuriated Redbeard, which, of course, led to Rupina's current, unfortunate situation.

Nonetheless, once they were out of earshot of the Dragon's crew, Rupina turned to Preston and grabbed his shoulders. "I've designed his steamer trunks with a significant flaw to make certain his plan fails. When it does, there will be no words I can say to prevent my fate. Once I'm gone, they'll turn their anger to you. Promise me, even if our plan fails, you'll find a way to leave before then, for nothing I do, or don't do, will stop him from achieving his goals."

"What is he planning on doing?"

"Something which will destroy our planet, as well as several others."

Quinton knocked on Redbeard's door.

"What?"

Redbeard was at his desk, studying Rupina's notes. Looking up, he gave Quinton a puzzled look and pulled out his pocket watch.

"Did the steel arrive already?"

"Not quite, Cap'n."

"Whaddya mean? Ye playing games with me?"

"No, sir. Uhm, she's here."

"Who's here?"

Quinton rolled his eyes, which caused Redbeard to let out a deep sigh and drop his head.

"Right. Well, see her in," he grumbled.

"I'll see me self in," Crownickers said as she pushed Quinton out of the way. "Well, ye got yerself a doorman. Aren't we all fancy and important now? And here I thought he was nuthin' more than the keeper of the clocks," she scoffed at him with disdain in her voice.

"Matilda, my sweet. How long has it been?" Redbeard said, stuffing his notes into his pocket before extending his arms to greet her. "Ye look as ravishing as always."

Quinton raised his eyebrows and backed out of the room, closing the door behind him.

"Don't give me yer sweet talk, ye slimy bag of bilge water," she said, dropping down into his chair. She opened several desk drawers and searched through them. "Where's my gold?"

"Gold? I don't understand. I've covered my part of the bargain."

"Ye shorted me three of those little ankle-biters. Now, either pay me for my troubles or use another port to drop that heap of yours into."

Redbeard stared at her and frowned. "Whatever happened to us, my sweet? Ye know, I believe it's yer fiery passion I miss the most."

"Ye'll get more than ye bargained for if I don't get what's owed to me," she said, leaping up and pulling a small dagger from her boot. With fire in her eyes, she lunged at Redbeard, shoving him against the wall and pressing the sharp tip of her blade under his chin, but he just smiled.

"There's ma girl. Ya know, this reminds me of our wedding night."

Crownickers sneered as she snorted at his insufferable comment. "Some wedding night. Ye left me to go drinkin' rum with those dogs ye call a crew."

Redbeard slowly reached up and pulled her hand down. "Now, ye know that couldn' be avoided. Plus, that meeting filled yer pockets and got us to where we are today, my love."

"Exactly my point."

The two leered at one another before Redbeard shook his head and reached into his waistcoat, pulling out a small leather pouch. "I believe this should make us square," he said, dangling the purse in front of Crownickers. She reached for it, but he snatched it away before she could grab it. "How's about a little peck on the cheek first?"

Crownickers grunted before leaning in with a crooked smile and puckered her lips. Just before reaching his cheek, she thrust her fist forward, punching him in the gut. Redbeard let out a gasp of air, then had a rolling chuckle, which exploded into a deep laugh. "Ye never change, my sweet."

"Don't ye forget it," she said, grabbing the purse and tucking it into her cleavage. She replaced the knife and scowled. "Now that we've conducted our business, where is she?"

Redbeard grunted and gave her a sullen look. "I would like to say she's preparing for our next expedition, but I fear treachery is afoot."

"Whaddya sayin'?"

"It seems our dear daughter has made an ally with this stray dog who's come across my path."

Crownickers scowled. "Who?"

"Some young scamp named 'Preston,' of all things."

A smile grew across Crownickers' face. "Hmm, young ye say ... Perhaps I can take him off yer hands. Plus, it'll help make up for the way ye shorted me."

"Are we still on this? I thought we was square now?"

"Ha! We'll never square up. Ye still owe me for the many years I wasted following yer sorry self around. Ye'd be quicker to swim to the bottom of that blasted ocean of yers than to make it square with me. Now whaddya say?"

"Hmm, tempting, but I'm not done with him yet. I believe he can get me somethin' I need. Somethin' stolen from me some time ago."

"Well, don't do anything rash. I could always use an extra hand in the slag heap. It's especially brutal work for someone deserving of that sort of thing. But it won't help if he's broken!"

Redbeard scowled. "Always tryin' to ruin my fun."

"Has he been transitioned?"

"No." Redbeard walked over to his globe. "Not yet at least."

"So, what's this delinquent's story?"

"Strange enough, he comes from yer realm."

"Really?"

"And I believe from yer sector."

"Well, isn't that interesting now?"

Redbeard spun the globe, standing silent for a moment.

"Ye still have yer contacts within the government there?"

"Ye know I do."

"Good. I need ye to check on something for me."

"Quinton!"

The door flung open. "Aye, Cap'n."

"Now that she's back on the Dragon, I need ye to gather up the crew on this list and prepare for a jump. Only the names on the list! Savvy?"

"Aye, Cap'n. I'll alert Savannah."

Redbeard's hand slapped the paper against the desk and he squeezed his eyes shut. "ONLY the names on the list."

Quinton stood silent, glancing around. "Uhm, of course, Captain. My apologies."

With a stern stare, Redbeard slid his hand off the sheet, which prompted Quinton to pick up the paper. On the top was a red triangle with the number "7" in the center.

Redbeard stared at Quinton. "It's time to unleash the Crimson Triad."

Redbeard walked over to the wall and flipped over a large painting. Attached to the back of it was a map with the same bold red triangle. Below this was a topographical chart for each realm.

"Plans have changed. The bombs yer building will be placed in the steamer trunks. We cannot waste any more time burying them."

"So Krinsworth can build the beacons?"

"Aye! But we'll still need the old man to complete the consoles. Once our new beacons are constructed, we will install them at the locations shown here. This will ensure the steamer trunks in our fleet are guided to their precise location. With each steamer trunk loaded with explosives, our youngins will spearhead them directly into these weak points."

"Yer planning on using youngins, sir?"

"Aye. Since the trunks will be transporting themselves, we do not need skilled pilots any longer."

Quinton cocked his head, confused. "Beg yer pardon, Cap'n, but since that is the case, can ye not just remove the kids and send the trunks on their own? Then we can pack in more explosives."

"Aye, but given the amount of strain on the trunks during the jumps, there's too much risk of them detonating before they reach their targets. Instead, we will instruct the youngins on how to trigger the devices once they arrive."

"If the bombs are the trunks, how will the youngins return?"

Redbeard raised an eyebrow to Quinton, who pursed his lips and nodded.

"But won't Savannah expect ye to be bringing them home?"

"Aye, and she will know no different, because this is what I want her to think." Redbeard said, directing Quinton to a chair at the conference table.

As Quinton sat, Redbeard walked over to a cabinet and removed two mugs. After filling them with ale, he pushed a pint of lager over to Quinton before taking his seat at the head of the table.

"Ye been with me since the beginning, Quinton. Ye helped me escape the hangman, and for yer loyalty, ye have been taken care of and have become my most trusted advisor. What I've told ye is only known by three."

As Quinton drank his ale, Redbeard walked over to the map on the wall.

"When ye think back through history, it only took one rock from space to wipe out the mighty dinosaurs in the 7th. Even though we don't have something as large and as powerful, we make up for it in numbers! Our fleet will drop down like rain from the heavens. Three prongs: 'Fire', 'Water', and 'Earth'," he said, taking his sword out and tapping the three points of the triangle. "After the assault, what doesn't immediately wipe out our enemies will dwindle their numbers over time as the ash snuffs out their sun," he said, pinching the flame on a candle until it went out. "With no sunlight, their crops will wither. Ash-soaked rain will fall upon them and poison their waters."

Redbeard sat back in his chair with his hands behind his head.

"All we have to do is have patience; to sit back here in paradise and wait. The survivors of the realms will wage war upon one another for the few scraps of food remaining. After several years, we will send our forces to these realms, and pick apart the last of their resistance."

"This is quite ambitious, Captain. But if I may point out a minor detail, we don't have enough youngins to carry out yer plan."

"Aye, true. We do not have those numbers. But my dear wife has a factory full of them."

"She's on board with this?"

"Of course! She wants to see me rise to glory and achieve my dream."

Quinton shot him a blank stare, to which Redbeard chuckled.

"Right ... Truth be told, that cantankerous fishwife of mine wants a chunk of land to rule over so she can fill her coin purse. Plus, these children mean nothing to her."

Redbeard finished his stout and looked out the window.

"The hour is upon us. What time is it in the 7th?"

Quinton reached into his vest and pulled out one of seven pocket watches tucked into pouches sewn into the lining. Each realm had its own timepiece.

"It's just about midnight, Cap'n."

"Perfect. Where's my lovely bride?"

"Back at the Dragon, sir."

"Prepare to sail and bring the new lot aboard. We shall make the jump and deliver the shrew her tidings."

"Aye, Cap'n."

Back on the Dragon's Curse, Redbeard stood at the rail drinking his coffee as he watched the morning sun. "Aye, it's gonna be a good day."

He turned his head toward town and spotted Quinton and several other pirates marching a line of children through the streets. There were twenty of them in total, ranging anywhere from thirteen years old to eight. Most of them were still wearing their school uniforms. Others wore ragged clothes and looked as though they had been plucked out of the sewers.

"Keep movin'," the pirate barked.

They marched up onto the ship, the younger ones crying. Some even called out for their mothers.

"Quit yer bellyachin'!" Quinton said. "Ye should be thrilled to be takin' this adventure for our glorious captain!"

The rest of the children kept their eyes down to the ground. As they boarded the ship.

"Take 'em below!" Quinton yelled before standing next to Redbeard.

"Everything is ready on yer command, Cap'n."

"Where did ye find this lot?"

"Some school a few islands over, as well as a few stragglers along the way."

Redbeard nodded. "Any trouble?"

"Nah. I told the teacher it was for the cause. She started to say sumthin', but the cock of a pistol seems to make 'em knot their tongues."

"C'mon with the lot of ye," a guard yelled, hurrying the children up the gangplank. "Breakfast comes early and there's lots to be done!"

Crownickers rubbed her tired eyes as she emerged from Redbeard's cabin with a crooked scowl.

"I trust ye slept well?"

"It's only been a few hours! My dreams just started to welcome me before all this racket woke me up!" But her eyes went wide as she watched the children being marched past them. "Where did ye find this precious cargo? I should get 300 a head for this lot." She then turned to Redbeard. "It's good to see ye finally keepin' yer word and hold up yer end of the bargain."

"Now is this any way to act after I brought ye such a lovely gift? I suppose this'll hold ye for a while?"

"Aye. Once I give the headcount to the state auditors and get my money, we'll arrange for ye to get the lot of 'em back for their 'adventure,' let's call it."

Redbeard laughed.

"How long before yer ready for 'em?" she asked.

Redbeard stroked his beard. "I'd say the steamer trunks will be ready in five to six weeks and I'll be needin' a week or two to get this lot ready. Are ye ready to play yer part?"

"I should receive my earnings in a few weeks. That'll give me enough time to train these urchins for ye," she said with a giggle. "Plus, with all the money I pilfered away from these rapscallions, I'll have enough to leave that deplorable place behind. After I get mine, it can crumble to the ground for all I care. I'll set myself up on the pretty little island we visited and wait for ye to finish yer plans and present me with my queendom."

They both let out a belly roll.

"Always scheming, ain't ye?"

"I blame you."

"When I call for 'em, how many can ye send?"

"All of 'em if ye so desire. With this gaggle, I'll have two-hundred and seventy-three. Whatever ones are left behind will be let loose in the street when we're done with all this."

"Ye better just send them all when I come callin'. Whatever ones don't work out, I'll put 'em to work, or give 'em to Krinsworth."

"Krinsworth? What does he want with 'em?"

"The good doctor tells me he has some fresh ideas he wants to try out."

"Oy, here we go again. Ye put too much faith in that man! He's the doorman for the devil, if ye ask me."

"He serves a purpose, doesn't he?"

Crownickers grunted. "Speaking of which, where's that traitorous daughter of mine?"

"Back in the keep. She doesn't need to be privy to this part of the plan."

"Excuse me, Cap'n ..."

Crownickers sneered as Quinton walked up to the pair.

"What is it?"

"We're ready to shove off."

"Well, my dear. Should we retire to my cabin?"

Crownickers frowned before turning and heading down the hall.

"Quinton, I don't want to be disturbed until everything is finished."

"Aye, Cap'n."

It was still dark when the Dragon's Curse secretly splashed down in the river next to Iron Hills. It's at this point where I feel it necessary to remind you since the steel mill was one of a handful of jump points within the seventh realm, it played an integral part in Redbeard's plan. With Crownickers as an ally, she kept a close eye on it. Shortly after their arrival, Quinton knocked on Redbeard's door. Before his knuckles pulled away from the wood, Crownickers flung the door open.

"Whaddya want?"

Quinton closed his eyes and bit his lip. "The Cap'n asked me to let him —"

"Get in 'ere!"

Redbeard slid his boot on and chuckled. "Don't let her get to ye. What's the update?"

"We've unloaded the cargo, and the steel is on board, Cap'n. We're ready to make the jump back home on yer command."

Redbeard looked back at Crownickers and took her hand. "Well, my dear, duty calls. Until we meet again," he said, tipping his hat and kissing her hand.

Crownickers rolled her eyes. "Yer not fooling anyone with that gallantry. I'll be ready. Just let me know when ye want 'em." She grabbed her bag and headed up on deck. Once she was gone, Redbeard turned to Quinton.

"As soon as that shrew is back on land, chart our course back to Breakaway Bay. There are a few things I want to set in motion."

BEFORE HE WAS INUNDATED with early morning chores, Preston rushed into town and met Amelia behind the Rusty Bucket for breakfast. With the Dragon's Curse away from port, they could relax and enjoy their momentary freedom.

"Where did Redbeard sail off to?"

Amelia shrugged her shoulders and dug her fork through her fruit salad, pushing aside the raisins. "Who knows? It's so much nicer around here when he's gone. Nobody's on edge."

"That's for sure." Preston said. "I'm glad they didn't drag me along." However, he would not have been so delighted had he known how close to home the Dragon's Curse was at this moment.

"Hey, what's the story with Savannah and your grandfather?"

"What do you mean?"

"Why don't they get along?"

Amelia set her baguette down. "I've tried to get them back together. They both blame each other for what happened to my father. It's a gigantic mess. The one thing they share is their insufferable stubbornness, so I don't think either of them will ever move past their anger."

"What did happen to your father?"

Amelia turned away. "I don't want to talk about it."

"Right. Sorry."

On top of the keep, the morning sun reflected off the massive copper tanks from the factory.

"Hey, what are those tanks for, anyway?" Preston asked, nodding toward the factory.

"They're the boilers for the steam used to run the factory and town. Since there is unlimited lava flowing through here, everything pretty much runs on steam power."

"Do they build anything in there?"

"Not really sure. I do know it's where they process the rock my grandfather is so infatuated with."

"How do they do that?"

"Come on," she said, grabbing Preston by the hand. "I'll show you."

They jumped onto one of the steam trolleys, getting off at the last stop, which was several blocks from the keep.

"Why don't they extend the tracks to the gate?"

"Some sort of security precaution or something."

Once they made their way into the factory, they descended the spiral stairs until they reached a floor where Amelia led Preston through a maze of carved out tunnels. After what seemed to be hours of walking, the path ended in front of a massive door guarded by two hulking men. Both of them stood as tall as Chuggs, but were not as muscular.

"Amelia?" one guard grunted. "What are ye doin' down ere?"

"The Captain wants me to check on the timeframe for the last load."

The guard squinted an eye at her. "That don't sound right. E's never asked for those before."

Preston stared at Amelia, subtly jerking his head for them to leave, but she ignored him.

"That's fine. You probably know what my grandfather wants better than he does. Come on, Preston. Let's go back and tell Redbeard we weren't given an answer because Gimbels here has it under control. Grandfather is already in a horrible mood, so I can't wait to see how he reacts," she said with a wicked smile, turning and walking away from the man with Preston right behind her.

"Wait!"

She stopped and turned back, watching as the two guards stood silent, their brows furrowing as they tried to decide what to do. With her patience waning, (she is her mother's daughter after all) Amelia glared at the two buffoons.

"Well?"

Gimbels' partner shrugged his shoulders, causing Gimbels to reluctantly agree. "Alright then."

They both set their pikes down and grabbed hold of the thick metal beam securing the door. With a hearty grunt, they heaved the drawbar up off its perch. Even with their immense strength, they struggled to move it aside, their muscles straining from the weight of the bar. Once it was free, they set it against the wall with a solid thud and dragged the door open. A blast of hot air washed over them, making it hard to breathe. By the amount of sweat pouring off them, you'd think this was as hot as it could get, but it felt like a crisp fall day compared to what awaited them inside. Had Preston not known better, he would've thought they were stepping directly into the sun. Preston dragged his feet as he followed Amelia inside. Harsh memories of his first day in captivity flashed into his head as the heat enveloped him.

"I hate this smell," Amelia said. "Reminds me of rotten eggs."

"Yeah, it's the sulfur from the lava," he said, barely able to choke out the words through the thick air.

The inside chamber was a large cave, its walls formed from solidified lava. Amelia led Preston up a narrow staircase sculpted out of the igneous rock. Once they reached the top, she walked over to a platform which overlooked a deep pit. Below, prisoners bound in chains were pushing carts full of Zimponium over to tables to be sorted. Crew captured from the galleon stood in pools of their own sweat as they picked through the piles, making sure nothing but Zimponium was collected. They kept their eyes down, feverishly working as guards walked up and down the line, carrying a cat-o'-nine-tails to keep them "encouraged." Several men bore wide scars along their backs as reminders of Redbeard's ambitions.

"What happens here?"

"This is where the Zimponium is melted out of the stone."

She led Preston across the platform where beneath them was a huge metal vat resting upon a set of rails. The bottom of the vat was fitted with mesh grates. Once the prisoners filled the container with Zimponium, eight other captured crew grabbed hold of metal bars extending out and pushed. The vat was so heavy at this point, their feet slipped as they tried to dig their toes into the ground. Slowly, the metal wheels turned, squealing as they rolled along.

"Put yer backs into it ye dogs!"

The crack of the whip caused the exhausted crew to groan out as they struggled to move the weighted tub to the end of the track. Two men collapsed before making it to the wall, but once the cart stopped, the rest of them scattered before a pair of prisoners yanked on a lever, causing a series of pulleys to open a metal trap door above them. As it slid to the side, molten lava spewed out of the opening, flowing down from the channel and covering the Zimponium. By the time the vat was filled, the lever had grown so hot, the prisoners wrapped their shirts around their hands to ease the pain from their burns. Within minutes, the stone surrounding the Zimponium melted away, leaving behind the precious metal. The melted rock and excess lava filtered through the grate at the bottom of the vat, disappearing into a deep underground chasm.

"Who would want to do that job?" Preston asked, watching the two men working the lever.

"Nobody," Amelia said, looking at the prisoners, who were covered in scars and burns. "That's why they send the prisoners here. Or whoever is unfortunate enough to get on Redbeard's bad side. Every now and then, lava splashes off the vat and those two bear the brunt of the burns. They don't usually last long in here," Amelia told him. "It's basically a death sentence."

"Why do it then?"

"Because if they can survive for six months, they earn their freedom — sort of. They don't get to leave the island, but they're given a job aboard one of Redbeard's ships. The other prisoners have to suffer for five years to make it out of here."

"Has anyone ever made it to the six months?"

Amelia shook her head. "Not too many. The last one I remember was Chuggs."

"Is that what happened to his arm?"

"Yeah. It just melted off."

Preston cringed at the thought of this. "Has anyone refused to work down here?"

"Unfortunately, yes," she said, pointing to a pool of bubbling lava.

Above the pool was a cage, built just large enough to hold one person, but only if they stood straight. Inside this cage was a charred skeleton. Its mouth hung open as a preserved reminder of a once torturous scream.

"If anyone refuses, then they take a rest in 'Satan's cradle.'"

Preston stared at the skeleton.

"Do they starve to death in there?"

Amelia snickered. "They wish. The cage is slowly lowered over the lava. It takes hours for it to reach the pool. At first, the sweat from their bodies evaporates as soon as it comes out. I heard it feels like your whole body is being pricked by hot needles. Once their body can't produce any more sweat, their blood boils, eventually cooking the person from inside. If they somehow survive all this, the cage will dip down into the lava and burn the prisoner alive. Either way, the pain is excruciating. It's done here, in front of the others, so they can see what happens if they refuse orders. It's fiendish, but it keeps them in line."

"Eh! Whaddya think yer doin?"

Preston jumped as Amelia looked over to the door and saw one guard from the entrance pushing some prisoners away from the water bucket.

"We better go. Those two idiots might get suspicious."

After leaving, Amelia took him up several levels to a part of the factory Preston had never been. It was cold and damp, unlike the rest of the mountain. Certainly, a welcomed relief from where they had just been. Water droplets zigzagged down the walls, pooling into tiny puddles along the walkway. They both peeked around the corner where rusted iron doors lined either side of the chamber. A pair of double doors at the end of the path were closed tight.

"Where are we?"

Amelia drew in a deep breath. "The transition center."

You must understand, this was a place Amelia never would venture down willingly. It was a heinous place of torturous screams and sadistic experiments; but she needed Preston to know — to understand. Once she saw it was clear, she skirted around the corner and crept over to the double doors. Twisting the knob, she pushed one door open and walked into the large space. Three blood-stained tables were centered in the room. Constructed from old wooden planks, each table was roughly seven feet long and four feet high. Leather cuffs attached to thick chains were bolted to all sides. Most certainly there to restrain the poor soul suffering at the hand of Krinsworth. Several tall wooden shelves positioned throughout the space were stocked with an assortment of sprockets, gears, cogs, and springs. It was a cornucopia of mechanical workings similar to the ones Preston had often used in his uncle's workshop. Along the back of the chamber were several empty prison cells. Preston walked up to them and stared through the iron bars. The small cells were windowless; the back wall made of solid granite. Straw was scattered along the floor, some piled on the wooden bed as one tried to create a bit of comfort for themselves; possibly their last.

"How did all of this start?"

"Redbeard nearly died during a battle," Amelia told him, lifting one of the leather cuffs and dropping it. "He was taken prisoner and chained to a wall in a dungeon where he was left to die. Fortunately for him, there was another who shared his fate — Krinsworth. In his previous life, he had a medical degree, but it was revoked because of some experiments he conducted. Once he lost it, he took to building and creating. When he saw the shape Redbeard was in, he bribed some guards for materials to help him 'fix' the Captain. Whatever he did worked, as you can see. Once Redbeard was strong enough, he escaped and kept Krinsworth with him should the need arise to use his skills once again."

"What did he do to Redbeard?"

"Initially, he just stopped him from bleeding to death, but his leg had turned gangrene, so he had to remove it and replace it with his peg. Over the years, Krinsworth has modified the leg. Now it can work all kinds of mechanical contraptions."

"Yeah, I noticed."

Amelia snickered. "Krinsworth was so excited by those results, he wanted to do some more experiments. So, while the two of them remained captive, he took some other prisoners apart and put them back together. Against their will, of course, but he paid some guards to help him, including Quinton."

"What did he use to pay them?"

Amelia's face twisted as though she were sucking on a lemon. "Mostly with gold fillings he collected from the teeth of patients who didn't make it."

"That's disgusting."

"Yeah. I wish that were the worst of it. Anyway, some of his trials worked, some didn't. Since I've been here, I've heard the screams of the people he works on; it's horrendous! You've seen the results. Those gears he implanted on the crew run their vital organs, so if they're wounded in battle, all Krinsworth has to do is replace the workings without having to cut the person open. Redbeard says it makes for stronger, nearly indestructible soldiers. Now, this maniac is experimenting with ways to control the mind as well. Once he perfects this process, Redbeard will be able to manipulate whoever he wants."

"At first, I thought Redbeard just wanted to loot the realms."

"He kind of does. I mean, he needs money and resources to keep his empire thriving, but I don't think it's his true focus."

"What is it then? Someone I spoke to thinks it's for technology."

"Makes sense. I mean, look at this place. Half of it is stuck in the past, and the other half is, well, you've seen."

Preston examined the tables, pulling on the chains.

"Who gets changed?"

"Pretty much everyone who has been on his crew for a while. Except for the ones he gets from battles. Those who agree to fight with him will not get transitioned for a few years. Once he's certain they are worthy. The other ones, the prisoners who refuse to fight, are often given to Krinsworth to further his experiments."

"What about you and Savannah?"

"He won't change her. Not anytime soon, at least."

"Why not?"

"Crownickers doesn't want her touched. I guess she still has some motherly flame burning deep inside her that she hasn't managed to snuff out yet. Plus, I think the Captain is afraid if he tries it, Savannah will mutiny. She has a pretty strong following."

"And you?"

Amelia grew quiet. She drew in a deep breath as she stared into Preston's eyes. Everything seemed to vanish around them as she pulled her long hair off her neck and turned toward him. Embedded in her skin on the back of her neck was a small box. She opened the cover and within this box were several spinning gears. She readjusted her hair and stared at the ground.

"Even though Krinsworth hasn't figured out the total process yet, I was one of the first to get fitted. Redbeard never wanted me here, but Savannah insisted I be near her, so he declared it was either this, or ..."

Preston sat silent.

Amelia raised her head and looked at him, but Preston turned away.

"Yeah, that's the kind of response I usually get." She reached over and raised his chin, drawing in a deep breath as her mouth dropped open, but no words came out. Preston still avoided her stare. She frowned and nodded before turning and walking over to the door.

"Amelia, wait, I just —"

"Don't worry about it!" she said, flattening her hair across the back of her neck.

Stomping through the tunnels, Amelia kicked a few stones as she wandered through an enormous cavern.

"Ey, girl. Whaddya doin' down ere all by yerself?"

Amelia closed her eyes and groaned. "Chummers! I should've recognized your stench. Well, if you must know, right now I'm doing my best to hold my breath. When's the last time you took a bath?"

"Oh, feelin' sassy, are ye? I like that," he said with a wide grin as he strolled up next to her. "Ye know, ye got me in a world of hurt for that li'l stunt ye pulled with that boyfriend of yers."

"What are you talking about?" she asked, her arms crossed.

"Hidin' in the Cap'n's trunk. Ye almost got me keelhauled. Now I'm stuck down in this hell hole on guard duty ferever. So, what are ye gonna do to make up for it?" Chummers reached forward and rubbed Amelia's shoulder with his dirty, sweaty hand.

"Get your slimy paw off me!" she said, pushing him away.

Taken aback, his expression turned sour, and he let out a low grunt. "I think ye owe me a debt, princess," he said, rubbing the greasy scruff on his face as he sauntered up to her, forcing Amelia to step back.

"You know, I believe you're right, Chummers. How about I ask Savannah to kill you quick for laying your filthy hand on me instead of what she would normally do, like give you a ride in Satan's Cradle? Or perhaps you'd prefer to dip your toes into the lava flow," she said, nodding over to the red glow deep below them.

Chummers looked down at the river of magma with its ripples of heat whispering into the air.

"At's a good idea, missy. Maybe when I'm through with ye, I'll drop ye into the flow. They'll think yer anger got the best of ye and ye just run away and all," he said, raising an eyebrow and chuckling. With a wicked smile, he licked his lips and crept up to Amelia. When he got close enough, he grabbed her by the throat. She gasped as Chummers sniffed her hair. "Mmm ... smells like coconut."

"Leave her alone!"

Chummers jumped back, tossing Amelia aside as he whipped around, drawing his sword. He looked past Preston, almost expecting to see someone else.

"Oy, yer alone? Eh, look, dearie. It's yer boyfriend. And he brought himself a stick."

Preston stood with his feet planted firm as sweat dripped into his eyes. He shakily held the rounded end of a broom handle toward the pirate. Chummers roared with laughter at the sight of this. "An' here I thought my blade was to be ignored," he said, twisting his rusted sword in the air as he inspected it.

He wasn't wrong. The thing he called a sword looked more like an ancient relic that had been dug out of the mud. Nonetheless, it put Preston's stick to shame. Chummers coughed out a few more chuckles before regaining his composure, but Preston wasn't amused and held his ground. With a furrowed brow, Chummers squatted low with his blade pointed at Preston.

"Right then. Looks like the li'l man wants to dance." He turned his head and winked at Amelia, who was still on the ground, holding her neck. "Don't worry, princess. This won't take long."

Before Chummers could turn, Preston raised the broomstick high above his head and swung down with all his strength. The wooden pole made a dull crack as it broke in half over Chummers' thick skull, causing the pirate to squinch as his head fell into his shoulders. He brought his hand up and felt his scalp, pulling it away to check for blood.

"Oh, yer gonna pay for that, laddie," he sneered as he swung his sword, barely missing Preston's chest. Preston dropped the broken stick and backed away as Chummers took another swing. This time the rough steel passed closer, the wind ruffling Preston's shirt. "What's a matter, boy? Never 'ad a proper fight before?"

Preston didn't know what to do at this point. He had never been in any kind of fight, so he kept backing away. Perhaps it would've been wise to retreat in a different direction. For now, he had to pause as the heels of his boots started to burn. Turning around, he noticed he was precariously teetering at the edge of the lava flow.

"Looks like ye got a choice to make now, don't ya? Tells ya what ... let's give ya a fightin' chance." The pirate reached into his sash and pulled out an even rustier sword than the one he held. "It ain't pretty," he said, twisting it in his hand, "but it's better than that stick of yers." He tossed it down at Preston's feet. "Now, ye can pick it up, and die fighting like a man, or ye can step yerself off the edge and take a swim in hell's porridge."

Preston looked over his shoulder before staring back at the pirate, who broke out in a maniacal laugh. Nobody in their right mind would willingly jump into that slop and suffer the intense pain of being burned alive, so Preston crouched low, slowly reaching for the sword. Seeing this, the pirate's eyes grew wide. With a deep grunt, he stomped on Preston's hand. The cracking of bone could barely be heard over Preston's painful yelp.

"Ye gotta be quicker than that, matey!"

Preston held his hand close to him as he dropped to his knees.

"Well, come on with ye, pick up the steel and let's dance."

But Preston didn't move. He looked over to Amelia, then back at Chummers, as he tried to come up with a plan.

Chummers dropped his hands. "Well, I'm gettin' bored of this. Plus, I'm keepin' m'lady waiting. Let's just end this so her and I can get on with our night. Don't ye worry though, she'll join ye later."

The pirate raised the sword high, but before he could drop his blade down onto Preston, he was side struck by Amelia, who came running from across the chamber and threw her shoulder into him. With a loud grunt, the pirate was launched off his feet and landed next to Preston, his ankle twisting as it hit the ground. Before Chummers could react, Preston lurched over, grabbing the sword. The pirate tried to stand, but his weakened ankle buckled under his weight, causing him to stumble, locking feet with Preston. Amelia ran over and grabbed the back of Chummers' shirt, yanking him away from Preston. Unbalanced, the pirate flapped his arms as he fell backwards over the edge of the ridge and into the molten magma. As he splashed down into the red-hot liquid, his piercing screams filled the chamber. Preston leaned over the edge, throwing his hand out in a feeble attempt to help the man, whose skin was instantly turning charcoal black as small flames burst from underneath. The screaming stopped as Chummers' face froze in a twisted look of agony. As the skin melted away from his cheeks, his eyes burst into flames. The ghastly sight caused Preston to reel back, and crab walk away from the ledge. Amelia stomped over and stared down at what remained of the man before spitting into the fire.

"Serves him right," she mumbled before turning to Preston. "What were you thinking?"

Preston's lip quivered as he held his hand and stared at her, shocked. "What are you talking about? I was saving you!"

"Saving me? What kind of arrogance is it where boys always think girls need to be saved? I was fine on my own," she said, storming away. Preston stood speechless until Amelia spun around and pointed her finger at the remnants of his broom. "And what kind of saving is that, anyway? You had a broom handle, you dolt!"

"At least I tried!" he yelled with his arms outstretched as she turned and walked away. "And you're welcome, by the way!" Preston kicked the broom handle, which dropped over the edge of the flow as Amelia spun around with fire in her eyes.

"Welcome for what? I didn't ask for your help. Or are you asking for praise after treating me like some sort of oddity who belongs in a circus?"

Her words took all the fight out of Preston. "It isn't like — I just couldn't believe someone would do such a thing to their own granddaughter."

"Well, believe it. And don't you have somewhere to be? Why do you follow me around all day like a stray dog?"

"You know something? You're impossible!"

"Apparently so," she said as she entered the tunnel. "And if you stay here looking all stupid and pouting, you'll get blamed for Chummers' disappearance," she yelled back, her words echoing down the corridor.

"Quiet!" Preston grumbled, scrunching down. "Seriously, what is her problem?" he whispered, hoping nobody had heard. Once he was certain he was alone, he scurried out of the chamber.

"Amelia, Amelia!" Preston called out in an anxious whisper. "Where is she?" Each cubby, hole, and corridor were thoroughly searched as he tried to find her. "She just killed someone. I helped! What if someone finds out?"

The image of Chummers' skull slowly sinking into the lava kept flashing in his head. A sick feeling swept over Preston, forcing him to pause as he tried not to heave. He leaned up against a stone wall, surrounded by nothing but prison cells and medieval iron torches hanging off the walls.

"Chummers would've killed me. He deserved what happened to him."

Back on the surface, the road leading away from the mountain fortress was empty.

"Someone's going to find out he's dead and that I'm involved. They're going to do the same thing to me."

Amelia was nowhere to be seen as Preston arrived at the edge of town, glancing in each store front window he passed as he searched for her. If he had been paying attention, he would have noticed Savannah, who had just jumped off the trolley and emerged through the steam.

"We have to get our story straight," Preston said with his head turned.

"What are you going on about?" Savannah asked.

Preston's heart exploded as he twisted his neck and came face-to-face with Savannah.

"Why are you so sweaty?"

Preston stood there fidgeting as he desperately tried to answer, but no words were coming out.

"Where were you? Somewhere swinging the lead?"

"Swinging the lead?"

"Slacking off, being lazy, I can guess."

"No, sorry. I was just."

"What's wrong with your hand?"

Red and swollen, Preston tried to hide his hand behind him. "It's nothing. I fell on a wet floor is all. It'll be fine."

Savannah leered at him. "So, you were swabbing the floors, eh? Where's this mop of yours then?"

Preston's eyes widened as he glanced around. *Did I leave the handle down there? What if someone finds it? Say something, you idiot!*

After a moment of awkwardness, Savannah shook her head. "I would've never guessed you could act even stranger than usual. Get back up to the Captain's office and make sure you didn't leave your mop in there. As soon as he wakes, he'll be headed here."

"He's not in port."

Savannah spun around.

"Whaddya goin' on about?"

"They sailed the Dragon's Curse away early this morning."

Savannah looked toward the bay and cocked her head. "Regardless, we need to be ready for his return. Get up there and scrub the place clean."

"Yes, ma'am."

Preston walked away, leaving Savannah staring out into the bay.

You always knew when Redbeard walked through the gates of the massive fortress because an unusual silence would permeate through the quad. Most of the time, the meandering miscreants guarding the fortress were either drunk or partaking in childish pranks on one another for their amusement. It's hard to keep cutthroats attentive when they're guarding a building built upon a volcanic mountaintop on a remote island in a realm controlled by a sadistic red-haired pirate. But once word spread of his arrival, each guard made certain they were in their assigned spot, bowing to the captain as he sauntered past them in mid-conversation.

"They have free will," Redbeard told Krinsworth before snickering. "That is until I decide they don't."

The two men shared a laugh.

"Are they almost finished?"

"We've just completed the last of the beacons. Upon your command, we will have them placed within the realms."

"I want to see."

After entering the glass building, Krinsworth took Redbeard to a hidden elevator. The faux brick wall spun, allowing the two men to enter the lift and descend deep below the surface. Singular lights marked each floor until they lowered so far below the surface, the lights disappeared, and the elevator abruptly stopped with a thud. Stepping out, Krinsworth threw a switch, which illuminated the corridor. At the end of it was a large steel door, and behind that, a burst of colorful lights flashed from within.

"Look at those beauties!" he said with a broad smile and his arms outstretched.

Lined up in two rows were three hundred beacons. Multicolored lights on the mechanisms flashed their unique sequence of six lights.

"Are they working, as did the elders?"

“Yes, sir," Krinsworth said, picking one up. "The pattern of lights will be set to the particular steamer trunk it is assigned. There will no longer be the need for the collection cups.”

Next to the beacon Krinsworth held was one of the new trunks, which flashed the same sequence of lights as the beacon. It was similar to the steamer trunk Preston arrived in; however, this one was made of Zimponium with a stainless-steel frame.

“Excellent news, doctor. And what of the beacons? How did the tests go?”

“I was very pleased with the results. Granted, these were tests from one side of the island to the next. However, the system was 100% accurate.”

Redbeard turned and glared at Krinsworth.

“From one side of the island to the other? I can get the same outcome with smoke signals. My concern is between realms. I instructed ye to run tests under those parameters.”

“I did as well, sir.”

“And?”

“Even though the designs you acquired were quite detailed, I believe some of the finer details were missing.”

“The results, Krinsworth!”

“73%”

Redbeard clenched his fists and then let out a deep growl. “I’d expected better from ye.”

“Sir, you realize that even with —”

“Enough!” he said, stroking his beard as he paced. “I will deal with this in another way. Ye disappoint me, Krinsworth!”

Krinsworth dropped his head as Quinton walked into the room.

“Quinton! What is the final number?”

"Of explosives? About 1,000 hectals in each trunk, sir," Quinton said, reaching into the one next to Redbeard and releasing the false bottom. The sound of metal scraping echoed as he lifted the panel out and showed Redbeard the bricks of explosives jammed tight into the compartment.

"And yer certain this will be enough?"

"Based on my trials and calculations, more than enough," Krinsworth interrupted, causing Redbeard to scowl at the man. "The Zimponium proved to be even sturdier than we had hoped. It maintains its structural integrity under immense pressure better than anything I've ever seen! After detonation, the pressure growing within the trunk will be extraordinary! It will build up so much from its containment that once the metal ruptures, it will have created an explosion one thousand times greater than the one that swallowed Port Royal!"

Redbeard nodded. "What is left to be done, then?"

"Just to attach the triggers to the control panels, sir. Once they are connected, we'll install the return panel," Krinsworth said, eager to get back into Redbeard's good graces.

Redbeard thought for a moment before turning to Quinton. "How much extra explosives can be added to the chest if we didn't have the return panel?"

"Maybe another 200 hectals."

Redbeard brought his hands behind his back and circled the trunk. "We have a new plan, then."

Krinsworth's mouth dropped as though he were gasping for air. He hesitated asking his question, worried he'd antagonize Redbeard any further. Nonetheless, he needed to make certain he heard correctly. "But ... sir ... the extra amount won't really change the outcome. The results will be just as devastating. Plus, how will the children get back?"

Redbeard paused.

"My plan never specified them coming back," he said, smiling. "Quinton, make it happen!"

"I see," Krinsworth said, creaking out a nervous smile. "Just one thing, Captain. I have some concerns about losing so many children. If you don't mind me —"

"Are ye getting soft on me, doctor?"

"Good heavens, no. It's just that I'm making great strides in my work and —"

"Never ye mind. Once this is done and I rule the realms, ye'll have plenty of playthings to keep ye occupied."

Krinsworth exhaled deeply. "Very good, sir," he said, bowing to Redbeard.

After the doors were sealed and the men left, Amelia emerged from behind the corner and threw her back against the wall.

"He's going to kill us all!"

Preston was soldering wires when Savannah stormed into the room.

"Hey, Fishbait, where's the old man?"

"He went down to the storage room to gather up some supplies."

"You're supposed to be the one helping him. Why didn't he send you?" she asked, squinting an eye at him.

"He thought it would take too long to explain what he needed, so he said he would just do it himself."

"Hmm ... I best not find out you've been lying to me!"

Preston cocked his head at her.

"Why don't you like me?"

"And why would I be doing that?"

"I don't know. We spend a lot of time together, so I thought you would have warmed up to me by now."

Savannah snorted. "You know, it all makes sense now."

"What does?"

"Well, when I first saw you, I thought you were a boy. But you act more like a princess every day, so I guess in this one rare instance, I was proven wrong. Perhaps later, we'll go into town, and I'll get you fitted for a nice pretty dress."

Preston smiled, quelling a laugh.

"Since I have you here, the Captain has given you a new assignment."

"What do you mean? I'm done being a cabin boy?"

"For the time being," she said. "There has been a selection process put into place for runts like you to pilot the steamer trunks in support of his master plan. I'm not sure why he chose you to be one of the pilots. I can only assume he hasn't been privy to the many tales of your glorious incompetence."

Preston dropped his screwdriver. "Me? He wants me to do that?"

Savannah rolled her eyes.

"Have you not been listening? I clearly just said that."

"What I meant is, I'm surprised."

"You and me both. Anyway, there'll be training sessions coming up on how to operate the steamer trunks, but in the meantime —"

"Oh," Rupina said as he entered the room carrying a wooden crate full of parts. "Is there something I can help you with, ma'am?"

"I'll get with you later," she told Preston. "Let's go, old man. There's a new plan for you."

Rupina set the box down, nervously glancing at Preston. "Uhm, okay," he said, his voice shaky.

"Where are we going?" Preston asked, walking behind them.

"Not you, Fishbait. Just this one. Return to the Dragon and have a dance with your mop. I'll fetch you later."

Savannah turned and led Rupina out of the room.

"Krinsworth must've completed his work! They're going to change him," Preston said as he watched them disappear down the hall.

The unbearable silence ate away at Rupina as Savannah led him down a long, shadowed corridor. The farther they went, the more he shook, to the point where he felt as though he would pass out.

"As I told the Captain, I've made significant progress," he said as they arrived at an elevator and took it down to the bowels of the fortress. When the doors opened, Krinsworth was standing there to greet them, causing Rupina to step back.

"Wonderful!" Krinsworth said with a wide smile. "Shall we begin?"

Savannah smirked and pushed Rupina out.

"I, I don't believe I've ever been down this far," he muttered, his eyes wide as his fingers shook against his lips.

At the end of the hall, Savannah unlocked the latch on the heavy metal door. Heaving it open, she pushed Rupina in. He froze when he saw what was ahead of him.

"What are these?" Even though he asked the question, Rupina knew exactly what he was looking at. After all, he had installed one similar in his clock tower back home. He so desperately wanted to check his pockets, wondering if he had left his scribbling of the design behind.

"So, you don't recognize them, eh? Well, these are beacons to guide our fleet. The captain wants you to alter the control panels so they align with these beacons and improve the accuracy. Right now, it's operating at 73%. I would advise you to get that number much higher by the time he comes calling!"

"But this is something completely new to me. I must have time to study this first before I can make any sort of modifications or adjustments."

Savannah snickered. "Something tells me you'll figure it out." She then turned to Krinsworth. "I'll leave you to it."

As she walked past Rupina, she pulled her dagger out and pinched the handle between her fingers, waving the blade in front of him like a pendulum swinging on a clock.

"Tick-tock, my dear fellow ... tick-tock."

She broke out into a hearty laugh as she closed the door until some rustling at the end of the corridor caught her attention. She drew her sword and crept along, pausing when a shadow appeared ahead. As she raised her blade, Amelia stepped out into the light.

"Amelia! You're not supposed to be down here. What are you doing?"

Amelia glanced around, tears filling her eyes. "Mom! We need to talk."

PRESTON RUSHED BACK TO the workshop and burst through the door, but Rupina was nowhere to be seen.

"No, no, no ..."

For what felt like hours, Preston paced until a loud clank made him jump. The door swung open, and Rupina walked into the room. As soon as the guard left, Preston went to the door to make sure he was out of earshot before turning to his uncle.

"What happened? I thought they were going to experiment on you."

"As did I." His uncle collapsed into a chair and rubbed his forehead. "I believe such news would be better than what I have to offer."

"How so?"

"Redbeard has assembled the beacons!"

"What? How?"

"I fear he has somehow found my design.

Preston thought for a moment. "There's more," he said. "Just today, Redbeard assigned me to pilot one of those trunks."

Rupina raised his head, elated. "Then perhaps all is not lost. If he knew of our relationship, he would never assign you to pilot a trunk. We just have to make certain to set it with the correct navigation sequence so you'll return home."

"WE will return home! I'm not going anywhere until we figure out a way for both of us to return. The only problem is we don't know which trunk is assigned to go where."

"True," Rupina said, pacing the floor. "Perhaps we can forge a sort of skeleton key, which can override the navigation system once it's inserted and lock into the beacon back home?"

"How can you be sure it's still operating? You've been gone a long time."

Rupina paused. "I'm not. But it's our only chance."

"Do you know how much time we have?"

"No. But Savannah made it perfectly clear I didn't have long."

"Have you tried this override when you built our steamer trunk?"

Rupina stopped and turned away from Preston.

"No, I've only learned how these machines work from the time I've been here. They're quite fascinating."

"Wait, what? Well, where did it come from?"

"Where did what come from?"

"Our trunk! The one that got me stuck here!"

Rupina shot up and scrunched his face. After turning back to Preston, he drew in a deep breath. "I stole it from Redbeard."

"What?"

Rupina tiptoed toward the door to check on the guard. Once he made sure it was still clear, he walked up to Preston.

"It was when I traveled to Georgia. I heard about the tunnel I told you about; the one below the tavern leading down to the river. It didn't make sense to me the city was surrounded, yet all these pirates were able to sail away with none of them being captured. Well, while walking along River Street, I stepped into a small antique store where I stumbled upon an old journal. The owner told me the book had washed ashore in Jamaica after Port Royal was swallowed by the sea. Most of the pages were water-damaged and indiscernible. Within the few remaining pages was an entry regarding a steamer trunk capable of traveling past the stars and through distant galaxies. There was also a schematic of the trunk, and a notation saying it was constructed in Savannah, Georgia. Even though it seemed ridiculous, I became obsessed with the thought of this kind of technology. Whether true or not, I had to see for myself. When I searched for the tunnel, I found hints of its existence, but the entrance had long since been sealed off. Come to find out, to shield it even further, they built a tavern over the site. Since then, the tavern had been converted into an inn, so I decided to stay. If nothing else, it would give me easier access to the site. Over the course of several weeks, I snuck into the cellar and began my excavation. Brick by brick, I disassembled the wall in secret until I finally broke through! After some exploration, I found the steamer chest; the one you arrived in. It was an absolute work of art!"

Rupina looked up at the ceiling, reflecting on glints of joy he once had. Those moments were now rare, only brought back to him through his memories.

"Of course, I had no idea how to work it, just a few clues I cultivated after studying the journal. In order to examine it further, I had to remove the trunk from its tomb before anyone discovered what I had done. Under the cover of darkness, I dragged the trunk through the tunnel, and down to the water where I had a boat waiting. I smuggled my hidden treasure upriver, away from prying eyes, and packed the chest into a shipping crate. Before anyone could figure out what happened, I had it delivered to my home where I could study it; where I could delve into this wondrous technology."

Rupina fell back into a chair and stared at the chains around his ankles.

"Alas, I never got a chance to travel anywhere in it before I was kidnapped. Fortunately, before I was taken, I had retrofitted the trunk with a secondary lock. It can only be opened —"

"By syncing its clock to the watch on my hat. Yeah, I know."

Rupina nodded. "Right. At least Redbeard hasn't figured out the secret yet."

Preston shook his head. "But you stole it from him! What were you thinking?" He paced and ran his fingers through his hair. "He, he must've been looking for it!" he said, throwing his hands up into the air. "Is this the reason my parents disappeared?"

"No! Absolutely not," Rupina said, standing. "I assure you neither their disappearance, nor you ending up here, had anything to do with my actions in Savannah."

"Actually, it did. It was because of that trunk that I'm here! So, what happened to my parents?"

"I, I don't know," he said, kneeling before Preston and grabbing his shoulders. "All I know at the moment is we are stuck here, and we now have a way to return there. Once we do, we can focus on your parents. But nothing can happen while we're imprisoned."

Preston closed his eyes and breathed deep. "Fine. What do we need to do?"

Rupina stood and walked around the room, tapping his head. As he passed a shelf, he reached into a box of scrap parts and pulled out a brass collection cup.

"These are installed on every trunk ..." he said before pausing, "or at least they were ... Ingenious design, really. You see, the samples in these cups help navigate the machine toward its targeted location, almost like a magnet is attracted to metal."

"Is this why you had all those jars of dirt in your study?"

"Precisely. But by designing it this way, it also insured the chests could not be redirected to a different target without new coordinates and new samples. Therefore, they were limited in their ability to travel elsewhere. Take this one, for instance." He dragged his finger through the powdery residue at the bottom of the cup. "What we have here appears to be limestone," he said, rubbing the dust between his fingers and sniffing them. "Now, I know through my studies Port Royal, Jamaica is a jump point, and the island is made up of 70% limestone, so I can assume, by inference, this trunk would have been slated to go there."

"Okay, so what if we retrofit the new trunk with one of these cups? There's a storage room full of old parts. I'm certain we can find one with elements from back home and rebuild it before anyone notices."

"Perhaps." Rupina let the dust sift from his fingertips as he held his index finger to his chin, leaving a thin white line along his skin.

"What do you mean?"

"Well, even though there would be an element present in the tray, the navigation system is still the true mechanism to pinpoint the location," Rupina said, tapping his forehead. "However, once we know which steamer trunk you'll be assigned to, perhaps we can figure out a way to override the new beacon and have it revert to a guidance system based only on the sample in the collection tray."

"So, we can use an element unique to something from back home."

Rupina thought for a moment. "There's the problem. Let's say we find chromium, for instance. You might think our destination would be Iron Hills, since there are vast amounts of this element there in order to produce stainless steel. However, there are ample stores of chromium elsewhere, such as South Africa, Turkey, India ... So, without coordinates entered, the steamer chest could be headed to any of those locations. Or even below the ocean, if there is an element present there as well. And those are just a few examples within our realm. Who knows for certain what the other realms hold?"

Preston thought for a moment. "I don't believe that's the case. If some of the other realms had chromium, Redbeard wouldn't be so dependent on Crownickers. Ours must be the only realm where it's produced. We just need to find my assigned trunk."

"Well, as long as you're certain, then be off with you! When I see you again, I pray you have good news," he said with a broad smile.

Preston scrambled out of the room as Rupina returned to work.

Savannah rushed into Redbeard's office, but he was nowhere to be found. From the window, she looked out to the bay to make certain the Dragon's Curse was in port.

"She's there, so he must be around here, somewhere."

The view of the bay aroused her memories, taking her back to a time as a little girl playing in the sand along the beach. But much like smoke drifting into the air, those memories, the memories of a happy young girl, were fleeting. So much has changed since then. The innocence of youth was gone. What's worse is her ambition stole those memories from her daughter as well. She never shared those same experiences with Amelia. Amelia's childhood was over before it began.

"I can't lose her!"

Quinton reluctantly stepped into Redbeard's cabin.

"Beg yer pardon, Captain. Yer misses sent something."

"More steel, already? We've only just returned."

"No, sir. A note."

Redbeard pounded his fist onto the desk. "Dang blasted woman! She knows we can't be wastin' our jumps! Especially now, when we're so close."

Quinton kept his distance and cleared his throat. "Ye may want to read it, Captain."

Redbeard stood, shaking his head as he walked over to Quinton and snatched the letter out of his hand. His eyes glided across the paper before his face turned bright red.

"Run and grab Aralia. I don't believe her and the boy have been properly introduced."

Just outside the door, Rupina noticed Aralia unlocking the padlock and removing the hefty chain.

Shredder... What does she want? Rupina's throat tightened and his hands shook as he stepped away from his workstation.

Shredder swung the door open and stepped aside as Redbeard sauntered in.

"Cap, Captain! You, why you honor me with your presence," Rupina said, wiping his hands with a rag. He walked over to a long counter and waved his hands over a series of brass boxes aligned on his workbench. "As you can see, I've made great strides since our last meeting. Sorry you haven't been able to stop in for some time."

"Aye, I've been sidetracked. It's not all rum and pillaging, ya know," he told Rupina as he slapped him on the back and belted out a hearty chuckle.

Rupina nervously laughed. "Well, I hope it is nothing serious distracting you."

"No, no," he said, holding up his hand and shaking his head. "Just an aberration involving some young scamp spinning some tales. Normally, I'd ignore such a trivial matter. But I was told this youngin may have something of interest to me."

"Oh, well, best of luck to you, sir."

"Ye sure do enjoy tinkering," Redbeard said, walking around the workshop, picking up and examining several items. "It may interest ye to know this rapscallion I speak of lives in a home with a grand clock built into it," he said, straining to watch out of the corner of his eye, waiting for Rupina's reaction.

Rupina froze as Redbeard walked up behind him, staring at the back of his neck. He could feel the bristly hairs of the pirate's beard brushing his skin.

"My dear wife has gone to collect the boy. It may take some time, though. It appears there are many places to hide in this home of his."

Rupina's shoulders relaxed.

He doesn't know!

Comforted they hadn't made the connection yet, Rupina cleared his throat. "Well, what can I do to, to, uhm, help you, sir?"

Redbeard shifted, now standing in front of the man, staring deep into his eyes as though the boy was hiding somewhere inside Rupina's soul. As he stood silent, feeling each breath Redbeard exhaled, Rupina focused on his heartbeat pulsing through him. From his toes to the top of his head, the pounding grew deafening. Suddenly, Redbeard smiled and nodded, the sprockets in his beard swinging as he did. He then circled the man.

"Perhaps ye can motivate yerself to finish my mechanisms. What say ye?"

"Sir, I would like nothing better than to finish these. However, you must understand, I've just learned of them, and they are quite complicated. I implore you to give me more time. I'm doing everything I can." Rupina turned his head, trying to follow Redbeard.

The pirate stopped in front of him once again, gripping the handle of his cutlass tight. "Of course," he said. "Take all the time ye need," he said with an unsettling smile.

Rupina nodded and let out a deep breath. Redbeard took three steps before turning and facing Rupina again while stroking his beard.

"Ye know, over the years, I've been taught many things by men and women who perhaps saw great potential in me. I assure ye, not many others did," he said with a slight chuckle. "These were outstanding leaders, who I very much admired. They were each unique in their approach to leadership. All of them differed in their ways, but there was one thing they all agreed as being the greatest motivator."

Redbeard shrugged his shoulders as he examined some more of Rupina's work.

"I was young, didn't understand all this leadership nonsense, but I knew they did," he said, waving his index finger. "Fortunately, I was wise enough at the time to listen, to learn. At one point during my training, I was asked what I thought this greatest motivator was; the one thing people feared most above all others. 'That's easy,' I thought, and

I quickly answered, 'losing one's life!' I was so proud of myself. Nailed my first test ..." He paused before spinning around with wide eyes. "But ye know something; I was wrong! Losing one's life was not the answer they sought! It surprised me when I was told this wasn't the highest motivating factor. Can ye believe it? I mean, what's worse than ye dying, right?" Redbeard asked, looking surprised. "Would ye like to guess what the greatest factor was? Ye might not be so surprised."

Rupina didn't move, didn't speak.

Redbeard pursed his lips and nodded, continuing to circle Rupina. "Eh, you'll never guess," he said, waving his hand dismissively. "Let me just tell ye." He nodded to his guards at the door, who dragged Preston in and threw him to the ground.

Rupina's eyes went wide as he and Preston glanced at each other. Redbeard withdrew his cutlass and held the shiny blade next to Preston's neck, which caused his eyes to grow wide as he shook uncontrollably.

"The greatest motivator, above all else, was to lose a loved one. I never understood it. Choosing to spare another's life over yer own," he said, shaking his head. "But in all my years, ya know, they were right! It never fails to make people do things they ... don't ... want ... to ... do." He replaced the sword in his scabbard and squatted down next to Preston, who continued to shake, sweat beading above his brow. "Even after all these years, I still can't wrap my head around it. Placing another's life above yer own."

He shook his head, snickering as he stood while the guards dragged Preston from the room.

"So sorry about that," Redbeard said in a soft, pleasing tone as he turned to Rupina. "I tend to ramble on and I forgot what ye told me." Then Redbeard's brow furrowed. "When exactly did ye say you'd have my control panels completed?" he asked through gritted teeth.

Rupina swallowed hard. "Uhm, by the end of the week, captain."

Redbeard scowled at the old man with a deadly stare. Time seemed to stop until Redbeard smiled once again and shook his head. "I just don't get it. But alas, great leaders are always right. Ye have three days!" he said before turning and leaving the room.

The guard slammed the door shut, locking it as Rupina fell to his knees and dropped his head. He reached up, shakily grasping the table. After taking in a deep breath, a tear rolled down his cheek. He stood, straightened his shirt, and returned to his work.

Preston was dragged through the halls and thrown into a room similar to his in the fortress. But instead of kegs of gunpowder, or the large cannon, this one had chains dangling from the walls, and blood spattered across the floor. With everything happening, Preston could only think of one thing:

Amelia ...

Before he could process any of this, Shredder walked into the cell, standing in the doorway, smiling with the coiled whip in her hand.

"Well, hello there!" she said, raising her eyebrows and closing the door. "Let's have some fun!"

Preston woke up with his head throbbing in pain and his face pressed against the cold stone floor. As he opened his eyes, he let out a quiet moan. The smell of straw was apparent as a seemingly distant voice echoed in his head, the words popping in and out as though someone was raising and lowering the volume in his ears.

"Pre ... ake ... up! Can ... me? Eston ..."

He still couldn't make out the words as he slowly raised himself off the ground. Dizzy, he pressed his hand against his scrambled head and felt a warm wetness. Taking his hand away, he brought it close to his eyes and noticed it was covered in blood. Things became clearer, as did the voice. It was closer now, and the words slowly pieced themselves together.

"Preston!"

It was Amelia.

"Are you alright? What happened?"

Preston looked over, and in the cell next to him stood Amelia. She stuck her hand through the bars and grabbed Preston's. "What happened?"

Now that he was lucid, Preston thought back and remembered what took place. He leaned his bruised head against the solid iron bars, which caused him to wince in pain. He shut his eyes, still holding on to Amelia's hand.

"I'm so sorry. This is because of me. Redbeard got a letter from Crownickers. One of her contacts with the police department back home told her about me. He even said I was living in my uncle's house, but disappeared. I can't believe you're in here. You should've never gotten wrapped up in this."

Amelia let go of his hand and turned away.

"It was just a matter of time. Redbeard's been looking for an excuse to get rid of me since I'm a constant reminder of my father." She turned around, her eyes filled with tears. "It's not your fault. It's mine."

"How so?"

"It was an accident. Savannah and I were at dinner, and I — she knows the old man is your uncle."

"How, how did you know?" Preston asked, dropping his head.

"One day, I came to find you and I overheard the two of you talking." She grabbed the bars next to Preston's cell, leaning her head against them. "This is all because of me and my big mouth. I let it slip by accident, I swear to you. She must've told him."

Preston sighed.

"I'm so, so sorry," she said.

Preston raised his head, reaching through the bars to grab her hand.

"None of it matters now. We have to figure out what to do from here, together."

Amelia wiped her tears and nodded.

"Whether you like it or not, we're friends now," he said sleepily.

This caused Amelia to smile and shake her head. "Nah. I have better taste than that."

"Wait! Your grandfather!"

Amelia shook her head. "I haven't seen him, so I'm certain he's in the tunnels by now. I just pray he doesn't come looking for me. Redbeard won't be as subtle."

Able to see clearly now, Preston looked around. "Where are we?" he asked. Just outside his cell, his hat was displayed on a chair in front of him — taunting him.

"Krinsworth's lab."

Preston raised his head. "The transition center?"

Amelia nodded.

"If they haven't killed me yet, it must mean my uncle is still working on the control panels. Maybe we can figure out a way to escape."

Back in his workshop, Rupina worked day and night to complete the panels as promised. By the time Redbeard returned, the mechanisms were arranged along several tables. Just as Redbeard prophesied, Rupina didn't care what happened to him. He was worried about his young nephew.

"Please spare, Preston," he whispered as he heard the door unlock.

Redbeard sauntered in and smiled as he saw the devices. After all these years, his destiny was nearly fulfilled. He could taste victory. He turned to Quinton. "After Krinsworth tests the accuracy, have the crew install these. If our esteemed guest has done his work well, we'll dispatch the beacons and prepare our pilots." He then stood within a breath of Rupina's face. "I'd hate to see what happens if they don't live up to my standards."

"Should I have this wretch executed for his betrayal?" Quinton asked.

Redbeard stared at Rupina. "Not yet. His value is still there, he just needs to be more ... motivated, let's say. Offer him up to the good doctor for an 'update.' One which will insure his loyalty."

The guards grabbed Rupina and dragged him out of the room. "No, wait!" he yelled before his voice disappeared down the corridor.

Savannah walked into the room and watched Rupina being hauled away.

"What was that all about?"

Redbeard scowled. "Just some changes to the organizational structure."

"Can I trouble you for your time? I've heard some unsettling rumors and have something urgent I need to discuss with you."

"Do ye now?" Redbeard scowled as he nodded and grabbed the handle of his sword, but something outside the window caught his attention, causing his face to light up. "Ahh, there she be!"

Savannah raised her eyebrows, then rushed over to Redbeard. Sailing into the harbor was a copper-colored ship, similar to the Dragon's Curse, but this one wasn't constructed from wood.

"Zimponium," Savannah whispered.

Much like its sister ship, this version had three steam boilers on the center deck, but its masts were made from black iron, which held the billowing black sails. Steam drifted out from the top of the towering masts as she pulled up to her moorings. Savannah inched away from the window, her mouth agape.

"You, you lied to me."

Redbeard scoffed at her.

"Ye knew everything I needed ye to know."

"Where did you get the Zimponium to finish this?"

"Only a fool shows their true strengths. Isn't she a beauty?" he asked as he beamed at the sight of the vessel. "She has a sturdy skeleton of stainless steel and a thick skin of Zimponium. It will make our jumps for the next hundred years." He turned and raised his index finger, shaking his head. "Let me correct my previous statement. It will make MY jumps for the next hundred years. I fear yer no longer part of the crew."

Redbeard nodded, signaling Chuggs and Quinton to take hold of Savannah.

"What is this? You're turning me?"

"I'm not certain what the doctor has in store for ye, but I guess we'll find out soon enough."

"But I'm your daughter!"

"Ye still will be," he said, but then put his hand to his chin and raised his eyebrow. "I think." Redbeard shrugged his shoulders. "Ah, well. We'll just have to wait and see how ye turn out." He walked over and plucked the Kraken pin from her lapel. Within his mighty fist, he crushed the pin and threw it to the ground in front of her. "Take her away! She can keep her worthless daughter company while Krinsworth 'tinkers.'"

As Savannah struggled, Chuggs swung his beefy arm and struck her in the face, causing her head to drop.

"Take her to Krinsworth," Quinton said as they threw her limp body into the hall.

Two pirates standing sentry at the door nodded and grabbed Savannah by the arms. By the time they reached Krinsworth's lab, Savannah was regaining consciousness.

"Wait!" she mumbled before coming to her senses. As soon as she did, she tried to break free.

"She's always been a feisty one!" the guard said, struggling to hold her tight. "Eh, get over 'ere and 'elp us!" As the third pirate came over, Savannah kicked him in the groin, dropping him to the ground. As she continued to grapple with her other two captors, they dragged her into the lab. All the commotion caused Krinsworth to turn.

"Ah! I've been waiting for this opportunity for some time."

"No!" she screamed, kicking and pulling with all her strength.

"Mom!" Amelia yelled, grabbing the bars of her cell.

Rupina was strapped down onto one table. As the guard reached for the restraints on the other table, Savannah yanked her arm loose, freeing herself from his grip. She immediately threw a left hook at the other pirate, sending his jaw shooting upward with an unsettling crack. Stunned by this, he lost his grip on her, falling backwards, his head striking the iron bars of a cell, knocking him unconscious. She took this moment of freedom to yank a hidden dagger out from underneath her corset. In one swift move, she turned and used the knife to pluck a large gear from the first man's chest. The remaining mechanics controlling his heart and lungs broke free and scattered along the floor. He immediately gasped and dropped to the ground. With the precision of a surgeon, she pressed the tip of her dagger into the last pirate's chest. The sprockets controlling his heart jammed against the steel blade. He looked down with wide eyes, knowing he didn't have much time.

"Now, you can release my daughter, or I can cut you into slivers of meat for the crabs to feed upon! Your choice, savvy?" she asked, a raging fire burning in her eyes.

He nodded his head so fast, his hat fell to the ground and beads of sweat dripped down his forehead as he fumbled with his keys. Savannah pulled the knife from within the gears but kept it close. "You do anything stupid, and I'll pluck these from your carcass before you can blink."

They made their way over to the cell, and Amelia jumped up, grabbing hold of the bars.

"Mom!"

"We'll have you right out of there."

The guard unlocked both cell doors, releasing Preston as well.

"What about him?" Preston asked, pointing to Krinsworth, who was on the ground, in a corner, shaking.

After grabbing the pirate's cutlass, Savannah walked up to the cowering man while Preston and Amelia locked up both pirates before releasing Rupina. Krinsworth shook as Savannah stood over him.

"The realm is better off without his kind," she said as she slowly pushed the tip of the sword into his leg. With a sadistic stare, she watched Krinsworth squirm, screaming out in pain as the blade split the skin. "Is this how all your victims sounded as you conducted your experiments?" she asked, twisting the blade ever so slightly.

"No, wait!" he sputtered. "I can — I can change her back!" His face grimaced in pain.

Savannah pulled back her blade, still gripping the handle tight.

"What are you going on about?"

Krinsworth pushed himself up off the ground, struggling to his feet, all the while keeping a hand in front of him, hoping to hold Savannah at bay. "The process ... I believe it can be reversed," he said, his hand shaking as he stood, pleading to Savannah for a moment to explain. A thin stream of blood seeped through his pant leg.

"Well, let your tongue start its dance before you lose it."

"Your father had sent some of his crew to me; you know, the ones who haven't been working out too well, if you gather what I'm saying."

Savannah didn't respond with words. Her eyes said it all, and Krinsworth got the message.

"Right ... anyway, he said I could use them to test my theory. A reversal of the automation process," saying it while waving his hands in front of him as though he just performed a magic trick. Krinsworth looked at Savannah with wild eyes and raised eyebrows as a wide grin spread across his face. He nodded rapidly, giddy as he spoke. "It's really fascinating," he said, looking around as though he was waiting for an audience to applaud his efforts.

Savannah glared at the man, disgusted he would treat this process as something to be revered and rewarded. But she was desperate to make her daughter whole.

"And?"

His smile shrunk. "Right ... Well, most of the time, I've been able to remove the mechanics and reattach the organs," he said, performing a phantom surgery with his two hands dancing in the air, "thus, returning the subject to their former selves."

"And what do you consider 'most of the time?'"

Krinsworth swallowed hard. "Well, it hasn't quite worked out as well as I had hoped," he said, fidgeting with his fingers and looking around nervously.

Savannah lunged at him, blade first. "And you think my daughter is going to be mixed in with your failures?" she asked, red in the face.

"No! No, of course not! What I'm saying is the results have been promising."

"Would your previous patients agree with you?"

An unfeeling man, Krinsworth didn't know what to say, nor was he even sure how to process the question. With an impatient, sword-wielding Savannah glaring at him, Krinsworth shrugged his shoulders and gave her an awkward smile with a haphazard nod.

Of all the responses to give, this was the worst. This became painfully apparent to the arrogant man as Savannah grunted in disgust before plunging her blade deeper into his leg. Krinsworth screamed out in agony as he fell back to the floor.

"And what do you calculate the percentage of me not slowly cutting you up into little bits?"

Krinsworth held his leg and grimaced, begging for a moment. "No, please! Uhm, I can increase those odds! Yes, yes! What I mean is I can do it. I just need a little more time; a few more subjects to help me perfect the technique."

"I'm not going to let you perform your sadistic torture on others. If you can't do this, then I have no further use for you!" She raised her sword.

"Wait! Mom, please," Amelia pled.

Savannah looked at her as she stood next to Preston. She then lowered the sword. "I'm sorry, Amelia, but I cannot allow this to continue." She raised the cutlass once again.

"Let him try it on me," Rupina blurted out.

Savannah turned to him. "What did you say?"

"Let him — let him try it out on me. Then you'll know."

Savannah shot him a sideways glance, confused. "You owe me nothing. Does your memory escape you? I am the one who placed you in iron."

Rupina looked over at Preston and Amelia. "It isn't about you or me; it's about them."

Savannah thought for a moment before grabbing Krinsworth by the throat. "If this man dies, you do as well! And I assure you, yours will take longer ... Much, much longer," she sneered.

Rupina lay on the table unconscious as the effects of the anesthesia took over. Savannah stood in the corner, picking at her nails with a dagger. Meanwhile, Krinsworth had patched his own wound and placed a helmet, similar to the ones the crew wore during the jumps, over his head. Each time he exhaled, a metal flap on the back of his helmet fluttered, allowing his breath to escape behind him, away from the patient. He pushed a cart carrying an assortment of surgical tools over to the table before turning on a pair of lights attached to his helmet.

"Why don't you help me keep an eye out in the hallway," Amelia suggested to a pacing Preston. As she led him out of the room, Savannah smiled and nodded to her.

"The first thing I need to do is disconnect the holding unit from the outer layers of flesh," he said as he slid the scalpel along the sides of the stainless-steel box in Rupina's chest. Blood seeped from the opening. Once Krinsworth dabbed the blood away, he gently slid his fingers into Rupina's chest and carefully lifted the box out. "Now, I need to make certain the arteries do not prematurely separate from the pump on the back of the container unit."

As the box came out, the gears inside it kept spinning. The arteries for the heart followed, stretching slightly, but leaving the heart in place.

"You see, the way this works is brilliant. If the heart stops beating, whether it be from battle or old age, the unit here serves as an override, allowing the machine to take over and keep the blood flowing."

Savannah gripped the handle of the knife tight as she stomped closer to Krinsworth. "I didn't ask you for a speech, so stop patting yourself on the back and stay focused. Treat it as if your life depends on it, because it does!"

"Right. Of course," Rupina said, dropping his head before returning to the task at hand.

He clamped off one artery before he removed it from the pump. "I have to be quick about this," he said as his hands raced between the cart and Rupina's chest. He snipped and tugged while cutting other pieces of flesh. Finally, he took a needle and thread, using them to sew the artery to the heart before grabbing a glass jar. With his finger, Krinsworth scooped out a dab of a clear goo and spread it in Rupina's chest where he had just sewn up the artery. This caused Savannah to rush over.

"Hey! What exactly are you doing?"

"Easy!" he said, holding up his hand with the goo dripping from his fingers. "I'm just applying some hamamelis on the incision area to help stop any bleeding."

Savannah stared at him.

"Witch Hazel, with some alcohol mixed in. It's perfectly safe, I assure you. However, you being so close is not. You are risking giving him an infection."

Savannah scowled and stepped back.

"There! One down," he said as he removed the clamp and transferred it to the other artery.

Repeating the process, he removed the second artery from the pump and began to reconnect it before he stopped and pulled his hands back.

"That's not right."

"What?"

Krinsworth quickly grabbed some tools and began cutting and sewing as fast as he could.

"I asked you a question!"

"I've had this problem before. Especially on some of my older patients."

"You mean lab rats!"

"Regardless, the artery keeps tearing."

As soon as the words left his mouth, blood began spraying out of Rupina.

"Quick! Get over here!"

Savannah growled, replaced the dagger and ran to the table. Hearing the commotion, Preston ran into the room.

"What happened?"

"His artery tore!"

"Squeeze this!" Krinsworth told Savannah, handing her the artery, which was gushing blood like some sort of garden hose. "I need to get more clamps. His artery cannot handle the pressure of blood flowing."

Savannah tried to press her fingers over the tear, squeezing hard, but blood continued to seep out from under her grip. Preston ran from the room.

"Where's he going?"

Rupina started to shake violently on the table as Krinsworth returned, feverishly clamping different sections of the artery.

"Move your hand!"

Savannah pulled her bloodied hand out and Krinsworth sewed up the opening, but every time he released the clamp, the stitches ripped apart.

"I need to find some stronger thread to sew the opening closed!"

"He'll bleed out before you do, you fool!" Savannah said, jamming her hand back into the man's chest.

While Krinsworth scrambled around the workshop, Preston came running back in. Between his fingers he held a square of stainless steel mesh, about the size of a postage stamp. Before handing it to Krinsworth, he took a bottle of alcohol and doused the mesh with it.

"What is that?" Krinsworth asked.

"Roll this into a tube and stick it in the opening, then sew it up!"

Krinsworth took the mesh and, after doing as Preston suggested, he slid it into the tear before sewing the artery together. Drawing in a deep breath, he carefully released the clamp. The room was dead silent.

"It's, it's working! The bleeding stopped!"

Rupina was lying so still, Savannah came over and checked his pulse, leaving three bloody fingerprints on his neck.

"It's weak, but I can feel it."

Krinsworth ripped off his helmet with his blood-soaked hands and stared with wide eyes.

"How did you —"

"I helped out on the Dragon's Curse when they were having issues with steam hoses bursting. After a few trials and errors, I inserted some stainless steel mesh just like this, and it worked. It contained the excess pressure, and the hoses stayed together."

Krinsworth shook his head and replaced his helmet. He then finished reverting the process before sewing the opening in Rupina's chest closed.

"Well, it's finished." Krinsworth said, removing his helmet as he examined Rupina. "Hold on. He, he isn't breathing."

Savannah dashed over to Rupina and put her hand on his chest. "Why isn't he breathing?"

"I, don't, I mean ... I'm not sure why."

Preston walked over to his uncle as Savannah drew her sword and charged over to Krinsworth. "I warned you!"

Just as she raised her blade, Rupina gasped and drew in a deep breath.

With her sword at the ready, Savannah walked up to Redbeard's office, where she found Chuggs standing guard. The massive pirate took a step back as he saw her. A look of concern spread across his face as he nervously placed his hand on his sword.

"Don't!" she said, staring him in the eye.

Chuggs was strong, but Savannah easily outmatched him in swordplay. Knowing he had no chance, he gritted his teeth, scowling at her as he removed his hand. With heavy feet, Savannah pushed past him and kicked the doors open. She then spun around and slugged Chuggs in the mouth with the hilt of her sword.

"That's for earlier!"

As she entered the room, she removed her pistol and pointed it at Redbeard's head.

"You told me I'd be ruling the realm!" she said, replacing the sword into its scabbard, never taking the muzzle of the pistol off Redbeard. "You said there would be no sacrifices made."

Redbeard held his hands up and smiled. "Ahh, just as I expected, ye passed my test and proved yer worthiness!"

"Test? You had me taken! I was going to be killed!"

"And yet here we are."

Savannah disregarded his attempt to sway her. She froze, staring just past him at the double doors, which were open, displaying all the completed steamer trunks set in neat rows, ready to be launched.

"Those trunks are to carry our children to their doom. There are no bombs in place; they're the bombs! You would allow my daughter, your granddaughter, to be sacrificed! What happened to all your promises? What lies will be flowing from your lips now? What shall I believe?"

"Ye shall believe whatever I tell ye is to be believed!"

"You told me the bombs were already in place and set to go. I saw the blueprints. We discussed the plans. The youngins were to detonate the devices and return home."

Redbeard nodded. "Circumstances arose, making changes necessary. It is true when I say the trunks will be used to deliver the final blow, washing away the scourge of the realms. These beauties are the most powerful devices ever to be created. They will rain down from the skies and plunge deep below the surface. The explosions will generate the cataclysmic events which will lead to my long-awaited reign."

"What sort of leader would send hundreds of children to their death?"

Preston walked in and helped Rupina into a chair.

"That scallawag ye align yerself with changed it all," Redbeard said. "Now Amelia will join the brave souls who will bring about the change. Songs will be sung of her sacrifice!"

Savannah's mouth dropped.

"She's your granddaughter!"

"And that's how she'll be remembered!"

Savannah stood silent, her mouth agape as she stared at her father, shocked at the sheer callousness of his words.

"I tried to do this without the youngins!" Redbeard roared. "This man forced my hand!" His finger stabbed at Rupina. "I had the devices built and in place. Everything was set to go, but he stole the one thing from me that would make this plan work, so I needed to adapt. If it weren't for him, all yer precious youngins would be spared!" he said, sweeping his arm across the room of chests. "My granddaughter, yer daughter, would be spared."

Savannah stared at Redbeard, her pistol at the ready, squeezing the grip hard. With gritted teeth, she turned to Rupina, panting as her anger grew.

Seeing this brought a smile to the pirate's face. "Yes, my dear. He is to blame. All he had to do was give me what I seek, and none of this would have been necessary."

"You could've stopped all this?" she asked, turning to Rupina.

Still weak, Rupina couldn't speak. Preston looked at him, then at Savannah.

"He's manipulating you! Don't —"

"Knot yer tongue, ye scamp!" Redbeard yelled. "Ye know it to be true. Did he not steal the trunk from me? Is he not behind the actions which ripped ye from yer parents, from yer home? Did this trickster not pilfer the blueprints which would have prevented all these sacrifices about to be suffered?"

Rupina sat there, his mouth quivering.

"The only question now is, will ye help me lead?" he asked, turning to his daughter. "Are ye willing to do what is necessary to achieve our dream? For us to sit side by side, leading this new empire of ours?"

A tear rolled down Savannah's cheek as she lowered her gun. She turned and stared at Amelia, then at Preston. "I'm sorry," she whispered to Amelia before raising the gun and pulling the trigger.

The flint from Savannah's pistol struck the metal frizzen, igniting the gunpowder just before an ear-piercing boom echoed throughout the room. Preston flinched at the noise, watching as Savannah lowered her arm, which had held the gun pointing directly at Redbeard's head, but before the lead ball could end his tyranny, Crownickers had emerged and threw herself in front of the shot. She gasped as the metal ball bore into her chest.

Savannah dropped the pistol, her eyes wide. She ran over to the woman, sprawled on the floor.

"No! Mother! I didn't mean to —"

A tear rolled down her cheek as she crouched down and lifted her mother's head into her lap. Crownickers opened her eyes and gazed up at Savannah, softly brushing her daughter's cheek with the back of her hand. From the corner of her mouth, she creaked out a smile before her eyes turned fierce and she looked over to Redbeard.

"I told ye she couldn't be trusted," she sputtered before thrusting her dagger into Savannah's stomach. With a deep gasp, Savannah's eyes flew wide. Falling back on her heels, a trickle of blood crept its way over her lip and down her chin. Crownickers coughed out a sinister laugh as she leered at Savannah and twisted the blade. Savannah heaved when

Crownickers yanked the blade from her and let it drop to the floor. Turning to Redbeard, Crownickers smiled at him as her eyes drew heavy.

"Now go fulfill yer destiny, ye worthless barnacle."

Redbeard smiled and turned. "Always the dependable one, my dear," he called out as he tipped his hat to her and hobbled down the hall.

Savannah pushed Crownickers away and brought her hand to her stomach. Blood oozed between her fingers as she held them up and looked at Amelia.

"I love you," she whispered as she fell next to her mother.

"Mom! No, please!" Amelia cried out, rushing over to Savannah. Preston was already tearing his shirt apart, using it to put pressure on her wound.

"You have to hold on!" he told her. "You can do this."

She pushed him away. "Leave me be."

"You're too stubborn to die," Preston said, pushing her hands away.

Rupina held onto his chest as he staggered over, dropping to his knees next to the woman, his long-time enemy.

"I hate to say this," he struggled to say, "but we need Krinsworth."

"No!" Savannah muttered. "I'd sooner wear the hangman's necklace."

Rupina smirked and turned to Preston. "I'm not moving well. Go get him out of his cell and tell him to bring his bag."

Savannah grabbed her daughter's hand. Her bloodied thumb caressing the back of the young girl's hand.

"Amelia, I'm sorry I haven't been the best mother to you."

Amelia smiled, tears rolling down her cheeks. "You made me strong."

Savannah's hand slipped from Amelia's, and she closed her eyes.

"Mom ..."

MOST OTHER PEOPLE WOULD have died from the wound Savannah suffered, but Savannah was not "most other people." In fact, it was rumored when death approached to claim her, she throat punched the specter. Now, I'm not certain this is true, but she somehow survived, so who am I to argue? Her father had taken his new ship and fled Breakaway Bay with most of the beacons and a majority of the crew. The others stood by Savannah's side, led by Shackles, who donned his old uniform and hid the steamer trunks before Redbeard could retrieve them.

"What will you do now?" Preston asked.

"My father will never give up," Savannah said, walking along the dry dock where what remained of the Dragon's Curse had been lifted from the bay.

Now resting on dozens of large wooden blocks, most of the damaged planks on the hull had been removed, leaving the ship with gaping holes, exposing the stainless steel frame beneath.

"He will do everything in his power to pursue his legacy, but I need to stop him. Now that I've taken hold of his flagship, I plan to disassemble the steamer trunks and use their Zimponium to strengthen the old girl."

"Will there be enough?"

"No, but we'll make do."

"What's the plan after you complete the retrofit?" Preston asked, running his hand along the brittle wood.

"I will sail to the seven realms so I can undo my father's work. From the charts I've studied before he took them, I've memorized dozens of keeps he's maintained within each realm. I'll search him out at each one if necessary. Tyranny will die with him. Nobody should suffer as my daughter has," she said, rubbing Amelia's shoulders. She kissed her on top of her head. "You ready? I have much to discuss with your grandfather."

Amelia nodded her head.

"I guess this is it then," Preston said to Savannah. "Take care of the Dragon's Curse."

Savannah smirked. "Don't you mean the Widow's Revenge?"

Preston smiled. "Perfect."

"Until next time, Fishbait," she said, punching Preston in the shoulder. Not much to some, but the most affection he's ever seen Savannah give to another.

Amelia walked over to Preston and looked around before kissing his cheek. "I'm going to make sure mother keeps one jump point open," she said, smiling at him.

"Iron Hills?"

"Iron Hills."

Preston brushed her hair back and looked at the device, still clicking away in her neck.

"What did you decide about this?"

She shook her head. "Your uncle said he'll study the technique before he returns. When he does, he offered to assist Krinsworth in removing it, if I so wish."

"Well, whatever you decide, I'll be there to support your decision."

With the sun rising behind them across the bay, Amelia smiled and touched her forehead against Preston's.

"Never goodbye," she said to him.

Preston smiled back at her. "Never goodbye."

She backed away from Preston, slowly releasing his hand as she turned to her mother, who led her toward Shackles' shed in the distance.

After they left, Preston returned to the factory and found his uncle flipping through papers on a clipboard as he stood over Preston's steamer trunk, preparing it for the journey back. As Rupina leaned over, tapping a gauge, Preston noticed the long scar in his chest where Krinsworth's pump had been removed. Around the wound, his veins had turned black, and his uncle appeared pale and weak. He looked up at Preston.

"Does the girl know?"

Preston smiled. "Not yet."

After dropping Amelia off at Shackles' hut, Savannah returned to the Widow's Revenge. She climbed up the ladder, the pounding of hammers filling her ears as carpenters ripped up old boards from the deck, replacing them with new ones. As she made her way to Redbeard's old quarters, ghosts of her father appeared throughout. At the ship's wheel, she swore she saw his repugnant face leering at her. Without a moment's thought, she threw a knife, which embedded into the wall. She wished it were him instead.

"I'm coming for you, father. And there's no place you'll be able to hide."

Inside his quarters, Savannah walked through the now empty space. Eager to separate herself from his legacy, she had most of his belongings removed, aside from a few charts, the orrery, and his desk. It was an impressive desk, to be certain. One she always admired. Dropping down into the chair, she pulled the drawers open. Inside one was a crumpled up sheet of paper.

"A note from my dear old mother," she said with a scowl as she grabbed her wound, remembering their last moments together.

Madame Crownickers:

The child you inquired about, Preston Cornsuckle, is Crispus Rupina's great-nephew. He had been living in Rupina's home but has since gone missing. You may recall the house as it has a large clock tower. The parents, Charles and Anastasia Cornsuckle have traveled to Ceylon to search for an artifact owned by Captain Redbeard. I believe it to be the one the three of us spoke of. I'm certain this relic you seek means much more to you than the boy. However, I've enclosed a photograph of the Cornsuckles. They shouldn't be hard to find. And you were correct. Redbeard's daughter, Aralia, and Charles bear a striking resemblance to one another. It seems the rumors are true. Happy hunting!

Your servant,

Constable McGreary

"Fishbait needs to know of this," she said as she leapt from her chair.

Rupina nodded and patted Preston on the shoulder as he approached the trunk, but then stopped.

"I don't know, nephew. It might be better if I were to stay behind a little longer to help Savannah remove the explosives from all those steamer trunks. After all, I feel responsible for assisting Redbeard in creating this mess."

"Your only concern at the moment should be to get well. You need to return to see some actual doctors!"

Rupina set his bag on the ground and patted his pockets. "Very well. I think I have everything I need."

"I've been meaning to ask. Do you know why the steamer trunk design was kept when the new fleet was built?"

Rupina laughed. "Well, as I see it, the design of the steamer trunk is the perfect conduit for realm transference. The limited size allows streamlined propulsion through the vortex with reduced drag; thus, it needs no excessive power source other than what we have here. With the latest construction using Zimponium and stainless steel, they will flex without breaking. And, most importantly, based on what I learned from you, it doesn't create a ripple effect, which awakens the Feeders. Plus, just look at it, dear nephew! It's a classic design! Loaded with character!" he said, his hands on his hips.

Rupina bent over to insert the sprocket into the lock and stood back as the lid lifted. As soon as it did, the lights inside flashed.

Rupina beamed as he saw the display of lights. "My dreams of returning home are finally becoming reality. I promised Amelia we would help reunite the children from Iron Hills with their families. I don't expect the news of Crownickers' demise will upset them much." He removed the key and replaced the sprocket into Preston's top hat before setting it back on his nephew's head, adjusting it with a slight tilt. "This looks far better on you than on me."

Preston smiled as he readjusted the hat. "Won't you need this for when you return?"

"The key? No. I have the extra one hidden about," he said with a wink before bending down and grabbing the handle of his bag.

"You do?" Preston asked, looking around. "So, where did you hide it?"

Rupina surveyed the surroundings as well before leaning down and whispering, "In a cylinder cipher, hidden within our home where no one can find it."

Preston's head sunk. "Uhm, mother found it."

Rupina's eyes widened. "Oh, my."

Preston nodded. "Yeah, and ahh, well, I opened it."

Rupina's mouth dropped as he rubbed his forehead. "That cipher was personally designed by me to take years to crack the code. It was even constructed from Zimponium so nobody would be able to break it open!"

"Yeah ... sorry."

"Impressive," he said, nodding his head. "No matter. Where is it now?"

"It's still back at the house in your desk."

"Wonderful," he said. "Well, I best be off. Much to be done."

"Wait, you didn't need to sync the clocks?"

"Ahh, yes, thank you for mentioning this. I made another slight adjustment," he said, tapping the pocket watch embedded in Preston's hat. "Now your clock is just that, a clock."

As Rupina stood, he winced and faltered, bracing himself against the trunk.

"Are you okay?"

"I'm fine, I'm fine," he said, regaining his balance and reaching for his hinged leather bag.

"Here, let me help you." Preston grunted as he heaved the bag up off the ground. "Wow, this is heavy! Maybe you shouldn't be carrying this."

"I must. Most of it is my research and designs, including the one to fix this old gal," he said, rubbing his hand along the steamer trunk.

Preston dropped the bag behind the seat before grabbing Rupina's arm. Crispus slowly stepped into the trunk and after settling into the seat, he spun the dials to adjust the coordinates.

"I dreamed of this day for so long," he said, pulling on the handle at the side of the cushioned chair. The trunk rumbled to life, vibrating and sputtering before coughing out some unusual noises. Sort of like someone gargling and sneezing at the same time; minus the inherent mess, of course. But the sounds didn't seem to bother Rupina as he fiddled with some wires under the console.

"Has much changed?"

"With the house? Uhm, kind of," Preston told him. "But it's all good. The colors may shock you at first. My parents told me you liked it to be gray."

"Why? What color is it now?" Rupina asked, looking up.

"Uhm, well, sort of yellow and purple."

Rupina's face twisted at the thought.

"Like an Easter egg?" he said, taking a moment to picture it in his head before shrugging his shoulders. "Oh well, with everything else I've endured, I believe I can get used to it." After making a few more adjustments, the steam trunk whirred and Rupina stood, smiling at

Preston. "As soon as I resolve my issues with the doctors back home, I'll make the necessary repairs to this old gal. I'm afraid she won't be able to make any more trips without a complete overhaul. As soon as I'm finished, I'll send her back to you. Are you sure you're okay being here for another few weeks?"

"Of course! It'll be a great surprise for Amelia. Plus, I can help Savannah get everything ready for their journey. Maybe we can even locate a few more jump points before they set off. Don't worry though. You'll find me right here when it's time."

"That reminds me. May I borrow your hat for a moment?"

"Sure," Preston said, handing it to him.

Rupina stepped out of the trunk, then plucked the smallest sprocket from the hat. Below the console was a small panel where he inserted the sprocket. Once it clicked into place, a hidden door popped opened, exposing a scroll and small notebook, which Rupina removed before pressing the door shut. After replacing the gear back into Preston's hat, he handed his nephew the top hat and papers.

"Make certain Savannah gets these."

"What are they?"

"A complete set of plans for the new beacons and control panels. Plus, there is a list of all the jump points scattered throughout the seven realms. As for the notebook, I'm not exactly sure what it contains. I was shanghaied before I had a chance to research it further."

"She'll be so excited to get these. You sure you don't want to be the one to give them to her?"

Rupina smiled. "No, no. You do the honors." He smiled and took a deep breath. "Well, I guess there's nothing left to do."

"Have a great trip, Uncle Rupina. If my parents are back, please let them know I miss them, and I'll be home soon."

"Of course," Rupina said before breaking out into a coughing fit.

"Are you sure Doctor Krinsworth can't help you?"

Rupina scoffed. "Doctor, indeed. I wouldn't trust that man to cut my toenails. No, I'm better off taking care of this on my own. After doing some research, I've come up with a plan." Rupina stared at Preston and smiled. "My dear nephew, you are truly an amazing person!"

"I have good roots," he said, hugging his uncle. "Plus, now I know where my interest in tinkering came from."

Rupina laughed. "I can see us inventing some amazing machines together."

"I can't wait," Preston said as he helped his uncle back into the trunk. "Oh, speaking of tinkering, you'll be happy to hear I fixed your clock."

With one leg in the trunk, Rupina froze. "Which clock?"

Preston laughed. "THE clock. The gigantic one on the side of the tower."

Rupina stepped out of the trunk and grabbed Preston by the shoulders. "My dear boy! Please tell me you did not restart the clock!"

"No, I didn't have the chance to, but I adjusted the gears. Why? What's wrong with the clock?"

"Remember the beacon I spoke of? Well, the clock is the beacon! Each time the clock reaches midnight, the navigational lights illuminate. If the pattern is known, the signal can be locked in from any of the realms using the redesigned trunks. Redbeard can find your parents!"

"Well, it should be fine. Mother and father don't realize the clock has been fixed. Plus, I'm not sure they would even know how to start it."

Rupina looked up and thought for a moment.

"The designs I drew up never accounted for the clock not running. It should be fine unless Redbeard figures out a way to bypass —" he muttered before turning to Preston. "Sorry, I forgot one important thing."

"What is it?"

"This!"

Rupina shoved Preston, who fell backwards into the trunk. Before he could react, Rupina slapped his hand against the flashing green button, causing the lid to close. After righting himself, Preston pushed against the lid to stop it, but it was too late.

"Uncle Rupina! What are you doing?" he screamed, pounding on the domed top.

As the trunk started to vibrate and rumble, Rupina leaned in close. "My dear Preston, we don't have much time, so I'm going to say this quick. You need to return, for there is much work to be done and if your parents are found and tell Redbeard about the tower, I fear all our efforts will have been in vain. It is up to you to protect them; to protect everyone! Above all else, do not let them travel to India! There is something hidden there that could be devastating to us all. It needs to remain hidden."

Preston continued banging on the lid. "Uncle Rupina! You have to go back!"

"Don't worry about me," he said, stepping away from the trunk as the gauges fluttered and wisps of steam drifted up from the bottom, coating the trunk with tiny water droplets. "I'll be fine. Now that the clock back home has been repaired, I need to finish something here to make certain all remains the same. But you need to go now! Return home, and whatever you do, no matter what it takes, do not restart the clock!"

"But Uncle Rupina! You won't make —"

Before he could finish his sentence, that maddening whistle screamed as the bright light blinded him once again. And as his steamer trunk nestled down deep within the hidden cellar at 2579 Willowbush Court, Preston knew he'd be returning to Breakaway Bay. But would he be too late?

Breakaway Bay
Redbeard's Fortress

OTHER WORKS BY G.L. GARRETT

To a ten-year-old, death is far from kind; it is imprisonment! To help the living get to their next day, Peter is required to work in the "Conservatory," a library where every person is represented by a "LifeBook." Turning the pages of LifeBooks is excruciatingly dull, so Peter plots his escape! However, that would ruin Apius' evil plan to obtain an Ancient Hourglass that controls time. With the hourglass in hand, all of the guarded souls in the LifeBooks could be his, making him unstoppable.

After escaping the servitude he suffered while being imprisoned in heaven, Apius — an ancient evil entity — calls out to Peter Nichols from beyond the grave. It was this "child" who thwarted Apius's plan for revenge as he sought out the destruction of humanity for the last several centuries. But Peter now owes Apius a blood-debt. Collecting on this debt, Apius captures the soul of Peter's mother, hoping to draw him near. Once he rids himself of Peter, he can then move to release his brothers from their guarded sarcophaguses and wipe away the scourge of mankind. However, fifteen-year-old Peter will not make it easy for him. After he discovers a hidden symbol, a series of events brings Peter back to heaven where his three lives converge. Besides freeing his mother, Peter has seven days in which he must locate and defeat Apius if he is to help prevent the apocalypse.

Apius is gone, but his legacy lives on with a brother's promise. Because of this promise, humanity is on the verge of extinction. Famine has swept across the globe as a mysterious pathogen is destroying the world's food supply. Even though agroterrorism is suspected, FBI Special Agent Peter Nichols knows there is much more to this. Haunted by his long-forgotten past, he hunts for answers — answers hidden deep below an ancient Ceiba tree in the heart of Mexico. Here, protected by a deadly maze of tunnels, is a mythical temple. According to legend, this temple serves as a gateway to the afterlife. It is here where Peter must travel in order to stop the eradication, and Apius's brother, Ezekial. But how does one stop the dead?

After losing his father, young Thomas Bristol is at risk of losing his dearest friend as well. Because of this, he and his trusted bear run away and seek refuge in Creekside Woods. Over the years, many stories have been told of Creekside, and secrets abound in this fabled forest. Creekside is full of dangers, and now, Thomas is being hunted by the most dangerous threat yet; a legendary dragon known as "The Screech." But Detective Claire Spillen doesn't believe in dragons and fears the worst. She finds herself in a battle of her own, against time. While Thomas struggles to escape this merciless monster, Detective Spillen hopes she'll be able to rescue him before it's too late.

www.ingramcontent.com/pod-product-compliance
Lightning Source LLC
LaVergne TN
LVHW090548110826
845146LV00001B/69

* 9 7 9 8 9 8 6 6 9 8 0 4 5 *